CH00820983

AMONG HIDDEN STARS

AMONG HIDDEN STARS

JOHN COON

SAMAK PRESS

AMONG HIDDEN STARS
Copyright © 2022 by John Coon

Samak Press
ISBN: 978-1-7324871-8-5

All rights reserved. No part of this publication may be reproduced, stored, or transmitted in any form or by any means, electronic, mechanical, photocopying, recording, scanning, or otherwise without written permission from the publisher. It is illegal to copy this book, post it to a website, or distribute it by any other means without permission.

This novel is entirely a work of fiction. The names, characters and incidents portrayed in it are the work of the author's imagination. Any resemblance to actual persons or aliens, living or dead, events or localities is entirely coincidental.

Cover Design: 100 Covers
Interior Design: Formatted Books

AUTHOR'S NOTE

Mythology and folklore have always fascinated me. I enjoy learning about stories ancient people created and passed down from generation to generation while trying to better understand their world. A love of myths and legends influences how I craft my own stories.

You can see that love firsthand with how the *Alien People Chronicles* evolves. Calandra and Xttra both embark on a classic hero's journey, starting when they make first contact with an alien race and gradually leading into a struggle to free their own people from a tyrant's clutches. *Among Hidden Stars* draws inspiration from myth, folklore, and ancient religion in bringing to life their journey to prevent Delcor from finding and taking possession of a powerful ancient relic. I hope you will be entertained and inspired by what Calandra and Xttra do in this latest chapter of their lives.

I am indebted to Jefferson Keyes and Sandra Coon for reading over early drafts of this story and supplying valuable feedback on plot and character development. Credit goes to 100 Covers for again creating a beautiful cover for this concluding chapter of my trilogy and Formatted Books for designing the interior of this novel so skillfully.—JC

For Dad, who has always encouraged me to keep persevering.

A cavern on an isolated moon offered a perfect hiding place. No doubt existed in Xttra's mind the chief sovereign deliberately selected this remote region. Delcor made an extraordinary effort to guarantee no one uncovered or interrupted his genetic experimentation. Multiple subsurface scans were required to confirm the subterranean lab existed.

Now that he and Kevin had uncovered the lab, they needed to document its existence and location to further bolster their case against Delcor and destroy the lab before anyone returned. Neither he nor his allies must be allowed to resume their operations inside the lab.

"Are you sure landing on this ice is safe?"

Xttra smiled and shook his head. Kevin's image flickered on the holoscreen above the helm console. Concern threaded through the Earthian's eyes.

"The ice on Pago is almost 12 peds thick and as hard as stone," Xttra said. "It won't suffer even a minor crack under the weight of your dart."

Kevin cast his eyes skyward while doing the math in his head.

"12 peds." His gaze returned to the holoscreen. "Isn't that like nine miles on Earth?"

"More or less."

"I'd hate to try to drill through that to go ice fishing."

Xttra laughed. He pushed the steering stick forward and began descent maneuvers. His Cassian dart rotated onto its side and shot toward Pago's icy surface. Deep fractures crisscrossed the frozen crust. Where solar wind blasted ice remained smooth and unbroken, light from the distant Lathoan sun gleamed off the surface.

Kevin trailed him, traversing the same aerial path in another dart. Both darts leveled out over a mountainous region and touched down on an expansive plain near the cavern entrance. Xttra powered down his dart's engines and rose from the pilot's chair.

"I hope this is the same place Calandra found in that travel log," Kevin said. "It looks like no one has landed here since…forever."

Xttra shrugged.

"Active ice volcanoes are all over Pago. Calandra told me all about them back when she worked at the Luma Observatory. No telling how quickly a few ice eruptions can reshape the surface."

"I hope you're right."

"The travel log hasn't steered us wrong yet."

Xttra switched off the holoscreen and powered down non-essential systems. He snapped his helmet into place. Environmental readings popped up on the tinted visor. Xttra slipped protective gloves over his hands and patted down his zero-gravity suit. No rips or tears in the fabric. His sensor readings showed nothing amiss.

The rear hatch door emitted a slight creak as Xttra lowered an exit ramp to the frigid ground. Plumes of ice crystals shot skyward around spots where the ramp touched the ground. Xttra fitted a tightly sealed chest pouch over his zero-gravity suit and started down the ramp. He trudged toward the cavern, taking deliberate steps across frozen ground. Maintaining solid footing on one long sheet of ice and snow was hard enough. Pago's weak gravity only complicated his movements.

Kevin caught him shortly after he reached the cavern entrance. His pace mirrored Xttra's own.

"I wish I owned a pair of sturdy snowshoes," the Earthian said. "Trudging across this iced over snow feels like I'm walking on marbles."

"Snowshoes?"

Xttra glanced down at his boots and then over at Kevin's boots. His eyes trailed back up to Kevin and he flashed him a puzzled look. Kevin scrunched up his face for a moment at the question before responding with an annoyed sigh.

"Footwear designed for walking on top of snow, so you don't sink," he said. "We wear them on Earth."

"What do they look like?" Xttra asked. "Maybe I can acquire similar Lathoan footwear."

"Some snowshoes resemble foot-shaped tennis rackets. Others look like small paddles."

"Tennis rackets?"

His explanation laced with other unfamiliar Earthian terms did nothing to dispel Xttra's confusion. Kevin raised his gloved hands and shook his head.

"You know what? Forget it. I'm not in the mood to give you a detailed breakdown of snowshoes."

A sealed metallic door blocked the entrance inside the cavern's mouth. Xttra saw no visible outer handle to push or pull the door open. His eyes trailed along the cavern roof and down the walls.

A spherical motion sensor jutted out from the upper left wall. His gaze lingered on the sensor. No blue or red light had appeared and scanned him and Kevin. Xttra wondered if the device malfunctioned amid continued exposure to extreme frigid temperatures. Perhaps someone deactivated the sensor. The second scenario seemed improbable. Xttra imagined Delcor and his allies would do everything possible to protect this secret laboratory from unexpected and unwanted intruders.

"Cutting our way inside is our only option." He glanced over his shoulder at Kevin. "Keep your eyes and ears open and search for any traps awaiting us."

Kevin nodded and extracted a small thermal tracker from a belt line pouch. Xttra unsheathed and activated a Ra'ahmian cutter. Sparks flew around the cutter as a blue laser circling the volcanic glass blade sliced in a straight line through the metallic door. Once the cutter reached the bottom, Xttra withdrew his blade and switched his tool off. He manually pushed the door back into a slot.

"I see faint heat patterns inside this cavern." Kevin glanced up from the tracker screen. "That means hybrids in stasis, right?"

Xttra frowned and pushed open a second internal door. His eyes settled on a newly exposed corridor winding deeper into the cavern. Kevin's thermal tracker confirmed his fears.

This subterranean lab still held living hybrids.

"If any are here, we better execute them quickly before anyone decides to return and awaken them from stasis," he said.

Fist-sized rectangular lights sprang to life on both corridor walls. A pale white glow illuminated the corridor, revealing stairs a short distance ahead. The second door did not automatically release from the slot and seal the corridor again, so Xttra and Kevin kept their protective helmets locked in place. The stairs wound downward until leveling out onto a cold sterile stone floor. An expansive laboratory constructed within a natural cavern lay before them.

A series of hibernation pods lined one wall on the opposite end of the laboratory. Blinking lights covered both sides of each pod. One pod door after another bore distinct Ra'ahm symbols imprinted on their surface. Each door held a round glass window, exposing the face of the pod's occupant.

Xttra's eyes rested on the hibernation pod nearest to him. A face with closed eyelids and distorted, grotesque features rested behind the glass.

Hybrids.

This was indeed the right place.

"It doesn't matter how many times I see these monsters," Kevin said. "They still freak me out."

Xttra glanced back and nodded. Seeing hibernating hybrids here made his heart race as much as fighting them face-to-face in the Aramus system four years ago. He silently thanked Ahm for the fact these creatures remained in a deep sleep. Xttra did not want a single hybrid to ever awaken. He and Kevin were here to turn their womb-like pods into tombs.

"I'll disable the nanotubes supplying nutritional supplements and water," Xttra said. "You cut the power supply feeding the pods."

Kevin nodded and headed over to a console embedded in a half-pillar rising from the floor. It bordered an adjacent wall running in a perpendicular direction from the pods. Xttra's eyes fell on the nearest pod. He knelt and examined clear panels above blinking lights on the side facing him. Each panel displayed data related to the pod's occupant. Heart rate. Brain activity. Nutrition reserves.

These pods preserved hybrids in stasis for a future purpose. No one needed to explain the chief sovereign's intentions to Xttra. These hybrids were once normal Ra'ahmians. Willing or not, they were monsters now, designed to be merciless destroyers of anyone who opposed their creator.

"That setaworm is willing to start a whole new war to retain his throne." Anger dripped from his words. "Places like this exist for no other reason."

"We'll make it un-exist."

A crooked smile formed on Xttra's lips as Kevin's reply settled into his mind. Earthians always conjured up such strange words and phrases.

Xttra drew out his cutter and activated it again. Sparks flew as the laser sliced through the pod's exterior shell above the data panels. He lifted out a square section and tossed the cut metal on the ground. An exposed network of nanotubes now lay before him. Xttra studied the nanotubes and pondered where to make his next cut.

An alarm started blaring.

Yellow and red lights flashed above his head. Xttra craned his neck skyward. Multiple warning lights lit up along lab walls behind him and facing him and flooded the entire room. His eyes widened like plates.

"Did we trigger an alarm?"

Kevin stared at the pod before Xttra as he posed the question. Xttra shook his head with vigor.

"That's a proximity alarm."

The Earthian cast his eyes back toward the stairs.

"I guess the Stellar Guard didn't buy the phony intelligence we planted."

"A safe assumption."

Sudden tremors shook the ground above the lab, consistent with precision strikes from an ion torpedo or a plasma cannon. Kevin stumbled and wrapped his hand around the side of the console to keep from falling. Xttra lurched forward and slammed into the hibernation pod. His cutter spilled out of his hand and slid across the floor.

"They're targeting our darts!" Kevin said. "We better wrap this up quick."

A second wave of tremors shook the lab. Xttra scrambled to his feet and stumbled toward the cutter like a drunken man. Kevin was right. Their window to sabotage these pods was closing fast. What those tremors represented offered a greater concern. No doubt existed in Xttra's mind that Stellar Guard operatives fired on their unguarded ships.

Kevin wedged open a panel on the power regulation console and planted a cylindrical Serbiusian neutron charge amid a collection of circuits and conduits. Each one ran from the console, traveled underneath the floor, and fed directly into a central membrane fused into the wall. The membrane connected to each pod's upper end like a web. Hibernation pods hung suspended above the lab floor like evenly spaced cocoons.

With cutter in hand again, Xttra severed each visible nanotube. Lights running along the side of the pod fell dead. He darted over to the neighboring pod.

"Help me disable the rest of these pods."

Kevin activated the neutron charge and sprinted to a pod on the opposite end from Xttra. Fresh tremors shook the lab. Both kept their footing by clutching pods directly in front of them until the tremors subsided again. Xttra and Kevin rapidly cut through the outer shells of each remaining pod and severed every exposed nanotube.

After disabling the last pod, Xttra whipped out a thermal tracker. His throat tightened. Multiple heat patterns moved down the corridor toward the lab. The tracker screen revealed four humanoid patterns.

All clustered together.

"Stellar Guard secret ops." Xttra's voice dropped to a whisper. "A quarter ped away from us and closing. We better take cover among these pods."

Kevin drew out an eliminator and ducked between a pair of pods. Xttra mirrored his actions. His visor's data showed an elevated heart rate. Each breath he took matched the intensity. Anxious thoughts cluttered his mind. How many Stellar Guard officers blocked their path back to the darts? Could they reach the cavern mouth uninjured? If they did, would either ship still be capable of flight?

Xttra clenched his jaw and forced these questions out of his head. His first concern entailed avoiding capture at any cost. The chief sovereign would love nothing more than to bring him and Kevin back to Luma for a public execution.

He refused to let such a scenario unfold.

Both he and Calandra had sacrificed so much. The same held true for Kevin and Bo'un. Delcor and his allies were overdue to make their own sacrifices.

"I have an idea."

Kevin peeked his head out from behind a pod.

"What?"

"We open some pods and let these hybrids create a distraction for us."

Kevin's eyes widened.

"Are you nuts?"

"We make a run for the corridor while they fight the hybrids." Xttra's eyes darted to the corridor and back as he silently mapped an escape route. "Once we reach the mouth of the cavern, we detonate the neutron charge and bury the whole lab under a pile of icy rubble."

"Once again…are you nuts?"

He snapped his head back at Kevin.

"Got any better ideas?"

"Stun pebbles?"

Xttra shook his head.

"Too risky down here. The flash could also blind us and leave us at their mercy."

Kevin glanced at the ground and back at him. The Earthian's stoic frown told Xttra he had concocted no other alternatives for combating the Stellar Guard officers headed their way.

"Wait for my signal."

Xttra refocused his attention on the tracker. Heat patterns were much further down the corridor now. He drew in a deep breath.

8

Subduing disoriented hybrids coming straight out of hibernation would not take long.

This had better work.

Two Stellar Guard officers popped out from the corridor. Their black zero-gravity suits and helmets confirmed their identities to Xttra. A special operations squadron had landed on Pago. Two others quickly emerged behind the lead officers. All four fanned out inside the lab. Their attention seemed focused solely on the power regulation console and workstations on the opposite side of the lab.

Exactly as Xttra hoped.

He activated a pod door release mechanism on a neighboring pod. A hiss signaled air escaping from inside the pod. The door began to lift up and away.

"Over there."

One Stellar Guard officer turned and faced the pods flanking Xttra. They drew an eliminator.

"Saboteurs! Stop them."

The other three officers wheeled around and faced the same direction. A second hiss made its presence known. Kevin followed his lead. Xttra gave a satisfied nod and trained his eliminator barrel on the nearest Stellar Guard officer. A hybrid stumbled out from behind the open pod door in front of him. The creature charged toward the special operations squadron once it found its footing.

Numerous shouts, eliminator bolts, and smoke from blast points filled the room.

Xttra cut down a Stellar Guard officer backpedaling toward the corridor. Kevin took out another near the first. The other two squadron members each battled newly awakened hybrids. Xttra and Kevin both sprinted back into the corridor.

"Ready for some fireworks?"

Kevin spouted another unfamiliar Earthian saying. Xttra assumed this one referenced the neutron charge he planted.

He nodded.

"Detonate the charge."

The Earthian drew out a small crystal remote and flipped a switch as they ran.

An ear shattering blast tore through the cavern.

Shock waves rippled through the entire corridor a second later. Xttra stumbled forward. He pressed a hand against the wall to keep his balance. Kevin also stayed on his feet. He seized Xttra's arm.

Cracks formed along both corridor walls. Rock, metal, and other debris rained down from the ceiling.

The cavern began collapsing.

Xttra and Kevin sprinted toward the entrance. They dove forward, throwing themselves outside the cavern to avoid being crushed under falling debris.

"Delcor and his minions won't be using that lab again any time soon." Kevin turned and cracked a grin. "Mission accomplished."

Xttra lifted his chin and pushed off the ice with his arms. He stared at the site where their darts landed.

"Not quite."

Both ships were smoldering wrecks. Plasma cannons obliterated primary and secondary engines on each dart. This action effectively stranded them on Pago's surface. Only one means of escape remained.

Finding and stealing the same scout ship that brought the Stellar Guard officers to the icy moon.

2

Xttra's heart sank while staring at the scout ship on the icy plain leading to the cavern. Boarding and capturing a scout ship was a more complicated task than anyone outside the Stellar Guard understood. Xttra went through extensive training to prevent such a scenario from unfolding before earning his master pilot rank.

The four dead Stellar Guard officers crushed under icy debris had crewmates who stayed behind to guard the ship. Anyone still aboard understood exactly what their assignment to protect the vessel entailed. Their duty would be to consign Xttra and Kevin to becoming frozen lifeless husks on Pago.

They had to outsmart those unseen officers. Fast.

"Suggestions?" Xttra asked, turning to Kevin.

The Earthian mirrored him and rose to his feet. He brushed crystalized ice fragments off the front of his zero-gravity suit. Kevin stared stoically at the scout ship from a hidden spot behind an ice ledge and pressed a hand against his helmet.

"Magnetic constrictors."

Xttra shot him a puzzled look. Where was his Earthian friend going with this?

"We knock out exterior magnetic constrictors holding the lower hatch door in place," Kevin said, elaborating on the thought running through his head. "From there, we unseal the hatch and lower the ramp."

"A risky plan," Xttra replied. "If a systems officer is waiting inside the cargo bay—"

"It's not a perfect solution." Kevin turned away and faced the lower hatch. "But we don't have many realistic options for boarding that ship."

Xttra answered him with a reluctant nod. He worried they lacked the element of surprise needed to execute this plan. Did anyone on the scout ship witness their flight from the cavern? Did a distress signal from inside the lab reach the ship before the Stellar Guard officers perished in the explosion and collapse that followed?

Wondering what awaited them on the other side of the lower hatch bred new doubts. These concerns swarmed through Xttra's mind like a horde of persistent ictus bugs.

"Let's hope Ahm smiles on us," he said.

Kevin stepped out from behind the ledge, raised his arm above his head, and fired an eliminator bolt at one corner of the lower hatch. Xttra followed suit and fired at the opposite corner. Both constrictors emitted sparks and let out an audible buzz. Vibrations jarred the lower hatch door loose. A broad visible crack formed between the unsealed door and both hull layers.

Step one completed. Now came the hard part.

Once they crept under the belly of the ship, Kevin dropped his arms down and cupped his gloved hands together. He boosted Xttra upward to put the lower hatch within his grasp. Xttra latched onto the crack and manually pushed the door inside a connected slot. When he created a large enough opening, Xttra used the part of the door still visible as leverage to climb inside the hatch. Sweat trickled down his skin underneath his zero-gravity suit. He silently expected to be on the wrong end of a deadly eliminator bolt at any moment.

"See anyone up there?" Kevin whispered.

Xttra's deep blue eyes trailed from wall to wall. Two aerorovers, sealed cargo containers, and assorted tools occupied the cargo bay. One notable absence stood out.

No sign of a systems officer.

"I don't think we were detected." Xttra echoed Kevin's earlier whisper. "Give me your hand."

He dropped to his knees near the lower hatch's edge and clasped Kevin's forearm. Xttra pulled the Earthian upward until he cleared the opening. Kevin resealed the door behind him so no crack remained, but it would not stay in place during flight without working magnetic constrictors. Making hatch repairs would be necessary once they took full control of the ship.

A door connecting the bridge to the cargo bay slid open. Kevin ducked behind the nearest aerorover. Xttra followed a step behind him. He crouched next to a rear magnetic wheel and peered over the vehicle's back end. A bald, bronze-skinned man stepped through the doorway. His Stellar Guard uniform displayed a systems officer's insignia over the left breast.

"I don't see any sign of…"

He trailed off and stopped just outside the doorway. The systems officer shot a suspicious glance toward the aerorover concealing them. Xttra gulped. Was the top of his helmet visible? Did he spot him or Kevin?

Fingers tapped his forearm. Xttra snapped his head toward Kevin. The Earthian signaled for him to close his eyes. Xttra glanced down at his belt line and met his gaze again. He mouthed the word "no" and shook his head. Kevin flashed a defiant smile, removing a stun pebble from his belt.

Xttra turned his head and pinched his eyelids shut right as Kevin lobbed the stun pebble over the aerorover's roof. A clank greeted his ears when it struck the floor.

A brilliant flash of light flooded the cargo bay.

An anguished shout followed.

"Intruders!" The blinded systems officer grimaced as he breathed out a warning. "In the cargo bay. Hurry!"

Xttra unholstered his eliminator. Kevin mirrored his action. They sprang to their feet behind the aerorover and pointed their barrels at the doorway. A black-haired man with a single braid running down his neck emerged from the bridge. His muscular frame fit a stone cutter more than a Stellar Guard officer. His uniform bore a master pilot's insignia. When he laid eyes on Xttra and Kevin, the master pilot instinctively thrust out his right forearm and targeted his armored sleeve at the aerorover.

"I will not let pirates take control of my scout ship." A deep scowl washed over his lips. "Surrender now and I may show you mercy."

Kevin and Xttra exchanged amused glances.

"Surrender?" Kevin scoffed. "Read the room, bro. You're in no position to make threats or demands."

The master pilot edged closer to the systems officer sprawled on the floor. His fallen comrade still cradled his eyes and let out an alternating string of moans and heavy breaths. Xttra gave him an annoyed sideways glance. Stun pebbles were painful, but his reaction bordered on excessive.

"The Stellar Guard will never negotiate with filthy Confederation agents like yourselves."

Their helmets obscured his face and Kevin's face enough to conceal their true identities. Xttra figured that was for the best. Subduing these Stellar Guard officers would be much more difficult if they recognized him and Kevin as Ra'ahm exiles inciting a rebellion against Delcor.

"We are not aligned with the Confederation," Xttra said. "We answer to no one but ourselves."

"Don't lie to me! I disabled your darts myself."

"You did. And now we're taking your ship."

The master pilot's forearm stiffened, his armored sleeve pointing straight at Xttra's throat. "Not a chance. You're not leaving this moon alive."

Xttra frowned.

"We don't have time to deal with this nonsense."

He fired his eliminator. A bolt struck the armored sleeve, blowing apart a long flat chamber concealing razor discs. The master pilot's eyes widened, and he staggered backward, banging into the wall behind him.

He reached for his holster. Kevin fired this time. The master pilot let out an angry shout and his hand recoiled back toward his chest. Smoke wafted out from a fresh hole in his hand, just below his fingers.

"You're not quick enough," Kevin said. "My army ranger training beats the hell out of whatever skills you think you own."

The master pilot's scowl deepened. He raised his uninjured arm. Xttra and Kevin disarmed both Stellar Guard officers and directed them to stand against the nearest wall.

"Let's find some restraints for our new friends," Xttra said, after confirming with his thermal tracker that no one else was on the ship. "Once we repair the magnetic constrictors, we can head back home."

***

Relief washed over Calandra with a suddenness akin to an ocean wave crashing on a beach. Her heartbeat slowed to a normal pace when Xttra and Kevin exited the unfamiliar scout ship. Their entry into Daraconian airspace provoked warnings from a formidable air defense system. The threat only subsided when Xttra relayed his identity and a landing code. At that point, the scout ship received clearance to land in Daracos.

A little hand slipped from her own as Calandra started forward. She glanced down at her knees. Alexa ran ahead of her as fast as her tiny legs allowed. The little girl stretched out her hands and a bright smile radiated from her lips.

"Diada!"

Xttra matched her smile with an equally bright one. He sprinted toward Alexa and scooped her off the ground and into his arms. Locks of her dark red hair fluttered in the breeze and brushed against Alexa's cheeks. The hem of her purple dress rested on his right armored sleeve.

"My precious little girl. I'm so happy to see you!"

He kissed her cheek as she threw her arms around Xttra's neck. Alexa laughed and hugged her father. Calandra caught up to them and threw her arms around both her husband and their child. Xttra planted a tender kiss on her lips.

"We found everything described in the travel log," he said, after pulling back again. "Subterranean lab. Medical pods. Bio code technology. All in working condition."

"Hybrids?"

"Dozens of pods holding fully formed hybrids."

Calandra stepped back and gazed at the scout ship. A deep frown formed on her lips.

"You and Kevin weren't alone on Pago, were you?"

"We were at first."

She cast her green eyes over at Kevin as he turned, smiled, and waved at little Alexa. Kevin quickly refocused his gaze on Calandra.

"Stellar Guard officers landed on Pago before we finished sabotaging the lab," he said. "Destroyed both our darts. So, we hijacked their scout ship and turned it into our ride home."

Calandra's frown formed into a crooked smile.

"You make everything sound so simple and easy."

"That's my story and I'm sticking to it." Kevin followed with a brief laugh and pointed his thumb back over his shoulder. "And, to put a cherry on top, we captured two members of a secret ops team."

She gazed past his shoulder at the scout ship again. An empty ramp greeted her eyes. Neither Xttra nor Kevin brought out a prisoner when they exited the vessel. Calandra flashed a questioning stare at her husband.

"They're still locked in restraints inside the cargo bay," Xttra said. "You're welcome to be the first one to interrogate the master pilot."

"Our Daraconian liaison wouldn't be thrilled with your idea," she replied.

Xttra cracked a knowing smile.

"Is Corvah ever thrilled with anything we do?"

Calandra answered him with a shrug. A satisfied grin washed over her lips. An image of Corvah's horrified expression flashed through her mind. She imagined a lecture would follow, urging Calandra to let the past stay in the past and focus on building a new peaceful life away from Ra'ahm instead of provoking trouble.

It all sounded wonderful in theory. Real life afforded no choice to embark on such a simple path. Calandra refused to rest while Delcor ruled Ra'ahm. She owed it to Alayna, her grandfather, and all other victims of his selfish, unchecked thirst for power to make the chief sovereign answer for his crimes.

This fight belonged to her until his rule met an end.

"I think I should talk to him." Calandra's eyes drifted back to the ramp leading into the cargo bay. "We need to uncover Delcor's next move, now that we've destroyed his final hybrid hibernation facility."

Xttra nodded and turned to Kevin.

"Can you watch Alexa for a while? An interrogation is no place for a small child."

Kevin cracked a broad grin.

"Did you need to ask?"

His eyes drifted over to Alexa, and he held out his arms. She mirrored his action. Xttra shifted her from his arms and into Kevin's arms. He often referred to himself as Alexa's uncle and Xttra and Calandra both eventually embraced using the same Earthian term.

"Are you excited to hang out with your uncle Kevin?"

Alexa answered with eager nods.

Calandra and Xttra turned away and headed toward the scout ship. She climbed the ramp with long-legged strides, and he matched her pace. Taking a prisoner from a secret ops team who managed the hybrids offered an unexpected and promising boon in their struggle against Delcor. Calandra hoped he possessed information about the chief sovereign's plans, locations of his network of agents, or something else to aid their quest to free Ra'ahm from his tyranny.

A stout man with short black hair, surrounding a distinctive shoulder-length Abidosian braid, occupied a small back corner in the cargo bay. Thick metal bands circled each wrist and both legs above his ankles. A high-powered magnetic field bound each band to a wall behind the prisoner, forcing him to stand against the wall.

Contempt radiated from the prisoner's face upon making eye contact with Calandra and Xttra. A new recognition flashed through his eyes. No doubt from seeing their images in messages they broadcast to clans from one end of Ra'ahm to the other.

"Traitors." He spit on the floor near their feet. "I have nothing to say to enemies of Ra'ahm."

Calandra scrunched up her nose and sidestepped the fresh saliva. She gazed back up at the Stellar Guard officer and shook her head.

"Your resistance means nothing in the end. Enforcing Delcor's tyranny is not a noble cause."

She met him with an unblinking stare. He averted his eyes and focused on the water vapor tanks.

"I would sooner die from Russakin venom than help you destroy my sovereign." His eyes slid back to meet her own. "May Ahm lengthen his rule to match his days."

Xttra sighed and shook his head.

"Thinking for yourself is normal. It won't harm you."

"I always think for myself." The prisoner focused his gaze on Xttra. "Ra'ahm needs strong men like the chief sovereign to protect our innocent clans from monsters like you. If I die in service to Ahm's chosen, I count my life as a small sacrifice for the greater good."

Pure anger simmered behind his eyes. Calandra expected nothing less from one loyal to the chief sovereign. No doubt this man would lunge forward and attack if restraints did not hold him in place. He could sit and brood until the sun dipped below the horizon. His prolonged pouting would never produce the effect he intended. Calandra refused to let him intimidate or impede her from getting necessary answers.

"We aren't here to listen to you recite propaganda," she said. "You know what our true purpose is."

"You're growing desperate."

"Desperate?" Calandra scoffed. "Delcor has failed to silence our broadcasts. We destroyed his hybrids and one hybrid creation facility after another over the last three years. We are not the desperate ones here."

"You will never unseat a ruler chosen and supported by Ahm himself."

"Ahm had no hand in raising him to his throne. Discontent with his rule grows daily. You can't see it only because you've chosen to be blind."

Her eyes drifted down to the master pilot insignia on the prisoner's uniform after saying these things. Xttra once held the same rank within the Stellar Guard. Calandra recalled his loyalty to Ra'ahm and how he faithfully performed his assigned duties. But he always had a strong spiritual compass. Xttra never did anything to threaten or harm innocent people.

The same could not be said for the prisoner standing before her.

Calandra learned enough from conversations with Xttra and Bo'un to understand Stellar Guard secret operations officers were a special breed of ruthless. She harbored no sympathy for their prisoners because they were complicit in helping Delcor crush all forms of dissent. This man knew all about hybrids and what their existence meant. Yet, he consented to being a merciless tool for the chief sovereign. Still, he had useful knowledge related to Delcor, his plans, and his activities.

Knowledge she hoped to draw out.

"What do you gain from this?" Calandra started pacing back and forth in front of the master pilot. "Why tie your fate to the chief sovereign? Why prop him up while he clings to power?"

Her questions only earned an eyeroll and a scornful smile. The master pilot paused, cleared his throat, and directed a forceful stare at Calandra.

"He is our one, true sovereign," he said, speaking in an equally forceful tone. "You are merely an ictus bug he will soon crush under his foot. Your rebellion has already failed. Your voice will fall silent."

"Your sovereign is the one who will be silenced."

Xttra approached the prisoner while making this declaration and tapped on a restraint circling his right wrist. Calandra's eyes trailed him, and she took note of the captive master pilot's bandaged hand for the first time. A sign he resisted Xttra with force. Her heartbeat accelerated at this subtle revelation of his attempt to steal away the life of the man she loved—nearly depriving Alexa of a father.

AMONG HIDDEN STARS

Calandra stopped, faced him again, and scowled. Her left hand balled into a tight metal fist, and she pushed back against a surging anger boiling like hot water within her chest.

"You do know you will not return to Ra'ahm, right?" Xttra said. "Daraconian leadership will hold you accountable for your role in perpetuating Delcor's crimes. Why throw away your life for him?"

The captive master pilot's eyes trailed from Xttra to Calandra and back again. A wry smile crept over his lips, as though he guarded secret knowledge.

"Trust my words when I say you will never defeat my sovereign. He will be your sovereign again soon enough. Every part of Lathos will fall under his domain."

Calandra crinkled her nose and her eyebrows knit together. She considered him a sane, if misguided, zealot until this moment. His claim sounded ludicrous.

"Delcor cannot rule an entire planet," she said. "He does not have enough troops or resources to stand—"

"He will soon engineer the galaxy's most powerful weapons." The master pilot cut her off. "When he does, his domain will exceed what the ancient Wekonn Empire itself once ruled."

Calandra snapped her head toward Xttra. A distinct horror filled his widening eyes. The same terror gripped her from head to toe. Their resistance had taken on a greater urgency.

Delcor planned to plunge billions of people on Lathos into a devastating war.

3

elcor slammed his fist on his writing table. A familiar loathsome image again materialized on his holocaster. How did this rebel and her allies continually penetrate digital barriers designed to silence their treacherous revelations? How long must he suffer from their insolence before his agents finally found and executed Calandra Menankar and Xttra Oogan, destroying their nascent resistance?

"The chief sovereign lies to Ra'ahm daily. He strayed from Ahm's true path and unjustly retains power over our people through fear."

A distinct icy fury infused each word. Her voice held the same fierce passion Calandra first showed on the day she used Peleusian technology to infiltrate his assembly chamber. Her brash words stuck like glue in Delcor's mind. She never rested in her self-appointed quest to expose what she characterized as his evil actions. Delcor leaned forward in his chair and wrapped his hands around the armrests, digging his fingernails into the fabric while staring at Calandra's unbroken image cluttering his holoscreen.

"We must rise against Delcor and his entire clan. He is a curse upon our people. My friends, you and I are the tools Ahm forged to break this curse."

A scowl washed over his face and deepened with each word Calandra spoke. Her tenacity in standing against Delcor only infuriated him. Every stratagem he enacted to silence this worthless astronomer had failed. Her voice only grew louder and reached farther. She had become an irritating ictus bug, forever eluding his grasp while scurrying from one dark hidden nest to another.

"Shut down all holocaster signals at once!" His voice thundered across the expansive throne room. "Her words must not poison my people's ears for another second."

Delcor's scribe, a young woman with elaborately styled hair seated across the table from him, set down a stylus atop a metal plate. She quickly pinched her eyes shut and bowed her head.

"Your will is my will, my sovereign."

She rose from her seat and sprinted with equal haste from the throne room.

Calandra's message continued, but the chief sovereign did his best to block out her remaining words. He resisted an urge to simply clap his hands over his ears. Seeking a distraction, his eyes drifted down to the partially inscribed metal plate. It bore an official message to Ahmmana's governor. Calandra's attempts at stirring an insurrection spread far beyond Luma and the northern province. Her words infected his people like a virus. Her message now found receptive ears in Ahmmana and other major cities throughout the southern province.

Delcor's well-scrubbed face concealed dark circles under his eyes arising from tossing and turning in his spacious bed. Night after night unwelcome thoughts took root in his mind and sprang forth like invisible noxious weeds. Those nocturnal thoughts popped up again with eyes wide open.

"You should have taken the threat she posed more seriously." His voice barely climbed above a whisper as he scolded himself. "The astronomer's treachery is a trial from Ahm you brought on yourself."

Delcor pushed back his chair and jumped to his feet. He shook his head in disgust at all the continued efforts to undermine his rule. These traitors mocked him with their ingratitude. Did they bring peace to Ra'ahm and deliver it from a brutal war with the Confederation? Were they architects of a prosperous nation that grew into the envy of an entire planet? He marched to a nearby window and stared out across the palace courtyard.

Everything good about Ra'ahm found life through his vision. The people should thank Ahm daily for the chance to call him their chief sovereign.

"I have not wavered in showing you evidence of Delcor's true character." Calandra's voice pierced his thoughts. Her words lingered between his ears with the painful persistence of a blinding headache. "And I promise I will never waver in my—"

Her voice vanished before completing the thought. Delcor turned away from the window and glanced back at the holoscreen. It lingered above the holocaster, now devoid of any images. He released a relieved sigh.

Calandra Menankar was silenced.

Again.

Delcor wrestled with forging a path for making her silence permanent. Building such a path offered a true dilemma.

Her allies hunted down one hybrid creation facility after another and destroyed them all. Every hybrid he created using technology and knowledge obtained from Rubrum scientists also met destruction along the way. Ahm opened a door for him to rule Lathos. Calandra and Xttra slammed that door shut while leading the effort to demolish his entire force of hybrids. These were tools created with a singular purpose of delivering the world to Ahm and his chosen ruler. And she dared to invoke Ahm's name while undermining his rule! Her traitorous actions boiled Delcor's blood.

Voices rose from the street. A scattered few soon morphed into a clamoring din of unwelcome noise. Faint at first before growing stronger and closer.

Shouts.

Chants.

Pure anger oozed from their cries.

Delcor snapped his head toward the window again. His courtyard presented a scene of serenity from blooming scarlet fraxa trees to rippling fountain pools. Outside the palace gates, a malevolent storm brewed.

A storm of flesh and blood.

A crowd gathered beyond the walls bordering his courtyard. Delcor's aging eyes did not discern their origins or numbers. He only perceived faces drawn into tight scowls and raised fists.

"A new sovereign must rise! A new sovereign must rise! A new sovereign must rise!"

Their repeated chant dug into his ears like a freshly sharpened blade. Delcor's jaw tightened, and he clenched his teeth. Every single traitor outside the palace gates would soon lament their insolence toward him.

The chief sovereign marched up to his throne and threw himself on the sapinoa hair cushioned seat. He mashed down a round green button on the left armrest. A holoscreen rose from a concealed arca vox in the platform below the throne. A city guard commander appeared on the screen hovering before him.

"Disperse the crowd." Delcor's voice masked his internal rage with deliberate calmness. "Seize the leaders. Make an example of anyone who dares resist. Disruptive behavior of this magnitude must be dealt with firmly in the name of public safety."

The commander answered with an abrupt nod.

"Your will is my will, my sovereign."

His image vanished from the holoscreen. Delcor rose to his feet a second time and returned to the window overlooking the palace courtyard. City guards lobbed stun pebbles into the midst of the protesters. Bright flashes enveloped parts of the crowd. Several protesters fell to their knees, clutching their eyes and screaming. Delcor's scowl fled from his lips. A satisfied smirk now conquered the same territory.

His eyes did not stray from the dwindling crowd. City guards charged toward protesters and surrounded their incapacitated leaders. They quickly bound their new captives and hauled them from Delcor's sight. Others fled down streets in several directions once their vision returned to normal, with multiple city guards in pursuit.

Footsteps filled the throne room, accompanied by a hushed argument. Delcor closed his eyelids and unloaded an irritated sigh. He did not bother to turn and look at his newest visitors.

Their voices betrayed their identities.

"We cannot let the traitor's message infect my people like a plague," Delcor said. "Open your eyes. Can you see the fruits of your failures on the streets of Luma?"

"I beg your forgiveness, father. We created a new complex algorithm to block their transmissions, but they uncovered our encryption key."

"This is more than a coincidence."

"If enemy agents operate within our ranks, I vow to swiftly expose their identities and bring them to justice."

Delcor opened his eyes and finally turned to face his visitors. His son stood before him, concern flooding his light blue eyes and manifesting in a stoic frown. The same concern burdened Delcor himself.

"How can you ever be a future chief sovereign, Giljax, if you can't keep Ra'ahm secure from its enemies?"

Giljax averted his eyes, brushed back wavy red bangs from his forehead, and instinctively glanced over at the empty throne. Delcor shook his head and refocused his attention on his other visitor.

A balding, bearded man also stood before him, dressed in a purple robe. Vertical white lines with dashes running at right angles on both sides from top to bottom covered each breast. Symbols of divine light offering a visual witness of his station as a supreme cleric within the Order of Ahm—specifically governing followers of Ahm who dwelt in Luma, the capital city.

"Ahm will never let you fall from your holy station, my sovereign." The supreme cleric cast his eyes downward and bowed his head. "These are his people. You are their chosen ruler."

Delcor studied him for a moment before finally approaching him. He laid a hand on his shoulder.

"Your faith assures me, Aginon. The truth you affirm strengthens my resolve."

Aginon's eyes remained fixed upon the floor.

"Your resolve, my sovereign?"

"I will never rest until I secure my right to govern until Ahm sees fit to bring me home to his dwelling."

A brief chuckle greeted Delcor's words. Fire flashed through his eyes, and he snapped his head toward Giljax.

"Do you find humor in our current situation?"

An enigmatic smile melted from his lips, and he stiffened. Giljax pressed his knuckles against his hips.

"My intent is not to mock you, father." His tone stayed calm and deliberate. "An inspired thought entered my mind. A solution to our current dilemma."

Delcor studied him suspiciously.

"Speak your mind."

Giljax nodded. His eyes never left his father, but he squared his shoulders toward Aginon.

"Why do we not find and use the Staff of Onrai?"

Delcor turned the same direction as his son. Aginon raised his chin and peeked at both men. His expression stayed stoic, but the supreme cleric's eyes betrayed an internal bewilderment.

"Begging your pardon, my sovereign. The Staff of Onrai is merely an ancient legend." Aginon straightened his back and made direct eye contact with Delcor for the first time. "No reliable source of historical evidence confirms it ever existed."

Giljax rubbed his hands over his cheeks and sighed.

"The Wekonn Empire itself bears evidence to the truth of that legend," he said. "No other people ever grew powerful enough to rule all of Lathos."

"Their empire failed more than 500 years ago."

"It stood unchallenged for a thousand years."

Delcor's ears perked up. A thousand years? Their argument continued, but his attention turned inward.

Historical records chronicled how ancient Wekonn rulers stayed a few steps ahead of their adversaries. He admired their strategic thinking, cunning, and tenacity. In the past, Delcor ascribed their unrivaled power to sound military strategy and wise governing. Still, passing such wisdom down through an unbroken chain of rulers stretching over fifty generations seemed improbable. Giljax's comments opened his eyes to a new possibility for the true source of their power.

Did the Staff of Onrai play a critical role in forming the Wekonn Empire? If knowledge obtained from the staff became a catalyst enabling their rule over Lathos, this made it more valuable than all riches he could ever own. The staff held an unmatched power he must claim for himself.

"Where is it now?"

Giljax and Aginon fell silent and wheeled around to face him. Both met the chief sovereign with blank stares. Each looked to the other to answer his inquiry.

"Where is the staff now?" Delcor repeated his original question in a firmer tone.

"Hidden away, my sovereign," Aginon said. "Lost to the mists of time. Legends say acolytes of Pyrah, an ancient oracle of Ahm, concealed the Staff of Onrai inside an isolated sanctuary where it remained protected far from the Wekonn Emperor's grasp."

Delcor crossed his arms and studied the supreme cleric's face. Aginon stiffened like a stone column. His fingers alone moved, fidgeting with a sleeve on his robe. The chief sovereign shifted his eyes to his son. Giljax also stared at Aginon. He gulped when he sensed Delcor's intense gaze returning to him and faced his father again.

"If the staff is hidden from the world, we must spare no effort to learn where the relic lies hidden," Delcor said. "I leave it in your capable hands, my son."

"My hands?" Giljax repeated.

"Gather our brightest scholars from the Order of Ahm and set them to work scouring ancient records in the Central Archives. If clues to the Staff of Onrai's location exist, we will find them within our vast repository of knowledge."

Giljax answered him with a quick nod. Aginon mimicked his action and added another customary bow. Both men rushed from the throne room to tackle the assigned task. Delcor glanced over at his writing table after they left and let a satisfied smile conquer his lips.

Their search had potential to turn into nothing more than a fool's errand. But if those efforts yielded fruit and they uncovered the staff's location, such a discovery promised to change his destiny and Ra'ahm's destiny.

His right to rule would continue unchallenged for as long as a single breath of life remained within him.

4

alandra watched Xttra with a skeptical eye. He tried to paint a supportive smile on his lips, but she instantly saw through his façade. He struggled to conceal his true feelings from her. Worry filled his deep blue eyes, betraying that smile. When Xttra turned away from her and sauntered over to a nearby window, Calandra followed on his heels.

He owed her an explanation. Why did her news stir a current of negative emotions he obviously labored to bury from her sight?

"You think this is a bad idea, don't you?"

Xttra tugged at a gray shirt sleeve covering his wrist and licked his lips. Whatever thought rested on his tongue, he fought to conceal and silence those words.

"He's my baby brother," Calandra said. "I'll be fine."

"Something doesn't feel right about this whole situation." Xttra replied. "Jemanoah hasn't spoken to you since we brought him to Daraconiah. Why is he taking a sudden interest in you now?"

Calandra cast her eyes toward an east window in their dwelling. She let them trail across a row of flowering acutyi shrubs.

Yellow buds only now began peeking out from each shrub. Her thoughts centered on her brother as she stared at the nascent flowers. Jemanoah used to be a treasured friend. Why could he not be her friend again?

She wanted her brother to be her brother again. Meeting with him offered a new, hopeful path forward. A first step toward a destination frustratingly eluding her reach for such a long time.

"Maybe he wants to mend old wounds," Calandra finally said, without making eye contact with Xttra. "I want to do the same."

"You shouldn't go alone."

"I can take care of myself."

"That's not the source of my worries."

She wheeled around and greeted him with a fierce stare. Xttra stepped backward and raised his hands. Concern claimed every inch of his face from a furrowed brow to a nervous frown.

"Jemanoah is a good man." Her tone grew brusque. "Why do you refuse to see what I see?"

Xttra drew a couple steps closer again and laid his hand on her shoulder. His eyes fixed on hers.

"People change, Calandra. And those changes aren't always better than what came beforehand."

Calandra brushed back a lock of auburn hair resting against her cheek. What was he implying? Xttra did not know her baby brother in the same way she knew him. Nor could he ever gain such knowledge. Jemanoah admittedly showed rough edges in need of smoothing—including a combustible temper. He also owned a kind and caring heart. She refused to believe his intentions were anything except honorable.

"You're not stopping me from seeing my brother." Calandra crossed her arms and refused to look away. "I want my clan to be a part of our lives again. I want Alexa to bond with them like I did as a child."

Xttra glanced over her shoulder toward their daughter's bedroom. Calandra turned and faced the same direction, letting her gaze drift through the open doorway. Alexa giggled and chattered with excitement while sitting on the floor and playing with Bella. The little cala batted at a small ribbon in Alexa's hand.

"I also want Alexa to bond with my clan," Xttra said. "This is equally difficult for me—seeing their attitudes sour toward us. I wish things were different."

Calandra returned her gaze to him.

"So let things be different. Ahm opened a door and Jemanoah reached out. Shouldn't I walk through and embrace him?"

Xttra tilted his head toward the ceiling and pressed his lips together. After a moment, he answered with a reluctant nod.

"I trust your judgment."

"As you should."

He turned to her. His brows knit together.

"Promise me one thing."

"What's that?"

"We'll go to the fountains together and you'll wear flex armor as a precaution."

Calandra let out an annoyed sigh.

"I never go anywhere without it."

Xttra had grown much too overprotective since their narrow escape from a phony street musician at the Sol Umbra Festival. Calandra grew weary of his frequent reminders to keep her eyes and ears open. She wanted a normal life that did not involve obsessing over agents of Delcor lurking hidden in shadows, waiting to unleash a surprise attack. Kevin and Bo'un did all the right things to conceal their location when they transmitted messages into Ra'ahm. Their encounter with an agent of Delcor at the Sol Umbra Festival counted as an unlucky fluke.

Still, Calandra donned flex armor beneath her long-sleeved black lace shirt and matching pants. Concealing her armor restricted her wardrobe choices, but Calandra found ways to make it work. She entrusted Alexa to the care of Ashelle, a neighbor who had grown into a close friend, and departed with Xttra in their aerorover.

They flew over the eastern half of Daracos. Rectangular towers dotted the cityscape. Each tower featured a partially embedded spiral column on every side and climbed skyward to a breathtaking height. The towers appeared much more striking and appealing than their own dwelling near the edge of the city. Xttra wanted a modest place designed to divert unwanted attention and he succeeded. Their home resembled a series of three giant staggered square boxes stacked atop one another with a flat roof covering each level's exposed portion.

Their aerorover soon circled above an expansive crimson grass field overlooking a small lake. Clusters of fraxa trees dotted the edges on both ends of the field. New leaves already filled their expansive branches. Calandra gazed upon an open-air stage surrounded by a staggered terrace cut into a half bowl shape. Seats covered each level. It offered a popular gathering spot to listen to local musicians perform. Right near the place where Jemanoah wanted to meet to talk.

Xttra landed on a small platform a short walk from three towering fountains spaced an equal distance apart. Each fountain resembled a mountain waterfall in its construction. Water cascaded into reflecting pools forming a half-circle connected to the bottom end of the waterfall façade. Evenly spaced stone pillars encircled the outer perimeter beyond the pools.

Calandra took Alexa to this same spot intermittently and they both enjoyed every minute they spent here. Each pool featured dancing waters. Mechanisms below the pools forced sprays of water to shoot upward at timed intervals and the water formed a dazzling array of shapes. Stone benches and tables built into the ground several steps away from the nearest pool's edge let people watch the dancing water without getting splashed.

It made sense Jemanoah wanted to talk in this place. He loved visiting and exploring waterfalls as a child. Calandra recalled his visible excitement after they discovered a unique waterfall on the first trail they explored together when he grew old enough to go with her on longer hikes through the Aurora Mountains.

"Callie! Callie! Come over here and see this!"

His excited words entered her mind as though Jemanoah said them only a day earlier. Her little brother darted ahead of Calandra on the trail earlier after sloshing and churning water grabbed their attention. When she reached the same bluff, she finally laid eyes on what sparked his excitement.

Jemanoah had waded into a shallow pool inside a cavern. Water sloshed around his legs, just above his ankles, as he journeyed into the cavern. An uneven rock wall surrounded the pool on three sides and a sloped rock ceiling connected one end of the wall to the opposite end. Water cascaded through a giant natural hole in the rock ceiling and splashed into the pool.

"This is so amazing!" Calandra could not peel her eyes away from the falling water as she stood outside the cavern. "We picked the right trail to explore."

She drew out her holocaster and captured a living image of falling water and another image of Jemanoah splashing happily through the pool. Once Calandra tucked the holocaster away again, she followed her brother and drew closer to the waterfall.

Calandra splashed through the pool and stopped underneath the fall itself. Water sprayed her hair and face with the force of countless concentrated raindrops. A wide grin enveloped her lips, and she closed her eyes.

"Best hike ever?" Jemanoah asked. His breathless voice barely rose above the falling torrent.

Calandra opened her eyes again and looked over at her brother. He claimed a spot next to her under the fall and wore the same happy smile.

"Best hike ever," she repeated with a slight nod.

Calandra closed her eyes again and enjoyed the cool sprays of water. If it were possible to spend an entire day at this waterfall, she would not hesitate to stay here. This place felt like a hidden paradise.

"I think I see your brother headed our way."

Xttra's voice snapped Calandra back to the present. Images of the waterfall faded back into deep corners within her mind. She spotted Jemanoah walking toward a stone bench and table on the opposite side of the far pool. Calandra opened the passenger side door and stepped out of the aerorover.

A peaceful slumber-like feeling permeated the area around the fountains. The whole place appeared deserted—not out of the ordinary for a late morning hour. Jemanoah's green eyes trailed up to Calandra as she and Xttra approached the same stone table. A small smile crept over his lips when Jemanoah first laid eyes on her, only to vanish with equal speed when he noticed Xttra.

"This is a surprise." His eyes shifted back to her. "I only expected to meet with you, Callie."

"What can I say?" Xttra replied. "Angry treemas could not drag me away from these fountains. I can't get enough of watching the dancing waters."

Calandra shot an annoyed half-frown at her husband. She did not welcome his sarcastic attitude. She came to mend old wounds with her brother, not open fresh ones.

"It's good to see you again," she said, turning and facing Jemanoah a second time. "I've missed you. We've gone far too long without speaking."

Jemanoah bowed his head and closed his eyes.

"It didn't need to be this way."

Calandra took a seat on a bench across from her brother. She rested her arms on the stone table and leaned forward. He kept his eyes closed as though engrossed in a silent prayer to Ahm.

"I had no choice," she said. "I needed to bring our whole clan here to Daraconiah to keep us all safe. You. Our parents. Everyone."

Jemanoah lifted his head again. His eyes settled on her, and a determined look washed over his face.

"I understand why you did what you did now. I honestly do. And it rends my heart to witness how things have turned out."

"Between us?"

"Of course. I regret lost time and empty memories."

Jemanoah brushed his face and scratched the bridge of his nose with his pinky finger. A crease formed in Xttra's brow when he made this gesture. He kept his eyes glued to Jemanoah, silently probing him like a suspicious stranger. His reaction irritated Calandra, but she brushed it aside and focused on her brother.

"We can chart a new course," Calandra said, offering a hopeful smile. "One starting right here."

"And become one clan again," Jemanoah added.

She straightened up and offered him her right hand. Her brother glanced down at her extended hand and then at the other one. His eyes traced over metal bones and rubber padding composing the end of the limb.

"You're not wearing a glove. I grew so used to seeing one after—"

"I embraced who I am." Calandra interrupted Jemanoah before he vocalized his full thought. "Hiding from yourself is never a wise idea."

Her brother made eye contact with her again.

"I suppose you're right. Face what's in the mirror and yield to Ahm's will so he can shape us like wet clay."

Jemanoah raised his hand and scratched his nose with his pinky finger again. On the exact spot he scratched the first time. Xttra's lips parted slightly, and he crinkled his eyes and nose at him.

"Is everything all right?"

Calandra's eyes darted from her husband back to her brother. Jemanoah quickly dropped his hand again and flashed a tight-lipped smile.

"Everything is fine with me. How about you?"

Xttra shrugged.

"I have no complaints."

Jemanoah shifted on the bench and tugged at one shirt sleeve followed by the other. Calandra eyed him suspiciously now. Her brother's nervous body language was out-of-character for him.

"Do you have somewhere else you need to be?" she asked. "You're making me nervous with your twitching."

Jemanoah leaned back and crossed his arms in front of his belly. The edge of the stone table blocked her view of his hands.

"Asking you to come here was not an easy decision," he said. "You can't imagine how much upheaval you created in my life."

Xttra dropped his hands to his hips and leaned forward on the bench.

"We should talk about something else. Do you like watching football?"

Jemanoah shot him a puzzled look.

"Football? I've never heard of such a thing."

Xttra painted a smile on his lips.

"Such an exciting game. I can't get enough of Seattle."

"I'm not familiar with that place."

"Seattle Sea…um…hawks. My favorite NLF team!"

Calandra's throat tightened. Her heart raced and she bit her lower lip. She knew exactly what those code words meant. Jemanoah tilted his head toward her and shifted in his seat again.

"Let's turn around and watch the dancing waters for a little while."
Her brother fought to keep a tremor from overtaking his voice.
Calandra stiffened. Her body grew as rigid as the stone pillars surrounding the fountains.

"No. You tell me what's really going on first."

He scowled. A second later, Jemanoah licked his lips.

"You're only wasting your time stalling." Xttra's eyes locked firmly on her brother. "No one is left to carry out your secret plan."

Calandra snapped her head toward him.

"Secret plan?" she repeated.

"Your brother has an ulterior motive for inviting you here." Xttra said, glancing over at her. "This isn't about reconciliation at all. That was never his intention."

Jemanoah unleashed a loud curse. He brought his body forward and raised his hands to push the table forward with a violent shove. It tilted and collided with Xttra and Calandra, knocking them backward off the bench. Her brother sprang clear of the bench and dug an eliminator out from a concealed pocket on his hip. The chamber held a full charge of blue laser bolts.

"You're a traitor to your clan and our sovereign," he shouted. "Only your death will redeem our clan's name!"

Jemanoah fired a bolt at Calandra as she scrambled away from the bench. She gasped and cried out. Pain rippled from her shoulders down to her tailbone.

As she fell, her brother unleashed a scream of his own. Calandra rolled on her side and lifted her head off the grass. Xttra had drawn his eliminator from its holster. The weapon pointed right at Jemanoah. His shirt sported a fresh, smoking hole below his ribs.

Blood oozed from beneath the torn fabric.

Jemanoah turned and stumbled forward. He regained his footing and raced toward a waiting aerorover beyond the far pool. Xttra fired off two more bolts. Neither one found their target.

Bo'un emerged from a cluster of fraxa trees where he concealed himself earlier. A long-range spear gun hung off his arm as he sprinted toward the fountains in the same direction as Jemanoah.

"Don't let him escape," Xttra called out. "Disable that aerorover."

Bo'un nodded and continued sprinting past the overturned stone table. Before he made it halfway to the aerorover, the engines ignited. The vehicle lifted off the ground with Jemanoah on board. Bo'un slowed to aim his weapon skyward and fired a spear head. It struck the intended target but glanced off a back panel without inflicting any considerable damage to the vehicle.

The aerorover climbed above the treetops and zipped away. Bo'un let the spear gun drop to his side again once he realized the vehicle escaped his weapon's range. He shook his head, turned around, and sprinted back.

"I didn't reach it in time," Bo'un said. "I'll find that coward and his aerorover somehow. You have my word."

"NLF?"

Calandra winced and raised herself off the ground into a sitting position when she heard Kevin's voice. Her entire back throbbed. He sprinted toward the others from a different direction. An eliminator hung loose in his hand near his hip.

"NLF?" Kevin repeated. "It's called the NFL! As in National Football League. Really not a hard acronym to remember."

Xttra tossed up his hands and shrugged.

"NFL. NLF. Close enough."

Kevin rolled his eyes. He stopped dead in his tracks when he spotted Calandra on the ground. His earlier annoyance vanished in an instant.

"What happened? Are you injured?"

Xttra wheeled around. Concern flooded his deep blue eyes. He rushed to her side and dropped to his knees. Xttra rubbed his hand over the spot where the eliminator bolt struck. When he brought his hand away from her back, his skin showed no traces of blood.

"A bolt struck you, but your flex armor absorbed most of the impact. That's a relief."

Calandra stared at him in stunned silence. The bolt striking her concealed armor and her fall was not the lone source for her pain. Her lips trembled and tears welled up in her eyes.

"My brother tried to kill me."

Those words left her tongue in a tortured whisper. Calandra said nothing else. She lacked the strength to restrain the rising tears any longer. They burst from her eyes and flowed down both cheeks as she buried her head in her arms, sobbing.

5

The right words eluded Xttra's grasp. He lingered in the doorway and pondered what he should say to Calandra, searching for some means of consoling her. She perched on the edge of the bed and stared at the opposite wall. Tears streamed down her cheeks while she buried her mouth in her hands. His inability to produce comforting words mocked Xttra. He wanted to ease her grief and pain but had no clue where to start.

Jemanoah's horrific actions shook her to the depths of her soul. They produced the same effect on Xttra.

Calandra's brother betrayed her trust and love for him in the cruelest manner possible. A singularly horrifying thought crossed Xttra's mind while he spirited her away from the fountains. It clung to him while he flew the woman he loved to safety.

Jemanoah would have murdered Calandra had I not been here to protect her.

That unwelcome realization ate at Xttra's heart. He longed to track her brother down and punish him. Inflict pain for everything he did to her. Calandra deserved better. Her clan—especially that setaworm of a younger brother—proved themselves unworthy of sharing the same name and the same blood.

Xttra decided to say nothing. What could he say? He walked over, sat next to Calandra, and encircled his arm around his wife's shoulders. She glanced up, her beautiful green eyes swimming with tears. Calandra turned into him and wrapped both arms around his back. He dipped his chin down and tenderly kissed her forehead.

"I loved him." A choked whisper cloaked her words while she clung to Xttra. "How could he do this to me?"

Xttra pondered the same question repeatedly. Jemanoah's continued devotion to Delcor and his newfound willingness to murder his own sister in the chief sovereign's name made no sense. No tangible path leading back to a life in Ra'ahm existed for her brother or anyone else belonging to Calandra's clan.

Not while Delcor ruled.

The same fate claimed Xttra's clan. Daraconiah became their home because it offered the safest refuge from Delcor's wrath.

"Miama?"

Xttra glanced over at the doorway. Alexa peeked her little head around the corner. She wore a worried frown. He beckoned to his daughter and invited her inside the bedroom. Alexa scampered over to her parents and stopped in front of Calandra.

"Why are you crying?"

"Miama is sad," Xttra said.

Alexa's eyes darted from her to him.

"Why?"

"Someone she loves hurt her."

"Why?"

"Because he's mean."

Alexa gazed up at Calandra again. Her lower lip jutted out and she kicked at the wooden floor.

"I'm sad too."

Calandra lifted her head away from Xttra's chest and turned to their daughter. She brushed away tears with her hand and formed her lips into a slight smile.

"You sweet child." Calandra held out an arm, inviting Alexa into their embrace. "Don't be sad. We can help each other be happy again."

Their little girl broke into a warm smile and sprang forward. Calandra scooped Alexa into her lap and kissed her left cheek. She held her daughter close enough for Alexa's long red hair to brush against Calandra's cheek and mouth. Ashelle braided it into simple braids earlier. White ribbons woven through two separate braids connected in small tight bows near the ends.

"You have a visitor."

Xttra and Calandra slipped out of their embrace and snapped their heads toward the doorway. Ashelle stepped inside the room. Her light brown hair also formed braids laced with ribbons— matching the styling on Alexa's hair. Kevin entered the room a couple of steps behind her.

"Still no sign of Jemanoah," he said. "But finding him might be the least of our worries."

Xttra exchanged worried glances with Calandra.

"What do you mean?" he asked, facing Kevin again.

"I got word through the grapevine a Ra'ahm minister spilled the beans concerning Delcor's master plan to a Confederation agent embedded with that minister."

"His plan to start a planetwide war? Calandra and I already gathered the same information from the prisoners we turned over to Daraconian custody."

"That only covers page one in his world domination playbook. Now I got a solid idea of what else he's scrawled on page two."

Ashelle turned and flashed a cute smile at him.

"You Earthians have a strange way of speaking."

Kevin responded with a brief laugh. He clasped his hands together and shook his head.

"I think you actually meant Earthians have the best way of speaking."

His subdued reaction to her remark defied Xttra's expectations. Of course, Kevin finding Ashelle attractive contributed to him downplaying her verbal jab. He shared his heartfelt desire for her on more than one occasion while accompanying Xttra on hybrid-destroying missions.

"What news have you learned?" Xttra asked, redirecting Kevin's attention away from flirting with their neighbor.

"The word is old Delcor plans to track down some ancient weapon called the Staff of Onrai," he said. "Ever heard of it?"

Calandra gasped and her green eyes widened. Her worried expression matched Xttra's internal reaction. They were both familiar with the Staff of Onrai and its role in Lathoan history.

Kevin did not bring a welcome piece of news.

"I've definitely heard of the Staff of Onrai." Xttra's tone grew subdued as he contemplated details of the weapon's history. "Delcor is taking much more drastic measures than any of us realized."

"It's only a legend, right?" Ashelle asked. "Is there any historical evidence this staff ever existed?"

"We can't afford to take that chance."

Xttra wheeled around after Calandra answered her. She set Alexa down on the bed beside her and sprang to her feet. Determination swallowed the earlier concern present in her eyes. Calandra pressed her lips together and marched over to a table occupying the opposite corner of the room. She scooped up a copy of the *Book of Ahm* and thumbed through metallic pages. Calandra stopped on a page approximately one-third of the way into the book and trailed down the page with her finger.

"The Staff of Onrai was forged by Onrai, an ancient prime oracle, under the guidance of Ahm." Her eyes remained fixed on the page as she studied a passage from the book. "He created the staff as a tool to build a civilization on Lathos governed by Ahm's teachings. It housed a portion of the divine creator's true power."

"His true power?" Kevin repeated. A puzzled look washed over his face. "Is this like your planet's version of the Ark of the Covenant?"

Calandra glanced up from the page at him.

"I'm not familiar with that object."

"It's a famous lost religious artifact back on Earth. Legends describe it housing the power of God. An alliance of 12 ancient Jewish tribes called Israelites carried the ark into battle to conquer a land called Canaan."

Calandra frowned.

"The Staff of Onrai was never designed to function as a weapon of war like your Earthian god's relic. Its true purpose became corrupted and that opened a door for the ancient Wekonn Empire to rise."

"What purpose was it originally designed to serve?" Kevin asked.

"Revealing hidden knowledge."

"What sort of knowledge?"

"Everything. The Staff of Onrai reveals the past, present, and future all at once."

Kevin's jaw dropped when he grasped the full implications of Calandra's statement. A somber feeling welled up inside Xttra and squeezed his heart with the strength of a giant shadowy hand. The Staff of Onrai grew into a cautionary tale among all Lathoan clans after the Wekonn Empire fell.

Xttra recalled legends passed down to him while still a child. Ahm created the staff to function as a repository of knowledge encompassing all important subjects. History. Agriculture. Science.

The divine creator designed it as a tool to aid Onrai in building a holy civilization on Lathos—one modeled after the eternal worlds where Ahm dwelt.

Xttra, like other Lathoans familiar with these legends, knew what happened when Onrai's successors grew careless in their roles as caretakers of Ahm's creation. Their arrogance and slothful ways created the right conditions needed for the Wekonn Empire to rise.

Galjokk, the first Wekonn Emperor, stole the Staff of Onrai from a temple housing the relic in a daring nighttime raid. He fled deep into the Aurora Mountains and used knowledge drawn from the staff to recruit and build a powerful army. Galjokk then swept down from his mountain base and conquered one city after another with ease. He succeeded in bringing every tribe and clan on Lathos under his rule within seven years of stealing the Staff of Onrai.

The Wekonn Empire stood for a thousand years before it finally broke apart after the staff was stolen and hidden. Untold billions suffered under the rule of one authoritarian emperor after another during that time.

Xttra had no clue if the Staff of Onrai ever existed. He wondered if the relic was nothing more than a myth created to explain why a single empire ruled an entire planet for so long. One thing was certain. If the staff did exist, and indeed held the power ascribed to it, they needed to uncover its hiding place before Delcor did the same. They could not allow him to create an oppressive empire rivaling what Galjokk once built.

"What does the Staff of Onrai look like?" Kevin's new question pierced a growing uncomfortable silence inside the bedroom. "How does it work?"

"I'll show you," Calandra said.

She exited the bedroom and walked down a set of stairs to the second level of their dwelling. Xttra, Kevin, and Ashelle followed her. Calandra slid open a door leading to a small room where she recorded messages which she regularly transmitted into Ra'ahm. A long shelf mounted on the opposite wall across from her recording equipment held a collection of metal books and parchments. Some were records Calandra rescued from a subterranean storage room before fleeing Ra'ahm. Xttra found others during his hybrid destroying missions and brought the records back to Lathos with him.

"I'm so happy I have the record we need on hand," Calandra said. "It saves us from an exhausting search in the public records depository."

She marched across the room and grabbed a parchment from the middle of the shelf. Calandra unrolled the record, revealing a series of hand drawn images. Each image detailed an important religious or historical relic originating on Lathos. Small rows of text below each image described the artifact it illustrated.

"This image is a depiction of the Staff of Onrai based on ancient texts." Calandra trailed her finger downward and pointed to the third image drawn on the parchment. "It has a unique appearance. It certainly doesn't resemble any weapon I've ever seen on Lathos or Earth."

She handed the parchment to Kevin. Xttra stood next to him and peered over his shoulder at the image. It depicted a shoulder high staff carved from polished fraxa wood. An oval white stone topped the staff on one end. Rays of white light emanated from the stone, symbolizing knowledge contained within the relic.

"No documented evidence exists pointing to where the Staff of Onrai is now." Xttra glanced up from the parchment at Calandra. "How will we track it down? Where do we even start?"

She shrugged.

"Sometimes, moving a mountain requires removing one rock at a time."

Xttra frowned. They could not afford to waste time on an endless search. Who knew how long Delcor's minions had been seeking the staff?

"We can't take a one-rock-at-a-time approach," he said. "I'm sure it works for hunting stars and planets. This is a whole different animal."

Calandra's eyes lit up.

"That's it."

"What?"

"I know where we need to take our search."

Xttra glanced over at Kevin and smiled. The same realization that came over her also struck him.

"And where is that?" Kevin asked.

"The Staff of Onrai is not on Lathos because it was hidden on another planet."

"Another planet?" Ashelle's mouth dropped open as she grasped Calandra's line of thought. "How could anyone take such an important relic from Lathos without being discovered?"

Calandra shrugged again.

"I can't answer that question. All I know is if I wanted to prevent others from misusing the Staff of Onrai, concealing it on a distant planet is an effective solution."

Her theory made sense to Xttra. It also meant an extensive search lay ahead. They needed to uncover which distant alien planet housed the Staff of Onrai before Delcor reached the same conclusion as Calandra.

6

o'un rubbed the scars along his jaw and neck as his eyes trailed
ancient text. His lips moved as he read, but he said nothing. When
Bo'un finally reached the end of the document displayed on the
holoscreen, his lips curled into a slight frown.

He looked as irritated and confused as Xttra felt.

"Another dead-end trail," he said.

Xttra lost count of how many books and parchments they combed
through inside the Daracos public records depository. Two hours into
their search and neither he nor Bo'un had taken meaningful steps
toward narrowing down a potential location for the Staff of Onrai.

Still, Xttra ignored the urge to quit now. A persistent hope
drove him forward. The next record he scrutinized would hold the
evidence they sought. If he quit before studying that record, they
would never obtain critical information they desperately needed.
And he would shoulder the blame for quitting too soon.

Xttra wondered how Calandra, Bo'un, and Kevin all patiently
sifted through historical records. They were steadfast and efficient,
particularly Calandra. He wanted to board a spaceship and take

direct action rather than sit around and read about civilizations rising and falling hundreds of generations before he existed.

"Anything catch your eyes?" Bo'un asked, glancing away from the holoscreen.

Xttra pursed his lips and shook his head. His holoscreen displayed a brief historical record chronicling an ancient battle. The record detailed how a band of Confederation rebels defeated a larger Wekonn army near the borders of Khuara—the modern Confederation capital. The Staff of Onrai received only a cursory mention as an ancient source of Wekonn power which vanished at some unknown point before the Battle of Khuara occurred.

This firsthand account of the Battle of Khuara, while an intriguing tactical treatise, uncovered no useful information not already in their possession.

"What are we missing?" Xttra said. "Calandra says the staff isn't on Lathos and I believe her. But these records are all so murky on when it vanished, who stole the staff, and where they hid it from the Wekonn emperor."

"I wonder if Calandra or Kevin are making better progress than us," Bo'un said.

Xttra wondered the same thing. He glanced down at his chest pouch and instinctively reached for his arca vox. His hand stopped short of digging into the pouch.

No.

Calandra did not need him pestering her repeatedly and hindering her and Kevin in their search. He would check in with her a little later.

Xttra turned his attention back to his own holoscreen. The screen floated atop a shoulder-high polished stone column rising from the floor of the ancient records room. Aracian script covered the virtual page displayed before him. He adjusted a black scrolling glove on his right hand and swiped the text in an upward motion.

His eyes hardened into a half-squint while trailing Aracian letters from right to left. Why did Daraconian scholars who preserved these historical records never bother to insert a Confederation Universal language translation into the holoscreen images? One extra step guaranteed to save time by giving him and Bo'un readable text to accelerate their search. He grew annoyed with deciphering every word from these ancient languages on his own.

Xttra opened a second parchment detailing a Wekonn march across the Sabadan Plateau in Ra'ahm. His gloved fingers scrolled down the holoscreen at a deliberate pace until he paused the screen with a jab of his index finger.

His eyes lit up.

This ancient account also mentioned the Staff of Onrai, but in a much different context than other records he and Bo'un scoured. After struggling through a difficult passage mentioning the staff, a verb phrase grabbed Xttra's attention with a suddenness matching a Mokai seizing prey with its talons.

We have hidden away the staff forever.

Hidden.

A smile formed on his lips. Xttra retraced the Aracian words repeatedly until he gained a firm grasp on a correct translation.

The parchment detailed how a band of rebels executed a successful raid on the emperor's palace and gained possession of the Staff of Onrai. These rebels fled across the Sabadan plateau from a legion of Wekonn soldiers. Only a few evaded capture and reached a sky port with the staff still in their possession.

Four rebels boarded a mining ship bound for the Ice Belt. The account detailed how they seized control of the ship and journeyed across a hyperlight route unknown to Wekonn authorities.

"You need to see this." Xttra glanced over at Bo'un. "I think I found our first serious clue to the staff's location."

Bo'un edged closer to him and stood behind his shoulder. Both men studied the words written on the holoscreen. After a minute or so, a matching smile slid across Bo'un's face.

"This has to mean something important," he said.

Their enthusiasm proved short-lived. Xttra scrolled further down the parchment but found no mention of the four rebels' destination.

Only a cryptic clue obscuring their path.

"Their destination lay across a hidden bridge passing through a darkened void," Xttra said, reciting the cryptic passage. "Years turned to days on the path to a land clothed in a familiar light."

"What in Ahm's name is that supposed to mean?"

Xttra glanced over at Bo'un and shrugged. He had no idea what the passage meant either. The scribe who created this ancient record spared no effort to construct an intricate puzzle for seekers of the Staff of Onrai.

"We better save copies of this parchment to take back to Calandra and Kevin," Xttra said. "It will probably take all four of us studying it together to solve this puzzle."

They captured images of relevant parchment pages on their holocasters and deactivated both search columns. Holoscreens floating atop each column vanished. Xttra and Bo'un crossed the records room at a brisk pace. Once they exited through the depository's main doors, Xttra pulled out his arca vox and signaled Calandra.

Her image soon popped up on a small holoscreen emanating from the circular pad.

"Any promising news?" she asked.

"I think we found a clue for the staff's location," he said. "We uncovered an ancient parchment that revealed how Wekonn rebels stole the staff and fled from Lathos."

Calandra's eyes widened at his discovery.

"Did you learn where the rebels took the staff?"

Xttra shook his head.

"Only a cryptic reference to the staff's location was in the record. Bo'un and I captured images of the relevant pages. We're bringing them back to you."

She smiled and nodded.

"Let's hope we can uncover their meaning."

Calandra's image vanished. Xttra deactivated the holoscreen and returned the arca vox to his chest pouch. He and Bo'un started walking toward a small landing platform around the corner of the building where they parked their aerorover. Bo'un gained a step on him and reached the corner first.

He froze.

Bo'un stretched out his left arm, signaling for Xttra to stay back. Xttra walked forward anyway and pushed the arm down with his right hand. At once, he saw what aroused his friend's concern.

A woman with short deep brown hair crouched beside their vehicle. She pushed the open side of a cupped hand against the underside of a front magnetic wheel cavity. When she straightened up again, the mystery woman turned and cast a glance in their direction. She wore a wrap-around long sleeve shirt and matching hood common with many Daraconian women. Her youthful face reminded him of Calandra when Xttra first met her several years earlier.

"She's tampering with your aerorover," Bo'un said.

"Not if I can help it," Xttra said.

He rounded the corner and charged toward her.

"What are you doing to my aerorover?" Xttra stabbed a finger at the Daraconian woman. "If I find any damage, you will purchase major trouble for yourself."

Her brown eyes darted between him and Bo'un. She backed away from the vehicle as Xttra drew closer. Then, she turned, and sprinted down the street.

Xttra took off after her.

"We can't let her escape," he shouted, glancing back over his shoulder at Bo'un. "Find a way to block her exit."

Bo'un turned and sprinted up a parallel street intersecting the mystery woman's probable path. Xttra maintained his pursuit, following on her heels. A couple walking out of a neighboring building stopped and stared at him as he passed. Xttra's breaths grew labored as he pushed himself to close the gap between himself and this would-be saboteur.

He intersected paths with Bo'un again as the young woman dashed toward a sky tram boarding junction. Xttra thrust a hand inside a pouch on his belt and drew out several Daraconian coins. Each oval shaped piece of metal bore a pair of deep grooves running end to end.

"Didn't count on needing to catch a sky tram today," he mumbled.

A few travelers meandered around the boarding junction while waiting for an incoming sky tram. Three giant glass boarding tubes surrounding circular platforms stood between the travelers and the edge of a narrow street. Each boarding tube featured a vertical rectangular hole at ground level. Similar holes were on the opposite side near the top. A pair of small columns stood before each tube entrance point and a clear door restricted tube access. Travelers had to feed coins into designated slots in either column to gain passage on the sky tram.

Xttra cast his eyes skyward at an incoming sky tram. The vehicle operated in similar fashion to an aerorover, only it had a much longer and wider body. A single tram had enough space to hold 20 passengers. The tram featured a peaked roof that sloped down to form a metallic lip running around the length of the vehicle. A windshield on the rounded front end covered the piloting station. Five square windows with rounded edges adorned both sides. Metal paneling as broad as a mature senosa tree branch separated each window.

The Daraconian woman shoved her coins into a designated slot at the nearest boarding tube. At once, the clear door slid open, and she stepped on the platform. The door sealed behind her again and the platform rose upward. Xttra and Bo'un wove between travelers approaching other boarding tubes and beat them to the spot. Angry shouts and curses followed.

"Ask the pilot to keep this tram parked," Xttra said, paying the fee at one tube as Bo'un entered the other. "I'll deal with her."

Bo'un nodded and the boarding tube door closed behind him. Xttra entered the neighboring boarding tube and his platform zipped skyward toward the exit door. He charged into the tram before the door fully slid open and his eyes darted toward the rear of the vehicle. The mysterious woman stood near the back end with her head bowed. Her hands trembled as she held a lit arca vox and punched crystal buttons in a sequential pattern.

"Don't you dare move." Xttra's loud and firm voice reverberated through the tram interior. "What did you do to my aerorover?"

The Daraconian woman froze. She raised her chin and greeted Xttra with a firm stare. Her eyes widened when she discovered he had positioned himself between her and the nearest exit.

The young woman plunged her hand into a hidden pocket and drew out an eliminator. Her arca vox fell from her other hand and clattered against the floor. Xttra matched her movements and drew his own weapon. Each barrel locked on the other person. Screams filled the tram as other passengers concealed themselves behind seats.

"It doesn't need to be this way," Xttra said. "Put away your weapon and let's talk. Final warning."

The Daraconian woman resolutely shook her head.

"I will not submit to a seditious traitor. I will never become your prisoner."

Before he could respond, she swung her weapon toward a tram window parallel to the spot where she stood. An eliminator bolt ripped apart the glass a second later. Glass shattering tore renewed screams from several passengers. Xttra's eyes darted to the broken window and back to her. She let out a determined shout and charged at the window.

"No! Don't jump!"

Xttra sprang forward to intercept the young woman. He stretched his arm out to grab her shirt sleeve, but the fabric eluded his grasp. The young woman clenched her teeth and plunged headfirst through the broken window. All four limbs sprawled out as she fell before landing on the stone street below the tram with a sickening thud.

Her broken body lay on the ground motionless.

Xttra glanced down and away with equal quickness. He swallowed hard and stuck his eliminator back inside its concealed holster. He lingered in front of the broken window, grimaced, and shook his head slowly.

"She killed herself rather than be captured?" Bo'un wondered aloud. "Did she truly think we were monsters who would do unspeakable things to her?"

Xttra wheeled around and faced him. Bo'un approached the neighboring window and stared down at the ground. His mouth hung partially agape.

"This is a definite sign she intended to murder us and make it appear like my aerorover malfunctioned," Xttra said. "She must have been a fanatical agent of Delcor. Where are his other agents lurking?"

Bo'un said nothing. Xttra cast his eyes out the window at the lifeless body again. He knew one thing. Flying his aerorover home was not an option.

7

C alandra embraced Xttra as soon as he walked through the open door to their dwelling. Her lips pressed against his and lingered, unwilling to release him. She ran her fingers through his medium brown curls, just above his ear. When he shared with her what happened on the sky tram earlier, a fearful chill gripped Calandra from head to toe. She had closed her eyes tight and uttered a silent plea for his safety. Laying eyes on him again washed away those unwelcome feelings.

"I'm so relieved you're not injured," she said after pulling away from his lips again.

Xttra flashed a warm smile and brushed his hand against her cheek.

"These last few days have turned out more stressful than we anticipated. Hopefully, the worst is behind us."

Calandra wanted to indulge in his optimism and believe their struggle would grow easier. Their shared experiences taught her a different, painful lesson. She subconsciously clenched her artificial hand.

"Bella!"

An excited half-squeal came from a nearby room. Calandra wheeled around and spotted the diminutive cala trotting from the room. Bella's bushy silver-and-gray tail stood erect. Alexa followed her with stretched out arms, trying to match her playmate's pace. She giggled as Bella darted into another room and disappeared through the same doorway. Calandra smiled. Alexa loved the little animal as much as she did. They formed an unbreakable bond once Alexa grew old enough to crawl across the floor by herself.

"Tell me more about this clue you found." Calandra turned and faced Xttra again. "You made more progress than Kevin or I did."

"What did you find?"

"Nothing noteworthy. Only legends related to ancient Lathoan gods bearing no relevance to the staff."

"Is Kevin still searching?"

She nodded.

"Kevin told me he wanted to track one more lead when I last contacted him on my arca vox an hour ago. He felt as frustrated as I did at our lack of progress."

"I thought we hit a dead end too, for a while."

Xttra turned and called out Bo'un's name. He stood outside the dwelling speaking with Selia, his wife, on his arca vox. Bo'un reassured the shy diminutive woman no harm came to him on the sky tram. He snapped his head away from the holoscreen and nodded at Xttra. Bo'un returned his gaze to Selia and bid her farewell. Her image vanished a moment later.

"Let's show Calandra the parchment pages we found," Xttra said.

Bo'un dug out an orange storage crystal from a small pouch on his belt. He removed a protective sleeve from the micro port and walked toward the dwelling. Calandra met him at the doorway and Bo'un dropped the crystal into her open, extended palm.

"I'm excited to read what you found." Her smile matched the excitement in her words. "I hope this will give us the breakthrough we've been searching for."

Calandra retrieved a holocaster from a front room shelf inside their dwelling. She plugged the storage crystal into a matching port embedded on the side of the holopad and pressed the main control button. An empty holoscreen materialized above the holopad. Calandra scrolled through multiple images and retrieved the parchment pages Xttra found earlier. Bo'un joined them inside. All three gathered around a table and Calandra set the holocaster down with the holoscreen facing her.

"Aracian letters?" She scrunched her eyes and nose. "The depository did not provide a modern translation?"

Xttra shook his head.

"What you see is what we found."

She refocused her attention on the holoscreen. Calandra trailed her index finger along the ancient text. Her eyes brightened as she read the account of rebels fleeing across the Sabadan Plateau. Their defiance of a worldwide empire inspired Calandra as she compared her own efforts to dethrone Delcor.

Her finger paused on the bottom half of the parchment image. Calandra's eyes narrowed as she retraced the Aracian words.

Their destination lay across a hidden bridge through a darkened void. Years turned to days on the path to a land clothed in a familiar light.

What did this cryptic passage mean? The destination for the Staff of Onrai lay hidden in plain sight. A puzzle waiting for someone wise enough to understand how to piece it together. Calandra cracked a smile.

She was wise enough.

"A hidden bridge through a darkened void. A land clothed in a familiar light."

Calandra repeated words aloud as she weighed their meaning. Why would rebels fleeing Wekonn soldiers hide the staff? Why not destroy it? Someone preserved the relic for an unknown purpose and left obscure clues for the right person or people to find the staff again when needed at a future time.

"Clothed in a familiar light...."

She trailed off and glanced over at a mounted shelf on the near wall parallel to the table. A worn copy of the *Book of Ahm* lay atop the slab of carved and stained fraxa tree bark. It rested near a sculpture depicting a maniogo climbing on a senosa tree branch. The maniogo raised its pointed muzzle skyward while its long slender tail wrapped around the branch to support balance. These items were among the limited possessions Kevin and Calandra rescued from the old apartment she shared with Xttra before fleeing from Luma.

"What is it?" Bo'un asked.

Calandra pressed her lips tight and ignored his question. She fixed her gaze on the copy of the *Book of Ahm* in particular. One phrase from the parchment stuck in her mind, lingering with the same persistence as a familiar note played on a syri'nai.

Clothed in a familiar light.

Those words connected to a familiar passage within the holy text. Surely, it held a helpful answer to the riddle this parchment revealed.

"I know I encountered these phrases elsewhere," she finally said. "In the *Book of Ahm* itself."

Calandra rose from her chair at the table and marched over to the shelf. She snatched up the book and flipped through pages cut from kerval skin and stitched together on one side. Some pages bore frayed corners. Neither Xttra nor Calandra sought to replace the holy book with a more durable metal plate version matching the one she already owned. Xttra's parents, Malar and Chloe, imparted this kerval skin copy to him as a gift. His grandfather Atrer had passed down the same copy to the couple at an earlier time. It held sentimental value within the Oogan clan.

The book's spine rested in her palm as Calandra continued flipping through pages. She stopped on a page one-third of the way through the record. Her index finger trailed down the page, stopping near the bottom.

"At that day, I will guide you to a choice land clothed in a familiar light," she said, reading the passage from the *Book of Ahm* aloud. "Wisdom, knowledge, and peace shall rain down on your heads in my holy place as do rays from the three suns which give warmth to the land."

Calandra glanced up from the page at Xttra. His brows knit together, and he rubbed his chin. Xttra cozied up to her side and glanced down at the same passage.

"Are you suggesting the Staff of Onrai is hidden in the Land of the Three Suns?"

Xttra's gaze trailed up to Calandra's eyes. His half-frown hinted at a latent skepticism driving his question.

"It makes sense," she said. "So many people dismiss the Land of the Three Suns as an ancient myth. I did until Kevin showed me where to find the three stars. Many ancient acolytes of Ahm memorized the *Book of Ahm* word for word. Seeing both records use the same descriptive language is no coincidence."

"Which one is it?"

Calandra snapped her head toward Bo'un. He rubbed his scarred jaw, leaned forward in his chair, and rested his arms on the table. Bo'un studied the parchment pages with a determined gaze.

"What do you mean?"

Bo'un turned in his chair toward Calandra.

"Which star does the Land of the Three Suns orbit? It's impossible to orbit all three stars at once. Which star is the home sun?"

A good question.

Calandra never considered learning which specific star the Land of the Three Suns orbited. Lingering curiosity about who dwelt in that place—and whether those people included Valadius, the former prime oracle—crossed her mind from time to time. She never followed through on pinpointing the exact planet. Their situation effectively ruled out space travel. Alexa was a small child. Spending several months sealed inside a hibernation pod would be detrimental to her daughter's body and mind at such an early age. And she would never leave Alexa behind on Lathos to undertake such a voyage.

"I know one foolproof way we can narrow three stars down to the right one."

Calandra snapped the *Book of Ahm* shut and passed it off to Xttra. She wheeled around and walked to another mounted shelf on the far wall. Her fingers wrapped around a trique laying atop the shelf. She pressed a button lit with blue light above the triangular device's bottom edge. A holoscreen activated. It displayed only a blank horizontal box.

Calandra pressed down on a second blue-lit button embedded in an opposite corner from the first one.

"Show me star spectral classes."

Columns of data, along with relevant images of diverse stars, materialized on the holoscreen. Lathoan explorers discovered and mapped each star noted in the images, starting a hundred generations before the rise of the Wekonn Empire up to the present time. Calandra scrolled to a three-dimensional holoscreen image of her home sun. New data appeared within adjacent columns detailing the sun's mass, radius, effective temperature, luminosity, and chromaticity.

"The phrase 'clothed in a familiar light' tells us the Land of the Three Suns orbits a star exhibiting the same characteristics as our own sun." Calandra glanced away from the holoscreen and fixed her eyes on Xttra and Bo'un. "It will have similar mass, luminosity, and so forth. In other words, this distant star—and the planet orbiting it—will resemble Lathos and our own sun."

Xttra narrowed his eyes and stared at the Lathoan sun. Calandra handed the trique over to him.

"Neither the Stellar Guard nor the Confederation mapped any of the three suns to my knowledge," Xttra said, without looking up. "How can we pinpoint which hyperlight path to take?"

Calandra smiled and brushed his cheek with her fingers. He finally glanced over at her.

"Those stars were mapped. Trust me."

"How?" A crease formed in his brow. "Unless a ship or a probe has traveled to that star, there's no way to—"

"Space telescopes orbiting Lathos have catalogued thousands of stars." She cut off his protest in mid-sentence. "Each telescope uses instruments sensitive enough to chronicle a mountain of data about every star within 100 parsecs of our planet. Existing data on those stars will pinpoint the home solar system for the Land of the Three Suns with near certainty."

Xttra exchanged an impressed glance with Bo'un and answered Calandra with a satisfied nod.

"Kevin will love this news. Once we sift through the data, Bo'un and I can start planning an expedition with him to the proper star."

Calandra bit down on her lower lip and ran her hands through her auburn hair. Xttra planned to go to this alien planet without her. Did he not realize the implications behind this decision? It took six months to reach Earth while traveling with hyperlight engines at a maximum safe speed. Journeying to the Land of the Three Suns would take a minimum of four months using available technology. Neither she nor Alexa could travel with him on such a long journey through deep space.

Staying home on Lathos, separated from Xttra, was also out of the question. Spending a year without seeing him or hearing his voice, and not knowing his fate, felt akin to pure torture. She did not want their child to also endure such a familiar excruciating emptiness.

"What's wrong?"

Xttra shot Calandra a puzzled look. She drew in a deep breath. "You can't go."

He crinkled his nose and squinted at her.

"What do you mean?" Disbelief permeated his words. "We uncovered a promising location for the staff. We must reach that planet before Delcor, or his minions, make the same discovery."

Calandra folded her arms and answered him with an unblinking stare.

"YOU can't go."

His eyes drifted from her toward the room where Alexa played with Bella. The little cala chattered from inside the room while their daughter laughed and spoke to the pet in unintelligible words.

"This isn't the same." Xttra refocused his gaze on Calandra. "No one else knows where we're traveling. We'll secure an unmarked vessel for the voyage. The danger will be minimal."

Calandra rubbed her hands over her cheeks and squeezed her eyes shut for a moment. She opened them again, glanced back at Alexa's room, and then at her husband a second time.

"How can you know that with any degree of certainty? You are terrible at properly judging risk. Our first contact mission with Earth ended up being more dangerous than we ever imagined."

"What do you want to happen?"

"Alexa needs her father and her mother." Calandra's tone and expression both softened. "How will it affect her—and me—if something happens to you and you never return home?"

"We can handle it."

Calandra and Xttra simultaneously snapped their heads toward Bo'un.

"Kevin and I can track the staff down and do whatever needs to be done to keep it out of Delcor's hands. You can trust us."

Calandra frowned.

"What about Selia? How will she cope if you're absent for a year?"

Bo'un studied the floor for a moment before meeting her gaze. A half-smile formed on his lips.

"Selia is an understanding woman. She stood by my side through every danger I faced in my Stellar Guard days. Plus, we obviously have no small children to worry about yet."

Xttra answered him with a slow nod. He handed the trique back to Calandra.

"I trust you Bo'un." He made eye contact with his former weapons officer again. "I'm comfortable staying here on Lathos. You and Kevin will succeed in this expedition. Now we only need to hire an experienced deep-space pilot with an unmarked vessel to take you where you need to go."

8

elcor paced inside a solarium on the north side of his palace. He retraced the same tight circular path between enormous arched windows and two solitary chairs facing those same windows. Sunlight struck his side, splashing an elongated shadow that swallowed both empty chairs and blanketed the eastern wall behind the furniture. He spent an hour concealing himself inside this unassuming refuge, alternating between listening to calm music and trying to meditate.

Searching for peace without success.

She did this to him. Such a vile woman. Ra'ahm's prosperity was endangered, and it was her fault alone.

Every measure he took to silence Calandra Menankar failed in one way or another. Her poisonous words and the seditious actions of her willing minions interrupted peace and order he brought to Ra'ahm. Her image and message reached too many eyes and ears.

Protests.

Dissension.

None dared act against him only a few years ago. He stood higher than all except Ahm in their eyes, and rightfully so. Calandra emboldened worthless agitators to spew endless discontented lies calculated to disrupt the foundations of Ra'ahm itself. She must pay for her sins and her treachery.

He would dispense justice. Soon.

"Your journey will meet a quick end, Calandra Menankar." Delcor spoke as though she stood in the room listening to his words and raised a well-manicured fist for emphasis. "A traitor's reward awaits you and everyone you love.

A loud rap on the solarium door greeted his ears. Delcor wheeled around and stared at the door.

"What is it?"

"Apologies for the interruption, my sovereign, but I bring promising news regarding the Staff of Onrai." An excited tone infused each word. "We think we discovered the place where it lays hidden."

"You think?"

"We are certain, my sovereign. This is the discovery you desired."

Delcor gave a satisfied nod and quickly opened the solarium door. Aginon stood before him with head bowed in submission. He cradled a metallic book between his forearm and ribs. The chief sovereign glanced down at the plates nestled in his arm.

"Show me what you found."

He directed the fearful man to step forward. The door slid shut behind him with a whoosh. Aginon cracked open the metallic book and flipped through pliable metal pages before stopping on a page two-thirds of the way through the record.

"Here." Aginon lifted his eyes and gazed at Delcor again. "Here is the clue we searched for."

Delcor cast his eyes down upon the open page. He snatched the metallic book from the supreme cleric's hand. Aracian lettering filled each page, a telltale sign of the record's ancient origin. Delcor studied the page Aginon showed him. A satisfied smile washed over his lips as he read.

"The staff was taken to the Land of the Three Suns?" Surprise tinged the chief sovereign's question. "I assumed it was only a myth. Do we know where to find this place?"

"Yes, my sovereign. We identified three specific stars matching what is written within the *Book of Ahm* itself."

He lifted his head and gazed at Aginon.

"That is welcome news. Where are these stars found in relation to Lathos?"

"Dharcha has more comprehensive details about the three stars than what I can share from memory. My understanding, though, is these stars are roughly two parsecs away from our sun."

Delcor's smile melted into a frown.

"That requires a four-month journey to reach the nearest star— even with hyperlight engines. I cannot spend a year away from Lathos without yielding ground to would-be rebels."

"Many capable and loyal Stellar Guard officers serve you, my sovereign, who can be entrusted to retrieve the staff and return it to Ra'ahm."

The chief sovereign's eyes hardened into an icy glare. Did this fool understand what he suggested? Whoever possessed the Staff of Onrai wielded tremendous power. He would never allow a simple Stellar Guard officer to learn the staff's secrets and use that knowledge to lead a rebellion against his rule.

"I alone will retrieve the staff." His tone hardened, matching his expression. "No one else will lay a finger upon this relic."

Aginon stiffened like a stone column before him.

"Perhaps…your son…Giljax could go…in your place." Hesitation cluttered his voice as he searched for a way to spare Delcor a trip to this unknown region. "Or a blessed…oracle from the Council of Oracles."

Delcor stabbed his index finger at the supreme cleric and shook it like a tiny club.

"No one else will go."

"Then how will we retrieve the staff, my sovereign?"

He cast his eyes down at the book and let them trail up to Aginon again.

"I will decree a travel ban to that specific star system," Delcor said. "We will station scout ships near every hyperlight lane leading to those three stars. Those ships will be under strict orders to turn back or destroy all unauthorized vessels in that sector."

Aginon averted his eyes and settled his gaze on the nearest solarium window.

"You risk open war with the Confederation." His voice grew softer. "And such actions will further enrage the Thetians, Serbiusians, and Peleusians. How will they respond to a blockade? I fear they may unite against us."

Delcor snapped the metal book shut and let it clatter against the floor. He pressed a hand on each of Aginon's shoulders and forced him to make eye contact.

"Learn to fear the proper things."

Aginon gulped.

"I care not about threats directed against me." Delcor's tone hardened again as he spoke. "I will do whatever is necessary to preserve this great nation. Give heed to my words—Ra'ahm will never be torn down by lawless rebels allied with Confederation agents."

The supreme cleric pinched his eyelids shut and aggressively nodded. Delcor's smile returned, and he relaxed his grip.

"Good. Now we both have a proper understanding of the circumstances."

Persistent muffled beeps greeted his ears. Delcor plunged a hand inside his robe and drew an arca vox from an inner pocket. He activated the holoscreen. Giljax's image appeared before him.

"We gained an advantage, Father." Enthusiasm infused his words. "One step closer to claiming the staff as our own."

Delcor raised his brows and flashed an uncertain frown. Did Giljax bring the same news Aginon shared?

"What is this advantage you speak of?"

"Let us talk face to face in your throne room and you can see with your own eyes."

His son's image vanished off the holoscreen. Delcor stared into the space his son occupied for a few seconds. He slipped the arca vox back inside his robe and returned his gaze to Aginon. The supreme cleric studied the floor around his feet. Delcor said nothing and marched past Aginon, exiting through the solarium door.

Footsteps followed the chief sovereign, but he did not bother to glance over his shoulder. His ears confirmed the supreme cleric tailed him like a treema desperate to satisfy hunger. Delcor's attention centered on what his son told him.

We gained an advantage.

Scenarios flooded his mind while he mulled over what specific advantage Giljax alluded to during their brief conversation. More footsteps greeted his ears. Delcor gave a passing nod to two palace guards who joined them as he and Aginon entered the grand hall.

He cast his eyes at the mural gracing the wall on his right-hand side. Vivid scenes in bright colors jumped out from the wall. Each part paraded before the eyes with the vibrancy of a living and breathing creature. Sharing stories culled from a rich history of a proud people.

Delcor already held a treasured spot in the mural. Winning the Separatist War assured him that honor. Once he claimed ownership over the Staff of Onrai, his story would outshine all others. Delcor contemplated which lesser men he should erase to free space to chronicle his continuing accomplishments. No other name in Ra'ahm, or on Lathos, would ever be greater.

Giljax stood before his writing table when Delcor entered the throne room. His son at once wheeled around and flashed a knowing smile. His unearned arrogance threatened future trouble. And unnecessary risk.

"This is what I wanted you to see."

Delcor let his eyes trail down to Giljax's hands. He held long strips of kerval skin parchment bound on one side with four rings. Ancient Aracian words covered each section of cracked and fraying parchment.

"I ordered a thorough search of secret ancient records belonging to the Council of Oracles," Giljax said. "Held back from the *Book of Ahm* itself. Not only do I know where the Staff of Onrai is, I also learned of a shortcut for reaching the relic."

A self-congratulatory smugness hung on his words. Delcor glanced up and narrowed his eyes.

"Shortcut?"

Giljax jabbed his finger at the parchment and pressed the tip against faded ink.

"Space bridge. This record speaks of a bridge known to ancient oracles connecting our system with the Land of the Three Suns. Years turn to days within the bridge."

The chief sovereign frowned.

"I've never read or heard anything about this space bridge. Is such a thing possible?"

"Pyrah concealed or destroyed all evidence of the space bridge and the true location of the Land of the Three Suns. The ancient prime oracle feared the Staff of Onrai would fall into the wrong hands again if its location became known."

Delcor's frown curved upward into a satisfied smile.

"The staff must still be on that planet."

"With this knowledge, the staff can be restored to Lathos and bless our sovereign in his wise and judicious rule over Ra'ahm," Aginon said. He turned and faced Delcor. "If reaching the Land of the Three Suns requires mere days instead of many months, you need not fear a long absence from your throne, my sovereign."

Giljax snapped his head toward Aginon.

"Absence?" He turned and refocused his gaze on Delcor again. "You plan to leave Lathos?"

Delcor cast his eyes toward his throne and gazed upon the sapinoa hair cushions encircled by a gold-plated frame. Many enemies would love to fill his throne or tear it down forever. Now, he would thwart their plans for his destruction before they gained strength.

"I will possess the staff, my son."

Delcor crossed his arms and puffed out his chest. His smile broadened.

"If I must depart from Ra'ahm for a few days to claim what belongs to me, then let it be done." He turned on his heel and his eyes fell upon Giljax again. "Not one soul shall tear down what I built."

His son's eyes shifted to the throne and back to him. A worried frown crossed his lips.

"Who will rule while you're gone? Ra'ahm cannot survive without a sovereign to guide her like a pilot steering a space vessel."

"This responsibility falls on you for now, Giljax. I will appoint you as acting chief sovereign in my absence."

Giljax stepped back, speechless. One hand clutching the parchment dropped to his hip. He pressed the other to his mouth.

"This is a great honor." Aginon vocalized the words Giljax did not. "Your son is an intelligent and capable leader. He shall not fail you."

Delcor nodded without making eye contact. His gaze remained fixed squarely on his son. Giljax's sky blue eyes showed a hint of fear lingering behind his confident expression.

"I will not fail you, father. I promise."

Delcor pressed a hand down on his shoulder.

"You can secure your place as my eventual successor with a single act."

"Name it and it shall be done."

"Silence Calandra Menankar and Xttra Oogan forever. Let the seeds of rebellion they planted die and wither away with them."

Giljax answered him with a slight, close-lipped smile.

"It shall be done as you desire."

9

S urface scans revealed only a small fissure. This new data dumb-founded Tressek. Their findings did not align with the mining surveyor vessel's earlier reports. He expected to uncover a larger chasm on the asteroid's far side. Fortunately, this did not pose a major obstacle. Plasma cannons neared full capacity. His crew could still do the job their supervising commander sent them to do.

"Coordinates for all three designated shatter points are confirmed in the targeting system."

Dray, his co-pilot, glanced up from her console as she shared this update. Her vivid blue eyes locked on him. Tressek stroked the prominent tuft of hair springing out from his chin and nodded.

"Let's see if this works."

Dray squeezed a trigger stick below her console. Plasma bolts fired out of the cannon's mouth. The fissure cracked wide open, spewing rock debris up and away from the asteroid's surface as expected. Dray rotated the plasma cannon on the belly of the scout ship and zeroed in on their next target. No adjustments were needed to compensate for subsurface quakes. More plasma bolts struck the asteroid, this time closer to the southern pole. A third volley entered the jagged fissure, splitting away toward the northern pole.

One massive chunk of rock rivaling the scout ship in size sheared off from the fissure. The giant slab kicked up an enormous plume of dust as it fractured. It spiraled past the belly of the ship after breaking away from its mother asteroid. Tressek refused to peel his eyes from the holoscreen until dust cleared sufficiently from the strike zone to reveal evidence of their success.

A blue-green line moved upward on the updated asteroid image. He let out a relieved sigh and sank back in his pilot's chair.

"We brought the vein to the surface," Tressek said. "If the flectum runs as deep as our surface scans predict, this will provide us with a thousand tons of high-grade ore for hyperlight engine construction."

Tressek wore a satisfied smile as he gazed out at the asteroid below their ship. Flectum was an essential ingredient in making the alloy forming the engine's outer casing and several inner components. The mineral had enough durability, flexibility, and strength to withstand friction buildup at hyperlight speeds.

This newly exposed vein held enough flectum to supply an entire fleet of scout ships. The chief sovereign himself would hear of and celebrate such a discovery.

Multiple rapid beeps cut through the bridge.

"Incoming communication," Dray said.

"Put them on the holoscreen." Tressek leaned forward in his chair. "No doubt the mining guild is clamoring for an update on our progress."

A white-haired man with an equally white mustache appeared on the holoscreen above the helm console. Tressek furrowed his brow. Definitely not their mining guild contact. His dark Stellar Guard uniform bore a distinctive commander's emblem over the left breast.

"Wow. That's Kharil, our new supreme commander."

Tressek glanced over his shoulder at the whispered voice. Jo'ber, his navigator, instinctively brushed back his wavy black hair above his ears and straightened up in his chair.

Kharil cleared his throat. Tressek turned and faced the holoscreen again. The supreme commander's blue eyes settled on him in a determined stare.

"You are officially being reassigned from mining preparation on Asteroid 1279," Kharil said. "Return to Lathos and report to the Stellar Guard shipyard at once."

Tressek frowned. His throat tightened. Did a mining guild leader lodge a complaint with the Stellar Guard over their excavation efforts? His eyes narrowed as he considered which guild official would take it upon themselves to cause trouble. Sure, he and his crew needed more time to complete survey work on Asteroid 1279 than they originally projected. But they also needed to be careful not to blast away too much surface rock and send the entire flectum vein flying off into deep space.

"Apologies, supreme commander." Tressek's voice betrayed the sudden tension seizing his nerves. "I know we're running a little behind schedule on the mining operation, but if you—"

Kharil waved his hand dismissively.

"This has nothing to do with your current operation. Our chief sovereign selected you to take part in a new mission. Report to the shipyard at once. I'll expect you in one hour."

The supreme commander's image vanished from the holoscreen a second later. Tressek sank back into his chair. A new mission from the chief sovereign himself?

"What sort of mission do you think our sovereign wants us to do?" Jo'ber gave voice to another question floating through Tressek's mind. "I'm surprised he assigned it to us."

Tressek said nothing. He gnawed on his lower lip. He remembered from his time serving as a systems officer under Xttra what spurred the chief sovereign's involvement in specific Stellar Guard missions. Mention of Delcor only heightened a severe anxiety overtaking him. This mission, no doubt, involved much larger stakes for him and his entire crew than finding new mineral deposits on random asteroids.

He became completely dismayed by the consequences resulting from discovering that Earth probe many years ago. A similar helpless feeling, akin to suffering a long fall from a towering cliff, gripped him now.

***

Tressek glanced up when a chair squeaked across the floor. Sarianna dropped down into the chair and scooted up against the edge of the table across from him. He continued to rest his jaw in his palm as he gazed at her. A questioning smile flitted across her lips.

"You look so glum. This is exciting news! A major opportunity for you."

Sarianna made an excellent point. Ever since he climbed to his current rank, Tressek sought a chance to prove his value as a master pilot. For better or for worse, that proving ground lay before him now.

"You're right." His mouth remained locked in a stoic frown. "I wanted to be a part of something larger than mineral surveys. Now, my time has come."

She shook her head.

"I expected more celebration from you. What about this mission bothers you?"

Tressek straightened up in his chair. His left arm dropped to the table, and he draped the right arm across it. Sarianna's perception was accurate. Going to a distant star system stirred curiosity and excitement in equal doses in his mind and heart. Learning of the chief sovereign's assignment also unlocked an apprehension seeping deep into his bones.

Nothing prepared him to join an entire fleet of scout ships on an odyssey to the Land of the Three Suns.

Tressek's jaw nearly hit the floor when Kharil first elaborated on the nature of this new mission. The supreme commander relayed how scholars in the Order of Ahm found the actual place written and sung about by acolytes of the divine creator for ten thousand years. And now his sovereign had chosen him to go there.

"Am I ready for this?" he asked.

"Is anybody ever ready for something like this?"

"I guess I'm more worried about the unknown than I care to admit to my crew."

Sarianna leaned forward and brushed back a bang of her short black hair. She offered him a reassuring smile.

"Exploration is the vehicle for answering questions we cannot answer any other way. That's why I'm in space. It's also why you're here. Neither of us would be happy stuck on Lathos. You know this fact as well as I do."

Tressek furrowed his brow.

"I don't understand my role on this mission. Why me? Why my ship and my crew?"

"You said they're hunting an important relic."

"That's what they told me."

"There you go. You already have your answer. Your experience in mineral surveys and mining operations qualifies you to take part in a search for this relic."

Tressek rose from his chair and approached a window extending from floor to ceiling. It offered a panoramic view of landing platforms from the northern control tower. He stood before the window, gazing at a landing platform where a scout ship prepared for departure.

"Something else is on your mind, isn't it?"

Tressek snapped his head to his right. Sarianna stood by his side. She did not make eye contact, focusing her gaze on the shipyard like he did only a moment earlier.

"What if this is a hostile planet?"

His voice barely climbed above a whisper. Tressek almost did not share the troubling question with her. It bordered on blasphemous to suggest a place described as a paradise created for true followers of Ahm could harbor evil. Still, he and Sarianna both witnessed what happened to their former crewmates who journeyed to Earth.

Tressek feared a similar fate lay in store for him.

"Not all intelligent alien species are as violent and cruel as Earthians." Sarianna answered him with a reassuring tone. "Prepare for the worst but believe you will find the paradise of Ahm."

"Look at how Earth changed Xttra and Bo'un."

She turned away from the window and faced him.

"That manipulative astronomer changed them more than any Earthian. She destroyed their Stellar Guard careers and dragged them into exile with her because of a personal vendetta against our sovereign."

Tressek glanced down at the floor and gnawed on his lip. Xttra and Bo'un leaving the Stellar Guard on a whim made no sense to him. He knew both men well and it did not track with their personalities.

"What if they're right?"

"Please tell me you aren't embracing her ridiculous propaganda."

He lifted his chin and gazed at his former crewmate.

"No. I always shut her messages off once I see her image or hear her voice. But I still wonder what turned everyone who escaped from Earth against our sovereign."

Sarianna slipped her left hand into his right hand and clasped it tight.

"Everyone has their own agenda, Tressek. Trust your instincts. You're already a good man. No one needs to tell you how to be one."

He finally allowed a smile to spread over his lips.

"I appreciate your faith in me. Hopefully, this journey will ease my fears instead of letting them fester like an open wound."

Like what already happened to Xttra and Bo'un, he added silently.

Tressek needed to sift through conflicting voices. Sarianna was right. He needed to trust his instincts. Those instincts told him the Land of the Three Suns held answers to his most important questions.

10

alandra crossed her arms as her green eyes darted from wall to wall. Dozens of rough looking faces—a mixture of Lathoan and various alien races—occupied a spacious dimly lit room. Some enjoyed drinks. Others played games. A din of countless conversations filled the room, cutting through Chitha strings producing harsh background music. Meeting with a pilot in a space port lounge seemed like a foolish idea now. How many lounge patrons noticed when she walked through the door and were already plotting some nefarious action?

"Relax," Kevin said. "You got nothing to worry about. No one will do anything in such a crowded place. They would be foolish to try."

A frown washed over Calandra's lips. She glanced over at him and shook her head. Kevin's bravado did not ease her tense nerves.

"Do you know any of these people? I already see a few who would probably tear your head from your shoulders rather than speak to you."

"I've seen rougher crowds on Fengar. We'll be fine."

Calandra snapped her head toward Xttra on her other side and shot him an annoyed stare.

"We both know how your last trip to Fengar turned out, don't we? I can't believe I let you talk me into visiting this place."

Xttra shrugged. Kevin cracked an amused smile.

"No one is looking for us here except Kujoth," their Earthian friend said. "And I can vouch for him. He's a good dude and an experienced deep-space pilot."

"Experienced?" Calandra repeated.

"Kujoth is the Lathoan equivalent of an independent contractor on Earth. He owns a transport vessel and takes shipments for private clients on Lathos, Serbius, and other planets throughout this sector of the galaxy."

"So, he's a smuggler in other words."

"Well, yeah, if you want to get technical about it."

"And you're perfectly comfortable trusting your fate to a common smuggler. Does Bo'un feel the same way?"

Kevin sighed and pressed his hands to his temples.

"He's not here complaining about our future travel arrangements, is he?"

Calandra gnawed on her lower lip and said nothing. She did not feel comfortable in the smallest degree about their impending meeting with this smuggler. Then again, few worthwhile realistic options for making a four-month trip to the Land of the Three Suns were available.

They weaved through the crowd toward a back booth Kujoth occupied. Calandra banged her shin into a chair and winced. An angry shout greeted her ears. She quickly glanced over at a table to her right. A bald, burly humanoid man with ash-colored skin stared up at Calandra. Numerous skin covered tendrils grew from the back of his skull and extended down past his shoulders. His black oval eyes narrowed, and he partially turned his shoulders toward her. Finger bands topped with spikes covered each knuckle on both hands.

He resembled a Taircona alien. She had seen images of aliens from the distant planet of Taircona and read about them. This was the first one she ever encountered in real life.

It was not an experience she wanted.

"Apologies." Her heart pounded as she backed away from the chair. "I didn't mean to disturb you."

"Watch where you're going next time!" he snapped with a breathy hiss.

Calandra dropped her hand to her side and fumbled around for Xttra's hand. Once she found his hand, she slipped her own into it and grasped his palm tight.

"Settle down. She didn't harm you."

Xttra pivoted toward the Tairconian alien and met him with a stare as firm as his words. The alien slammed down a fist and slid back his chair. A long narrow glass in front of him toppled over, spilling out a foul-smelling sky-blue liquid across the table's surface.

He sprang to his feet.

"Shut your mouth, Lathoan." The Tairconian stabbed a lanky index finger topped with a sharpened nail at him. "Or they'll carry your bleeding husk away in pieces."

Xttra dug into a pouch on his belt and produced a stun pebble. He held it out, so the hostile alien saw the smooth, round device resting in his palm.

"How will you attack me if you're blind?" Xttra's tone grew icy. "Now sit back down, order yourself another cerulean bark tea, and leave my wife alone."

The Tairconian answered with a low growl. Xttra did not flinch. Kevin stepped forward and drew an eliminator from his belt.

"You heard him. Sit your ass down."

The alien's black eyes darted from Xttra to Kevin and back again. He tossed up his hands and dropped down into his former seat.

"You're not worth it," he mumbled.

"Smart choice," Xttra said.

Calandra continued clasping her husband's hand until they put a few steps between them and the Tairconian. She glanced over her shoulder a final time and then breathed out a relieved sigh.

"Are you alright?"

Concern washed through Xttra's deep blue eyes. Calandra offered up a weak smile and gave his hand a gentle squeeze.

"A little scared." She paused and released another deep breath. "At least we're all safe."

"Tairconians are a bunch of hotheads who thrive on intimidation," he said. "You stand your ground, and they move on to an easier target."

Kevin led them toward a booth along the lounge's back wall. A stout Daraconian man with shaggy red hair beckoned them forward. His broad smile revealed a chipped front tooth, and a scar divided his chin.

He raised a chalice fashioned out of frosted glass as they reached his table.

"You went toe to toe with a Tairconian. Such a move requires a major dose of courage. Or foolishness."

Kevin glanced over his shoulder at Xttra and Calandra and back at the Daraconian. His amused smile returned.

"When you've seen and endured what we have over the past few years, dealing with a grouchy Tairconian asshole doesn't really move the needle," he said.

The red-haired Daraconian man took a swig of orange Aurantia wine and set his chalice down again. He leaned forward on a bench forming a semi-circle around one half of the table.

"I guess not," he said, adding a laugh. "Still, I'd love to see an Earthian like you duel a Tairconian in a Wekonn battle pit. Just to see who prevails."

Kevin countered with his own laugh.

"Save the daydreaming. You already know I win that battle, Kujoth."

Kujoth shrugged and nodded. His eyes trailed over to Calandra and Xttra. She eyed him suspiciously when she felt them lingering on her. Kujoth quickly tore his gaze away before she said anything.

"I assume these are the passengers you want to transport?" He refocused his gaze on Kevin. Kujoth pointed back at Calandra with his thumb. "She looks familiar. I know I've seen her elsewhere."

"If you set foot in Ra'ahm recently, you've probably seen a lot of Calandra," Kevin said. "Or at least her holoscreen image anyway."

Kujoth's gaze trailed over to Calandra a second time. His eyes lit up and he cracked a grin again.

"Of course. You're the one denouncing their beloved tyrant. You must be popular in Ra'ahm."

She pressed her lips together for a moment before releasing them into a fierce smile.

"My popularity does not matter to me. What truly matters is people in Ra'ahm hear my message and revolt against their wicked chief sovereign."

Kujoth motioned for them to take a seat. Calandra, Xttra, and Kevin planted themselves on another bench forming a semi-circle around the opposite side of the table across from him.

"We aren't the ones taking a journey beyond Lathos," Xttra said, pointing to himself and Calandra. "Kevin—and Bo'un, who isn't here at the moment—are the ones who need to hire your vessel."

"I'm happy to take you anywhere—for the right price, of course."

Kevin leaned forward and drew a trique from his pocket. He retrieved a holoscreen displaying symbols for Confederation currency. Four numbers were listed next to each symbol.

"You're getting your money," he said. "I told you I'd take care of it."

Kujoth squinted at the holoscreen, and his expression grew stoic. His eyes trailed over the various numbers. The Daraconian pilot glanced back at Kevin after a few seconds and gave him a satisfied nod.

"I trust you," he said. "Still, you know my ship doesn't pay for itself. She runs on Confederation mynars as much as antimatter fuel."

"It's all there," Kevin said. "Count it up as many times as you want if it makes you feel better."

Kujoth clapped his hands together and smiled.

"5,000 mynars is acceptable. We have a deal."

Calandra focused on the holoscreen when she heard the amount. 5,000 mynars struck her as a modest fee to undertake a deep-space journey lasting four months each way. A little too generous for a smuggler. Did Kujoth possess an ulterior motive or conceal a secret plan? Knowing their status as exiled traitors of Ra'ahm supplied a tempting motivation for betrayal.

"I expected a higher price for a four-month trek to and from an alien star," Xttra said, revealing he shared the same doubts as Calandra. "You will remain on the planet and bring them back, right?"

Kujoth answered him with a hearty laugh.

"Four months? Your timetable is wrong. Let me see the destination coordinates."

Kevin retrieved a different holoscreen on his trique. A hyperlight route map materialized on the screen, displaying coordinates from Lathos to the alien star orbited by the Land of the Three Suns. He handed the device to Kujoth, who surveyed the data for a few seconds before shaking his head.

"This is far too complicated." He returned the trique to Kevin. "If you want that route, I'll need to triple my fee. Or we can take a simpler, faster route to this specific star system."

Calandra scowled. She and Xttra worked through the numbers repeatedly and programmed coordinates for their origin and destination through a navigational computer to produce this hyperlight route. It was the fastest, safest route for a ship to take to this alien planet. She did not appreciate him casually disregarding and mocking their efforts.

"No faster way exists." Her voice remained calm but forceful. "Xttra and I calculated all the relevant numbers. Even at a hyperlight engine's maximum safe speed, it will take four months to cover the two-parsec distance."

"Trust me," Kujoth replied, adding a dismissive wave at the trique. "This is the long way."

Calandra crossed her arms and released a brief exasperated sigh.

"Share with us this better route you found. No need to be cryptic."

Kujoth extended his hand toward Kevin.

"Do you mind if I borrow your trique again?"

Kevin shrugged.

"Be my guest."

He handed the triangular device back across the table. Kujoth set it down in a stable position and pressed the manual input board release button. A razor thin square pad popped out. Numerous letters and numbers covered the pad's surface. He entered a series of characters and coordinates. Once the trique processed the new data, an alternate hyperlight route materialized on the holoscreen.

Calandra leaned against the table edge and peered at the new route provided by Kujoth. Her mouth dropped open. His new route belonged in the realm of impossible. It reduced travel time from Lathos to the Land of the Three Suns down to a few days.

She glanced over at Xttra, and his eyes told her he entertained similar doubts about this implausible route.

"You cannot cross such a vast swath of space so quickly," Xttra said, staring at Kujoth. "It isn't possible, even with the fastest hyperlight engine on Lathos powering your ship."

"You can if you use a space bridge," Kujoth said.

A crease formed in Xttra's brow. He peered at the holoscreen a second time and then at Calandra. She offered him a blank stare. She knew of no space bridge anywhere, much less one connecting Lathos to the Land of the Three Suns. Such bridges were a fun theoretical concept but lacked real-world scientific evidence. She searched for space bridges fruitlessly many years earlier at the Luma Observatory.

"If a space bridge connected Lathos to the Land of the Three Suns, it would be common knowledge in Ra'ahm," Calandra said. "And anywhere else where true followers of Ahm dwelt."

Kujoth straightened up and focused his gaze on her.

"Not if you keep it a proprietary secret to stay ahead of competitors," he said. "Hidden space bridges work to your advantage when moving goods at a set price."

Hidden.

Making space bridges hidden.

Calandra's eyes lit up and she drew a sharp breath. A cryptic passage Xttra and Bo'un uncovered a few days earlier barged into her mind once again.

Their destination lay across a hidden bridge.

She turned to Xttra and saw the same recognition seared into his eyes.

"Their destination lay across a hidden bridge through a darkened void," he said.

"Years turned to days on the path to a land clothed in a familiar light," Calandra added, completing the original passage.

Xttra flashed a triumphant smile matching her own.

"We know what that passage means now."

"Years turning to days…hmm…kind of sounds like traveling through a wormhole to me."

Calandra snapped her head toward Kevin.

"Wormhole?"

"Yeah, it's an Earth word used to describe a tunnel connecting two distant points in space."

"That's exactly what a space bridge does."

Kevin tilted his head back, pumped his fist, and let out a brief celebratory shout. A few heads turned in their direction for a moment, but most lounge patrons ignored his outburst.

"This is a total game changer," he said. "Bo'un and I will reach that solar system and track down the staff before anyone realizes we left. Score one for Kujoth."

Kujoth smiled indulgently at his celebratory moment.

Calandra crinkled her eyes and nose and deepened her smile. Finding the Staff of Onrai suddenly became a much simpler task. Reaching it before Delcor did turned into a more attainable goal.

Kevin was right.

Score one for Kujoth indeed.

11

Xttra noticed a sealed bottle sitting outside their dwelling only after Calandra tapped his shoulder and pointed at the ground. He squinted curiously at the bottle, reached down, and snatched it off a broad flat stone flanking one side of their acutyi shrubs. A reddish liquid swished around inside the volcanic glass bottle.

"Looks like either pirica nectar or Ashmuthian red wine," Calandra said. "I always wanted to try both. Do you suppose someone sent this to us as a gift?"

Calandra crouched by the shrubs and her eyes darted about as she searched for a message paired with the bottle. She snatched up a flat metal square wedged under a smaller stone next to the front wall of their dwelling. A simple message written in the Ashmuthian language adorned the square.

For the truest friends under the sun.

Xttra's lips tightened into a frown as he studied the bottle in greater detail. A metallic strip circled the bottle confirming an Ashmuth origin. Other identifying markers were scrubbed from the glass, arousing his suspicion. Imbibing an exotic mystery drink held no appeal for Xttra. Few wines and nectars from Ashmuth were ever worth drinking—even when sent as an anonymous gift.

"Let's see if Ashelle knows anything about this," he said. "Maybe she can also take my share."

Calandra scrunched up her nose and shook her head.

"How do you know it will taste bad before you even take a sip?"

"I have an intuition for these things."

"I'm sure you do."

She laughed and planted a quick kiss on his lips. Their front door slid open, and they stepped inside. Alexa darted out of her bedroom to greet her parents.

"Miama! Diada!"

Pure joy threaded through her voice. Xttra stopped, set the bottle on the floor, and quickly scooped his favorite little girl into his arms. How could any Lathoan resist such an image of sweet innocence? A smile matching Alexa's own spread across his lips.

"Shouldn't you be sleeping, little one?"

Alexa wrapped her short arms around his neck and laid her head on his shoulder. Long locks of her red hair fell across her cheek.

"I'm not tired."

Calandra leaned over and kissed their daughter on her forehead. She smiled and brushed back Alexa's fiery tresses with her fingertips.

"Your eyelids are growing heavy, my sweet baby. Time to let your eyes rest and enter the land of dreams."

"I want to sleep later."

"She keeps telling me the same thing," Ashelle said. She emerged from Alexa's room and approached Xttra and Calandra. "I think there's too much excitement and she's afraid of missing out."

"I'll sing to her." Calandra held her arms out. "That usually works."

Xttra passed Alexa to her. Calandra wrapped her hand around the little girl's back and started down the hall. Xttra stooped down and plucked the bottle off the floor.

"Don't drink all our mystery beverage without me." Calandra said, adding a laugh.

He rolled his eyes.

"You're hilarious."

Xttra sauntered into their kitchen and approached a medium-sized wash basin sculpted from polished gray stone. He set the bottle down in the basin and retrieved three glass chalices from a shelf above his head.

"Is that wine or nectar?" Ashelle asked.

"Not certain to be honest," Xttra said. "Someone left the bottle as an anonymous gift at our door."

"Really? I didn't see or hear any visitors outside your dwelling while I watched Alexa."

"You're welcome to stay and try it with us."

She cracked a smile.

"Why not? I'm always willing to try new things—mystery beverages included."

He smirked at her appropriation of Calandra's mocking term for this anonymous gift. Xttra turned and handed her two chalices. Ashelle set one down and clutched the other in her left hand. She smiled, waiting for him. Xttra wheeled back around and set his own chalice on a narrow ledge behind the basin. He plucked the bottle from the basin and angled the cap toward the drain to catch any spills. Xttra twisted it off, dropping the cap in the basin. A bit of the reddish liquid bubbled out of the open bottle and splashed near the drain.

"Here goes nothing," he said.

Xttra grabbed his chalice again and poured out some of the liquid. He turned toward Ashelle and raised the chalice to his lips. Xttra paused. He sniffed the liquid. A pungent aroma wafted into his nostrils.

"Our mystery drink had rotten fruit for an ancestor," Xttra said. "Whatever this is, it smells awful."

He handed the chalice to Ashelle. She stuck the chalice under her nose and inhaled. Ashelle coughed a second later.

"Wow. That's disgusting."

Xttra's eyes trailed down to the bottle in his hand. He froze and his brows knit together. A sizzling sound greeted his ears. Coming from the wash basin. He jerked his head up again. Concern threaded through Ashelle's widened eyes.

"Steam is rising from your wash basin."

Xttra dashed over to the basin. The liquid he spilled earlier had dissolved the stone's polished surface. Now it ate holes in those landing spots.

"Don't drink it!" he shouted. "Don't let a single drop touch your lips!"

Xttra spun around. His heart raced as he realized what fate nearly overtook them. Ashelle's hand started to tremble; her eyes fixed on the chalice.

"Set it down carefully. On the table."

Ashelle did as he ordered. Xttra gingerly set the open bottle next to the chalice. Shoes smacked against the hall floor. Calandra popped into the kitchen a second later.

"What happened?"

Xttra drew in a deep breath, trying to calm his rapidly beating heart to normal rhythms again.

"That's not nectar or wine."

"What is it?"

"A highly corrosive acid."

Calandra's green eyes widened, and her lips started to tremble. She ran her hands through her auburn hair and clasped them behind her head.

"Are you saying someone tried to murder us?"

Xttra nodded and pinched his eyelids shut.

"They certainly would've succeeded if we drank. A mouthful of this acid is enough to eat through your mouth, throat, and belly. A quick path to a painful death."

Calandra sank into a chair at the table, next to a still-standing Ashelle. Their neighbor stared unblinking at the bottle and full chalice. She cupped her hands to her face. Calandra fixed her gaze on the same objects.

"What are we going to do?" she asked, squaring her shoulders toward Xttra.

"I don't know if one of Delcor's agents found our dwelling or if Jemanoah tried to finish what he started," he said. "Either way, we can't stay here any longer."

"I'm sure Corvah can find us another safe dwelling in a different section of the city."

"Does a safe place exist in this city? Or on Lathos? If Delcor can track us here, where can we elude his reach?"

"What are you saying?"

Xttra approached the basin and examined the acid-created holes a second time. Steam finally stopped rising. Multiple cavities remained behind as scars marking a path of acidic destruction.

"We need to leave Lathos," he said, avoiding her gaze. "Me. You. Alexa. Not one of us is safe here."

"This is our home." A nervous lilt threaded through Calandra's voice. "Where would you have us go?"

Xttra turned and faced his wife again. It pained him to uproot their little clan and flee elsewhere. They already fled their homeland once. No other choice remained. Death awaited them even outside Ra'ahm. No part of Lathos offered more safety than Daraconiah and it was no longer safe enough. Delcor had many ways of enacting revenge if his agents had truly pinpointed their home.

"We'll journey with Kevin and Bo'un to the Land of the Three Suns," he said.

***

Calandra pulled a hooded shawl tight around her mouth as she carried Alexa in her arms toward a landing platform in the Daracos space port. Xttra walked at her side, carrying an enclosed nest holding Bella. He matched her long-legged strides toward the waiting transport vessel. Head coverings and shawls partially concealed all their faces, so they resembled random refugees to onlookers amid their hasty departure.

She hated hiding herself in this fashion. Calandra hated Delcor for what he had done to them and for what he tried to do. Alexa's early memories should not be moments of fearful events and violence. He was nothing more than a vile monster. Still, her efforts to end his reign were not sufficient to counter the threat he posed. She had not swayed enough Ra'ahmian minds and hearts.

Her failure weighed down her soul.

"Welcome, fellow travelers."

Kujoth stood at the bottom of a ramp leading upward into the belly of his massive vessel. The ship's sheer size astounded Calandra. It dwarfed Xttra's former Stellar Guard scout ship. Kujoth's vessel was massive enough to comfortably fit two Cassian darts and a third small escape craft inside the cargo bay. The rear half of the outer hull resembled a gray metal bubble flanked by giant cylinders on each side. The front reminded her of a massive saucer bisecting an equally imposing Earthian bullet.

"My old scout ship could fit inside this one with room to spare." Xttra craned his head upward as they reached the ramp. "We definitely won't be inconspicuous entering another star system in this thing."

"Maybe it will deter stray scout ships from following us out of our solar system," Calandra said.

He lowered his head and smiled at her. She rarely saw Xttra so visibly impressed by a spacecraft. For a moment, his expression channeled an excited child who spent their nights dreaming of flying for the Stellar Guard.

"We can only hope."

The ramp raised behind them once they reached the top. Xttra stopped in the middle of the cargo bay and turned toward Kujoth.

"Where are Kevin and Bo'un?"

Kujoth scratched his chin and pointed at a corridor leading out from the cargo bay.

"They arrived here earlier. Both are setting up in the sleeping quarters down that way. You better hurry before they claim the best rooms for themselves."

Calandra's shoulder ached from carrying Alexa and she set her down on the ground. Her daughter gave Kujoth a wary glance and slipped a hand back inside Calandra's now free hand. She partially ducked behind a leg, using the limb as an impromptu shield, and peeked out at him with one eye.

"Alexa's shy around people she's never met before," Calandra said, glancing up at him.

Kujoth flashed a broad smile and let out a hearty laugh a second later.

"Your child is a smart one. I exercise caution around unfamiliar faces myself."

"If Kevin and Bo'un are already staying down that corridor, we can find another room there," Xttra said. "If that works for you."

"Sounds fine," Kujoth replied. "Let me show you to the bridge."

Xttra raised an eyebrow.

"Don't you have a crew to assist you?"

"Kevin tells me you were once a master pilot in the Ra'ahmian Stellar Guard," Kujoth said. "I'd be a fool not to learn from your experience while you're here."

Xttra shot a satisfied grin at Calandra.

"Can't argue with that logic."

As much as she wanted to join her husband on the bridge, Calandra needed to settle Alexa in their room. Shooting through an expansive blue sky and into the wide swath of star dappled space above Lathos would overwhelm a small child. It would do no good to send her into a panic attack.

"I better take Alexa back to our room," Calandra said. "I'll catch up with you again after we've left Lathos' atmosphere."

Xttra nodded and handed the enclosed nest to her.

"Take Bella with you. She needs some time outside of her nest."

He tucked the nest inside her arm. Small circular windows and matching air holes dotted each side of a dome topping the nest. Bella pressed her little nose against a window and chattered at Calandra.

"Don't worry, little Bella," she said. "We'll let you out for fresh air soon."

Xttra and Calandra shared a brief kiss and then parted ways. Alexa's small hand firmly clasped her own as they walked down the corridor. Each room they passed had a glass entry door. The design did not invite privacy, but also made claiming an unused room easier.

Calandra found an empty room near the end of the corridor. She set the nest on a small diamond-shaped table once she sealed the door behind her and Alexa. When Calandra lifted the dome covering, Bella sprang out and scurried down a table leg. The little cala stretched out on a low, rough carpet covering the floor and cocked her head toward her owners.

"That's much better, isn't it?" Calandra said.

Bella dropped her snout and started nosing around in the carpet, investigating new scents. Calandra turned her attention to her daughter. Alexa also explored the room for several minutes before unleashing a yawn. She gazed at her mother with a protruding lower lip.

"Are we going to a new home?"

Tears brimmed in Calandra's eyes. She reached up and brushed them away with her fingers before they rolled down her cheeks. No. This was not a suitable time to cry. She had to be strong for her little girl.

"We are going to a new home, sweetheart. An evil man wants to harm us. We need to hide from him for a little while."

"I want to go home."

"I know." Calandra sniffled as she suppressed new tears. "I miss our home too."

She dropped to her knees and pulled Alexa into an embrace. Calandra unwrapped her head covering. The fabric fluttered to the floor. She brushed back Alexa's red hair and tenderly kissed her on the cheek.

"We can make a new home. I love you deeply. So does your diada. No matter where we are, if we are together, that is enough of a home for me."

Calandra stayed on the floor with Alexa and scooted up against the edge of the wall behind the table. She held her in her arms and sang Alexa's favorite song, a traditional Ra'ahmian lyrical poem.

Her daughter's sadness reflected the grief also drowning Calandra's soul. For the second time in four years, she and Xttra fled their home. And now Alexa had to endure a trauma she worked tirelessly to prevent.

How foolish to think she could end Delcor's tyranny while dwelling in exile on another part of Lathos! Her messages reached all parts of Ra'ahm. Reports from Corvah, their Daraconian liaison, confirmed as much. Still, she did not make the impact she sought to make. No widespread uprising had occurred. Delcor's tight grip on power and unquestioned air of divine authority remained intact. Worse, many Ra'ahmians dismissed her words as vicious lies. They heard, and yet chose to ignore her.

In four years, all Calandra succeeded in doing was turning her clan and Xttra's clan against them. They had destroyed Delcor's reprehensible hybrids and his secret hybrid production facilities. But she and Xttra were no closer to ending his stranglehold over Ra'ahm than when they first fled to Daraconiah.

This realization pressed down on her like a thick stone threatening to grind her to powder. Where was Ahm during this ordeal? Why did he allow an evil tyrant like Delcor to wield power in his name? Her parents and the Order of Ahm taught Calandra throughout her childhood how the divine creator loved and watched over his creation. She struggled to see tangible evidence of such love in her life. Only repeated pain and grief for her and those whom she loved.

"We will be passing the outer planets soon. I thought you might want to be present when we reach the space bridge."

Calandra lifted her chin and gazed upward. Xttra stood over her and Alexa, smiling. His smile quickly morphed into a worried frown.

"What's wrong? Are you okay? Is Alexa okay?"

She brushed away fresh tears rolling down her cheeks. Alexa's head rested on her chest, and she lay fast asleep. Calandra drew in a deep breath.

"We've sacrificed so much because of one evil man. You. Me. Our child. I honestly believed we would make a difference against him. Have we done anything that truly mattered?"

Xttra licked his lips and sat next to her. He wound his fingers through a lock of auburn hair resting against her cheek while fixing his gaze upon Calandra.

"We've made a difference. Delcor's grip over Ra'ahm grows more tenuous daily. He's desperate and his actions are the actions of a desperate man."

"What if we don't find the staff and he does?"

"Traveling on the space bridge gives us a head start. We're smarter, more resourceful, and Ahm is on our side. We can't lose."

"Is he?" Calandra closed her eyes and lowered her chin. "Is he on our side?"

"Of course. Why would you believe otherwise?"

"Then why must we endure so much pain? Why so much heartache? Why must we be driven from our home yet again?"

Her voice climbed in pitch with each question that tormented her. Xttra's hand trailed under her chin, and gently raised it. His lips connected with hers, interlocking and pressing into a lingering kiss. Calandra opened her eyes again when his lips pulled away.

"I love you. Alexa loves you. Delcor cannot destroy that bond of love from our lives no matter what he does. Why am I confident Ahm is on our side? Because we are together. Our unity terrifies Delcor. It makes us strong enough to stand against him."

Xttra's reassuring words pierced the shadowy cloud surrounding Calandra. A small smile finally graced her lips as she gazed into his loving eyes and warm face.

"I love you so much. Your willingness to stand with me and sacrifice for us means everything."

"I'll always stand with you."

He encircled Calandra and Alexa in an embrace. She rested her head against Xttra's shoulder. For the first time in ages, Calandra felt a renewed peace and purpose.

12

Every part of Calandra's body tingled with excitement as their vessel approached the space bridge. She studied theories behind space bridges while training to become an astronomer and created her own proof of concept holographic models of a bridge. Nothing she read and learned fully prepared her for the thrill of standing inside Kujoth's vessel and seeing one in real life.

The space bridge resembled a giant spherical tunnel more than a bridge. When it first appeared after their vessel crossed beyond the Ice Belt's outer reaches, Calandra initially thought they wandered into the orbit of a rogue giant planet or failed star. Then, as the vessel drew closer, the sphere stretched out. Surrounding space curved and bent around the sphere. Rings composed of affected light and matter looped around the space bridge.

"It's so beautiful," she said.

Calandra stole a quick glance at Xttra. He stood still with a steady gaze on the space bridge. Bo'un and Kevin sat in fixed chairs behind him, equally enraptured by the sight greeting everyone on the vessel's bridge.

"I've witnessed so many incredible things in space," Bo'un said. "This one tops them all."

Kujoth let out a hearty laugh.

"You Ra'ahmians are easily impressed."

His cynicism did not dim a sense of pure wonder enveloping Calandra while she stared at the space bridge. She ignored his comments but appreciated Kujoth's calm demeanor. Miscalculating their route through the space bridge posed a truly serious threat to their lives. His nonchalant approach softened her tense nerves.

Calandra's eyes trailed rings of light as the vessel entered the bridge's mouth at hyperlight speed. Each ring stretched and rotated, turning distant stars and nebula clouds into colorful elongated bands of light and gas. Light danced on her fellow travelers' eyes when she stole a peek at their faces. Though only an optical illusion, the ship itself appeared to pull and stretch like soft rubber inside the bridge.

Calandra had no clue how much real time elapsed once their vessel exited the other side. From her perspective, only a few minutes elapsed, and the entire cosmos changed as constellations shifted from their familiar positions. They crossed a vast swath of deep space. Their destination star resembled a brilliant point of light no larger than a tiny moon from this distance. The space bridge spit the vessel out into the outer edge of this alien star system. A harsh region typically populated by unexplored comets, asteroids, and planetoids.

"This wormhole took us to the correct star, right?" Kevin asked. "I mean the place is called 'The Land of the Three Suns' for a reason."

"This should be the right destination," Xttra said. "I gave Kujoth's crew all the star data Calandra researched."

Kujoth traced his fingers over the scar on his chin and gazed thoughtfully at his passengers.

"I'll send out a survey probe," he said. "We'll wait here on the outer edge of the system while our probe collects data on the alien star and habitable planets. We should find the answers we need within a day."

Calandra expected a few hours to pass before they were ready to venture further into the system. Waiting was a prudent choice. She pressed her metal hand to her chest and dove into her thoughts. Her experiences on Earth a few years earlier taught Calandra a harsh lesson. Rushing in blind to make first contact with an alien planet proved reckless and dangerous.

"I should check on Alexa while we wait on the probe," Calandra said, turning to Xttra. "She's probably awake and worried about us right now."

He smiled and nodded.

"I'll tell you when the probe sends back useful data."

Calandra exited the bridge and walked down the corridor to the room she shared with Xttra and Alexa. Rows of pellet-shaped white lights on each wall lit the corridor. When the door slid open and she stepped inside, she found Alexa laying on a small bed jutting out in a semicircle from an interior wall. Her eyelids remained closed, and a little arm draped over the side of the bunk. Bella had curled into a ball under the dangling limb and joined the little girl in her slumber.

If only she had a holocaster to capture this peaceful image. Xttra packed one among the few possessions they brought with them on this journey. Calandra hesitated to search for it, largely because she did not want to disturb their rest with inadvertent loud noises.

She perched on a larger semicircle bed directly across from Alexa on the opposite side of the room. Calandra rubbed her hands over her cheeks and gazed down at the shawl and head covering she wore when boarding the ship earlier.

"He loves you, Callie."

Her mother's voice popped into her mind. Images followed. She was a child again, not yet 10 years old. Her mother, Alyssa, crouched down before her under the shade of a senosa tree. She wore a paint-ed-on smile, contrasting the pout adorning Calandra's own face.

"Then why did he leave?" Sadness choked her voice. "I don't want him to leave."

Tears trickled down Alyssa's cheeks and she brushed them away.

"Your grandfather needed to leave for a special reason. One day you'll understand."

"Why can't I go see him?" she asked between sobs. "I want to see him."

"I know, sweetheart." Alyssa drew a sharp breath to stifle a sob and pinched her eyes shut for a moment. "I want to see him too. But we can't go to Laxa. It isn't safe for you."

Her mother's final words repeated in Calandra's head as she snapped back to the present moment. She had to keep Alexa safe. Many years later, she grasped the depth of her grandfather's sacrifice. Janthore fled Lathos to save his clan after he learned of Delcor's crimes. Calandra was not old enough at the time to understand why he left and struggled to forgive her grandfather.

Now she understood.

"Your earlier data is spot on."

Calandra turned her head and glanced at Xttra. She had grown so immersed in thought she did not hear him enter the room. He carried a trique with an active holoscreen and handed the triangular device to her.

"Initial probe readings confirm this star is a near-perfect match to our own sun. Mass. Luminosity. Chemical composition."

She stared at the holoscreen and scrolled through what the probe recorded. The data matched what they gleaned from the observatory within an acceptable margin for error.

"This is welcome news," she said.

"Kevin and Bo'un boarded the darts in the cargo bay," he said. "They're scouting for habitable planets and will send word once they've found a potential location for the Land of the Three Suns."

Calandra rose to her feet and handed the trique back to him. The holoscreen flickered briefly as it passed through his arm.

"Now all that's left is finding the Staff of Onrai, right?" She shook her head and grinned. "If only it were so simple."

Xttra clasped her arm and offered up a hopeful smile.

"We're one step closer." He trailed his fingers down to her elbow. "That's what matters."

A sudden powerful tremor rippled through the length of the room. Calandra stumbled forward into Xttra. They both collapsed to the floor amid the shaking. She landed face first on his torso. Alexa rolled out of bed and awoke with a scream. Bella scurried away from her as she fell and darted across the room, searching for a hiding spot from the shaking.

An alarm blared through the corridor outside the room. Flashing red lights followed, swallowing soft white light which previously illuminated the corridor. The violent tremors ceased once these emergency lights sprang to life.

"Did we collide with an asteroid?" Xttra asked.

His eyes darted toward the door. Calandra rolled off him and he scrambled to his feet. She crawled past Xttra and wrapped her arms around Alexa. Tears flowed from their daughter's eyes as she sobbed.

"I'm here, sweetheart." She held Alexa close to her chest. "Don't be afraid."

Alexa buried her face in Calandra's shoulder. A second shockwave rippled through the room.

That was no mere asteroid.

Their vessel was under attack.

"Please help us, Ahm." Calandra closed her eyes and whispered a desperate prayer. "Please spare our lives from whoever is threatening this vessel."

She opened her eyes again, brushed back Alexa's hair and kissed her forehead. Calandra peered over at the door. Where was Xttra?

Did he reach the bridge? Did the second shockwave injure him? Her instincts pushed her to charge out of the room and search for him.

She pushed back.

Alexa needed her mother.

She did not want to expose her child to unknown dangers outside the room. Leaving her alone—even for a few minutes—was out of the question. Calandra refused to add to the fear threatening to devour Alexa.

"I won't let any harm come to you," she said, trying to reassure her. "We'll be safe."

The door slid open. Calandra's eyes locked on Xttra again as he sprinted into the room. Fear permeated his reddened face. Heavy breaths escaped his lips.

"We need to abandon ship."

"Are we under attack?"

Xttra nodded.

"Kujoth detected signals from three scout ships and a ground force carrier when we reached the outermost planet. They opened fire on our vessel."

"Delcor found us?"

A tremor raced down her spine. Calandra scrambled to her feet with Alexa still in her arms. Her eyes darted around the room, seeking Bella. Their pet had vanished.

"Help me find Bella. We can't leave her behind."

Xttra motioned to the door.

"Take Alexa to the escape craft. I'll grab Bella and be right behind you."

Calandra sprinted out into the corridor, still holding their daughter. Troubling questions flooded her mind while racing toward the cargo bay. When did the Stellar Guard reach this star system? Were they too late to find the Staff of Onrai and keep the relic out of Delcor's hands? The chief sovereign discovered the space bridge first. Calandra silently cursed her foolish belief they would gain an advantage over him so easily when he had the full resources of Ra'ahm to implement his agenda.

A new batch of tremors rippled through the cargo bay. Calandra stumbled again. Both kneecaps smacked against the hard floor. She winced and shifted Alexa to one arm. Her daughter clung tight to her shoulder, sobbing inconsolably. Calandra pushed herself to a standing position with the other arm and made a renewed dash toward the escape craft.

She reached the outer door before any new shockwaves shook the cargo bay. Xttra popped out of the corridor, wearing a chest pouch holding their holocasters and carrying Bella's enclosed nest in the crook of one arm. He extracted an external controller from a front pocket on his pants. He peered intently at the wrist-length cylinder with flat sides before pressing an indented button near the top. A pad outside the rear hatch flashed from red to blue. The hatch door opened. A small ramp extended outward and lowered to the ground.

"Kujoth gave me an external controller to open the escape craft," he said. "He's purchasing us time so we can fly out of here unharmed."

Calandra glanced down at his hands as they darted up the ramp. His left hand bore a fresh scratch from his thumb to his index finger. A trickle of blood oozed from the wound. A long deep tear crossed his shirt cuff above the scratch.

"You're injured."

"The most recent shockwave hit right after I found Bella," Xttra said, shaking his head. "She was startled, but I got her inside and closed the nest."

Calandra winced again when she cleared the ramp.

"I think I bruised my knees when that shockwave sent me tumbling to the ground."

A worried frown appeared on his face.

"I hope you don't have a fracture."

"Me too. Fortunately, the bone strengtheners I've used since we've lived in Daraconiah seem more effective in combating my brittle bones."

She drew in a deep breath and started moving again after Xttra resealed the hatch door. Calandra did not experience sharp stabbing pains a fracture produced with movement. Ahm had smiled upon her if the injury proved to be only a bruise. She prayed her brittle bones would not endanger their mission.

Calandra found a seat for Alexa behind the pilot and co-pilot chairs and strapped her behind a safety harness. Tears stained her little cheeks. The fabric on Calandra's long-sleeved shirt had grown cool and damp where Alexa buried her face after the first shockwave.

"Miama and Diada are both here." She stroked her child's cheek. "This will be over soon. Be brave."

Alexa's lips trembled in a frightened pout, but she nodded obediently.

Xttra settled into the pilot's chair and started pressing a series of buttons and flipping switches. Calandra slid into the co-pilot chair. She took deliberate breaths, trying to calm her frayed nerves, and uttered another silent prayer to Ahm.

A holoscreen materialized over the helm console. Kujoth's image appeared. Chaos had overtaken the bridge behind him. Sparks and smoke flew from shattered screens and broken consoles. Only emergency lighting functioned on the bridge, like in the corridor and the cargo bay. Three of his crew members lay sprawled out across the floor, unmoving.

"Primary systems are online," Xttra said. "Hurry. I don't know how much longer I can wait for you."

Kujoth shook his head.

"You'll never make it far enough from this ship if I leave this bridge."

Xttra's eyes widened.

"I can't leave you here to die."

Kujoth laughed. His laugh lacked the usual hearty carefree quality Calandra had come to expect from him. This was a quiet laugh of a man resigned to his fate, and ready to meet Ahm in the eternal worlds.

"Find the relic you're seeking," the smuggler said. "You're our best hope to stop that setaworm Delcor from bringing every part of Lathos under his control."

His response shocked Calandra. Kujoth offered no obvious signs before now of having a higher purpose for taking this journey beyond enriching himself.

"This was never only about money, was it?" she said.

Kujoth shrugged.

"No. Not completely." He mashed down an unseen button on his console. "Now go. Hurry!"

His image vanished from the holoscreen. An alarm blared as the massive vessel's rear hatch opened. Xttra ignited the escape craft's primary thrusters and pulled back on a steering stick. Their small craft shot forward. Calandra clenched her teeth and wrapped her hands around her chair's armrests.

The escape craft zipped away from the rear of Kujoth's vessel. Calandra got her first clear view of the damage to the ship as they put space between it and their smaller craft.

She gasped.

His vessel's protective energy shell had dissipated under heavy attack. Smoke and metallic shards floated into space from a massive hull breach on the far side. The breach cut across a primary thruster, leaving a deep jagged gash. Sparks and flashes from within the breach offered telltale signs the thruster was growing unstable. Pock marks and blackened smoldering holes peppered the hull above and below the bridge. Kujoth's vessel drifted, trapped within a deteriorating orbit, and spun slowly toward a giant planet.

No chance any survivors remained on board.

"He held them off as long as possible," Xttra said. "Let's hope he purchased us enough time to escape."

Calandra could not peel her eyes away from the wrecked vessel. Kujoth and his crew joined a never-ending list of victims who suffered cruel fates because of Delcor's tyranny. Their status as a band of smugglers was irrelevant. They deserved better.

Oh no.

Calandra drew a sharp breath.

Where are Kevin and Bo'un?

No visible trace of their darts appeared on the sensors. Neither ship was still inside the cargo bay when she fled the main vessel with Xttra and Alexa. Did they evade and escape the scout ships or suffer a similar gruesome fate as Kujoth and his crew?

No, Ahm. Please let them be alive.

Those words formed a desperate plea inside her head. Calandra could not bear the thought either one perished in an alien star system. They saved her life and Xttra's life on multiple occasions. Kevin and Bo'un were their friends in the truest sense of the word.

They needed them on this journey.

"I'm detecting another ship on the sensors," Xttra said. "I hope this thing has a viable energy shell."

He gave the steering control stick a sudden jerk to the right and angled the escape craft downward and outward from the giant planet. A massive smoldering metallic husk spiraled past the roof of their ship. It sank deep into the planet's gravity well and tumbled downward toward an impending collision with the thick upper atmosphere.

"I think we avoided the ship." Calandra breathed out a relieved sigh. "Or what's left of it, anyway."

Xttra shot her a concerned look.

"That's not the ship on the sensors."

His warning barely left his lips when a second ship popped out from behind a tiny moon in a tight, close orbit around the planet. Calandra's heart sank when she peeked over at Xttra's holoscreen. This was no shattered remnant from a space battle.

A fully operational scout ship engaged an intercept course toward their escape craft.

13

Once a scout ship appeared on the sensors, a creeping trepidation settled over Xttra and crawled down his skin like an ictus bug.

Their small escape craft stood no chance of surviving a direct confrontation with a scout ship. His weapon, a single neutronic blaster, would never match their arsenal. No visible sign of Kevin or Bo'un in their darts only decreased the odds he, Calandra, and Alexa would get past this unfamiliar planet safe and alive.

"What do we do now?"

Fear threaded through Calandra's question. The same fear wrapped around him with the strength of a mokai's sharp talons. No answer reassuring enough to put into words formed in his mind.

"We can't outrun that scout ship," Xttra finally said. "We won't survive more than three direct hits in a battle. Our only choice is to outsmart these setaworms."

Worry swam through Calandra's green eyes as they settled on him and the implicit desperation behind his words became clear to her.

"I hope you know what you're doing."

He frowned while swimming in deep thought.

"So do I."

Xttra activated an energy shell around the outer hull. Holoscreen data showed it only functioned at two-thirds power. He silently cursed that unwelcome revelation. Two or three direct hits would dissipate the shell to zero, leaving their small vessel entirely vulnerable. Then plasma cannons or ion torpedoes would tear their hull apart and send whatever remained spiraling down toward the giant planet.

Xttra's eyes brightened.

An unorthodox idea burst into his mind. A dangerous idea. Still, it offered their best chance for escape.

If he drew the scout ship into the gravity well, and disabled all primary thrusters, the ship would not escape the upper atmosphere. Gravity would pull the ship down and incinerate the whole thing in lower atmospheric layers, equaling certain death for all Stellar Guard officers on board. If his plan worked, he would create enough time to escape and reach the Land of the Three Suns before reinforcements arrived.

"I have a plan to get us to safety," he said, glancing over at Calandra.

She licked her lips and stole a hurried glimpse at their daughter. Alexa sat with her arms crossed, lips trembling and hugging herself while staring straight ahead.

"What's cooking inside your head?" Calandra asked in a wary tone, refocusing her gaze on Xttra.

"We're going to force the scout ship to collide with the giant planet and burn up in the atmosphere."

Her eyes narrowed and she swallowed hard.

"That's insane. You already said we can't fight them or outrun them. If we trap them in the planet's gravity well, how will we escape?"

A sharp series of beeps grabbed his attention. Xttra snapped his head back to the holoscreen. The scout ship had drawn closer into visual range. Their vessel had also entered the other vessel's weapons range.

"It's a calculated risk," he said. "But we have no time left and no better options."

Calandra drew a sharp breath and closed her eyes. Xttra understood the helplessness besieging her and Alexa. The same feeling held him hostage. Fear also claimed ownership of Xttra. Their lives were in his hands. His piloting skills, and a little luck, formed the only thin line between living and dying.

He pushed the steering stick to the left, toward Calandra's seat. The escape craft veered in the same direction and circled back toward the planet. The scout ship matched their change in course and continued pursuit—exactly as Xttra hoped. Two new signals suddenly appeared on the sensors as his ship and the other vessel drew closer to the giant planet.

Two more ships.

From another direction.

Neither vessel had entered visual range yet. Xttra had no way of determining if these ships originally attacked Kujoth's vessel or were fresh reinforcements. Either possibility meant a swift end for him, Calandra, and Alexa. A sudden prolonged beep cut through the relative silence building inside the escape craft. Calandra's eyes shot open, and she stared intently at the holoscreen.

"Someone wants to open a channel."

"I know what they will say to us. It won't be worth hearing. I don't want their taunts and threats of destruction to be the last words we hear."

Her lips parted and she gave him an incredulous look.

"Would you rather see them blow our ship apart without a word? I favor talking things out before shooting them out."

Xttra sighed and mashed down on a button activating the escape craft's communicator.

"You win. We'll try it your way."

A holoscreen materialized before the piloting console. Relief splashed over him like a cool ocean wave. The image belonged to Bo'un.

"I didn't expect to see you," Xttra said. "I worried you didn't make it."

"Kevin and I were already a fair distance from Kujoth's ship when the ground force carrier and a scout ship opened fire."

"Where's Kevin?" Calandra asked. "Is he safe?"

Bo'un glanced over at another holoscreen before him and nodded.

"He's fine. We both entered pole to pole orbits tight against the upper atmosphere to mask our darts within the planet's natural magnetic field."

Xttra smiled as he pondered their ingenuity. Bo'un and Kevin both evolved into skilled pilots over the past four years. While the darts made their situation less dire, their odds of destroying a scout ship without suffering casualties were not favorable. Xttra preferred to outsmart one master pilot instead of launching a full-scale battle against an entire crew of seasoned Stellar Guard officers. They trained endlessly to survive and win when faced with such scenarios.

"A scout ship is still on our tail," he said. "I'm drawing them closer to the planet, so we can disable their ship and force it into a deteriorating orbit where it will burn up in the atmosphere."

"That's a bold plan," Bo'un said. "How do we help?"

"Sneak behind the scout ship, while I skim the upper atmosphere, and target their primary thrusters."

He nodded and pressed down on an unseen button. Bo'un's image vanished from the holoscreen. Xttra pulled down a lever on the pilot console. The primary thrusters gave an extra kick as the escape craft accelerated.

"Have you lost your mind?"

Calandra's eyes widened and flooded with fear matching her distressed tone. She instinctively turned back to check on Alexa again.

"If we hit that upper atmosphere at this speed," she said. "Our ship will be torn apart by gravity."

Xttra shook his head. He understood her concern, but he was an experienced pilot. Their ship had excellent acceleration for its diminutive size. It could handle a brief dance with a giant planet's upper atmosphere.

"We'll be fine if we skim it." He adopted the most reassuring tone he could muster. "Our velocity constrictors can handle increased gravity if we don't linger in a tight orbit for too long."

The scout ship pursued their escape craft toward the upper atmosphere. Two darts entered visual range and sped toward their position from opposite directions. One above and one below.

A tremor engulfed their ship, shaking Xttra in his seat, as a plasma cannon bolt slammed into a section of energy shell covering the hull's back end. Bella chattered nervously inside her nest. Alexa cried out in terror. Calandra snapped her head toward their daughter again.

"This will end soon, sweetheart." Tears filled her eyes as she tried to comfort Alexa. "Close your eyes. Ask Ahm to bring us peace."

Xttra stole a glance over his shoulder and saw tears streaming down from under her closed eyelids. He hated witnessing Alexa suffer through this ordeal. She deserved better. They all deserved better.

He checked the ship's energy shell status. It dipped under half-capacity, drained to 40 percent power. One or two more direct hits would finish the shell off and leave them unprotected.

"What are they waiting for?" Xttra said. "I can't evade this scout ship forever."

Their small ship zipped along the giant planet's equator. Colorful swirls laced through the uppermost clouds. Beautiful and deadly. Xttra performed several other evasive maneuvers to prevent a second plasma cannon bolt from making contact. Plasma bolts fired wide of their intended mark as he dodged their fire.

Sensors showed two darts slip behind the scout ship from polar positions. It changed course and faced these new vessels. Xttra mirrored their action, turning to face the pursuing scout ship. Both darts fired plasma cannon bolts. Their weapons' aim held true.

A cloud of sparks, smoke, and metallic shards emanated from the Stellar Guard ship's primary thrusters. It spun out of control toward the giant planet. Xttra accelerated thrusters and their smaller escape craft zoomed outward. Both darts also reached escape velocity and broke orbit around the planet.

A second explosion behind the three ships ripped apart the scout ship's bridge. Xttra caught a brief glimpse of the wreckage and his eyes trailed back to the holoscreen. Sensors showed remnants from every ship and floating corpses on a collision course with the giant planet's atmosphere. Thick clouds would absorb all the wreckage in a brief time. Those metallic husks, along with his one-time Stellar Guard colleagues, would eventually be crushed down to their last atom.

An extended beep from the ship's communicator signaled an incoming message. Xttra activated the holoscreen. Kevin's image appeared a second later.

"They just had a close encounter of the deadly kind!"

He cracked a grin. Xttra and Calandra both flashed relieved smiles. Their happy expressions had less to do with reacting to Kevin's odd Earthian humor and more to do with surviving a battle with multiple scout ships while suffering no damage to their vessel.

"I'm happy you and Bo'un are safe," Calandra said, leaning over toward the holoscreen. "When we didn't see your ships on the sensors, we feared the worst."

"Don't worry," Kevin said. "You won't be rid of me that easily. Takes more than a few scout ships to bring down Kevin Riley."

Xttra glanced down at the sensors and back at the holoscreen. No sign of other vessels in the system beyond their own. That did not mean freedom from meeting further resistance on their way to the Land of the Three Suns. Since the Stellar Guard had also discovered the space bridge, more scout ships would arrive soon.

He hoped a larger fleet had not already reached the planet. Perhaps Ahm smiled on them, and these ships were only an advance party sent ahead of the chief sovereign to prepare the way. If that were the case, they may yet obtain the Staff of Onrai first.

The ship's communicator emitted a second prolonged beep. Xttra opened a second window on his holoscreen. Bo'un popped up next to Kevin's image.

"Kujoth transmitted probe data to our darts before coming under attack," Bo'un said. "His probe identified a planet orbiting in this star's habitable zone and sent back a long-distance image."

"That's promising news," Xttra said. "How far away is the planet from us?"

Bo'un punched a few unseen buttons on his console.

"I'm relaying all the probe data to you now," he said. "Based on the coordinates, it will take four hours to reach the planet traveling at your vessel's maximum subluminal speeds."

"Keep your eyes and ears open," Xttra replied. "We don't want to run into other scout ships in this system. Fortune may not favor us a second time."

He and Calandra calmed Alexa enough during their trek to the habitable zone for her to fall into a light slumber. Bella also grew quiet again after Calandra comforted the little animal inside her nest. Their cala joined Alexa in sleeping through the bulk of their four-hour journey into the inner part of this alien star system.

Xttra did not let himself relax for a second. His nerves and muscles remained as tight as fresh Chitha strings woven end to end inside a circular fraxa wood frame. One detail ate at him. Kujoth reported detecting three scout ships and a ground force carrier near the giant planet. Xttra counted wreckage from only three ships before leaving planetary orbit.

What happened to the fourth scout ship? The implications of a surviving ship gnawed at his mind. Xttra feared the ship fled to gather reinforcements with no one to stop it.

He slowed the escape craft to standard interplanetary subluminal speed once they reached the habitable zone. A large moon loomed on the horizon. Craters dotted the surface like giant round scars. It bore some resemblance to Laxa and Fengar. Unlike either Lathoan moon, this alien satellite showed no visible evidence of permanent colonies.

Xttra maintained open channels with Kevin and Bo'un while traveling from the giant planet. Kevin's image reappeared on the holoscreen when they rejoined the darts in a tight orbit around the moon. His expression turned stoic.

"I intercepted radio waves from the planet's surface," he said. "Bo'un and I are working to pinpoint their origin."

"That's not a surprise." Calandra jumped in before Xttra had a chance to respond. "We suspected this place is inhabited."

Kevin rubbed his hands over his cheeks and bit down on his lower lip. Xttra narrowed his eyes.

"What about these radio waves aren't you telling us?"

"You won't like what I found out." Kevin sighed and pursed his lips. "We identified multiple voices—all speaking English."

Calandra's eyes widened like plates, and she drew in a sharp breath. She pressed her hand against her mouth. Xttra's heart started pounding as rapidly as it did while evading the scout ship. He dared not speak the question already forming in his mind into existence.

Kevin confirmed their worst fears anyway.

"Whoever lives on that planet came from Earth."

14

S tunned silence smothered Calandra. She stared, eyes unblinking, at the holoscreen. Her lips parted slightly. None among the barrage of words swarming her mind escaped from her tongue, fading away like flames turning into dying embers. A nightmare scenario unfolded in their quest to find the Staff of Onrai.

Earthians.

Why did they have to encounter Earthians on this planet? These aliens went from owning no hyperlight travel capabilities whatsoever to infecting the Land of the Three Suns with the speed of a virus in only a few short years. It seemed impossible. Did they now face a new danger rivaling the one Delcor already posed?

Kevin's revelation frightened Calandra down to the depths of her soul. If other Earthians thought and acted like him, she would welcome a reunion. But he stood out as an exception. She glanced down at her artificial limb anew. For Calandra, it offered jarring proof of the volatile danger Earthians presented when meeting visitors from other planets.

"Can you talk to them? Maybe you can assess the threat these specific Earthians pose to us."

Xttra shot a quick glance at Calandra while posing the question before refocusing his gaze on Kevin. Worry sprang from his eyes and manifested in a deep frown. She knew he shared her fear at learning the Earthians built their own deep space colony.

"What do you want me to say?" Kevin replied. "I'm a deserter from the US Army and considered a traitor against Earth. They are probably Americans, and I face arrest and a court martial if I reveal my identity."

Calandra leaned back in her chair and stared at the ceiling of their small ship. A workable solution eluded their grasp.

Kevin already sacrificed so much to save their lives when she and Xttra made first contact with Earth. They could not expect him to continue making sacrifices on their behalf. Still, returning to Lathos while Delcor clung to power remained out of the question. His agents found them in Daraconiah. If the chief sovereign obtained the staff, no part of their home planet offered sanctuary from his retribution.

"We'll stand with you," Calandra said, finally breaking her silence. Her eyes drifted back to the holoscreen. "Whatever fate awaits you; we'll share it together."

He shook his head.

"I can't ask that of you."

"You didn't. I owe my life to you. Xttra and I have each other, and Alexa, because of what you did to save me on Earth and on Lathos."

Kevin cast his eyes downward. He studied his pilot console, as though uncertain of which action to take.

"I'll make contact." He met her gaze again. "I'll leave my arca vox connected, so you all stay in the loop with me. Wish me luck."

Calandra leaned forward. Her muscles grew rigid as Kevin flipped a switch to activate an inter-channel audio communicator on his piloting console. The device let him communicate with more than one person at a time while still isolating an individual channel for one-on-one communication when necessary.

"This is Kevin Riley," he said. "I'm an American from Earth. We're not here to cause trouble. We only want permission to land."

Calandra trailed a finger through a dangling lock of her auburn hair while awaiting a response from the Earthians. She expected him to conceal his identity. Did the Earthians on the planet's surface know him? How would they respond to his message if they did? Billions of aliens lived on Earth, so the odds of these Earthians knowing him had to be slim. Still, sharing his true name created an unnecessary risk.

"Your name isn't listed in our colony database. How did you end up out here so far away from Earth?"

A skeptical tone permeated the responding voice. It sounded like a young male Earthian. Calandra's throat tightened. The unseen Earthian obviously did not believe Kevin was one of his people. No doubt the Earthians brought weapons to this planet. Would they attack their ships like on Earth? Their energy shell lacked enough power to withstand another direct attack after tangling with the scout ship.

"It's a really long…story." Kevin paused as though he silently debated how much information he ought to share. "Listen, I'm happy to dive into the details with you all once we're on the ground."

An exasperated sigh greeted his words.

"I have no way of verifying who you say you are. If you can offer proof of—"

"Proof? Good Hell."

Kevin slammed his fist on his helm console. His image flickered on Xttra's holoscreen.

"What do you want from me? My driver's license? My social security number? A list of recent Super Bowl winners?"

Silence greeted his outburst. Worry swam in Xttra's eyes as they slid over to Calandra. She shared his concern. Kevin's deteriorating temper did not help their situation. Antagonizing the Earthians while stuck in such a vulnerable position was not a smart decision.

"These Earthians aren't being persuaded to open their arms to welcome us," Xttra whispered, cupping his hand over his mouth. "He's compromising our chance to land."

"Hey! I heard that." Kevin snapped his head toward his holoscreen. "I'll have you know I got this situation perfectly under control."

Xttra and Calandra exchanged incredulous glances.

"Have they attacked us yet? Sit tight. I'll get us down there. Show me a little faith."

Each second passing without communication from the planet's surface stirred a growing dread inside Calandra. It climbed her spine and spread like a web through her limbs. She ran her hands through her hair and glanced back at Alexa. The earlier trauma had drained the little girl's energy. Her eyelids were closed, and her head turned to the side. Calandra hoped she stayed fully asleep.

"Permission to land is granted." The unseen Earthian finally spoke again. "I'm sending you landing coordinates several miles outside our colony. A landing party will retrieve you at those coordinates."

Calandra pressed her hand against her chest and let out a relieved sigh. Xttra and Kevin both smiled, their expressions also reflecting a measure of hopeful relief.

"I read you loud and clear," Kevin said. "See you soon."

He transmitted the landing coordinates to Bo'un and Xttra and his image vanished from the holoscreen. Xttra activated the primary thrusters again and their small craft sped from the moon toward the planet they believed to be the Land of the Three Suns.

Conflicting feelings battled for control within Calandra when she laid eyes on their destination—a small blue and white planet. No one could deny the natural beauty it owned. One half lay blanketed in deep shadows. Sunlight kissed the other half, revealing swirls of white clouds and clear blue oceans. A giant land mass tinged with abundant red shades and hues peeked out from beneath the clouds. Large islands dotted an expansive ocean surrounding the reddish continent on three sides.

Lathos and Earth both owned a similar external beauty. And yet both planets revealed an inner ugliness manifested in so many of their inhabitants. Calandra wanted desperately to believe this planet would turn out different as they plunged into the upper atmosphere. Her heart urged her to embrace hope. Her mind argued that evil flourished everywhere. Why would things be different in the Land of the Three Suns?

"Alexa, you should look at this." Xttra's voice pierced the gloomy thoughts swarming Calandra. "You love the ocean. Now you can see it from the sky."

Calandra turned and gazed at their daughter. Alexa's eyelids opened gradually, and she let out a yawn. She gazed through a small circular window to her right. A joyful smile adorned her face, the first one since before they fled Kujoth's vessel. She glanced over at Calandra and beamed at her.

"It's so blue." Alexa's voice filled with wonder. "Can we go to the ocean?"

A matching smile appeared on Calandra's lips.

"We'll go there soon, sweetheart. I promise."

Xttra steered their ship toward the giant land mass. They approached the eastern coastline. His sensors showed Kevin and Bo'un flanking his ship in their darts. Other unidentified aerial signals, out of visual range, appeared on the holoscreen as the ship plunged through white billowing clouds. Calandra guessed they were hidden Earthian vessels tracking the incoming ships.

Cliffs climbed skyward a short distance from pristine white beaches along the coastline. Towering waves crashed upon the sand extending outward from the rocky cliffs. Each white foamy wave formed one jagged line after another, buffeting the sands with their fury and receding into the next approaching wave. Lush trees and grasses of varying red hues, mirroring familiar Lathoan foliage, topped a flat plateau leading away from the cliffs.

The scenic panorama before Calandra matched how she always pictured the Land of the Three Suns based on her readings of the *Book of Ahm*. It resembled all the most beautiful parts of Lathos. This place fit the ancient description of a land of refuge created by Ahm himself.

A beautiful, secluded world placed among hidden stars.

Kevin's dart took the lead and veered inland away from the coast. Bo'un and Xttra followed in their ships. They approached the plateau. Strange vehicles dotted a small section cleared of trees and bushes, bearing vague similarities to Earthian cars Calandra recalled seeing many years earlier. Six spherical tires jutted out from a broad rectangular body separated into a pair of compartments. The forward compartment presented a downward sloping gray metallic face. The rear compartment formed a hexagon with each sky-facing side topped by four clear black rectangular panels.

Doors opened on several vehicles as the ships drew closer to the designated landing coordinates. Multiple human-like aliens stepped out from the vehicles below. Many wore shaded glasses over their eyes. A few resembled Earthians by their dress. Others wore clothing matching popular Lathoan designs. This offered a sure sign some of these colonists never called Earth home.

"They aren't all Earthians," Calandra said, sharing her conclusion with Xttra. "Some of the colonists are wearing Lathoan attire."

Xttra squinted at the assembled colonists and their vehicles. A frown deepened on his lips.

"I can make an accurate guess where those colonists came from."

Their ship faced the fleet of strange-wheeled vehicles as landing gear touched solid ground. Earthians closest to the ship thrust up their arms, shielding their faces from plumes of dust and grass kicked up by the ship landing. Calandra's throat tightened as the aliens approached their ship. They showed evidence of carrying arms, although they pointed no weapons at them.

"Everything will work out. Have faith."

Xttra's uncertain mimic of Kevin's earlier admonition convinced Calandra he did not believe his own words. She appreciated his efforts to offer encouragement, but she also remained skeptical of the Earthians' intentions.

The rear hatch opened. An exit ramp extended to the ground. Calandra gathered Alexa out of her seat and into her arms, holding her daughter close against her chest. Her little heart matched the elevated rhythm inside Calandra's own ribs.

Xttra caught up to her as she started down the ramp. He wore a stoic expression. His empty right hand idled at his hip while his left hand rested on her shoulder blade. Calandra cast a worried glance at the holstered eliminator on his hip. Surely, Xttra would not start blasting away at Earthians if something went wrong? They were severely outnumbered. Taking a peaceful approach was a smart choice and the only practical choice.

Calandra squinted near the bottom of the ramp. Sunlight flooded across the plateau. As her eyes adjusted, she took in vivid colors of surrounding grasses and distant trees. An Earthian woman clad in a black sleeveless shirt and tan pants approached the ramp. She wore shaded glasses. The ends of her short wavy brown hair dangled just above her shoulders.

"I'm Lily Rhoads." She extended a hand. "I'm a physician here in Cascadia. Welcome to our colony."

Alexa stared curiously at the Earthian before hiding her face again when Lily met her gaze. Calandra wanted to do the same. She drew in a sharp breath and shot a quick glance at Xttra. He shrugged and motioned at Lily, inviting her to return the friendly greeting. She clasped Lily's wrist in traditional Ra'ahmian fashion, earning a curious look from the surprised Earthian woman.

"My name is Calandra. I'm a visitor from a distant planet called Lathos."

Lily removed her shaded glasses, revealing light brown eyes. Her eyes brightened after learning Calandra's name and she cracked a smile.

"Calandra?" Lily repeated her name in an excited tone. She snapped her head toward Xttra. "Does that mean you are Xttra Oogan?"

Xttra's eyes narrowed. He gave her a sideways glance.

"How do you know my name?"

"She knows your name because I told her about you." A familiar voice behind Lily called out to them. "I told all the colonists about you and Calandra."

The voice belonged to a man with thin brown hair, graying at the temples. He strolled from a nearby vehicle toward the ship, before stopping a few steps from the ramp. His belly bore a slight paunch. The man removed shaded glasses, matching ones Lily wore, and smiled. He extended his hand.

"Hello, Calandra. Hello, Xttra. What are the odds we'd run into one another again?"

Lily glanced at her fellow Earthian and slid her eyes back to them. Her smile widened.

"I guess no introductions are needed here."

Calandra scowled. Lily was correct. She already knew this specific Earthian's identity quite well. Sam Bono was not an alien she expected to meet on this planet nor ever wanted to see again.

15

ncountering Sam on another planet only confirmed a lingering
fear crawling through Xttra's mind since leaving Earth for a second time. The Confederation returned to the Aramus system and
plunged straight into helping Earthians develop their own hyperlight
technology. Kyra and Cavac completely ignored his repeated warnings
during their return voyage to Lathos. Their meddling opened a door
for a hostile alien race to creep out into the wider galaxy.

How long before the Earthians reached Lathos and plunged
his home planet into a devastating war?

Xttra internally shuddered at the thought. He found himself in
a difficult spot. Earthians posed an eventual threat to Lathos. Still,
they did not present the same immediate danger that the chief sovereign did. Delcor revealed his true nature long ago as a desperate
tyrant who would stop at nothing to extend his rule.

Maybe Ahm had a greater purpose behind facilitating this
reunification. Sam understood firsthand the threat Delcor posed
after he and Xttra battled hybrids side by side four and a half years

earlier. If any Earthian leader agreed to support their cause, Sam would be the first one to make such a commitment.

"Why are you here?"

Calandra's abrupt question pierced his thoughts. Fury filled her eyes as she stared down the Earthian. Xttra did not blame Calandra for her reaction to him. Not for a second. Sam deserved the cold greeting he received. She bore permanent physical and emotional scars from the violence Earthians inflicted on her under his leadership.

Sam withdrew his hand. His eyes rested on her exposed metallic hand and wrist.

"I'm sorry for all the pain I caused you," he said, making eye contact again. "If I could turn back time—"

"You can't turn back time, can you?" Calandra shot back. "What's done is done."

Sam dropped his head and stared at the ground. An uncomfortable silence permeated the landing site. Xttra gazed at others who came with Sam. Few were willing to make eye contact.

"Did you honestly expect a warm greeting?" Xttra's question dissipated the thickening silence. "Your soldiers' unwarranted attack almost cost Calandra her life and eventually robbed her of an arm. You're one of the last aliens in this galaxy she wants to see."

Sam hung his glasses from the collar of his long-sleeved beige shirt. He glanced up at Xttra and rubbed both hands over his cheeks.

"I tried to make amends," he said. "I helped reunite you with Calandra after you were brought to Mars against your will."

"You can't simply expect immediate forgiveness after inflicting life-altering injuries," Xttra said. "And you know it."

Lily's eyes darted between Xttra and Calandra. Her happy smile morphed into a questioning frown, and she pivoted toward Sam.

"What exactly did you do to her?"

Her phrasing made the question sound more fearful than accusatory. Lily's reaction offered illumination. Xttra realized Sam had not been forthcoming to his fellow colonists concerning his sordid past with visitors from other planets.

"If you're here to arrest me and drag me back to Earth, be prepared for one hell of a fight."

Xttra turned away from Sam as soon as Kevin's voice greeted his ears. He and Bo'un approached the group at a brisk pace from where they landed their darts. Kevin kept one hand hovering over his eliminator, ready to draw and fire at a moment's notice.

A half-dozen flying animals soared over their heads, calling out to one another as they traveled toward the ocean cliffs. Skin membranes covered their long wings instead of feathers. The alien creatures had lanky furry bodies matching an adult cala in size.

"We're not going to arrest you, Sergeant Riley." Sam turned to face him, welcoming the chance to ignore Lily's uncomfortable question. "I wouldn't let you land in our colony if I considered you an enemy to the United States or Earth."

A look of recognition washed over Kevin's face when he laid eyes on the Earthian leader. He matched Calandra's scowl with his own.

"I should have known the Earth Defense Bureau's fingerprints were all over this colony. Not satisfied with tracking and killing innocent aliens on Earth? Did the bureau decide to branch out and build its own galactic empire?"

Sam closed his eyes and pinched the bridge of his nose between his fingers.

"We are not your enemy." He let out an exasperated sigh. "Look, I made huge mistakes in the past. Mistakes I deeply regret. But beating me over the head with my flaws does nothing."

Before Kevin could unleash a snappy comeback, Xttra raised his hand and shook his head vigorously. Kevin tossed up his hands and beckoned at him to speak.

Xttra refocused his gaze on Sam.

"I hate to admit this, but we need your help."

"Help?" he repeated, crossing his arms. "What kind of help?"

"We journeyed to this planet to stop Delcor from extending his rule over all of Lathos."

A crease formed in Sam's brow.

"Delcor? Didn't he create the hybrid who nearly destroyed our colony on Mars?"

Xttra nodded. A collective murmur went through the small band of colonists who accompanied Sam.

"Indeed. Now he's traveling here to collect an ancient device that will give him unlimited knowledge and power if he gains possession of it."

Sam's mouth dropped open. Fear flooded his eyes. Xttra knew he understood better than any other Earthian, apart from Kevin, the danger Delcor posed if he acquired greater power.

"Is this Delcor an alien dictator?" Lily asked.

"He's like a Lathoan Stalin," Kevin said. "We're all in exile because of him. If he succeeds with his current plan, the entire planet of Lathos will fall before him."

Sam glanced skyward. His eyes slid back down to Xttra and Calandra. He drew a sharp breath, releasing it in a worried sigh.

"I'll take you to meet the other colony leaders," he said. "We need to get everyone on the same page concerning the threat facing us."

***

Traveling in Earthian ground vehicles offered a rougher ride than Xttra anticipated. The vehicles traversed worn trails crisscrossing the plateau. None had a smooth surface like a true road. Each bounce from driving over partially buried rocks or ruts sent a corresponding jolt through his body.

"We should have landed closer to your colony," Calandra said. She raised her voice to make herself heard over the tremors of the shaking vehicle.

Xttra knew her complaint was primarily out of concern for their daughter and their pet. Alexa sat between them on a long seat behind a pair of bucket seats near the front of the vehicle. She clung to Bella's enclosed nest resting on her lap. The little cala chattered, voicing her displeasure at continual bouncing, and being stuck inside the nest for so long.

"Sorry about the rough ride," Lily said. "We need to send our robots out to grade these roads again."

Both of her hands grasped a steering wheel. Lily had donned her shaded glasses again and fixed her eyes on the road ahead of their vehicle. She constantly corrected their path to avoid the worst of the broken way forward. A second Earthian occupied the other front seat. He had a bald head but wore a full beard and clear glasses.

"Zipping through grasses on a plateau makes this feel like home." His voice oozed nervous excitement. "Of course, the grass is literally greener on that side of the fence if you know what I mean. Not this alien red color here. Have you ever seen anything like it?"

Xttra gave him a sideways glance.

"No. I don't know what you mean. I don't know where you're from. Or your name."

The bald Earthian smacked his forehead.

"Sorry. I didn't even introduce myself before we crawled inside the rover. My name is Joel. Joel Haslam."

Xttra raised his eyebrows.

"That's definitely an Earthian name."

Joel answered with a shrug and a laugh.

"Earthian, huh? People have called me worse things. But you're right. I'm from Earth. A place called Little Horn, Kansas—better known as God's country."

"Which god owns that country?" Calandra asked. "Are you referring to Kevin's Earthian god?"

Joel let out a chuckle and slapped his knee.

"There's nothing except prairie grass for miles outside of Little Horn," he said, ignoring her question. "Some people find it boring. I find it relaxing. I could stare out at grass fields all day."

Calandra pressed her lips together and sighed. Xttra recognized the telltale sign of her growing annoyance. Similar feelings stirred inside him toward Joel. The Earthian seemed friendly enough, but also appeared quite oblivious to the magnitude of differences between peoples from different planets.

"You didn't answer her question, eh?" Lily said.

She cast a quick glance over her shoulder at Calandra and flashed an earnest smile, contrasting her sharpness with her fellow Earthian.

"He's talking about a god many people on Earth worship," Lily said, refocusing her eyes on the road. "How familiar are you with my home planet?"

"I know a few things," Calandra said. "Kevin talks about Earth occasionally. We don't discuss his home planet often—for my sake."

"Well, I want to hear all about Lathos after you meet with Cascadia's leaders. And I can tell you all about Canada—my home country back on Earth—if you're feeling up to it."

Calandra finally let a small smile emerge on her lips. Lily showed an open and welcoming nature. Xttra recalled Calandra once dreamed of meeting aliens like Lily on Earth when she first discovered the Earthian probe many years earlier.

"I'd love to hear about Canada."

Endless grasses soon yielded to a series of dwellings. Alexa craned her neck toward the window and her eyes lingered on each structure. Xttra and Calandra also turned and stared at the alien buildings. The Earthians laid out their colony in a square grid pattern, giving it a rudimentary resemblance to various Earthian cities Xttra once visited. Evenly spaced dwellings flanked both sides of broad dirt streets. A single narrow path led from the street to each dwelling's entry door. Stone walls formed boundaries between the streets and the dwellings.

Many dwellings resembled a giant stone cube topped by a second smaller stone cube. Multiple embedded windows and doors adorned each cube. A flat roof topped the larger cube, while a peaked roof topped the smaller one. Thin metal railings marked the perimeter, guarding against falls from atop the larger cube. Long stout columns stood only a few steps from the main door and supported a sloping roof that connected to the dwelling above the door. Two columns supported a similar sloped roof above the door in the second-floor cube.

Their vehicle drove past several dwellings and approached a few cylindrical towers near the colony's center. These structures matched ones Xttra saw on Mars in their design. The towers loomed over other colony buildings like a small band of stone giants.

"This is downtown Cascadia," Lily said. "Only took us a year to construct these towers. Robots and 3D printers did all the leg work."

"Robots?" Xttra repeated.

"AI. Artificial Intelligence," she replied. "Using them saved us considerable time and money. Robots don't need food or sleep. Once you program a task to complete, they are quite self-sufficient and work around the clock."

Artificial lifeforms.

Xttra's mouth twisted into a scowl. The Earthians' reliance on so-called robots put them only a few steps away from becoming like the Melders who lived among the Confederation of Northern Tribes. Melders sought to blend organic and artificial lifeforms into single symbiotic beings. They worshipped their technology itself and shunned Ahm—their own creator.

Lily slowed their vehicle to a crawl and stopped in front of the easternmost tower. Both rover doors cracked open, forming two separate halves. The top half extended outward and upward. The bottom half lowered to the ground, turning into an impromptu ramp.

Primitive, but functional.

"This is our stop," Joel said. "Welcome to Cascadia."

Alexa instantly hopped out of her seat. The enclosed nest slid off her lap and settled at her feet. She tugged at the dome, trying to crack open the nest. Bella urged her on with a pleading coo and pawed at the dome.

"No, sweetheart." Calandra pressed her hand down on the dome atop the nest to keep it in place. "We can't let Bella out yet."

Alexa's lower lip jutted out into a pout. She crossed her arms and stared upward—first at her mother and then over at Xttra.

"I want to play with Bella."

Calandra leaned over and caressed her cheek.

"You can play with her once we go indoors. We need to find out if this is a safe place for little Bella before we let her run around outside."

Alexa cast her eyes at the ground and nodded. Calandra hoisted the nest off the floor and rested it in the crook of one arm. She grasped Alexa's palm with her free hand and helped her out of the vehicle.

Other rovers carrying Bo'un and Kevin, along with Sam and other colonists from the greeting party, parked beside their vehicle in front of the same tower. A path led from the street to the tower's main door. Crushed rock covered the path. Crimson grass and shrubs bordered each side.

"This whole place feels like an odd blend of Earth and Lathos," Xttra said.

"Took me a while to get used to seeing red grass everywhere," Sam said. "But it's growing on me."

He wheeled around, gazed at Sam, and shook his head once he connected the dots. Did all Earthians possess Kevin's strange sense of humor? Calandra pressed her lips together to fight a smile from forming. She still harbored bitter feelings toward Sam and Xttra figured she did not want a spontaneous reaction to his silly remark to create a different impression.

Others in their group were not so quick to conceal their feelings.

"Ugh," Lily said. "That's a terrible dad joke."

The tower door slid open when they reached the end of the path. Sam led them inside to a spacious room. Scarlet vines encircled a single vertical column rising from the middle of the room. The column climbed to a skylight in the ceiling. Intricately carved rock walls surrounded the column on three sides. Water cascaded down the walls to a narrow pool at the foot of the column. Various paintings and lifelike images adorned walls throughout the room. The artwork portrayed unfamiliar places, people, and animals. Xttra assumed they all had a connection to Earth.

Sam directed Xttra, Calandra, Kevin, and Bo'un to a long white table and orange hardback chairs on the western end of the room. An Earthian woman with olive skin, deep brown hair, and equally dark eyes lifted her head as they approached the table. A laptop rested on the table before her.

She rose to her feet.

"I'm Erica Carson." She extended her hand. "I'm the governor of Cascadia. Welcome to our colony."

Bo'un stepped forward and clasped her wrist in a traditional Ra'ahmian greeting. Erica glanced down at his hand and offered a brief crooked smile.

"You don't shake hands on your planet, I take it?"

Bo'un instantly withdrew his hand and dropped it to his side. He shot a questioning look at Xttra and Calandra. Xttra turned and stared incredulously at Kevin and Sam. This Earthian wasted no time insulting one of their most basic customs.

Kevin rolled his eyes and sighed.

"People from Lathos clasp wrists when they greet one another," he said, facing her. "Try not to insult my friends 30 seconds after meeting them."

Erica licked her lips and looked down and away. She also dropped her hand to her side.

"I meant no offense." The Earthian woman's eyes darted from Bo'un to Calandra and then Xttra. "I'm so used to American customs and never—"

"It's fine." Calandra said, interrupting her. "Every planet has different customs. We're not here to fight you. We need your help."

"Help?"

Erica leaned forward and rested her hands against the edge of the table. Her brows knit together.

"What kind of help?"

Calandra set the enclosed nest down on the floor to rest her arm shouldering all that extra weight. Alexa let go of her other hand and scurried to the nest. She dropped to her knees and unsealed the dome. Xttra reached out a hand to stop her. His reaction time proved too slow to keep the dome sealed. Bella's little head and the top half of her bushy tail popped up from the nest. Her yellow eyes darted around until they fell on Alexa.

"Bella!"

She held out her arms, inviting the little cala to race toward her. Bella accepted the invitation, letting out a chattering coo along the way.

Erica and Sam both snapped their heads toward the diminutive animal.

"Is it safe to let that animal out in here?" Sam asked.

Calandra glowered at him.

"Bella's safer than you."

Xttra glanced over at Bo'un.

"Can you make sure they stay in this room?"

He nodded.

"I'll watch them like a mokai guarding its eggs."

Bo'un guided Alexa and Bella over to the rock wall fountain to play near the pool at its base. Xttra and Calandra turned and faced the Earthian leader again.

"What sort of help do you need?" Erica asked, repeating her earlier question.

"We came to this planet for a specific purpose," Calandra said. "We need to find the Staff of Onrai before it falls into the wrong hands."

"The Staff of Onrai?" Sam repeated. "What is that?"

Calandra cast a silent warning glance at him but said nothing. Her eyes slid back over to Erica.

"The staff is an ancient tool, once misused to establish a world-wide empire on my home planet," she continued, ignoring Sam. "We must stop the tyrannical ruler of Ra'ahm—our home nation on Lathos—from finding it."

"I have no idea where this staff is," Erica replied. "This is the first time I've ever heard of it. What makes you think it's here on Colonia?"

"Colonia?" Xttra shot her a quizzical look. "Isn't your Earthian colony named Cascadia?"

Erica shifted her eyes over to him and smiled.

"Our colony is named Cascadia. I picked the name myself because this plateau reminds me of my Oregon hometown. But we named the planet Colonia."

Were they on the wrong planet?

Calandra's worried sigh matched his concern. She turned to face a window a few steps beyond the end of the table. Xttra's eyes trailed in the same direction.

Two alien suns crossed the western sky outside the window. Their rays bathed a landscape decorated with red plants and trees that confirmed this planet was indeed the Land of the Three Suns. The main sun ducked partially behind swirls of white clouds. A second smaller sun followed a path set back behind the larger sun. Xttra did not inquire about the third sun. Calandra once told him it was a tiny red class star and not visible from the planet's surface without a telescope. Still, it shared the same blue sky and connected with the other suns in an eternal symbiotic relationship.

"On Lathos, this planet is called the Land of the Three Suns,"
Kevin said. "What do you know about this place? Are any ancient
alien temples or sanctuaries around here—places built to house a
religious relic?"

"We selected this spot to build our colony based on aerial surveys," Erica said. "One of our drones found some stunning ancient
ruins only a few hundred miles northwest of Cascadia. We also
stumbled upon a small settlement in the same region where an alien
tribe lives."

Xttra's ears perked up. An alien settlement?

"Did you make contact with these aliens?" he asked, facing her
again. "Are they native to this planet? Perhaps they possess knowledge concerning the staff's location."

"We couldn't communicate with them well," Sam said.

He retrieved a smartphone from his pocket and tapped on the screen.

"I suspected they're from your home planet, based on their
language," Sam continued. "But we didn't have access to the same
translators you wore when you visited Earth to enable an extended
conversation."

"I can listen to it and translate for you," Xttra said.

"Eliah, one of our consultants from the Confederation of
Northern Tribes, already translated the message I recorded when I
visited the aliens." He handed his smartphone to Xttra. "The alien
man said little. He identified himself and others living in their settlement as the People of Valadius—whatever that means."

Xttra snapped his head toward Calandra and then Kevin. Their
eyes both grew as wide as plates. All three understood exactly what
that phrase meant. His heart pounded faster when Xttra gazed at
the smartphone screen and confirmed the translated message's con-
tents for himself.

The Earthians stumbled upon a colony started by Valadius, the
former prime oracle who fled from Delcor.

O nce the unmarked transport vessel entered visual range, Tressek realized it did not originate from the local star system. Sensors showed the vessel approaching a giant planet bordering the system's outer edge from the same direction the fleet's advance ships traveled to arrive here. Not only did that detail arouse his suspicions, but the approaching vessel also resembled giant blockade busters which pilots from Daraconiah used to access restricted hyperlight routes.

Smugglers or dissidents.

This unmarked vessel must belong to one or the other, Tressek silently reasoned. No transport ship engaged in legitimate activities would intentionally scrub out its universal identification markers. The vessel's purpose here posed a mystery to him.

A mystery he needed to solve.

"Open a communication channel." Tressek glanced over at his assistant pilot. "I'm certain that's a Lathoan ship and I want to learn why it's out here."

Dray pressed a square green button on her console, activating an empty holoscreen.

"We are Stellar Guard officers tasked with security for this sector," she said. "Identify yourselves."

No image materialized on the holoscreen.

"Please identify yourselves," Dray repeated, after waiting a few seconds for the vessel's pilot to appear.

Her second hail met with an immediate response. A stout man with unkempt red hair and a scarred chin appeared on the holoscreen. He sat behind an expansive helm console. Crew members manned various stations behind his chair.

"Stellar Guard?" The red-haired pilot flashed a broad smile, revealing a chipped lower tooth. "You do understand neither you nor Delcor have any authority in this place, right? Why don't you go ahead and return to Ra'ahm so we can conduct our business in peace?"

Tressek scowled at the holoscreen image.

Smugglers transporting illicit cargo had no voice in deciding where and when the Stellar Guard chose to travel. The chief sovereign had prohibited peddling dangerous exotic wares in Ra'ahm street markets. Tressek felt duty bound as a master pilot to intercept the vessel, detain the crew, and confiscate unauthorized goods.

"The Stellar Guard does not tolerate selling and transporting prohibited goods to or from Ra'ahm," Tressek said. "Prepare to submit your vessel for a thorough inspection."

"I am Kujoth Ehlcan of Daraconiah." The red-haired pilot's smile vanished, and his tone grew firm. "You have no right to board my vessel. Daraconiah is a free nation. We don't answer to Ra'ahm, the Confederation, or any other rival Lathoan nation. We are not in your territory or subject to your authority. Move along."

Tressek muted the sound on his console and cast a glance over at his assistant pilot.

"It isn't a smart idea to start a skirmish with smugglers. Suggestions?"

Dray tilted her head and her eyes drifted to the opposite end of the bridge. She snapped her fingers a few seconds later and shifted her gaze back to Tressek.

"What if we program a tracking beacon to follow their vessel? It can track them through the system while we stay back a safe distance."

Tressek smiled and nodded.

"I like that plan." His eyes drifted back to the holoscreen. "It should work to our advantage. Following them is bound to help us identify habitable planets in this system and determine which one best matches the description of the Land of the Three Suns from the ancient texts."

An alarm reverberated through the bridge. Tressek shot a quick glance at the navigation station.

"Did they fire on us?"

Jo'ber turned toward the helm and shook his head.

"No. We received an alert from a fellow scout ship. Two smaller vessels exited from the transport vessel's cargo bay. I don't think we've stumbled upon a simple smuggling operation."

Tressek dropped one hand to his knee and brought the other up to his chin.

"Don't tell me—"

"Their sensors are detecting Cassian darts speeding toward the giant planet."

His throat tightened. Jo'ber was correct. This had become a much more serious encounter than intercepting random smugglers. This blockade buster transported either Confederation agents or exiled dissidents to this system. Their presence confirmed one thing to Tressek. They found the home star system for the Land of the Three Suns. He felt it deep in his bones.

The unmarked vessel harbored enemies of Ra'ahm and must not slip past their ships and venture further into the system.

Tressek restored sound to the holoscreen.

"Surrender or we'll be forced to disable your ship."

Kujoth snapped his head away from a second holoscreen at his helm and faced Tressek again.

"I'll give you the same warning I gave one of your other master pilots," he said. "You're not touching my ship without a fight."

Tressek muted the communicator's sound again.

"Target their secondary thrusters and weapons systems." He glanced over at Dray again. "Let's disable their ship, so we can bring the crew in for questioning."

"We're too late," Dray said. "The other scout ships opened fire!"

Tressek's eyes darted back to the helm. Multiple ion torpedoes zipped toward the vessel from scout ships on his right and left. One torpedo after another struck the vessel's energy shell until it disintegrated.

"What are they doing?" Tressek shouted. "We can't destroy their ship! We need to capture them and bring them in for interrogation."

Kujoth remained true to his word.

His vessel sprayed bolts from embedded plasma cannons back at the scout ships. He drew attention away from the departing darts while trying to take down all four Stellar Guard ships in a direct attack. Plasma bolts bombarded the ground force carrier.

A spinning ball with flashing spikes launched from the belly of the vessel a few seconds later. Tressek's eyes widened. The ground force carrier did not have a chance.

It lay in the direct path of a Vulian hull smasher.

"Brace for a shockwave!" he shouted.

The warning barely left his tongue before the hull smasher slammed into the ground force carrier's front end. An explosion followed. The hull instantly cracked like an egg and the carrier split into two sections. A cloud of metal chunks and shards sprayed outward like a fountain. Multiple Stellar Guard officers spiraled out into space, their unprotected bodies turning to frozen corpses within a few seconds.

A tremor shook the bridge as a shockwave from the ground force carrier rippled through Tressek's scout ship. It flung him from his chair and sent other crew members crashing to the floor. Tressek noted no severe injuries to his crew. Their energy shell absorbed the bulk of this explosive force but drained down to a fraction of its normal strength.

Tressek pressed a hand against his chest and drew a sharp breath. He fought an urge to vomit after seeing so many lives extinguished with such suddenness. Good men and women serving their sovereign. They deserved a better fate than this. He would not let their sacrifice become meaningless.

"Unload our plasma cannons on those traitors," Tressek said, after raising a second holoscreen. "Death is the only thing they deserve now!"

The other undamaged scout ship executed his orders and unleashed a fresh pair of ion torpedoes. Both slammed into the side of Kujoth's ship facing away from the nearby giant planet. One cut across a primary thruster. The other blasted a hole just below the bridge. Metal fragments and smoke sprayed out into space at both impact points.

"Direct hit." The other master pilot's image appeared on the second holoscreen. "I don't think those smugglers can escape from the giant planet's orbit now."

Tressek glanced up and glowered at his primary holoscreen. The smuggler captain Kujoth had cut off the open channel, leaving the screen blank.

"Keep your eyes open for escape vessels," he said. "I'm pursuing the darts."

The other master pilot nodded and vanished from the holoscreen. Tressek closed both screens and steered away from the wreckage. A second Vulian hull smasher ripped through the center of another scout ship unleashing a new wave of ion torpedoes. He barely escaped a lethal impact the resulting shockwave would have delivered.

Only two Stellar Guard ships remained intact.

Tressek flew his ship around to the giant planet's far side. He entered a high orbit near the equator. His sensors showed no evidence of the darts escaping further into the star system. Still, the planet's magnetic field prevented a clear reading on their current location, making their fate uncertain.

"Those Cassian darts must be lurking around here somewhere." Worry flooded Dray's blue eyes as she studied the holoscreen. She brushed back a blonde Abidosian braid from her shoulder. "I don't think our ships destroyed either one."

"I have the same feeling," Tressek said.

He stayed in a loose orbit around the giant planet. An intense gravity well would wrap invisible tentacles around their scout ship if he veered too close to the upper atmosphere. Once their ship sank downward and reached a point of no return, increasing atmospheric pressure would rip the vessel apart until only indistinguishable particles remained.

A proximity alarm blared through the bridge. Tressek peered at his holoscreen. Their sensors tracked two ships, closing toward the equator.

Both were Cassian darts.

"We found them," Dray said.

Tressek leaned forward and traced their individual trajectories with his eyes. Each dart originated from a different polar region.

One below.

One above.

They planned to simultaneously attack the scout ship from opposite directions.

"How much of our energy shell is left?" Tressek asked.

He glanced over his left shoulder at Kelum, his weapons officer. Kelum turned away from his console. He licked his lips and shook his head.

"19 percent. We need an hour to replenish the shell to full strength again."

Tressek returned his gaze to his holoscreen. Destroying two Cassian darts simultaneously was no simple task. With a full-strength energy shell protecting the outer hull, Tressek had no problem taking a calculated risk and battling both ships. Dealing with a drastically depleted shell required a cautious approach. He had no right to place himself or his crew in jeopardy.

Tressek slammed his fist on the console before him.

"We're retreating," he said. "Jo'ber, enter a hyperlight route to the designated rendezvous point near the space bridge. We'll wait for the main fleet to arrive and return with reinforcements."

Tressek engaged his primary thrusters and broke orbit before either dart reached optimal weapons range. He pushed the main engine to top subluminal speed and the giant planet quickly receded behind the ship.

"Send an encrypted message to the other scout ship," Tressek said. "Alert them concerning the darts and tell them to follow us back to the space bridge once the threat here is eliminated."

"We can't leave this system." Dray's voice climbed higher as she protested his action. "The other scout ship shouldn't face those darts alone. You'll put that crew in danger for no reason."

"Your protest is noted, Dray." Tressek's tone grew icy. "One day you'll understand being smart and staying alive is better than being a hero and dying for nothing."

Dray glowered at him and snapped her head back to her console. Tressek understood the stakes better than she did and made his decision accordingly. Encountering resistance in that system offered compelling evidence they found the Land of the Three Suns.

No task was more important, for the moment, than relaying their findings to the chief sovereign himself.

17

alandra studied the Earthian eyewear, turning it over in her hand. Shaded lenses blocked out glare from excess sunlight, mimicking other pairs of glasses many colonists wore outside of their dwellings. She shaded her eyes with her arm and glanced up at Lily.

"Thank you." Calandra smiled at her. "This is a wonderful gift."

"Try them on." Lily gestured at the glasses resting in her hand. "These sunglasses will make watching this soccer game so much easier on your eyes."

Calandra unfolded the temples, slid the glasses over her nose, and hooked them behind her ears. The eyewear dimmed the twin suns' brightness enough that her eyes finally relaxed. Her eyelids had tightened into a perma-squint since she first walked outside of the tower where they met Erica.

Lily unfolded a fabric chair and plunked down beside her. Calandra chose to sit on the cool red grass with Alexa on her other side. Other spectators gathered a few steps behind a long horizontal white line to watch Earthian and Confederation colonists run all over a wide grass field. Calandra barely missed a chance to watch

Earthians play one of their sports when she visited their planet. She had never seen one before today.

The soccer game offered a blend of simple play and frenetic action. Colonists divided into two teams, each numbering eleven people. Both teams pursued the same purpose—kicking a medium-sized ball with alternating white and black polygons down the field into a net. Colonists set one large net on each end of the field to act as targets. Both nets resembled a three-sided metal rectangle with the ground forming the fourth side. Netting connecting to posts and a crossbar hung down from the backside. Each team guarded one net and attacked the other net on the opposite end.

Calandra did not find soccer as intense or exciting as a slotball match on Lathos. The players only used their legs or feet to move the ball. She did not understand why no one grabbed the ball and ran with it. Still, the Earthian sport grew on her as the match progressed. Calandra gazed over at Alexa. Her daughter seemed oblivious to all the activity on the field. She entertained herself by ripping out tiny handfuls of blades from surrounding grass and peering intently at the roots and dirt.

"If someone told me five years ago that one day I'd watch a pickup soccer match on an exoplanet orbiting Alpha Centauri B, I would've laughed long and hard in their face," Lily said. She now sported sunglasses matching the pair she gifted to Calandra. "Days like this are still so surreal to me. I never realized how much intelligent life existed beyond Earth until I joined the Earth Defense Bureau."

"I've known of other alien races my whole life," Calandra said. "Lathos began making first contact with other planets hundreds of generations before I was born. I always dreamed of discovering a new alien race."

She paused and drew a deep breath to calm herself as a swirl of emotions churned inside her.

"Then I discovered Earth and met your people."

Lily studied her face carefully and reached out to touch Calandra's metal wrist.

"What happened when you came to Earth?" Her voice grew quiet, as though she feared stirring up painful memories. "What did we do to you?"

Calandra looked down and away. No uncomplicated answer to Lily's question existed. Seven years removed from first contact did not supply enough time and distance to fully mitigate the pain and trauma tied to the events of those few days. She wanted to heal her soul more than anything.

The healing touch eluded her grasp.

Calandra glanced up at the Earthian colonist again.

"Didn't Sam Bono tell you the whole story?"

"No." Lily shook her head. "I tried to pry details out of him. He told me your names and how he made first contact with you out in Utah. But he refused to share anything beyond the bare bones."

"I'm not surprised he concealed the depth of his violence and cruelty."

"What did he do to you?"

Calandra blinked back tears forming under her sunglasses. She removed them momentarily to wipe her cheeks with her hand.

"After we landed in the place you call Utah to make peaceful contact, your Earthian leaders attacked, hunting us down one by one. They murdered three of our crew members and captured me after shooting down my aerorover."

"That's awful."

"I broke my left wrist and some ribs while trying to elude capture. Sam and an Earthian woman named Paige interrogated me. They tortured me when I didn't supply answers they liked."

Her voice began to break as she recounted the ordeal. Calandra paused and pressed her hand against her forehead.

"Their doctors inserted pieces of metal in my wrist to reconnect my broken bones. The metal caused a bone infection during my journey home. My clan doctor had to amputate my left hand and wrist to save my life."

Lily pressed a hand to her mouth. Tears trickled out from under her sunglasses and glistened on her cheeks.

"I am so sorry," she said. "You never deserved any of that, Calandra. No person should ever suffer what you endured. I'm mortified at how my people treated you. I would despise Earthians in your position."

Calandra blinked back her tears a second time.

"When I saw him here, so many frightening memories rushed back to me," she said. "It's like those events happened yesterday. All that pain…I can't…What he did to me…I can't forgive him."

"I don't blame you," Lily said.

A boisterous cheer arose among several players. Calandra stared out at the field. One Earthian jumped around and pumped his fist. Others wearing matching green uniforms sprinted from multiple directions and embraced him. The black and white ball lay in the back of the net on the south end of the field.

Her eyes trailed from the celebration back to Lily.

"You're not like him," she said. "You're how I hoped the Earthian leaders would be before we made first contact with your planet."

A warm smile spread across Lily's lips. She leaned forward and clasped Calandra's metal hand. Locks of her wavy brown hair fell forward and brushed Lily's cheeks.

"You and your family will be welcome in this colony as long as I have any say about it," she said. "The galaxy is too large and dangerous for us not to be friends."

***

Xttra studied detailed aerial images on Sam's laptop, his deep blue eyes tracing every contour and feature of the ancient ruins. Broken, crumbling walls surrounded an outer courtyard. Stone towers climbed skyward in every corner where walls intersected. A central square building with a staggered curving roof occupied the courtyard's middle section. Portions of the roof and walls had crumbled away on the central structure.

The structure's layout resembled a fortress more than an ancient sanctuary or temple of Ahm. It offered an ominous starting point for their search to uncover the Staff of Onrai's location.

"Are these the only ruins you found here?"

Xttra pressed against the hardened back of his chair and stared at Sam. The Earthian met his gaze from the other side of the table. He sat in the same chair which Erica, the leader of Cascadia, occupied when they spoke with her inside the spacious chamber a day earlier. Sam shrugged and rose to his feet.

"Searching out abandoned ruins wasn't high on our to-do list before you arrived here," he said. "I'm sure other ancient cities and structures exist. Around rivers or lakes. This continent is as large as Russia."

Xttra tilted his head and cracked a bemused frown.

"Russia? I'm unfamiliar with that place."

A condescending laugh greeted his statement. Xttra snapped his head toward the opposite wall. Eliah, a Confederation colonist who helped conduct the aerial surveys, flashed a broad grin.

"You're expending so much energy worrying about a relic that never existed." Contempt permeated his words. "The staff of Onrai is a useless myth—like Ahm himself."

Xttra's face grew hot, and his cheeks flushed red. His eyes hardened as they settled on Eliah.

"Watch your words, heretic."

Eliah sighed and rolled his eyes. He scratched the part of his shabby medium brown beard covering his chin.

"Neabu is the one true god," he said. "He leads the Eternal Nine who formed our galaxy and created all life. All who number themselves with Ursat, my ancestral tribe, have treasured this truth since our world began."

His statements crossed an unthinkable line. Xttra slammed down a fist, shaking the laptop. This pile of Ebutoka droppings had no right to denigrate his most treasured beliefs to his face.

"Every word you said is a lie! Ahm created the galaxy and seeded life on every habitable planet. Deny it and he will not smile upon you or your clan."

Sam waved his arms, nearly stumbling as he dashed around the table and placed himself between them before their argument had a chance to turn physical.

"We're not here to argue the existence of one god or multiple gods," he said. "We're seeking out possible ancient technology before a known tyrant finds it first, right? You have the rest of your lives to debate creation myths. Right now, we all need to settle down and focus on the task at hand."

Xttra crossed his arms and glared at Eliah. The Confederation colonist mirrored his action. Neither said a word nor blinked an eyelid.

"We can send out drones to do other aerial surveys," Sam said, slicing through the thickening silence. "It will broaden the search area and rule out many places where this relic could be hidden."

Xttra finally slid his eyes away from Eliah. His gaze settled on the Earthian.

"How many Earthian drones do you have available?"

"A dozen or so." Sam said. "Enough to survey the continent from coast to coast."

"How much territory does a single drone cover?"

Sam rubbed his chin and gazed up at the ceiling.

"I don't know exact numbers, but our drones are all solar powered 2039 models. Top of the line. Each one can fly indefinitely on a sunny day and cover hundreds of square miles."

Xttra's eyes trailed back down to the aerial images on the laptop screen. Deploying several Earthian drones would trim considerable time from their search. He would never admit to being impressed with any Earthian technology in front of Sam. Still, based on image quality from earlier surveys, they could easily pinpoint logical hiding places for the Staff of Onrai with new images.

A satisfied smile crossed his lips and he leaned back in his chair. Ahm had a deeper purpose behind reuniting him, Calandra, Bo'un, and Kevin with the Earthians.

"Your assistance in our search should give us a crucial advantage over Delcor," Xttra said. "Hopefully, these aerial surveys will help us uncover the staff before the Stellar Guard regroups and returns to the system."

"What do you plan to do assuming this relic exists, and we find it?"

Eliah emphasized "assuming" and scowled as he unloaded an accusing glare at him. Xttra leaned forward again and planted his arms on the table. His unblinking stare reemerged.

"I plan to destroy it."

An incredulous glint surfaced in Eliah's eyes. He glanced over at Sam as though silently pleading for help to make Xttra see reason before meeting his gaze again.

"You can't destroy an ancient artifact without a second thought." An anxious lilt crept into his voice. "Think of the historical value. Such a relic should be preserved and studied."

Xttra cracked a sardonic grin.

"Why do you care? The staff is a 'useless myth,' right? Your words, not mine."

Eliah furrowed his brow and gnawed on his lower lip. Xttra gained some silent pleasure from trapping the Confederation colonist in his own denigrating words. He did not need to be an oracle to deduce Eliah's thoughts. If he learned where the staff lay hidden, Eliah would no doubt steal the relic and apply whatever knowledge he gained toward his own dark purposes.

Lathoan history already convinced Xttra to trust no one to act as a caretaker. They or their successors would succumb to the temptation the Staff of Onrai offered and open a door for a second Galjokk to rise. It fell on Xttra's shoulders to permanently dismantle the relic once found. No one must turn the staff into a world conquering weapon a second time.

"I don't understand." Sam's eyes shifted over to Xttra. "What makes this staff so dangerous? Calandra described it as an ancient tool earlier. Can't a tool be put to beneficial use?"

Xttra shook his head. Sam owned no working knowledge of Lathoan history. The Earthian's questions were ignorant at best, dangerous at worst.

"A clear stone crowns the Staff of Onrai and grants complete knowledge of the past, present, and future on any subject. It imparts such knowledge to whoever holds the staff and stares directly into the stone."

Sam's mouth fell open and his eyes widened.

"Complete knowledge?" he repeated. "In other words, they can see and predict the future?"

Xttra leaned back in the chair and folded his arms.

"Exactly," he said. "Give a tyrant complete knowledge of the future and they will predict every single move their enemies make. They will see the outcome of a thousand different actions. With this power, they can effectively rule an entire planet within only a few years."

"How is such a thing possible?" Sam asked. "It doesn't align with what we know of modern science."

"I'm no scientist," Xttra said. "I can't explain why or how the staff works the way our legends say it works. But if it is real, we can't risk it ending up in the wrong hands."

Sam stared straight ahead. His eyes focused on a distant point beyond Xttra. A worried frown crept across his lips. No doubt the

Earthian leader began to realize the danger the staff posed if Delcor gained possession of the ancient relic.

"We can't let that staff see the light of day," he said. "Your people can travel to Colonia and Earth. What's to stop this Delcor from trying to conquer my home planet?"

Xttra did not respond, but he did not need to say anything. Even as the question left Sam's mouth, they all knew the answer. Nothing would stop Delcor from expanding his empire beyond Lathos if he found the Staff of Onrai first.

18

Witnessing the simultaneous setting of two suns offered a breathtaking beauty Calandra never imagined. The primary sun painted surrounding clouds with an ethereal orange glow. It illuminated mountainous ocean waves out beyond the sea cliffs. Flying animals soared above the waves. Such a serene and gorgeous scene. Made to capture in a painting.

Calandra marveled at the intricate web of life. Unique creatures she never imagined in her most vivid fantasies called this alien planet home. Gifted ancient poets devoted countless lines to detailing the beauties of the Land of the Three Suns. Their greatest writings did not fully capture what Calandra witnessed with her own eyes.

"I'm happy this place is real."

Calandra turned at the sound of his voice and beamed at Xttra. Her feelings mirrored his words. Alexa stood at their feet, gazing upward. Her eyes also grew transfixed by the swirling clouds painted by the twin suns.

"There's no one else I'd rather share it with than you and Alexa."

Xttra circled his arms around her back, and she drew closer. Calandra gazed at him through her eyelashes and her hand pressed against his neck. Her lips parted and she pressed them against his lips as they also parted. They lingered in a warm, passionate kiss.

"I love you so much," she said, following the kiss.

"My love for you runs deep." Xttra wore a smile as broad as hers. "Through worlds without end."

Calandra slouched a bit and nestled her head against Xttra's shoulder. He trailed his fingers through her auburn locks and down her neck. A pair of little arms suddenly wrapped around her legs. Calandra's eyes trailed down to Alexa who decided to turn their moment of affection into a three-way hug. She hungered to pause this moment and stand near sea cliffs indefinitely, enjoying limitless happiness from experiencing an alien sunset with her husband and daughter.

"We better hit the road soon," a voice behind her said. "We don't want to bleed the rover's power reserves dry."

Calandra and Xttra both reacted with a startled jump. She slipped out of his arms, and they turned to face Joel. The Earthian had climbed out of the solar rover driver's seat and rested his arm on the vehicle's roof while standing behind an open door. She had forgotten about him completely while watching the suns retreat from the sky. Xttra flashed an annoyed frown at Joel for spoiling their moment alone.

He turned back to his daughter and the setting suns, stooped down, and held out his arms. Alexa dashed over to her father.

"Time to return to the Earthian village, my little flower." He scooped her up in his arms. "It's growing late. Night will arrive soon."

Xttra kissed Alexa's forehead and held her close as he returned to the rover. Calandra lingered for a moment longer, taking one final look at the evening sky framing twin alien suns. If only she had a telescope with her to gaze upon the third diminutive red sun not visible to the naked eye. She hurried to catch her husband and child and reached the vehicle right as Xttra set Alexa down. The little girl climbed on the backseat, wedging herself in a spot between her parents.

Joel fired up the rover engine once both the lower and upper doors closed behind Calandra. The Earthian vehicle journeyed back over a rugged makeshift road the colonists built from their village out to the sea cliffs. Each jolt bounced Calandra from head to toe. She agreed with Lily's earlier observation. The Earthians needed to make their roads smoother and easier to traverse. This short trip across the plateau made her better appreciate the ease of speeding through the sky in an aerorover.

"Your timing for visiting Colonia is perfect." Joel said. "If you came here even a week later, you would have missed our Settlement Day celebrations."

Calandra and Xttra exchanged confused glances. Did the Earthian not grasp the true reason they were here?

"We did not travel to this planet on a whim," Calandra said. "A deeper purpose guides us on our journey."

Joel grinned.

"You know what they say about all work and no play?"

Xttra answered him with a weary sigh. Calandra realized Joel wanted them to ask what his phrase meant. Neither ceded to the temptation.

"We can't neglect our true purpose here," Xttra said. "The threat we face—one which our people also face—is real and imminent."

"I'm sure things will turn out fine," Joel replied. "Relax and savor the moment."

"I refuse to let my guard down." Xttra's tone turned cold. "The last time I did, some of your fellow Earthians slaughtered my crew."

An uncomfortable silence settled like a dense fog inside the solar rover. Joel cast a brief frustrated glance at the backseat before refocusing his gaze on the road. Calandra figured he had good intentions, but Joel did not seem to sense the urgency involved in their journey.

If they took their focus off finding the staff, Delcor would gain another advantage over them. He already had too many advantages. Relaxing with Earthians equaled time yielded to the chief sovereign and his minions. Finding scout ships in this star system proved the Stellar Guard was already on the same track. Calandra refused to fool herself. Destroying those vessels earlier would do nothing beyond slowing them down temporarily. Delcor was as stubborn in his resolve as she and Xttra.

They could not afford to dismiss the frightening reality of his unrelenting will.

The solar rover stopped in front of a wide grassy field. They were within walking distance from the same spot where Earthians played soccer earlier in the day. Now, at twilight, two dozen colonists gathered in chairs forming a half circle under a stone pavilion with a cone-shaped roof. The chairs surrounded a long rectangular platform rising two steps above the surrounding ground.

Two colonists sat on stools occupying the middle section of the wooden platform. One colonist, a Confederation woman, pressed her lips to a syri'nai. Her fingers danced rapidly over nine hollowed out senosa sticks of varying lengths while she slid the ancient instrument across her lips. The other colonist, an Earthian man, strummed a strange musical instrument.

Calandra gazed at the Earthian instrument with fascination. Tight strings stretched across a wooden object with a long narrow neck and a circular hole in a broader body. It produced pleasant music. Kevin called the instrument an acoustic guitar. He once shared with Calandra how he and his younger brother owned similar guitars when they were children.

Several other colonists lined up in front of a cube-shaped stone column topped with a brick dome, tapping their feet to the music.

Smoke billowed out from a pipe poking out from atop the dome. An opening forming a half-circle on the front of the dome revealed flames gorging on a pile of wood inside the structure. One colonist pulled out a flat square board with a wooden handle from inside the dome.

"Hope you all like homemade pizza." Joel pierced the silence permeating the rover. "Maybe you all can let your guard down long enough to enjoy a slice or two."

He flung open his door and sprang out of the vehicle before Calandra or Xttra had a chance to respond. A delicious aroma wafted through the open door. Xttra glowered at the departing Earthian but bit his tongue to trap angry thoughts lingering in his head. Calandra opened the back doors and clasped Alexa's hand. She led her down the short ramp out of the rover.

"Isn't that the Earthian food we made for Kevin one time?" Xttra asked, glancing back at Calandra.

"We tried."

She smirked as images of their version of an Earthian pizza flooded back into her mind. Calandra did not have access to any Earthian ingredients, so she and Xttra substituted with Lathoan vegetables, grains, and meats they hoped were similar.

Their pizza never approached what Kevin described in taste or appearance. And he proved quite vocal in sharing that fact.

His sour grimace and clenched jaw offered the first visible clue their aspirational pizza experiment failed. Kevin chewed slowly and then swallowed hard after finishing off his slice, chasing the last bite down with a strong beverage.

"What do you think?" Calandra asked him at the time, a hopeful lilt threading through her voice.

"It's unique," he said. "Not what I expected."

Her face fell as she grasped what Kevin left unsaid.

"You don't like it?"

"I appreciate the effort and…your thoughtfulness." He hesitated as he considered his words. "But it doesn't taste…the same as pizza back home."

Xttra grabbed a slice and took a big bite. He smiled after swallowing.

"We used fresh Ebutoka meat and cheese, pressed solano sauce and whole poechea grain flatbread. This is a work of art." He nodded with eyebrows raised at Calandra. "I think it's delicious."

Aroma from fresh Earthian pizza brought Calandra's mind back to the present. Several round pizzas adorned a long table, each one cut into triangular slices. Predictably, Kevin stood at the front of the line when Calandra, Xttra, and Alexa approached the table. His eyes lit up when he spotted the little clan.

"You've got to try this." He lifted a slice off his plate. "Authentic pizza. Marinara sauce. Mozzarella. Pepperoni. Exact same ingredients they use back on Earth."

Kevin folded the slice in his hand and chomped down with a wide grin. Calandra studied the pizzas laid out across the table. How was it possible they were as fresh as ones prepared on Earth? Preserving food while traveling through deep space was impossible without freezing or dehydrating everything into a disgusting inferior copy of its fresh equivalent.

His claim piqued her curiosity.

"I'd love to try some of your pizza."

Kevin passed the plate over to her. Calandra let go of Alexa's hand. She picked up a slice, sniffed it, folded it like she had seen him do earlier, and took a tentative bite. A tangy red sauce buried under meat and cheese delivered a pleasant flavor to her tongue. But the crispy meat atop the pizza slice tasted gross and the slice felt like someone doused the whole thing in an unidentified oil.

The same oil dripped off the bitten end.

"I like my version better," she said.

Kevin scrunched up his face and laughed.

"Your version isn't real pizza."

Calandra dropped her partially eaten slice on the plate and handed it back to him. She flashed a tight-lipped smile.

"Enjoy the rest of your version."

Sam approached them, holding a plate with a pair of pizza slices on it. Thin circular slices of meat did not top these slices like the ones on Kevin's plate.

"You could argue our version isn't authentic pizza either. Not like how it was first made," Sam said. He turned to Calandra. "We have cheese and veggie options if you don't like pepperoni. Help yourself."

Calandra met Sam with a cold stare.

"Why do you insist on pretending you're my friend?" Anger permeated her question. "You so desperately want me to forget what you did to me."

She stabbed a finger at him.

"I will never forget."

Sam's jovial smile dropped off his lips and he stiffened like a stone column. His eyes drifted from Calandra down to his plate. Kevin and Xttra exchanged uncomfortable glances with one another.

"Why don't I help you find some food for Alexa?" Kevin shifted his plate to his right hand and held the left one out to the little girl. "I'm sure she's hungry."

Xttra answered him with a silent nod. He and Alexa followed Kevin to the far end of the table. Calandra stood unmoving; her eyes fixed squarely on Sam. The Earthian drew in a deep breath and lifted his head.

"I know you may never forgive me." He met her stare with an apologetic frown. "To be honest, I can't forgive myself. What I let my people do to you...I can't...it rips apart my soul."

Calandra noted contrition woven through his voice and written on his face. He sounded genuine. Still, how could she believe his words or trust his intentions after what he did to her? This man stood by and did nothing while his fellow Earthians harmed her in a multitude of irreparable ways.

Earthian soldiers shot her and Lance down in a ravine. She broke several bones when they captured her. Then, Sam and other Earthians held her captive on their secret base while they tortured her and poisoned her with their so-called medicine.

She glanced down at her metal hand and wrist. A part of her. Still a lesser copy of the original limb. It offered a sobering reminder he could have prevented all the pain created through these actions.

"Forgiveness isn't the only issue here," she said. "How can I ever trust you, Sam? How can I ever look at you and not suspect you might order soldiers to hunt me down and imprison me again?"

"I would never do any of those things to you a second time. I didn't know then what I know now. I don't know what else to say."

"I already know the answers. We came to your people in peace. You greeted us with violence and death."

Conversations around the pizza table abated as an expanding ring of silence grew. Many pairs of eyes shifted their gaze toward Calandra and Sam.

Let them stare, she thought. *He deserves to feel uncomfortable.*

"Go back to enjoying the festival." Sam pierced the silence without meeting the eyes of his fellow colonists. He carefully set his plate back on the table. "This is between me and Calandra."

"Why don't you share the full story with them, Sam?" she insisted. "They deserve to know."

Her eyes drifted down to a young boy half as tall as her walking toward them. He wrapped his arms around Sam and the Earthian rubbed his hand through the boy's brown curly hair.

"Mom wanted me to go find you Grandpa," the child said. "She told me to rescue you from making a scene."

Calandra studied the face of Sam's grandson. Sorrow for him stung her. He looked only four or five years older than Alexa. Too young and naive to be aware his grandfather was secretly an inhumane monster.

"You're a good boy, Jared." Sam painted a smile on his face for the child. "Thank you for 'rescuing' me."

His eyes met Calandra a second time.

"I guess I'll work harder to earn your trust," he said. "I hope one day to convince you I'm not the evil son of a bitch you think I am."

Sam grabbed his plate again and followed Jared away from the table. Calandra's eyes trailed him until he started mingling among other colonists near the pavilion. Now that she made her raw feelings about him clear, perhaps he would finally stay an acceptable distance from her during their temporary alliance with the Earthians.

19

elcor scowled deeply while studying data returned from their survey probe for a third time. No fresh details he overlooked earlier grabbed his attention. Surface scans revealed a planet with a slightly smaller mass than Lathos orbiting inside the red alien star's habitable region. Data culled from the planet offered discouraging signs. Atmospheric readings revealed surface temperatures hot enough to boil oceans down to trace amounts of liquid water. The thin atmosphere held scant oxygen. If this planet harbored intelligent life at one time in the past, it long since perished.

The Land of the Three Suns was not in this system.

All evidence on the holoscreen before him persuaded Delcor he made a critical miscalculation when his flagship exited the space bridge. He chose to scout the wrong system among the three alien suns.

"Sending a scout ship to the alien planet may be a prudent action, my sovereign."

Delcor lifted his chin and gazed down at the man who spoke from the helm. Nihu, the master pilot for his flagship, turned and faced the chief sovereign's chair. It rested on a raised platform over-looking the helm near the rear bridge wall.

"It's possible the rebels who stole the staff hid it inside a cavern on a planet hostile to life," he continued. "A single ship can scour natural caverns and crevices to rule out the planet."

Delcor shook his head. He liked Nihu's strategic thinking. Hiding an important weapon on a lifeless planet was a shrewd way to conceal it from potential enemies. But the ancient records they studied revealed a different strategy for concealing the staff.

The Staff of Onrai lay hidden in a mythical place. The Land of the Three Suns. No relevant planetary data matched ancient descriptions of that blessed land. A curse from Ahm burdened this planet rather than a blessing.

"I appreciate your initiative, master pilot Nihu Zell," Delcor said. "Your natural intelligence always filled your father Doni with pride. Still, our mission is quite clear. We must find a planet match-ing known details of the Land of the Three Suns. Only then will we uncover the staff's true location."

"Your will is my will, my sovereign."

Nihu faced the helm console again. He pressed three buttons on a vertical column in a numbered sequence.

"Shall we rendezvous with the rest of your fleet at the space bridge?" he asked.

"How long is the return journey?"

"If we depart immediately, we will reach the bridge within a day. That should supply your other ships enough time to complete their system-wide scans of the other two stars."

Delcor slouched in his chair and planted his elbow on an arm-rest. He buried his chin in his hand while considering their options. Increasing his time away from Ra'ahm did not please him. Still, Delcor dared not return to his people empty-handed.

Perhaps his son succeeded where he failed. Even now, Giljax could have pinpointed where Calandra Menankar and Xttra Oogan dwelt inside Daraconiah and ended their threat to his rule forever. Still, Delcor refused to make assumptions. Ahm blessed him with a long and prosperous reign specifically because he used his wisdom to predict and counter actions of his enemies. Relaxing his vigilance, even to obtain the Staff of Onrai, would only turn into a fatal mistake.

"Return us to the space bridge at once," Delcor said. "Send out a general order for our ships in this system to rejoin the rest of our fleet."

Nihu relayed the command to his navigator who entered the space bridge coordinates. A new hyperlight route materialized on the helm console holoscreen. Delcor hoped for promising news when his flagship reunited with the rest of his fleet. If one found the correct planet, time squandered in this system would not carry as potent of a sting.

Delcor retired to his private room once the ship entered the chosen hyperlight route. He settled into a plush chair cushioned with sapinoa hair seated before a broad senosa wood table. Ornate carvings etched into the table's surface depicted a treema standing atop a rocky ledge. Two big gloomy eyes and an extended furry muzzle pointed toward unseen prey beyond the outcropping. The animal arched its sleek back and crouched on long lanky arms and legs while an equally long tail covered in dense fur hung loose over the ledge.

Delcor's eyes lingered on the treema. He secretly desired to own a pet treema ever since he first laid eyes on one. Their exotic appearance and energetic demeanor appealed to him. Still, he dared not obtain one to dwell with him in his palace.

Rubrum was their homeworld.

Delcor labored to destroy any lingering evidence of his ties to Rubrum following the Separatist War. Treema ownership would highlight an undeniable connection to an enemy alien race. Such a revelation would strengthen the cause of his enemies and weaken his people's faith in him. And yet, his extreme caution proved insufficient. Liars and rebels, led by Calandra herself, destroyed the careful narrative Delcor constructed. They emboldened other extremists and traitors with their treachery.

He sighed and pulled out a drawer underneath the tabletop. Delcor retrieved an aging copy of the *Book of Ahm* from the drawer and resumed reading from where he left off.

"Perhaps the words of ancient oracles will grant me comfort and guidance," he told himself. "Illuminate my path on this quest."

Delcor thumbed through one metallic page after another, searching for relevant passages. He paused on a page one-quarter of the way through the ancient record. His eyes lingered on a single cryptic passage mid-page, repeatedly retracing the words.

Let the one who bears the staff imbued with Ahm's power possess the heart of a child.

Heart of a child?

Delcor furrowed his brow while he contemplated this phrase. The ancient oracle who composed this poetic language spoke in useless riddles. A child could never wield such a powerful weapon. Surely, the sheer volume of knowledge contained within the Staff of Onrai would destroy an immature mind.

Wielding the staff required a strong mind. He felt certain of this fact. No one fit such a qualification better than Delcor himself. His own far-sighted wisdom won the Separatist War for Ra'ahm and led the nation through an unrivaled era of peace and prosperity.

A sliding whoosh greeted his ears.

"Apologies for the interruption, my sovereign." A quavering servant addressed him. "We have an incoming communication from a master pilot. They requested a direct audience with you."

Delcor glanced up from the sacred book toward the now-open door to his private room. His eyes met a Stellar Guard officer who formed part of Nihu's regular crew. He studied the blonde-haired man for a moment. What was his name? Nihu introduced the entire crew when Delcor first boarded his flagship, but their names were not crucial to his mission. No one should expect him to remember lesser people he barely knew when weightier matters occupied his attention.

"Thank you," Delcor said. "Instruct Nihu to feed the transmission here into my private room."

The Stellar Guard officer nodded and bowed.

"Your will is my will, my sovereign."

Delcor pressed a button on his table. Two slots opened in the treema's eyes and a massive holoscreen projected through the open slots. A master pilot's image materialized before him. He instantly bowed before the chief sovereign.

"I am master pilot Tressek, my sovereign." A distinct nervous lilt gripped his voice. "Thank you for permitting me to speak with you."

"I trust you bring me good news," Delcor said.

Tressek swallowed hard.

"Forgive me, my sovereign…I…" he stumbled over his words while searching for the right ones. "I fear…it is not all…good news."

Delcor scowled. He had no time for trivialities. Or insipid trepidation.

"Speak your mind, master pilot."

Tressek cleared his throat.

"I believe we found the home star system for the Land of the Three Suns. But I fear we may meet heavy resistance on the planet itself."

Delcor grew rigid in his chair.

"Have you already encountered resistance? Did you travel to the planet to confirm it is the one we seek?"

"A smuggling vessel from Daraconiah entered the system shortly after our arrival. We intercepted the vessel near a giant planet on the outer edge just as it launched a pair of Cassian darts."

Cassian darts?

Delcor's temperature climbed as his fingernails dug into his chair's armrests. How did the Confederation find this system before he did? He restricted knowledge of his plans to his immediate clan and most trusted advisors. Encountering Confederation and Daraconian ships was no mere coincidence.

Were they also searching for the Staff of Onrai? This revelation was unacceptable.

"Did you destroy all three vessels?"

"We took heavy casualties, my sovereign." Tressek bowed his head again, no doubt a ploy to avoid meeting Delcor's gaze. "Two ships perished—a scout ship and a ground force carrier. We destroyed the other vessels. One scout ship stayed behind to finish off the darts while my crew and I spared no speed to return and give you a full report."

Delcor stared silently at the holoscreen. He fumed at Tressek's cowardly action. The master pilot merited a strict punishment for abandoning a fellow scout ship to fight enemy vessels alone, even if they were inferior Cassian darts. Still, if he had not fled to the space bridge, Delcor would have entered that alien star system unprepared for a Confederation presence.

Bringing back critical knowledge offered Tressek a reprieve. For the moment.

"You gathered valuable intelligence, master pilot Tressek. I commend you for bringing it to me."

Tressek lifted his head and met Delcor's gaze. Visible relief showed in his eyes.

"It is my honor to serve you, my sovereign."

"Yes, it is."

Delcor stabbed a finger at him.

"Never abandon your fellow Stellar Guard officers again. The Stellar Guard is one clan. You must defend one another as you would defend a clan member connected to you through blood. Never forget it."

Tressek gulped and nodded.

"Your will is my will, my sovereign."

Delcor deactivated the holoscreen and the master pilot's image vanished. He rose stiffly from his chair. The effects of deep space travel already wore down his body. Aches afflicted his knees and ankles when he stood on his feet again. He steadied a hand against the edge of the table and drew in a sharp breath. Delcor ran a hand through his hair and took a few halting steps forward.

Hiding his advancing age grew difficult with what he had to endure these days.

He forced his gait to mimic the vitality of his youth and his pace quickened when he reached the corridor. Delcor walked straight to the bridge and settled into his chair again.

"Calculate a route to the orange class star, Nihu, and depart immediately for that system. Instruct the rest of the fleet to advance to the same destination. We found the Land of the Three Suns."

Nihu answered him with a quick nod.

"It shall be done, my sovereign."

Relief washed over Delcor as his flagship departed from the space bridge toward its new destination. Ahm smiled on him this day. Another crucial step closer in their quest for the Staff of Onrai.

20

ew images from aerial surveys offered promising clues for the
Staff of Onrai's location. Xttra studied a fresh batch that Earthian
drones sent back on Sam's laptop. These images showed evidence
of a second ancient structure standing near a mountain river. A dense
forest surrounded the structure, which rested below a towering cliff.
Much like earlier ruins Sam showed him, this structure lay a few
dozen peds directly west from the Ra'ahmian colony.

Visiting the colony assumed greater importance than satisfying
simple curiosity.

Valadius founding a colony near two different ancient structures
must carry a deeper purpose. Xttra refused to dismiss his decision as
a coincidence. Did the former prime oracle know where the Staff of
Onrai lay hidden? When he staged his death during Xttra's childhood, Valadius must have fled to the Land of the Three Suns with
acolytes of Ahm and appointed himself as a guardian of the relic.

"These new images are our map revealing our destination."
Xttra peered over the laptop at Bo'un. "I'm convinced of it."

Bo'un rose from his hardback chair on the opposite side of the table. He set down an active trique. An image of an ancient parchment page flickered on the holoscreen. Xttra turned the laptop screen toward Bo'un as he rounded the table and tapped a finger on the upper half of the screen.

"Look at how close the colony is to these two sites the Earthian drones identified."

Bo'un squinted at an aerial image of the dense forest. The color drained from his face, and he shuddered. His eyes darted down to a topographical map displaying travel distance between the colony and the forest.

Xttra shot him a curious look.

"Is there a problem?"

Bo'un pressed his hand against his forehead.

"Flashback." He pinched his eyes shut. "Alien forest. Bad memory."

"From our landing spot on Earth?"

"You're perceptive."

Bo'un opened his eyes again and exhaled deeply. He instinctively trailed his fingers over jagged scars on his jaw and throat.

"It was a long time ago." Xttra adopted a reassuring tone. "The chances of another large alien animal attacking us here—"

"I know the odds," Bo'un said, interrupting him. "I agree it's an unreasonable fear. But it lingers inside the shadows of my nightmares all the same."

Xttra gave him a sympathetic nod. Bo'un nearly died after an Earthian bear mauled him less than two peds from their scout ship. Medical hibernation, followed by painful surgeries and rehabilitation, were bound to leave mental scars running deeper than the rough ridges of flesh on his head, neck, and arm.

"Of all the places where Valadius could have started a colony, why this spot?" Xttra leaned back in his chair and redirected his friend to the map on the screen. "Where he settled must hold some significance."

"From a practical angle, he has enough resources to sustain a thriving colony," Bo'un said. "Countless trees for building materials. Fresh water. I imagine enough vegetation and animals are in the area to create a steady food supply."

"Those descriptors fit many places in the Land of the Three Suns," Xttra replied. "No. A deeper reason must exist for choosing this place over another. A prime oracle would not settle near ancient ruins with closed eyes."

Bo'un crossed his arms and his eyes settled on Xttra.

"You think Valadius came here to find the staff?"

Xttra tapped his temple with his finger and smiled.

"Makes sense, doesn't it? Fleeing Lathos for him wasn't solely about escaping from Delcor's clutches. He wanted to find a means of defeating the chief sovereign. He must have acquainted himself with stories about the staff. Perhaps he also sought the relic's power—as a tool for dethroning Delcor."

Bo'un blinked rapidly and studied the laptop screen again. His eyes trailed back to Xttra, and he flashed a surprised smile.

"I never considered it in that light. An intriguing idea. Then again, learning Valadius never died in a tragic accident took time to accept."

The door leading to the room they occupied inside one of Cascadia's central towers slid open. Xttra rose from his chair as Calandra entered. He met her a few steps from the door, and they embraced.

"What did you learn from the new aerial images?" she asked, peering over his shoulder at the laptop.

Xttra pulled back and flashed a triumphant grin, signaling the image still displayed on the device's screen.

"A second ancient structure is less than 50 peds from the Ra'ahmian colony," he said. "Cleverly nestled inside a dense forest by a cliff."

Calandra followed on his heels as Xttra walked back over to retrieve the laptop. He handed the Earthian machine to her. A bright smile conquered her lips as she studied the images gracing the screen. For Xttra, a clear sign she drew the same conclusion as him.

"We need to visit that colony." Calandra handed the laptop back to him. "If they are 'the People of Valadius' as they claim, perhaps they will share useful information about the staff with us."

"Will they share information with us?" Bo'un asked. "We don't know anything about them beyond how they introduced themselves to the Earthians."

Bo'un made a good point. If they knew nothing about these colonists beyond their identity, thinking they would support their cause was a bold assumption.

It struck Xttra as strange that neither Valadius nor his people tried to return to Lathos and dethrone Delcor. Not to his knowledge anyway. If they journeyed here to find the Staff of Onrai and uncovered its location, why not use the relic to liberate Ra'ahmians suffering under his tyranny? Two possibilities sprang into his mind. Either the People of Valadius never found the staff or they uncovered its location but harbored no intention of liberating Ra'ahm.

Calandra tilted her head at Bo'un and pressed her lips together. Her eyes narrowed as she shook her head.

"We can't discard these colonists as potential allies before meeting them," she said. "We must contact them without delay and learn if they can help us."

Bo'un shrugged and nodded. Calandra shined a different light on the situation. Xttra quickly realized she had the right perspective. Neither Valadius nor his people seeded a rebellion against Delcor. Perhaps they hesitated to oppose him for a valid reason, waiting for the right people to join the fight. Allies with enough resources and courage to stand against the chief sovereign.

Erica offered a solar rover to Xttra and Calandra when they shared their plans to visit the distant colony with the Cascadian leaders. Xttra declined. Traveling in a land-based vehicle required a day-long journey from Cascadia to the colony. He preferred the flexibility of air travel. A ship provided enough time to visit the colony, speak with their leaders, and return with valuable information before both visible suns set.

Sam arranged for a Confederation star cruiser to fly from Cascadia to the colony and back. Xttra liked the choice. The star cruiser used a sleek design featuring a triangular nose and V-shaped body and matched a scout ship in size. Cassian darts did not fit more than two travelers comfortably in such a tight space. Beyond comfort considerations, a star cruiser was equally capable of handling atmospheric flight and deep-space travel.

Borrowing the Confederation vessel, however, meant an unexpected concession which pleased neither Xttra nor Calandra. Xttra shook his head in disbelief when Sam revealed his stipulation for using the star cruiser.

"What do you mean you're going with us?"

"We share a planet with these colonists," Sam said. "Our priorities are not limited to finding an ancient relic. We want to establish trade and diplomatic relations. Since you're also from Ra'ahm, we can make real progress communicating with their leaders."

Xttra sighed.

"You'll distract us from our purpose." His hands dropped to his hips. "You can do those other things at a future time. The task ahead of us requires greater urgency and a singular focus."

Sam crossed his arms and flashed a defiant smirk.

"If I don't go, neither does the star cruiser."

Xttra cast a glance over at Calandra. Her lips twisted into a half-frown, and she shrugged while running a finger through a lock of her auburn hair. They had little recourse to counter Sam's demand.

Spending an entire day traveling to the colony in a solar rover was unwise. A creeping fear lingered in Xttra's mind during quiet moments. The chief sovereign commanded a formidable military machine. More scout ships would turn up in this solar system sooner rather than later. Destroying a few vessels only slowed the inevitable onslaught. Time squandered bickering with Earthian and Confederation colonists over travel arrangements yielded ground to Delcor and his minions. Making concessions to the Cascadian leaders was the only logical choice, even if their agenda conflicted with more important matters at hand.

"Gear up." Xttra turned to Sam again. "Let's fly before sunlight yields to moonlight."

Sam was not alone among Earthian colonists joining their expedition. Lily volunteered to go, bringing their travel party to five people. Xttra, Calandra, and Bo'un all chose to make the journey. Kevin agreed to stay in Cascadia to take care of Alexa.

Lily drove the group out to a massive shipyard. It stretched over a section of the plateau where Cascadian colonists cleared out a broad swath of trees, brushes, and grasses years earlier. Kevin and Bo'un were already familiar with the shipyard from landing their darts there a day after arriving on the planet. Xttra did the same with Kujoth's escape craft. Cascadia housed a dozen space vessels— both large and small—inside its shipyard.

The shipyard featured a single control tower, built using a design matching cylindrical towers populating Cascadia but incorporating much larger windows. Lily and Sam pointed out this project also bore the handiwork of construction robots. Their ingenuity impressed and frightened Xttra. These Earthians built a thriving colony from scratch in less than four years. What would they do in a single generation?

Lily parked their rover near the control tower and Sam led the travel party to the star cruiser. Sunlight shimmered off the vessel's lustrous metallic outer hull. Its triangular nose pointed south, and a ramp extended from the belly of the vessel.

"I always wanted to pilot a star cruiser." Awe tinged Xttra's voice while he studied the scout ship's Confederation counterpart. "I'm curious to see how it handles compared to a scout ship."

A dismissive laugh greeted his words. Xttra snapped his head toward the ramp. His face fell when he spotted the source of the laugh.

"Wonderful," he said. "This ship belongs to that Neabu worshiping fool?"

The object of his scorn stood at the top of the ramp with hands resting on his hips and offered up an amused smile.

"No, I'm not Eliah," he said. "I'm Gulah, his twin brother. But I'll make a mental note to share your opinion of him."

Xttra kept his gaze fixed on Gulah and frowned. He avoided letting his eyes wander and learning how the others reacted to him making a fool of himself. Escalating a conflict with these brothers would be unwise. He tried to play down the insult.

"Trust me. He already knows."

Gulah laughed again and pointed his thumb backward at the star cruiser.

"If your heart is set on piloting my ship, prepare to be disappointed. No one sits in the pilot's chair except me."

Xttra's frown snapped into a smug grin.

"I don't care where I sit. Just redirect your piloting controls to whichever station I'm occupying."

Gulah stared at Xttra, mouthed the word "no," and shook his head with a slightly exaggerated motion before waving everyone forward. Lily and Sam climbed the ramp first. Bo'un, Xttra, and Calandra trailed them. Calandra nudged Xttra with her forearm halfway up the ramp.

"Smooth first impression," she said, laughing and adding a playful wink.

Xttra shrugged and pursed his lips.

"I'm happy you're enjoying this."

The ramp raised into a slot as they stepped inside the cargo bay. A hatch door resealed with a sudden whoosh and clank. Xttra silently noted every detail, helpless against an overwhelming urge to compare every star cruiser component to scout ships he spent many years piloting. Gulah led everyone to the cruiser's bridge. Eliah already stood on the bridge when they entered, checking navigation console switches. He instantly met Xttra's gaze and flashed an irritated scowl.

"Eliah looks thrilled to see you," Bo'un whispered, adding a chuckle.

"The feeling is mutual." Xttra's tone said otherwise.

They settled into seats scattered across the bridge. Gulah delegated monitoring navigation, propulsion, life support, and other ship functions to Xttra, Bo'un, and Calandra. He tasked Lily and Sam with relaxing and enjoying the ride.

Gulah settled into the pilot's chair and ignited the engines. The star cruiser lifted off the landing platform gradually and shot skyward with a sudden burst. He leveled the vessel out once alien trees surrounding the plateau resembled clusters of miniature shrubs.

Xttra's eyes drifted over to the eastern coastline. Foamy waves battered sea cliffs, slamming against the rock face with relentless energy. He gazed at rolling ocean waves stretching beyond the horizon and wondered what secrets the choppy water concealed beneath its surface. Xttra wished time allowed him to explore everything, starting from the white sand beach down to the ocean floor. Calandra and Alexa would enjoy sharing those adventures with him.

He faced forward again as the cruiser turned inland and the ocean receded from his view. Reddish grasses yielded to dense clusters of crimson and scarlet trees. A narrow road the Earthians built laced through a section of the alien forest. Xttra counted himself fortunate for insisting on flying. The broken ribbon of a road presented a rough trail guaranteed to send jolts up and down his spine with each bump the solar rover absorbed.

"There's the river from the aerial images," Bo'un said, pointing straight ahead. "It appears the water flows straight down into a wide valley on the horizon."

A herd of unusual animals roamed across foothills above the valley. Xttra never encountered another animal as exotic in all his travels. Each alien creature had a long furry body, four skinny legs and a trunk extending from their forehead down to the middle of their front legs. A few sported a pair of horns between giant floppy ears.

"Odocos!"

Lily let out a happy gasp. She quickly leaned forward in her chair as the star cruiser neared the foothills.

"I love watching odocos so much," she said. "I wish I could keep one as a pet."

"I liked my name better," Sam said.

Bo'un cocked his head toward the Earthian.

"What was your suggestion?"

Sam grinned.

"They resemble a hybrid of an elephant and a mule deer—two Earth animals. I thought we should call them elladeer. Or deeraphants."

Lily rolled her eyes. Her lips twisted into a half-smile.

"That's exactly why you're not allowed to choose animal names," she said, wagging a finger at Sam and shaking her head.

Xttra concurred with her observation. Sam had a distinct lack of imagination. Xttra's eyes stayed glued to the odocos. A few raised their heads and used their trunks to strip leaves from nearby trees and drop the food into their mouths. He stole a glance at Calandra. The alien animals enchanted her as much as him. Her eyes followed odocos in their movements so deeply she was unaware of his gaze.

"We've reached the other colony," Gulah said. "I'm landing two peds outside their main village. Hope no one minds a short walk."

"Why don't we land closer to the village?" Xttra asked.

"I got a distinct impression on my last visit these colonists might react poorly to seeing a star cruiser at their door," the Confederation pilot said. "I don't want them to refuse to speak with us out of fear."

The star cruiser touched down in a small meadow only a ped from the foothills. Xttra unlatched a safety restraint and rose halfway from his chair when a persistent beep echoed through the bridge.

He dropped down into the chair again.

"Proximity alarm." Eliah tapped a finger on a monitor embedded in a console before him. "Multiple large animals stampeding in our direction."

Calandra's eyes widened and she pressed her metal hand to her chest. Bo'un clutched both armrests on his chair and his breathing quickened. Their reactions matched a growing nervousness spreading like a mist inside Xttra. His heart thumped harder and faster.

What unseen menace would provoke a peaceful herd of animals to suddenly charge toward their ship?

21

When Calandra first laid eyes on the odocos, the herd of tree-eaters struck her as peaceful animals. She silently echoed Lily's desire to interact with odocos up close. Now the herd bore down on their cruiser in an unexpected stampede. They faced no real threat of injury inside the ship. But Calandra also understood they risked damaging the cruiser's landing gear if the ship stayed in the path of the frightened, brown-furred animals.

A damaged ship meant being grounded until Gulah and Eliah made necessary repairs. It would strand her and Xttra far away from Alexa for several hours—an unacceptable scenario for them and their little girl.

"How fast can you get this ship airborne?" Sam asked. "Staying on the ground isn't wise unless we can slow these odocos down."

"I'm powering up our main engines again." Gulah threw a control lever on his console forward. "This will be a close one."

He retracted the landing gear and the cruiser lifted off the ground moments before a lead wave of odocos swept into the meadow. Tracking sensors showed the herd closing fast. They galloped under the belly of the airborne vessel and out past the bridge. Terror filled the widened eyes of every odoco.

Three animals covered in black fur charged from the foothills. Their narrow eyes focused on a pair of juvenile odocos. Tusk-like incisors protruded from the upper and lower jaws of these predators, contrasting their short broad snouts. Saliva dripped from panting mouths over taut lips; visible hunger threaded through their light-brown rounded faces. Their long stout legs and broad bodies formed a harmonious balance of speed and power, allowing the three predators to match the strides of their fleeing prey.

"Are those bears?"

Bo'un's question left his tongue in a near-whisper. His lips quivered and he swallowed hard.

"Saber-toothed arcodons." Lily corrected him. "We first discovered them when…"

She paused and snapped her head toward him.

"How did you know about bears? That animal species is native to Earth."

Bo'un instinctively rubbed the jagged scars along his jaw and throat.

"The word 'bear' became seared in my mind when Kevin named the animal which mauled me on Earth. You don't forget an alien creature that nearly stole your life from you with the swipe of a massive paw."

Calandra stared at the fleeing animals, while the cruiser hovered overhead at a safe distance. Her heart raced faster as she followed churned soil and broken trees to judge the stampede's trajectory. The odoco herd galloped straight toward a small village west of the ship.

"Look! The odocos are fleeing toward that village." Calandra stabbed a finger at a low stone wall surrounding a cluster of dwellings. "We need to divert the herd before they trample innocent people."

Xttra stole a glance at the tracking sensors. A resolute frown washed over his face.

"I know how to deal with this situation. Bring the ship down again."

"Have you lost your mind?" Eliah's voice grew animated. "You don't give orders here. Especially when they make no sense."

Xttra shot him an irritated glare. Calandra hoped he would curb his temper, even though Eliah seemed determined to provoke a conflict with his bluntness.

"I grew up on a farm," Xttra snapped. "My parents raised a herd of kerval along with planting and harvesting our usual crops. Trust me."

Gulah shrugged and started the landing cycle anew.

"Show us what you're thinking."

Xttra rose from his chair once the cruiser returned to its former landing spot. He marched to the helm and hunched over the console. His eyes trailed over long rows of buttons, levers, and panels.

"Send out an ultrasonic blast," Xttra said.

Gulah furrowed his brow.

"Ultrasonic blast?"

"It works well for slowing terrified kerval," he said. "We should be protected from the effects inside the cruiser, but the blast will disorient both odocos and arcodons enough to stop the stampede."

"Is that ultrasonic blast lethal?" Calandra's eyes darted from the animals to the helm. "They're innocent animals. We don't have a right to slaughter them for doing what comes naturally."

Xttra turned and flashed a reassuring smile at her.

"It will only stun them temporarily. Maybe give a few a slight headache. They'll be fine."

Gulah frowned but relented in the absence of better ideas. At Eliah's nod, he tapped a blue-handled lever controlling the sonic emitter's decibel level with his index finger. Gulah toggled the lever into ultrasonic range and pressed a square button below the lever.

Outside the ship, all three arcodons stumbled forward into thick red grass when the ultrasonic wave spread out from the cruiser. Several odocos also lost their footing as the herd veered off from the village while scrambling to escape the high-pitched sound. One stumbled into a small boulder and came up limping.

"Now, we need to surround the arcodons and stun them before they resume their chase," Xttra said.

He turned and glanced at Gulah.

"How many shock sticks are in your armory?"

Gulah cast his eyes at the ceiling to avoid eye contact.

"Well...That's not an easy question—"

"Don't pretend you have none on hand." Xttra cut him off. "Beddeo builds and ships out bushels to every fellow Confederation tribe."

The Confederation pilot's eyes shifted to his twin brother. Eliah answered him with an immediate shrug and pointed back at Xttra.

"I guess we can spare one or two," Gulah said.

Calandra rubbed her hands across her cheeks and let out a heavy sigh. Were they not supposed to be allies in this case? This Confederation of Northern Tribes versus Ra'ahm conflict did not apply to her and Xttra and helped no one in the situation at hand.

"Will those shock sticks kill the arcodons?"

Lily voiced a question floating through Calandra's head before she spoke it into existence. Xttra shook his head vigorously.

"Beddeoian shock sticks are a stun weapon," he said. "We'll incapacitate the arcodons long enough to restrain and transport them a safe distance from the odocos and the village."

Lily frowned. Xttra's explanation appeared to do little to ease her concerns for the animals' safety.

"You can tag along and help me stun and restrain the arcodons if you wish," he said. "I harbor no intentions of harming or killing those creatures."

Lily, Gulah, and Sam followed Xttra into the cargo bay. Calandra opted to stay on the ship with Bo'un and Eliah. She could not bear watching the others stun and restrain disoriented animals even if their actions protected the people of Valadius from a stampede. She did not blame the stout black-furred predators for following their instincts and searching for a meal among grazing odocos.

Calandra cast a glance at the others beside her on the bridge. Eliah studied a screen tracking the arcodons and relayed data to Gulah on the ground. Bo'un stared at a distant point beyond the bridge. Concern flooded his eyes, and his fingers tightly gripped his chair's armrests.

"This must be terrible for you," she said. "A reminder of your trauma on Earth. Can I do anything to help you?"

His eyes softened and Bo'un met her gaze.

"Such an irrational fear. I shouldn't fall to pieces when a large predator appears. It's so foolish."

Calandra offered him a reassuring smile.

"You aren't foolish for being troubled about a source of tremendous pain for you. Nothing is wrong with feeling scared when confronted with scary things. People who claim to fear nothing are the foolish ones. And liars."

A grateful smile crossed Bo'un's lips. He drew in a deep breath. Her eyes drifted down to his hands. His fingers untensed and indentations on the padding covering the armrests quickly vanished.

"You always find the right words to ease a worried mind," he said. "I admire that quality in you."

Anxious minutes passed inside the cruiser. Bo'un's eyes drifted back to the ceiling. Calandra planted an elbow above her knee and rested her chin on her balled-up fist. She followed Eliah's conversation with Gulah from a distance. Based on the snippets she heard, and his calm demeanor, Xttra and the others met no significant resistance after stunning the arcodons.

Xttra is safe. He will stay safe.

Calandra silently repeated those words even as her nerves tightened like stiff ropes. She pressed her eyelids shut and focused on drawing in steady, calming breaths.

"The arcodons are fully restrained," Eliah said to her, glancing up from his screen. "No one's injured, including the animals. Praise Neabu. They're loading them into the cargo bay now."

Her eyes cracked open again. Calandra leaned back in the chair and let her arm fall to her side. Her tense nerves loosened, and a smile flooded her lips again.

Xttra was safe.

She sprang from her chair as Bo'un rose to his feet. They hurried to the cargo bay, entering right as Xttra and Lily hauled the last arcodon up the ramp. A muffled snarl came from the animal's muzzled mouth. Magnetic restraints prevented the arcodon from thrashing its limbs. Similar restraints bound all four limbs on the other predators.

"I'll take Eliah and Lily to help me drop off these arcodons in the forest a few peds from here," Gulah said. He turned and faced Calandra and Bo'un. "You're free to head over to the village and greet the People of Valadius. We'll rejoin you after we've moved the animals."

Xttra distributed gear and weapons to Calandra drawn from the cruiser armory. Bo'un still wore gear and weapons originally stored on his dart. Calandra, like Xttra, took no weapons or gear with her when they fled Kujoth's vessel. Only her flex armor underneath her regular clothing.

Calandra donned a chest pouch and cinched up a belt with multiple pouches and a holster around her dark blue pants. She stuck an eliminator inside the holster for self-defense. It held a full charge of blue laser bolts. Xttra strapped armored sleeves on each forearm over his long-sleeved dark green shirt, while taking a similar belt and eliminator for himself.

"I don't see a pressing reason to be armed," Xttra said. "Still, you can't be too careful. Who knows how these colonists will react to us?"

Calandra glanced down at her holstered weapon. Her eyes trailed back to her husband, and she nodded grimly. Harsh lessons learned on Earth taught her the importance of self-defense. Calandra loathed carrying a weapon, but she no longer clung to a naïve outlook concerning their value. Multiple brushes with death taught her to never assume good intentions and to always protect herself.

Bo'un hurried past captive arcodons and sprinted down the ramp. Sam, Xttra, and Calandra followed at a more subdued pace. The ramp retracted once their feet touched spongy grass and the hatch door sealed with a mechanical whoosh. Xttra and Calandra sprinted to catch up to Bo'un. Sam jogged to reach a safe distance from the ship before Gulah ignited the engines again and slowed to a more relaxed gait as he neared the others.

"This isn't a race. Wait for me."

Heavy breaths escaped Sam's lips. Xttra glanced over his shoulder at the Earthian.

"We're not out here for a stroll. Move faster or stay on the ship next time."

Sam grumbled a few unintelligible words but lengthened his strides. Calandra wanted him to stay behind in Cascadia from the start. Bringing him along threatened to undermine their primary reason for traveling to this colony.

The odoco herd fled toward an open field once they regained their senses and footing. They veered south past the village. Calandra stopped at the village outskirts and watched a pair of stragglers gallop to close the gap between themselves and the main herd. Each movement was fluid and graceful as the lovely creatures bounded through thick sprays of red grass.

A flustered shout greeted her ears. She snapped her head toward the village. Xttra and Bo'un both stopped a few steps ahead.

A solitary man wearing a headwrap sprinted out through an open gate in the perimeter wall. His worried eyes trailed the fleeing animals. He shouted in their direction a second time and uttered a few Ra'ahmian curses.

"What did he say?" Sam asked.

His hands hugged his hips and the Earthian let out heavy breaths after catching the others.

"I better not repeat his words in your language." Xttra shot him an amused smile. "What he said might deeply offend you."

The villager pivoted in their direction when Xttra spoke. He crossed his arms and a crease formed in his brow as he eyed the foursome suspiciously.

"We are peaceful travelers from Lathos." Calandra shifted from English to Confederation Universal. "We've journeyed here to find the people of Valadius."

"You scared off my herd." His eyes hardened into an intense stare matching his harsh tone. "I sent them out to the foothills to graze. Now their fright will carry them far away. Finding and bringing them home will require an entire day—or longer."

Xttra glowered at him.

"We didn't do anything to harm your precious odocos. You should thank us for saving them from becoming an afternoon meal for nearby predators."

"Odocos?" The man gave Xttra an incredulous look. "That is not their name. I don't think you understand—"

"We will help you find your animals again." Calandra spoke over the top of his rant. "You have my word. But first we need to speak with your leaders."

"I am Marteen Glenaar. I'm a trusted leader among my people."

Marteen stood taller and puffed out his chest while declaring his own leadership. Calandra rolled her eyes but fought to suppress an irritated sigh forming inside her throat. She disliked his blunt demeanor. Still, they could not risk alienating other colonists even if Marteen acted like a self-aggrandizing simpleton.

"Can we speak with Valadius?" Her tone remained polite but grew firmer. "We must discuss an important matter with him."

Bo'un turned and cupped his hand over his mouth.

"Do you think he's still alive after so many years?" he whispered. "He vanished from Lathos so long ago."

Marteen's eyes trailed from Bo'un back to Calandra. He pressed his lips together and studied her. Suspicion permeated every corner of his face. His direct prolonged gaze made her feel uncomfortable.

"Why do you think Valadius lives here?" Marteen finally asked. "Everyone knows he perished in a tragic accident a generation ago. We left Lathos and settled this peaceful land to carry on his name."

He squared his shoulders to the south where the odocos fled and stared at the horizon. Marteen concealed the truth. Calandra read his body language like a book. He misled them either out of contempt or from a misguided desire to protect the prime oracle.

"We already know he survived and led you here," Xttra said. "End your charade and take us to him."

Marteen turned and squinted at him. An amused smirk conquered his lips.

"Why should I comply with your demand?"

"We believe he holds valuable information we need to defeat Delcor," Xttra said. "Do you want the chief sovereign to find the Staff of Onrai and use it against all Lathoans?"

Marteen's smug smile melted off his face. He stiffened like a stone column. A distinct fear flooded his light blue eyes. Calandra felt an urge to smile herself.

They finally commanded his attention.

22

Entering the village stirred a peculiar sensation within Calandra. She compared herself to a traveler who slipped through a portal and journeyed back in time a hundred generations. This Ra'ahmian colony resembled places she read about in historical texts in simplicity and beauty. Her eyes trailed from place to place after she followed Marteen past a narrow stone wall surrounding the village perimeter.

Simple homes built from wood and stone lined both sides of narrow dirt streets. Each two-level dwelling followed a common design template. A giant stone square bisecting a rectangular stone block formed the ground level. Stairs at one end led to a flat roof and a second smaller cube-shaped block. A peaked roof topped the second level block.

Each home occupied the center of a perfect square lot. Neck-high perimeter walls, complete with a street-facing entry door, surrounded each lot. Immaculate inner courtyards filled space between entries and homes. Modest gardens and wells adorned many courtyards. A few also housed spacious pens for grazing animals.

A small stone temple occupied the village center. The sanctuary resembled three equilateral triangles cut from stone blocks and stacked atop one another, each triangle smaller than the preceding one, in perfect symmetry. A single column pierced the middle of the top triangular section, crowned by a seven-pointed star symbolizing Ahm himself. The holy structure incorporated a distinctive architectural style mirroring ancient Lathoan temples from an era predating the Wekonn Empire.

Several colonists labored outside their homes, tending to animals or gardens. They were clad in simple attire. Hand-sewn long-sleeved shirts and pants or dresses. Headwraps and shaded eye bands designed to protect their faces from excessive sunlight. Marteen wore the same simple clothing himself.

"Does this place resemble an ancient Ra'ahmian village to you?" Calandra whispered to Xttra.

"It's uncanny how much this village reminds me of Tu'atan." His eyes slid from a nearby dwelling back to her. "Or, more accurately, how I imagine my home village looked in ancient times before the Lathoan technological revolution."

"We embrace a simple life in Genahm." Marteen's voice swelled with pride. "Our people are not subservient to advanced technology. We focus our energies on serving Ahm with our whole souls and devote our lives to building a land of peace."

Genahm.

Calandra recalled what the *Book of Ahm* said of Genahm in several passages. A city of light and peace in the Land of the Three Suns. A twinge of disappointment rippled through her mind like a pebble skipping across a pond. Surely this was not the same place ancient oracles described. A smattering of humble homes and a small temple did not match her internal vision of an opulent and perfect city.

She matched Marteen stride for stride for almost three peds before he veered off the street toward a distinct home near the temple walls. This one incorporated the same base design as other dwellings except the courtyard housed a distinctive wooden tower overlooking a perimeter wall that rose above their heads. Marteen approached the wall and rapped his knuckles against a wooden entry door. A square slot opened within the upper part, above a thick metal handle, and revealed a wire screen.

"Who calls upon this house?"

A man with blue eyes and a sharp nose peered out from behind the screen. The thick wooden door obscured the rest of his face beyond those features.

"Travelers from Lathos seek an audience with the true prime oracle." Marteen paused and his eyes darted around. His voice dropped to a near whisper. "They bring with them a disturbing omen."

"What omen?"

"Delcor seeks the Staff of Onrai. They claim to have journeyed here to prevent it from falling into his hands."

Silence greeted Marteen's revelation. The sharp-nosed man pulled back from the screen and resealed the square slot. Calandra studied the unmoving wooden door and shook her head, shooting a sideways glance at Xttra and Bo'un. Xttra pressed his lips together into a slight frown. Bo'un glanced toward the door, back at her, and shook his head as well.

"Is he coming out to talk to us?" Sam asked.

The Earthian's eyes settled on Marteen. The villager returned a blank stare. Sam wore no translator in his ear. Nor did he speak the Confederation Universal language with any degree of fluency. Calandra wondered why he bothered saying anything. Marteen heard Sam's Earthian language only once before today. Why assume the villager would understand and answer his question?

Bo'un gave Sam a cursory glance and shifted his eyes back to Marteen. He translated the Earthian's question and Marteen's mouth twisted into a frown.

"No." He addressed Bo'un, ignoring Sam. "We will enter to converse with him."

Bo'un shifted back to English and repeated Marteen's response, indulging Sam's attempts to communicate.

"Maybe you should ask Gulah or Eliah for a spare translator Sam can use," Xttra said. "Constantly repeating everything will eventually wear on everyone's nerves."

The perimeter wall door swung open, revealing an aged man with short white hair. A thin white beard adorned his face. He wore a hooded purple cloak over a sand-colored shirt and pants. His left hand rested on a polished wooden staff with a rounded end.

"Marteen, my friend. I always enjoy your visits."

The white-haired man took a few deliberate steps forward and embraced him. Seeing his unobscured face confirmed his identity to Calandra. Like stumbling upon a long forgotten but familiar image stored within her holocaster. A quick glance at Xttra and Bo'un revealed the same recognition in their eyes.

Valadius stood before them.

Alive.

Calandra did not fully believe her own eyes. She accepted the myth of his tragic death for many years. Even after learning the truth, she never truly entertained the possibility she would ever meet him in the flesh.

That impossible day had arrived.

Valadius pulled back from Marteen and studied his other visitors. His eyes settled on Calandra and seemed to probe every corner of her soul while she stood before him.

"Who are these travelers who desire to speak with me?" He offered a warm smile and extended his right hand. "If Ahm wills it, I hope to impart whatever wisdom and knowledge you seek."

Valadius beckoned them forward, inviting them to join him in his courtyard. Marteen closed the door once everyone passed beyond the perimeter wall.

"Wait." Xttra cast his eyes back at the sealed door. "We should leave that door open."

"Why? I sense fear in you. Are we not friends here?"

Valadius raised his eyebrows. His sky-blue eyes filled with the same suspicion infusing his questions.

"Others came with us," Calandra said. "They stayed behind to transport arcodons threatening an odoco herd to another part of the forest. They'll return soon and we hope they will soon rejoin us."

The prime oracle blew out his cheeks and nodded.

"You need not fear," he said. "I am not familiar with those animals, but your friends are welcome if peace fills their minds and hearts."

"I think they're referring to my herd of hemantines," Marteen said. "I'm not sure what the other animal is."

Hemantines.

Calandra silently cringed upon learning what Genahm colonists called odocos. Lily would be justified in also banning them from naming animals if she were here.

Valadius strolled along a stone path leading to a modest well. It rose from the opposite corner of the courtyard across from the tower. He leaned on his staff to reinforce his balance as he walked. The prime oracle hunched over slightly and moved at a methodical pace. Calandra found it remarkable to see life still flowing within him. 28 years had passed since he fled from Lathos. He was in his 63rd year when he staged his solar flare accident. Living on a distant planet removed from the normal comforts of civilization had not led to a premature demise.

"How did you find Genahm, my children?"

"Genahm?"

Sam repeated the village name with a puzzled look, after Bo'un translated the question.

"I named our village Genahm as a symbol for why we settled here." Valadius acknowledged the Earthian with a brief nod after

Bo'un relayed his question back to the prime oracle. "We focus our whole souls on creating an oasis of peace and faith devoted to Ahm, far removed from the corruption and violence of Lathos."

Valadius settled into a circular seat made from white bricks near the well and set his staff against the well itself. His hands rested on his legs and his eyes settled on his visitors.

"More importantly," he continued. "Has the chief sovereign discovered our peaceful land?"

Calandra pressed her lips together and crossed her arms. She directed an intense stare at the prime oracle.

"Why did you flee Lathos all those years ago?" She blurted out the first question which sprang into her mind rather than answer his inquiries. "You had the ability to stand against Delcor and end his rule."

The warm smile decorating Valadius' face melted into a frown. A distinct sadness washed over his eyes.

"Child, you overestimate my influence in Ra'ahm. Delcor had grown too powerful before Ahm opened my eyes to his crimes."

"You left us to fend for ourselves," Calandra said. "We endured needless suffering under the whims of a tyrant. All because one chosen to lead the Order of Ahm chose to not lead."

Valadius pinched his eyelids shut and bowed his head.

"I saw a grim path ahead if I spoke out against him." His voice trembled as he spoke. "Endless civil war. Blood and fire engulfing the streets of Luma and other Ra'ahmian cities and villages. Ahm compelled me to leave the matter in his hands."

"Leave the matter in his hands?" she snapped. "You fled like a coward!"

Her cheeks grew warmer. Fury drenched Calandra's eyes. How dare he twist his own failure as a spiritual leader into a divinely sanctioned action? Valadius cared more about protecting his own skin than delivering people relying on his guidance from an evil tyrant's clutches. He was nothing more than a sanctimonious fool.

Xttra grasped her arm gently. Calandra instantly snapped her head toward him. His eyes locked on her own, silently pleading with her to hold her tongue and subdue her wrath so she did not jeopardize their original purpose for seeking the prime oracle.

"Ahm has given you a second chance to make a better choice," Xttra said, facing Valadius. "You hold the key to liberating Ra'ahm from Delcor's rule forever."

The prime oracle lifted his chin and his eyes shifted to Xttra. He tilted his head and his brows knitted together.

"If you're referring to the Staff of Onrai, I cannot help you." His tone changed from apologetic to firm. "The sacred tool is not mine to claim or give to another. It must remain hidden from evildoers until Ahm receives the staff into his own hand."

"You know where it is?" Bo'un asked.

Valadius countered his question with other questions.

"Why do you want to find the staff? What is your intention, should you take possession of this gift?"

Xttra crouched down to his eye level, trying to compel Valadius to meet his gaze. His eyes hardened with determination after settling on the prime oracle.

"We plan to destroy the staff," he said. "Delcor must never be allowed to fulfill his dark purposes."

Valadius stared past him toward the perimeter wall. A worried frown bled across his lips. He reached for his own staff and pulled it to his side.

"The Staff of Onrai is a gift meant to be treasured and used as Ahm intended." He countered Xttra with a bluntness mirroring a parent lecturing an unruly child. "You must not destroy Ahm's tool to bless his creation."

"If Delcor obtains the staff, he'll extend his rule over the rest of Lathos," Bo'un said. "And that will be only his first conquest. If we can thwart his plans and end his rule, we will not flee or hide from doing our part."

"Ahm decreed we must preserve his gift unto the latest generation," Valadius said. "You will not decide the staff's fate. Trust in Ahm to remove Delcor from his throne in his own time and own way."

Xttra rose to his feet again. His eyes did not veer from the prime oracle. They remained frozen in a stony glare. He shook his head with disgust.

"My father failed in his quest to incite a rebellion against Delcor." Xttra jabbed an index finger at the prime oracle and then pointed at Calandra. "Her grandfather resigned as first minister and exiled himself rather than bring Delcor to justice. We've paid a steep price for their failures—and your failure—far too long."

Valadius countered his hard gaze with a deepening frown and a sideways glance.

"Who are you?"

Calandra crouched down this time and stared, unblinking, into the prime oracle's eyes.

"He is Xttra Oogan. I am Calandra Menankar." A subdued fury filled her voice. "We will liberate Ra'ahm from the chief sovereign—with or without your help."

Valadius leaned on his staff and rose to his feet. Any lingering pretense of warmth and peace vanished from his face. His lips hardened into a scowl. His eyes revealed a rising fear he tried to conceal. A look of recognition also lingered in those eyes.

Neither Calandra nor Xttra met the prime oracle before today. But his silent reaction revealed a deeper, hidden knowledge. Valadius betrayed a familiarity with Malar and Janthore in his body language. Their clans played key roles in a traumatic past he wanted to bury.

Calandra and Xttra unburied it against his will.

"Leave my presence and depart from Genahm." A distinct tremor laced through his voice even as Valadius tried to make himself sound imposing. "You will only bring needless destruction and death upon true followers of Ahm who dwell here."

Sam's eyes darted between the prime oracle and Calandra. He cupped his hand against his mouth and leaned toward Bo'un.

"What's going on?" he whispered. "My command of your language is limited, but I'm not getting good vibes from the tone of your head oracle here."

Bo'un answered him with a worried frown.

"He refused to help us," he said, matching Sam's subdued tone.

Xttra cast a quick glance back at them and nodded. His eyes shifted to Valadius again with equal speed.

"We don't need your help," he said. "I, for one, don't want to align with a coward who turns his back on his people to save his own life. We're perfectly capable of finding the staff without you."

Valadius stretched his free hand skyward.

"Hear now the words of Ahm—"

"We will hear his words," Calandra said, interrupting the prime oracle. "From someone fit to lead Ahm's people—not you."

A thousand other accusations raced through her mind she wanted to vent in anger toward Valadius. They should have known better than to expect help from him. He cared more for his own life than the people who believed he perished and revered his memory.

Marteen signaled for them to honor the prime oracle's request and leave his presence. Calandra and Xttra both turned away without saying another word and marched back to the perimeter wall door. Their own intelligence and observational skills would be their tools for finding the Staff of Onrai. Valadius refused to stand against Delcor when he had a chance. Given an opportunity to redeem his earlier lack of action, he again proved useless in opposing the chief sovereign.

His failure could not become their failure.

23

Xttra had no interest in hearing Sam's complaints while retracing their path back through Genahm. The Earthian gazed back longingly at the small tower rising above the home of Valadius. He grumbled about dwindling trade prospects between Cascadia and Genahm when he met Xttra's gaze again.

"Enough!" Xttra snapped.

He shot Sam a stony glare. The Earthian retaliated with a dejected scowl and kicked emphatically at a pebble laying in his path.

"You and Calandra hijacked our meeting right off the bat and stormed out when this head oracle—or whatever you call him—didn't tell you what you wanted to hear." His voice couched a slow burning anger. "We made an agreement. You completely ignored why I came here and shut me out once it suited your purposes."

Xttra stopped and wheeled around. Sam stood unmoving in the narrow dirt street, arms crossed, and glowered at both him and Calandra.

"Your needs are different from ours," Xttra said. "They are not more important. Defeating Delcor before he obtains the means for conquering Lathos is essential to our survival."

"What about our survival?" Sam threw out his hands with a sweeping motion. "We experienced widespread crop failures during our first summer here. An alien neural virus swept through the colony during our first winter. Burying one colonist after another over the span of a few months still haunts me at night."

A tremor grasped his voice as he shared his painful memories. Xttra cast his eyes down at the street. He had acted like a selfish fool. Building a colony laid harsh burdens on these Earthians. Sam's tired eyes reflected the depth of pain and loss he experienced on a planet far from his home.

Xttra glanced over at Calandra. Her eyes and lips softened, and she bowed her head. He did the same. Sam lost his own people on an alien planet—a pain they understood too well. They had continually rebuffed Sam's efforts to make amends for his actions on Earth. What good did it do? Their bitterness threatened to alienate a potential ally at a crucial juncture.

"I want to help you." Sam's voice grew subdued again. "But I can't ignore Cascadia. These colonists in Genahm have lived on Colonia for an entire generation longer than us. They can help us build a permanent home here."

Xttra raised his chin and met Sam's gaze again.

"Apologies. You deserve better. We were enemies at one time, but we're no longer on opposite sides. I promise things will be better between us going forward."

He drew closer to the Earthian and extended his arm, inviting reconciliation. Sam clasped his wrist. Xttra then pulled back and shook his hand. Calandra finally faced Sam as well and extended her arm.

They clasped wrists for the first time.

"I don't want your people to suffer," she said. "An ancient Lathoan proverb applies to us: A stump cluttering the soil blocks a new sapling from greeting the sun."

Sam's lips melted into a grateful smile.

"A wise saying."

Bo'un and Marteen doubled back once they grew aware the other three no longer followed them. Their argument had also drawn curious looks from two passing villagers toting baskets filled with brown flatbread and fresh vegetables. Marteen waved and assured the villagers nothing was amiss. His smile hardened into a frown when his eyes settled on Xttra again.

"Your angry words are interrupting the tranquility of our village," Marteen said. "I insist you honor our prime oracle's directive and leave Genahm."

He swept an arm toward the wall surrounding Genahm, still a ped away from their current position. Calandra sighed.

"Why do you obey Valadius without question?" she asked. "We destroyed four Stellar Guard vessels already lurking in this solar system when we arrived. More will follow. You must tell us where the Staff of Onrai lies hidden before it grows too late."

"You heard what Valadius said."

Marteen turned away and marched purposefully toward the village wall. Calandra exceeded his stride and circled in front of him, blocking his path.

"Do you believe Delcor will leave you alone?" she asked. "Have you convinced yourself he'll simply ignore Genahm and return to Lathos once he gets what he wants?"

"We are not a threat to his rule," Marteen said. "We are a peaceful people."

He shifted to one side to walk around her. Calandra mirrored his movements to stay in his path.

"Your existence is a threat to him," she said. "Trust me when I tell you this fact. Delcor will never be satisfied to rule Lathos alone. He will also conquer the Land of the Three Suns. When that happens, where will you and your people go?"

Marteen furrowed his brow and his lips tightened at Calandra's declaration. He stopped and snapped his head toward a humble dwelling on the right side of the street. Xttra wondered if the home capturing his attention belonged to Marteen himself. His eyes trailed to the same spot. Broad leafy scarlet plants poked out from a garden hidden behind a perimeter wall. Tiny round green fruit adorned visible branches. A voice belonging to an unseen woman in the garden hummed a lovely melody.

"I was only a child when I fled Ra'ahm with my clan." Marteen's voice descended to a near whisper. "My father held a seat in the National Assembly until he spoke out against Delcor's invasion of the Animo Islands. They called him an insurrectionist and a traitor. We escaped arrest by a hair and fled from Lathos."

Calandra drew a holocaster from her chest pouch. She activated the holoscreen and brought forth an image of Alexa playing with Bella. A radiant smile covered her face as she laughed and batted at the silver and gray furred cala crouching on a carpeted floor.

"My daughter is exiled from the only home she's ever known." She stuck the active holoscreen under his nose. "Alexa is in the fourth year of her life. Like you, a child forced to flee from Delcor's tyranny."

Marteen stared unblinking at Alexa's image. Concern manifested in widened eyes and a deepening frown.

"You can help her," Bo'un said. "You have the power to help everyone here."

He pinched his eyelids shut and exhaled sharply.

"What would you have me do?"

Xttra flanked Marteen and laid a hand firmly on his shoulder. The villager's muscles grew as tight as Chitha strings under his touch.

"Tell us where the staff is," Xttra said. "Is it with Valadius? Or does it remain hidden elsewhere?"

Marteen opened his eyes again and faced him.

"No. The prime oracle does not possess the Staff of Onrai," he said. "It is hidden in a sanctuary, preserved since the Wekonn Empire fell."

"Will you take us to it?" Calandra asked.

"Valadius once told us Ahm had forbidden anyone from entering the sanctuary uninvited," Marteen replied, turning to her. "Anyone who violates this decree will be slain by Ahm's hand."

Xttra tilted his head at Calandra. Her narrowing eyes and creased brow told him he was not alone in thinking Valadius fabricated this prohibition from Ahm. All Ra'ahmians were taught their divine creator was a loving and compassionate being. It formed a core tenet of their faith from the beginning.

What Valadius claimed contradicted that belief.

"I don't believe him," Xttra said. "Ahm is not spiteful or vindictive. My guess is Valadius concocted this decree to dissuade anyone else from searching for the staff."

"I can't go myself." Marteen met his gaze, and his hushed tone returned. He pointed to a spot behind Xttra's shoulder. "My actions would create an unwelcome division in Genahm. What I can do is show you the way."

Xttra turned and faced the direction where Marteen pointed. He peered at trees climbing to meet the sky on foothills beyond the perimeter wall. Earthian drone images revealed an ancient building lay nestled within a dense forest in that same direction.

"My home lies beyond this wall," Marteen said. He stood behind Xttra, so he did not see the villager point out his dwelling as he spoke. "I will retrieve a copy of the ancient guide Valadius brought back. It shares wise teachings, but also describes the sanctuary's layout and reveals how to navigate the ancient structure's defenses."

"Defenses?" Xttra repeated. He turned and saw Marteen was already halfway to his dwelling.

"Ancient technology protects specific rooms." Marteen kept walking without looking back. "The guide reveals how to safely reach the Staff of Onrai."

Marteen entered through a gate to his dwelling and marched briskly down a narrow path leading to a broad wooden door. Xttra turned away. His eyes settled on Sam. A puzzled expression blanketed the Earthian's face as he unsuccessfully tried to follow another conversation in the same unfamiliar language.

"We finally know where the staff is," Xttra said, switching back to Sam's native language. "Calandra is quite persuasive when she needs to be."

Sam cast a sideways glance at her and nodded.

"You can say that again."

Multiple long beeps emanated from Sam's pocket. He retrieved his smartphone and peered at the screen.

"It's Lily," Sam said, grinning at Xttra.

He pressed down his thumb. Lily started rambling breathlessly about discovering a giant waterfall where they released the arcodons. Static threaded through her voice after a few words.

"I'm not getting a good signal here," Sam said. "Meet us outside the alien village. We've gathered useful intelligence on the whereabouts of the Lathoan relic."

"We're en route," Lily said. "Took us longer to haul all three arcodons out of the cargo bay than we expected, but it's done. We'll arrive in a few minutes."

Sam thanked her and pressed his thumb on the screen a second time. He stuffed the device in his back pocket again and glanced up at Xttra.

"You're probably wondering how I can still use a smartphone so far from Earth," Sam said.

"Not at all," Xttra said. "That question never crossed my mind."

"It's actually a funny story." Sam punctuated his statement with a chuckle. "To put a communications satellite in orbit here, we had to—"

"We need to pinpoint the fastest and safest path to reach the sanctuary," Xttra said, interrupting him. "Given the forest's density, we'll need to hike a moderate distance from our landing area."

"Two darts packed with supplies should be enough for us and Kevin," Bo'un said, pointing to himself, Xttra and Calandra. "What's our plan if Stellar Guard troops track us to the sanctuary?"

Xttra pressed his fingers to his right temple as he contemplated that dilemma. Stellar Guard vessels already used the space bridge to reach the system. Destroying a few vessels would not deter Delcor. Time worked against them in avoiding further confrontation.

"Can you help us combat a Stellar Guard fleet?" Xttra turned to Sam again. "How many ships from Earth did you bring to this planet?"

Sam gave him a sideways glance.

"Fleet? Exactly how many spaceships are we talking about here?"

Xttra hesitated to answer his question, suspecting what he said would alarm the Earthian. Delcor could theoretically send dozens of vessels to the Land of the Three Suns. He would never risk sending his full fleet and leave Ra'ahm vulnerable to an uprising. But the chief sovereign had more than enough ships to crush any potential resistance.

Marteen passed through the gate again while Xttra contemplated Sam's question. He carried a broad, flat parchment. Another villager leading a single odoco with a thick rope circling its neck passed in front of him as he crossed the street. Marteen thrust the parchment at Xttra. It felt like a flattened sheet of smoothed tree bark in his fingers.

"This has everything we know about the sanctuary," Marteen said. "Study it thoroughly before you depart, so you may enter without bringing harm upon yourselves."

"We are in your debt," Calandra said. "Your help will not be forgotten."

"I pray my help will be forgiven," Marteen replied. "But Valadius is an old man whose vision has dimmed. I want to keep my clan and the rest of Genahm safe. If leading you to the Staff of Onrai will guarantee us peace, then I am willing to help."

He bowed and bid them farewell before returning to his dwelling. Xttra flashed a hopeful smile and passed the guide to Calandra. Her eyes trailed down the reddish-brown parchment. After stealing a quick look at what information the guide held, Calandra rolled it into a tight scroll and stuck the parchment inside her chest pouch.

Obtaining the guide did not bring the peace of mind Xttra expected. His heart pounded as they reached the village wall. These elevated rhythms were not simply from their long walk. A nagging, unwelcome feeling told him Delcor, and his fleet, would strike soon.

Lily sprinted off the Confederation vessel's extended ramp, when they passed beyond the village wall, and raced toward the group. Xttra's throat tightened upon seeing the Earthian's deepening frown and panicked brown eyes.

"What's wrong?" Sam asked. "You look like you've seen a ghost."

"Gulah received word from Cascadia." Heavy breaths escaped her lips. "A small fleet of alien spaceships are approaching Colonia. They passed our moon and will reach our planet within a half hour."

Xttra gasped and pressed his hand to his mouth. His intuition proved alarmingly correct. The Stellar Guard found the Land of the Three Suns. Everyone on this planet faced incredible danger.

24

Calandra faced a tangible living nightmare. Delcor arrived at the Land of the Three Suns with his full fury. A predator no longer satisfied to lurk in shadows. The chief sovereign sprang into the light and would soon chase down his prey.

A fleet of ships?

Lily's revelation sent a chill racing down her spine. Another armed confrontation with the Stellar Guard was unavoidable after the destruction of Kujoth's vessel. Still, Calandra felt unprepared to travel the path before her.

Everyone sprinted to the bridge and threw themselves into their seats as Gulah ignited the primary thrusters.

"How many ships do you have?" Xttra asked, glancing over at Lily.

"Ships?" she repeated. "Like spaceships?"

"What can we throw at Delcor's fleet? We cannot let his ships land."

Lily swallowed hard and stared past him as Gulah's vessel lifted off the ground and shot skyward. Fear flooded her eyes.

"Drones...and a handful of ships we use...for deep-space travel." She hesitated while searching for the right words. "I don't think we own anything capable of withstanding an alien armada."

Calandra's eyes settled on a point beyond the bridge. Their vessel zipped over treetops as they raced back to Cascadia. How would they preserve their lives amid this impending attack? Every record she recovered from beneath Ominade's shop four years earlier revealed Delcor's true history and character.

The chief sovereign would crush any resistance he met with brutal force. If he discovered she and Xttra had also journeyed to the Land of the Three Suns, his wrath would only worsen.

"We need a safe spot to conceal ourselves and Alexa," Calandra said, turning to Xttra. "If Delcor or his followers learn we're here..."

She trailed off before finishing the bleak thought darkening her mind. Xttra's deepening frown and worried demeanor expressed what Calandra left unspoken. Their status as feared exiles and fugitives made them a priority target. Their capture would offer Delcor a victory as satisfying as obtaining the Staff of Onrai. He would broadcast their public execution as a warning message to all Ra'ahmians who entertained thoughts of opposing him.

"Every tower in Cascadia has an underground bunker," Sam said. "We built shelters for protection from violent coastal storms. We can hide you inside one until the coast is clear."

Hiding.

One word defined much of Calandra's life in the past four years. Hiding from Delcor. First in Daraconiah. Now in an Earthian colony far from Lathos. This is the path she chose, and each step forward grew tougher than the one preceding it.

"You brought a terrible fate upon us."

Her mother's complaint crept into her mind unbidden. An image of Alyssa standing before Calandra with crossed arms skulked in her mental shadows, paired with those terse long-ago words. Palpable anger and frustration threaded through every part of her mother's aged face when Calandra last laid eyes on her.

"We were uprooted from our homes and our lives because of choices you made," Alyssa said. "You had no right to speak against our sovereign."

Calandra had turned away and approached a window offering a breathtaking panoramic view of the heart of Daracos. Rectangular towers with partially embedded spiraled columns greeted her eyes in every visible direction. Beyond those structures, sunlight sparkled across a flat lake stretching toward the Aurora Mountains hugging the eastern horizon. She gazed at the distant lake, cradled her pregnant belly, and shook her head at her mother's outburst.

"He's a tyrant." Calandra closed her eyes as she formulated her counterargument. "I could never stay silent once I learned of the awful crimes he committed. How can you expect me to ignore the truth and simply pretend he is Ahm's chosen ruler?"

"You were deceived by Confederation propaganda," her mother said. "If our sovereign truly acted against Ahm's will, Callie, then the prime oracle would have known. The Council of Oracles would have removed Delcor and anointed a new ruler over our people."

Calandra's eyes snapped open. She pivoted from the window and faced her mother again. Alyssa leaned against a padded chair facing the same window.

"You're wrong, mother." A somber tone threaded through her declaration. "He forced Valadius to flee into exile when he made a move to oppose him. And he did the same to grandfather."

Alyssa scowled and cast her eyes down at the rough gray carpet covering the dwelling floor.

"You should have learned from Janthore's example." A quiet anger bubbled in her voice, threatening to boil into a louder rage. "Sacrificing for the greater good is better than selfishly endangering your whole clan over a misguided acceptance of foolish lies."

Her mother's refusal to believe the truths Calandra learned still stung nearly four years later. Their argument faded back into a dark corner where other unpleasant memories dwelt, but the pain Alyssa's words produced lingered in her heart. Calandra's eyes settled on the cylindrical control tower growing larger on the horizon and she ran her hands through her auburn hair.

"We are stronger than him."

She turned and shot a questioning stare at Xttra. A weariness rested in his smile. Did his efforts to comfort her and reassure her faith mask creeping doubts? Calandra did not blame him if their struggle against Delcor silently wore him down after so many years.

A flurry of activity enveloped the bridge as Gulah landed his star cruiser inside the Cascadian shipyard. Their discussions became an indiscriminate blur for Calandra as she hurried to the cargo bay. Alexa's smiling face consumed her thoughts. Hiding her in a safe place, until Delcor's incoming fleet had been dispersed and destroyed, mattered more than anything else.

"Any word from Kevin?" Calandra glanced over at Xttra again as they dashed off the ramp.

Xttra drew his arca vox from his chest pouch. He activated the holoscreen and signaled Kevin. Their Earthian friend's image materialized a few seconds later.

"I was just about to call you." Kevin's eyes darted from the holoscreen to a blaring siren over his left shoulder. "We intercepted signals from the Stellar Guard fleet. They passed Colonia's moon and reached orbital range. We're all getting nervous."

"We received word at Genahm." Xttra said. "Spared no speed returning here. Is Alexa safe?"

Kevin met his gaze again and gave a vigorous nod.

"I took her over to a little community center in central Cascadia," he said. "They have an underground bunker stocked with plenty of food and water where we can ride out the storm."

"Stay where you're at," Calandra said. "Xttra and I will meet you there."

Kevin nodded.

"Godspeed," he said.

His image vanished from the holoscreen. Xttra stuck the arca vox back in his chest pouch. He took Calandra's hand into his own and gave it a gentle squeeze. They dashed toward a waiting solar rover.

"She must be so frightened," he said.

Calandra lifted her eyes skyward. She understood such feelings far too well. Unrestrained fear raced through her from head to toe. No Stellar Guard ships roaming in a low orbit were visible to the naked eye. Such a detail offered no comfort. A hidden monster was still a monster. Neither Delcor nor his minions harbored peaceful intentions. She would never deceive herself into thinking otherwise.

"I feel the same way." Calandra cast a nervous glance at Xttra. Her eyes trailed back to the solar rover ahead. "If I had the power to snap my fingers and steal Delcor's final breath from him, I would not hesitate."

"Better for one man to die than an entire planet to suffer under his tyranny."

A biting coldness tinged Xttra's words. Both understood the stakes as the Earthian vehicle's doors opened and they crawled inside. Finding and destroying the Staff of Onrai was only one step in orchestrating the end of Delcor's reign.

***

Xttra perched on the edge of his solar rover seat. His eyes darted between Calandra and the windshield. Lily and Eliah were returning to Cascadia with them to help organize a general evacuation to underground bunkers. Sam, Bo'un, and Gulah stayed at the shipyard control tower to help combat the invading fleet. Worry threaded through Calandra's face. Her emotions matched his own as Xttra listened to Lily speak with other Cascadian leaders via a smartphone. The device rested in a mounted console beside the rover's steering wheel.

"Have they responded to any transmissions?" Lily's tone betrayed an increasing anxiety. "Which radio frequencies did you try?"

"I lost count," a male voice replied. He spoke the same Earthian language as Lily, but his rolled vowels and heavy accent hinted at a different origin from her. "We're trying everything possible to avoid a direct confrontation."

"Keep us posted," Lily said. "We've arrived at the community center. I'll be in contact again after we've settled colonists inside the bunkers."

Her smartphone clicked off. The screen reverted to a background image of snow-covered mountains overlaid by the current air temperature, time, and multiple square icons—each one holding a different micro image. She cast an anxious glance back at Xttra and Calandra after parking the vehicle.

"Is their radio silence normal?" Lily asked. "If we only could reason with them—"

"You can't reason with them," Xttra said. "We can safely assume Delcor handpicked zealous Stellar Guard officers for this expedition. They will lay down their lives for him—and won't hesitate to take your lives if you obstruct his path."

"Then what do we do?" She swallowed hard and licked her lips. "There are tons of frightened people here, including me. My duty as a physician is to save lives."

"We need to stand against him," Calandra said. "Fight Delcor and the Stellar Guard to our final breath, if that's what is required of us."

Lily pressed a button on the steering wheel and all the rover's doors simultaneously opened.

"Let's hope our situation doesn't become so dire," she said. "Follow me."

Xttra, Calandra, and Eliah followed on Lily's heels to the community center. Colonists streamed toward each cylindrical tower occupying the heart of Cascadia. Some held children or small animals tight against their bodies while fleeing to assigned shelters. Their widened eyes betrayed a palpable fear sweeping through and settling over the Earthian colony like a dense fog.

Kevin greeted them at the door. Once they entered the tower's bottom level, Alexa dashed to her parents from a small play area. Seeing joy woven through her sky-blue eyes and broad smile soothed Xttra's racing heart for a moment. His little girl was safe. A relieved smile also washed over Calandra's lips. They took turns embracing Alexa before Calandra scooped her into her arms.

"How many ships have the Earthians detected in orbit?" Xttra asked, refocusing his attention on Kevin. "We need a plan to stop them from landing."

Kevin clasped his hands behind his head.

"Cascadia has a communications satellite we used to capture images of the oncoming fleet. I counted 21 ships in images sent back to the planet."

21 ships.

Xttra's throat tightened, and his heart throbbed like a hammer kept striking that exact spot. He wished to show strength and a plan. Instead, his eyes instinctively slid over to Calandra hoping she had ideas. Her mouth dropped open, and her eyes turned skyward. The same fear casting a shadow over him also swarmed her. Only a fraction of Delcor's entire fleet traveled to this system. Still, Xttra doubted the Earthians had any meaningful ability to withstand him.

Their nascent shipyard held only a dozen vessels. Many were not built for war.

"What will we do?" Every scrap of confidence fled from Calandra's voice. "We need a miracle to destroy so many scout ships."

"Erica and Sam will launch as many switchblade drones as we can spare," Lily said. "They're small enough to fit inside a backpack and possess enough explosive force to penetrate armored ground vehicles."

Xttra snapped his head toward her.

"Can they crack through an energy shell?"

"An energy shell?" she repeated.

"A protective energy field surrounding a spaceship's outer hull." Xttra formed an imaginary energy shell with his hands. "Designed to prevent projectiles and energy weapons from piercing the hull."

Lily frowned.

"I don't know. We don't usually run into that level of advanced technology on Earth."

"We'll need to send up a few short-range fighters." Xttra turned and faced Kevin. "The drones won't do much if we can't crack those energy shells first."

"That's a damn suicide mission," Kevin said. "We are seriously outmanned and outgunned."

"Our odds are worse staying on the ground," Xttra replied. "If every scout ship and ground force carrier lands, we'll be dealing with anywhere from 500 to 1,000 Stellar Guard troops. We must destroy as many ships as possible to thin their ranks."

"That's not your only problem." A new voice behind Xttra joined the conversation. "We need guards to protect all bunker entrances."

He wheeled around. Joel approached the group from an open bunker doorway. His usual relaxed demeanor had vanished, and a stoic frown graced his lips.

"A platoon of Army rangers is stationed on the outskirts of Cascadia," Joel said. "But 50 soldiers aren't a ton of manpower compared to what we might be facing. They're already stretched thin defending our colony."

Xttra turned away from the Earthian. His eyes lingered on Calandra and Alexa anew. Xttra's first instinct told him to climb inside a ship and fight the Stellar Guard directly. Peering into their faces inspired a competing instinct. Guarding his wife and daughter took priority over leading an aerial attack.

Calandra trailed her fingers through Alexa's fiery red hair. The little girl rested her head against her shoulder. A melancholy frown settled across her lips as Calandra met Xttra's eyes. Her expression offered a sign she reluctantly accepted sending him down a path she dreaded.

"Your place is in the sky," she said. "You know scout ships inside and out. No pilot here is more skilled or better qualified to stand against Delcor's fleet."

Xttra cast a worried glance over his shoulder at the corridor leading down into the bunker. He refocused his eyes on her again and shook his head.

"My place is down here with you." Xttra ran his hands through his medium brown hair. "I can't run off and leave you and Alexa vulnerable."

Kevin drew close and laid a hand on his shoulder.

"I'll keep them safe. You go and do your part."

Xttra gnawed on his lower lip to suppress new tremors from escaping and pinched his eyelids shut. So much changed in four years. Flying still brought him joy—but not this version. Every risk grew progressively more calculated because of the special place Calandra and Alexa occupied in his life. He did not fear his own mortality as much as he worried about their safety or how his absence would affect their lives.

An awful truth chewed on him like a wild animal picking clean the bones of slain prey. Defending Cascadia required pilots skilled enough to bring down multiple ships. If Earthian drones were ineffective, they had little recourse against a fleet able to decimate the colony from above. Xttra saw no realistic path to victory if that bleak scenario unfolded. Still, he vowed to make any needed sacrifice to protect the wife and child he loved.

"I'll go." His voice fell to a whisper as he opened his eyes. "If Delcor wants a battle, I'll give him one he won't soon forget."

Xttra gazed at Calandra and Alexa. He drew close and embraced them, planting a kiss on his daughter's left cheek and another one on his wife's lips.

"I'll return to you alive," he said. "You have my word."

25

Xttra's eyes trailed nervously over the helm controls in his Cassian dart. He was not accustomed to flying a dart in combat situations. Hesitation would prove deadly against a seasoned Stellar Guard crew. He glanced over at the helm holoscreen as his dart climbed past a dense cluster of billowy white clouds. Flashing red dots showed where Ra'ahmian ships orbited the Land of the Three Suns. The chief sovereign's fleet formed a tight cluster above the northern hemisphere. Seven vessels broke orbit and descended from the cluster into the upper atmosphere. The holoscreen showed a trajectory leading straight to Cascadia.

An attack was imminent.

"Our drones are tracking multiple alien ships." Nervousness gripped Sam's voice as it crackled over a small speaker in the dart's communicator. "We finally communicated with one of the pilots."

"What did they say?"

Xttra already suspected the answer before posing his question. He entertained no realistic hopes of receiving a non-hostile response from any Stellar Guard ships approaching the planet.

"Gulah translated the pilot's words," Sam said. "They ordered us to submit to our new sovereign and assist him in obtaining the Staff of Onrai."

Xttra licked his lips and straightened up in his chair.

"What did you say?"

"I told them they could kiss my ass."

Xttra stared straight ahead. A resolute smile crossed his lips. Having the Earthians on their side offered a strange reassurance. Delcor would underestimate them as a threat because of their small numbers and inferior technology. Still, the Earthians would challenge his fleet and surprise him with their wrath. Xttra relished the idea of witnessing that moment.

A prolonged beep from the dart's communicator signaled an incoming transmission. Xttra flipped a control switch. The holoscreen split into a second window and Bo'un's image floated above the helm. He sat in the pilot's chair of another Cassian dart. His light gray eyes settled on a hidden spot offscreen.

"Most of Delcor's fleet hasn't broken orbit," Bo'un said. "What are they planning?"

Xttra leveled out his dart before climbing high enough for an ionized gas envelope to form around the outer hull. The dart zipped above the clouds at a constant speed. He glanced at his map tracking every Stellar Guard vessel. Seven ships continued their descent through the upper atmosphere. The vessels broke from a linear formation, diverging as each one fanned out above the continent both colonies called home.

Xttra shrugged.

"An aerial survey?"

His eyes darted from the holoscreen back to his flight path. Why did the bulk of the fleet hold their position above the planet instead of plunging into a direct attack? It conflicted with what he recalled concerning Stellar Guard battle strategies. Even with a small fleet, Delcor owned a definite numerical and technological superiority over Cascadia and Genahm.

A proximity alarm echoed inside the dart. Xttra snapped his head back at the holoscreen. Dozens of new smaller objects shot downward from oncoming vessels and scattered in all directions.

One raced toward his position.

"Are you seeing this?" Bo'un asked.

"One is headed straight at me," Xttra said. "It's approaching visual range."

A crease formed in his brow when the object entered his line of sight. Four rectangular rods extended from a diamond shaped frame surrounding a central disc. Three flat metallic fins lined the edges of each rod from end to end. Glowing circular lights covered each rod on the side facing Xttra. His eyes widened.

Thermal compasses.

Their strategy became instantly clear. He toggled the communicator switch to Sam.

"Launch your drones at once," Xttra said. "They've released dozens of thermal compasses."

"What are thermal compasses?"

Sam sounded more bewildered than frightened at his revelation. That would change once he understood the danger those devices presented.

"They scan for signs of advanced technology," Xttra said. "The compasses scan and mark sources of power generation. Then other ships will follow and turn your entire colony to rubble."

Sam shouted hasty instructions to other Cascadian colonists inside the control tower, ordering them to track and destroy thermal compasses. Xttra quickly toggled the communicator back to Bo'un.

"They launched thermal compasses—"

"I see them." Bo'un cut him off. "I'm tracking a pair spinning toward my dart."

"You know what we need to do."

Bo'un pressed three buttons on his helm console in a numerical sequence.

"Powering my plasma cannons now."

Xttra pulled down a lever and loaded Thetian ion mines into a launch tube embedded in the belly of his dart. Typically, Cassian darts did not carry Thetian weapons. Xttra, Bo'un, and Kevin customized their darts to use ion mines for an added self-defense measure on hybrid destroying missions. Praise Ahm they had enough foresight to install these alien weapons. A few mines, paired with plasma cannons, should quickly lay waste to many thermal compasses.

"I hope we're not too late," Xttra said.

He squeezed a trigger stick connected to the launch tube twice. Two ion mines resembling metallic eggs shot from an open port. Both spiraled toward an approaching thermal compass. The first flew past its intended target. The second collided directly with the compass.

A small fireball engulfed the thermal compass and the device shattered, forming a cloud of metallic shards. Remnants spiraled downward, destined to incinerate in the atmosphere far above the ground. Two more dots vanished from the holoscreen, signaling Bo'un obliterated both compasses in his path.

Xttra cracked a relieved smile at seeing their success.

"Let's plow the field."

Bo'un grinned on the holoscreen. Xttra executed a sharp turn and his dart barreled toward a small cluster of thermal compasses descending over Cascadia. Bo'un's dart flanked his ship a short distance away. They tore through one compass after another with plasma cannons and ion mines. Their weapons ripped the devices apart like threadbare fabric.

Dots tracking thermal compasses rapidly dropped off the holoscreen. Still, they cut down only one-third of the total number. A few compasses made it past their vessels and neared scanning range over the colony. Where were the switchblade drones Lily mentioned earlier? What were the Earthians waiting for?

Xttra toggled the communicator back to Sam.

"We're running low on time here." An agitated tone wove through his words. "Bo'un and I can't destroy all these thermal compasses alone."

"We had to wait until they dropped to a lower altitude." Static interference caused Sam's voice to crackle over the communicator. "Our drones can't climb into the upper atmosphere."

"Where are your drones?"

"Lt. Gates tells me the ranger platoon just launched the first wave of switchblade drones."

Xttra glanced over at the holoscreen. Several blips rose from the outskirts of Cascadia. The drones shot skyward on a collision course with multiple thermal compasses that made it past him and Bo'un.

"Be careful where you send those drones," Xttra said. "I don't want your soldiers 'accidentally' firing on us."

His emphasis on "accidentally" instantly grabbed Sam's attention. The Earthian uttered a muffled curse under his breath.

"You have nothing to worry about," Sam told him. "The platoon has marked your spaceships. They know we're on the same side."

Insistent sharp beeps cut through the dart's interior. Another proximity alarm. Flashing lights in Xttra's peripheral vision joined the persistent noise. He snapped his head over to a compact stationary screen. It flanked his helm console opposite from his holoscreen. His face fell when he laid eyes upon the fresh sensor data.

Two scout ships were on his tail.

Xttra rolled the dart onto its side and plunged through a cluster of clouds. He pushed the ship to a hypersonic speed as he turned in a 180-degree arc. Maneuvering the dart so he faced both oncoming scout ships became his top priority.

"Keep your eyes and ears open," Xttra said, after switching his communicator back to Bo'un. "The scout ships are moving into an attack position. Two are already pursuing me."

Bo'un cast his eyes offscreen and frowned.

"Two other ships are headed my way."

Clouds obscured Xttra's dart as he positioned himself for a strike. He looked away from the holoscreen and launched a pair of ion mines. Both egg-shaped explosives spiraled forward and struck the lead scout ship. Twin fireballs enveloped the front of the energy shell protecting the outer hull. When the flames cleared, Xttra sprayed plasma cannon bolts across the hull. Blue-white shimmering ripples fanned out from each impact point.

He rolled the dart on its side again and veered away from the lead ship. Xttra understood how scout ships worked inside and out. Enduring so many direct hits in rapid succession drained the power supply feeding the lead ship's energy shell to a critical level. With patience, he could bring down both ships pursuing him quickly and painlessly.

Xttra flew in a zigzag pattern to evade plasma cannon bolts targeting his dart. He swung back to attack position and unloaded two more ion mines into the near side of the second scout ship. Their energy shell suffered the same effects as the one surrounding the lead ship. A fierce grin sprouted on Xttra's lips as his dart climbed higher to evade retaliatory fire.

A proximity alarm sounded again.

Tremors rolled from end to end in the hull. Plasma cannons struck the energy shell protecting his dart. He clenched his teeth and plunged into a descent maneuver.

Xttra scolded himself over his impatience and poor timing. His dart could endure only two or three more direct hits before the shell dissipated and left him vulnerable. Then a few blasts from a plasma cannon, or a strike from an ion torpedo, would incinerate his dart and end his life.

He peered at the stationary screen tracking airborne switchblade drones. Five drones screamed toward both pursuing scout ships. They passed through his line of sight and veered underneath his vessel. The Earthian weapons resembled a flock of metallic birds soaring with fully spread wings.

Explosions ripped through the sky.

Each drone disappeared from the tracking screen one by one. Xttra executed a sharp turn and faced the scout ships again. Those switchblade drones inflicted as much damage as he hoped.

The drone cluster targeted primary thrusters and blew apart antimatter fuel chambers upon impact, setting off chain reaction explosions engulfing each Stellar Guard vessel. Earthian weapons featured a primitive design and technological sophistication compared to weapons Lathoan engineers created. Still, they proved equally effective tearing through an enemy ship.

Both vessels were nothing more than flaming husks. They plunged toward the plateau.

He let out a relieved sigh.

"Any good news, Bo'un?"

Xttra glanced over at the split holoscreen again. Bo'un and his dart were still intact. He winced. Flickers disrupted Bo'un's image— evidence of a shockwave from plasma bolts or an ion torpedo rippling through the protective energy shell around his vessel.

"One scout ship is down," he said. "The second one spotted and destroyed the Earthian drones before they pierced its outer hull."

"I'm headed your way," Xttra replied. "We'll destroy the other ship ourselves. Do what you can to evade it until I reach your position."

Earthian drones continued to obliterate thermal compasses. Only a small fraction remained from the original batch. Xttra wanted to celebrate, but he reminded himself that destroying compasses was only a starting point to repelling an invasion. Compasses alone offered a minimal threat. The true battle still awaited in their defense of the planet.

Only three scout ships purged from 21 vessels. Four prowled the sky, drawing ever closer to Cascadia. The rest refused to break orbit. Xttra presumed the other vessels were biding their time, awaiting a command to descend and rain complete destruction upon the colony. Why had no manned Earthian or Confederation vessels launched? Did the colonists expect him and Bo'un to turn back an impending onslaught alone?

As Bo'un's dart crossed into his peripheral vision, Xttra flashed a concerned frown. Smoke billowed from a gaping hole in a primary thruster. Xttra checked his plasma cannons. They had drained to 50 percent capacity. He unleashed a wave of plasma bolts at the scout ship pursuing Bo'un. Bolts peppered the hull from the bridge to the primary thrusters.

Explosions erupted across the scout ship. Flames and smoke shot out from the bridge and engines alike. The vessel plummeted through the clouds to the plateau. Xttra pushed back at thoughts of the dead scout ship crews clawing into his mind. Former friends and allies were plunging to untimely deaths in the atmosphere of an alien planet. But they were determined to destroy him and everyone he loved. Showing mercy was no longer a possibility.

"Get out of here, Bo'un." Xttra cast a deepening frown at the holoscreen. "Flying around with one working primary thruster is too dangerous."

Bo'un shook his head.

"I'm not abandoning you up here. You can't battle all these ships by yourself."

Xttra admired his courage and loyalty. Still, Bo'un had endured far too many brushes with death. His continual sacrifices ate at Xttra's conscience. He refused to let Bo'un endure the same fate that claimed Lance back on Earth. Delcor and his minions needed to lay down their lives for their cause. Let them suffer loss and sacrifice for a change.

New beeps greeted Xttra's ears. His eyes slid over to the other holoscreen window. A second wave of ships appeared on the sensors, traveling in a skyward trajectory from the surface. Manned Earthian and Confederation ships were joining the fight.

"I won't be alone." Xttra refocused his gaze on Bo'un again. "Reinforcements are on their way. Return to Cascadia while you still can."

"How many ships?"

Xttra squinted at his map and studied each new dot.

"I'm counting five, maybe six."

"That's it?" Bo'un shot him an incredulous stare. "I still count 17 ships up here. How will they turn back Delcor's fleet with so few attack vessels?"

Xttra shrugged.

"Maybe you can help them devise new strategies once on the ground." He jabbed a finger at the holoscreen. "Now go. Hurry!"

Bo'un's image vanished. Xttra closed the empty window, toggled his communicator back to the Earthian channel, and expanded the sensor map to fill the entire holoscreen. Only a smattering of thermal compasses remained from the original cluster. Compasses rapidly dropped off sensors as new switchblade drones destroyed one after another across the skies above Cascadia.

Xttra changed his trajectory once Bo'un left. He charged toward a scout ship chasing down and destroying drones before they reached their targets. The ship's crew seemed oblivious to his approach from above their right rear flank.

That's how he wanted it.

His sensors showed seven other vessels breaking orbit and plunging into the upper atmosphere. Two nearby vessels from Cascadia made quick work of one scout ship and a few thermal compasses. The Stellar Guard's numbers diminished as the aerial battle progressed. If they brought down only a few more ships, losses incurred by the Stellar Guard would force survivors to retreat and return to Lathos. They still had a realistic chance to repel this invasion with minimal loss of life on their end.

Sudden tremors rocked Xttra's dart.

Plasma bolts.

He checked the stationary screen. His energy shell had dipped below 12 percent. Xttra broke off his pursuit and began evasive maneuvers. His dart dipped below the clouds toward the plateau.

A single scout ship rode his tail.

Xttra turned a dial and pressed two panels below it. These controlled the ion mine launch tube. He angled the tube to point backward past his primary thrusters. Xttra peered at the warning light on his stationary screen.

Depleted mines.

Only six remained.

He had to make these shots count.

Two ion mines spiraled from the launch tube and blasted the pursuing ship's energy shell in rapid succession. The impact failed to shake their close pursuit.

"I need a new strategy," he mumbled.

Xttra veered off from above the colony and drew the scout ship toward the coastline. His eyes evaluated the steep sea cliffs and towering waves crashing ashore. A simple plan formed in his mind. If he forced the enemy vessel to skim the ocean surface, a mine targeting their primary thrusters would knock the ship off course and sink his pursuers below the waves.

A new shockwave rippled through the dart.

His energy shell vanished.

Xttra gulped and increased his speed. His dart straddled the shoreline, weaving back and forth across an invisible line while he tried to dodge plasma cannon bolts. The dart's proximity alarm sounded again as the scout ship drew closer. The enemy vessel soared directly over ocean waves now.

He mashed down a button and released another ion mine. Fresh tremors rippled through his dart after firing the weapon. A different alarm sounded, long and steady. A death knell for any pilot.

He lost his primary thrusters.

A second explosion followed.

Reflected flames shimmered on the ocean's surface behind him, an uneven match between fire and turbulent water. Xttra's dart spun toward the churning surface. The enemy vessel twisted past him. His ion mine had blasted a giant hole through the bridge. Smoke and flames billowed past broken glass while the scout ship plunged toward the ocean. White churning water sprayed skyward as the vessel crashed and sank beneath ocean currents.

Xttra gripped the steering controls with both hands, trying to prevent his dart from drifting over the deeper part of the ocean. Steering failed. His vessel plummeted. He clenched his teeth and focused his energies on slowing his velocity any way possible. Xttra silently prayed for Ahm to spare his life.

He was going to crash.

The nose of his dart struck first, plowing into the shoreline. Frothy water and sand blasted through the air as the triangular ship barreled forward. It veered away from a shallow tide pool and crashed straight into oncoming waves. A towering and churning wall of water tipped the dart over like a tree battered by a ferocious wind. The force of the wave buckled the hull on one side.

Xttra sat partially suspended upside down in his pilot's chair when the dart stopped moving. A persistent throbbing squeezed his entire head with the strength of a giant hand. His vision turned grainy like white sand blanketing the nearby shore and darkness overtook his eyes after only a few excruciating seconds.

26

alandra insisted on watching Xttra's dart climb into the upper reaches of the atmosphere with her own eyes before consenting to seal herself inside an underground bunker. She silently petitioned Ahm to keep him safe, repeating her prayer until the vessel grew too small to see with the naked eye.

Calandra stared for a moment longer where the dart was last visible before turning away from the window to face Kevin.

"Now, I'm ready to go."

Kevin led her and Alexa through an open bunker doorway. Joel stayed back and sealed the door behind them. Hanging lamps with circular lights illuminated a narrow corridor. Thick stones bound with gray mortar formed walls on both sides. Calandra said nothing as she followed Kevin down the short corridor. She simply took her daughter's hand in her own, walking listlessly between her and the far wall.

They descended a short set of steps made from polished stone. A din of hushed voices greeted her ears.

"Here we are," Kevin said. "We're sharing this bunker with a few other colonists. Hope you don't mind getting cozy with temporary roommates."

Calandra's eyes trailed over the underground room. Describing this hiding place as cozy was generous.

Four hardback chairs surrounded a round table in a back corner. Shelves filled with assorted items lined the back wall. Two cots flanked opposing walls. Both large enough to hold an adult human and each stretched along more than half of the wall's length. Only three steps separated both cots from one another and from the table. Rugs woven from coarse fabric covered spots on the cement floor between the table and stone steps.

If Calandra shared this room with only Xttra and Alexa, squeezing into such a cramped spot would be bearable. Occupying the same space with 10 colonists—none of whom she recognized—made her feel trapped. Like food or gear crammed inside a shipping container ahead of a deep space flight.

How much oxygen was in the room? Air vents adorned each wall. But she grew suspicious of the Earthians' ability to feed enough breathable air into such a congested underground space.

"This room has a flawed design," Calandra said. Her elbow touched Kevin's arm. "Too many people in a cramped space. We'll run out of oxygen in a few hours."

Kevin glanced up at an air vent and back at her. He tossed up his hands and shrugged.

"I don't think that will be a problem, honestly. Besides, you're all safer underground while Stellar Guard ships clog the skies."

Calandra frowned. He was right. They faced a greater danger outside the underground room than inside. Still, such knowledge did not ease her trepidation about her current circumstances.

Alexa squeezed her hand tighter. Calandra dipped her chin, and her eyes settled on her daughter's face. A nervous fear laced through the little girl's blue eyes.

"I know it's scary, sweetheart." She tried to adopt a soothing tone amid her own nervous fear. "I'm here. I won't let anything happen to you."

"Where's Bella?" Alexa glanced at the stone steps leading out of the bunker. "I want to play with Bella."

"Your uncle Kevin gave her to Lily, so she could keep a close eye on her." Kevin jumped in before Calandra formulated an answer. "Bella's hanging out with her animal friends in a safe place."

Alexa's lips started to tremble.

"I don't like this place." Fresh tears trickled down her tiny cheeks. "I want to go home."

Calandra faced her daughter and gently clasped her other hand. She knelt before Alexa and met her longing, worried gaze.

"We need to stay here for a little bit longer," she said. "Until the bad people leave."

"No!" Alexa tried to pull her hands away. "I want to be with Bella…and Diada…and…"

Sobs choked out her words. Calandra drew her daughter closer and embraced her. She brushed back her bangs and kissed Alexa on her forehead. Calandra started to sing her favorite song to her in a gentle voice, trying to calm the terrified little girl.

"Can you keep your little brat quiet?" an irritated voice interrupted her song after one verse. "She's endangering us all with her tantrum."

Fury consumed Calandra's eyes. She cast an icy stare over her shoulder. A bald Earthian man wearing a circle beard countered with a steely glare. He rested in a chair with an outstretched right leg. A heavy brace supported his knee.

"How dare you speak ill of my child!" Her voice climbed higher as she shook with rage. "She's been torn away from her home, taken to an unfamiliar planet, and doesn't understand why. Leave her alone."

The man wearing the brace leaned forward in his chair and jabbed a finger at Calandra.

"Colonia was a perfect planet until you showed up in our solar system. We should have never sheltered you or the other aliens. Our lives would be better for it."

Calandra turned away from him and pinched her eyes shut. She held Alexa in her arms like a mother mokai sheltering new hatchlings under her wings.

"You are a heartless pile of ebutoka droppings." Calandra clenched her teeth. "I hope no child is cursed to suffer with you as a parent."

The chair slid across the hard floor behind her. She glanced back again and saw him lumbering to his feet with a deepening scowl.

"What did you call me?"

Kevin cracked a derisive grin as he stepped between the man wearing the brace and Calandra.

"She called you a steaming pile of shit. And it's a spot-on description from where I stand."

The bald Earthian lunged forward. A woman with short blonde hair and glasses reached out and grasped the back of his arm.

"Leave them alone, Chase. We don't need to be at each other's throats down here."

Chase stopped his movement toward Kevin and turned his ire to the blonde-haired woman.

"Stay out of this, Emma." His voice grew increasingly strident from anger. "I don't need you rushing to defend these aliens. How about being on my side for once?"

Chase's hand twitched at his side and the fingers hinted at curling into a fist. Emma flinched and shrank back. Calandra's eyes darted to Kevin, silently pleading to him to silence this menacing Earthian. Kevin stared at Chase's hand for a moment and shook his head.

"If you strike any woman or child in this room, I promise it won't end well for you." He drew closer to the bald Earthian. "Sit your ass down before I force you to trade your knee brace for a full-body cast."

Chase quickly cast his eyes to his left and then to his right, searching for support for his antagonistic attitude. The other colonists averted their gaze or shook their heads at him. He finally relented and sank into his chair.

"If something bad happens to me because of them, I'm coming after you." Chase shook his finger like a club at Kevin. "Then we'll see who's tougher."

Kevin answered him with a dismissive wave.

"You don't want to embarrass yourself by getting your ass beat in front of everyone. Trust me."

Calandra turned back to her daughter. She sat on the floor against the stone steps and lifted Alexa into her lap. Her tears finally subsided, and she simply rested her face against her mother's chest.

A tense silence settled inside the room. Two colonists grabbed a box from a nearby shelf and emptied small rectangular wood blocks onto the table. Calandra watched with fascination as they built a small tower using the blocks. Three blocks stacked parallel to one another formed each tower level. Blocks shifted at a right angle on alternating levels. Once completed, the two colonists took turns extracting single blocks and placing them atop the tower. They pulled each block backward at a deliberate pace, being careful not to disturb surrounding blocks.

They were playing an Earthian game. Calandra had never seen it on Lathos. The game looked simple enough to learn. Perhaps she and Alexa could play once her little girl did not feel so scared.

The wooden tower started teetering when several middle levels had only one block left. Vibrations forced the remnant to collapse in a heap. One colonist pumped their fist and let out a celebratory shout. They instantly cupped their hand to their mouth, eyes darting apologetically from face to face in the bunker.

In the silence that followed, new vibrations shook the table. Various blocks bounced along the rigid plastic surface and the tower's ruin became unrecognizable. A haphazard jumble of flat blocks. Calandra's eyes darted to the ceiling. Lights swung above their heads and flickered. She met Kevin's gaze. A concerned frown crossed his lips.

"Those sure felt like plasma cannon blasts to me." He tried to conceal his feelings as soon as her eyes fell on him. "Delcor's fleet must have reached the colony."

Xttra.

Is he safe? Did a scout ship shoot him down?

Frightened thoughts washed through her mind in a sudden deluge. Calandra dug into her chest pouch and retrieved an arca vox. The uncertainty ate at her.

An empty holoscreen materialized when she pressed the crystal activation button. Calandra punched Xttra's contact code into the circular pad, pausing before the final symbol. Distracting him amid aerial combat may prove deadly. Still, the Stellar Guard had commenced a ground assault. Indecision tore at her until Calandra could bear it no longer. She entered the final symbol. A message greeted her eyes moments later—one she hoped to not see.

Not Available.

Were they too far underground for a clear signal to reach him? Calandra hoped for that scenario. She pushed back against another unwelcome thought fighting for space inside her head. A terrible, nightmarish thought.

Xttra did not respond to her on his arca vox because he was dead.

A fresh wave of tremors rattled the underground room from ceiling to floor. Lights flickered more violently this time. Items fell off shelves. Wooden blocks spilled over the table's edge and scattered across a nearby rug.

"They're right above us."

Calandra barely heard Emma's frightened whisper above the fearsome shaking. Her heart raced while she stared at the stone steps and her eyes trailed over each one up into the corridor. The Earthians detected 21 ships approaching the planet. How many landed? Were Stellar Guard troops already infiltrating Cascadia?

She pressed a hand to her mouth to keep herself from hyperventilating. Calandra kept her other arm wrapped tightly around Alexa. Her daughter clung to her. Fabric from Calandra's long-sleeved green shirt balled up inside Alexa's trembling hands.

"Protect us Ahm," Calandra whispered, lowering her voice to conceal her desperate prayer from the colonists. "Encircle us in your loving arms."

The shaking stopped. A booming rumble greeted her ears. She clenched her teeth. Calandra recognized the sound from when Xttra landed scout ships. Primary thrusters and the main engine were powering down.

Stellar Guard troops had landed in Cascadia.

"What are we going to do?" She snapped her head toward Kevin. "If they discover people are hiding down here and recognize me…"

Calandra trailed off before completing her fearful thought. Catastrophe would unfold if one of Delcor's minions stumbled upon her hiding in this bunker. Her face and voice were known throughout Ra'ahm. A public execution awaited Calandra back on Lathos.

Kevin ran his hands through his short, curly black hair and clasped them behind his neck.

"I need to move you to a safer place outside the colony. We're trapped like rats down here. I should have game planned this damn situation better."

"What about the rest of us?"

Chase crossed his arms and stared at him with renewed intensity. Eyes belonging to other colonists also fell on Kevin and Calandra.

Their worried expressions revealed a concern that he would abandon them to perish in an unsafe place.

Kevin buried his face in his hands and sighed. He rubbed his hands over his cheeks.

"You can come with us under one condition." Kevin raised an index finger. "Don't give Calandra, Alexa, or me any shit. Anyone itching to be a pain in the ass can stay."

Silence greeted his demand. Calandra studied the colonists' faces. Their sense of peril swallowed up angry feelings over his gruff demeanor.

"We won't do anything out of line," a freckle-faced female colonist at the back of the room said. "Let's leave while we still can."

Kevin drew an eliminator from his belt. He turned and started up the stone steps.

"Stay behind me."

Calandra lifted Alexa into her arms and followed him up the steps. The 10 colonists formed a single unbroken line behind her. Their whispered concerns and protests filled the narrow corridor.

"Cut the chatter." Kevin glanced over his shoulder. "We need to stay silent and focus on our surroundings."

He approached the bunker door and turned a middle wheel functioning as both a lock and handle. Kevin popped the door open and peeked his head through the doorway. He drew back a few seconds later, turned, and nodded at the rest of the group.

"The coast is clear." He waved them forward with his eliminator. "Let's hurry."

Calandra sprinted out into the community center a few steps behind Kevin. Alexa lifted her head and looked around as the group jogged across the expansive room.

Smoke, fire, and explosions buffeted other structures beyond the main door. Kevin stopped and mumbled an angry curse. Calandra shared his dismay. Fleeing from the cylindrical tower was not an option.

"Time for Plan B," he said, facing the colonists.

"Plan B?" Emma's voice shook as her eyes darted over to the chaos unfolding beyond the tower door. "What's Plan B?"

"We'll build a barricade against the back wall," Kevin replied. "Grab tables, benches, and anything else not bolted down and bring them over to me."

The colonists dispersed to follow his orders with grim determination. New tremors shook the cylindrical tower as explosions erupted near the town hall. Alexa screamed. Calandra stumbled to the floor. She twisted awkwardly to keep from landing on top of her daughter. Alexa tumbled from her arms.

Calandra winced when she pushed off the floor with her right arm. She drew in a deep breath and pulled herself into a sitting position.

"Are you hurt, sweetheart?"

Alexa dropped her head again and refused to look up. Tears streamed down the little girl's cheeks, and she sat on the floor hugging herself. Calandra scrambled to her feet and hoisted her daughter up into her arms again.

"Miama is here." She kissed her tear-stained cheek. "Be brave my little flower."

The ground level door leading into the tower opened. Joel, Eliah, and two army rangers ran inside while firing their weapons at an unseen pursuer. Joel's eyes darted from the open bunker door to the colonists assembling the barricade.

"Why aren't you all down in the bunker?" he shouted. "Alien troops are headed this way."

"It wasn't safe," Kevin said. "If Stellar Guard troops broke through the bunker door, they would have massacred everyone down there."

Joel let out an exasperated sigh.

"Like hell it isn't safe. You just supplied hostile aliens several easy targets."

Calandra stared wide-eyed in the same direction from where Joel and the others retreated. New explosions outside the tower sounded much closer than the ones earlier. Screams and blasts from eliminators followed. Her breathing quickened and her heart raced.

They were losing the battle. Delcor's fleet threatened to overwhelm the colony.

Calandra took Alexa and ducked behind the beginning stages of a barricade. Overturned tables, chairs, and benches formed a growing makeshift wall.

"The Cascadian council will fly to pieces when they learn what you've done." Joel stabbed a finger at Kevin. "This is an unnecessary risk. If you—"

He let out a sudden violent gasp and stiffened. Joel's face contorted and smoke wafted from the middle of his back. He pivoted around in a lumbering gait. A Stellar Guard officer faced him with a drawn eliminator.

Joel raised his Earthian rifle.

Two more eliminator bolts struck his chest. The Earthian groaned and staggered forward. His weapon fell from his hands and clattered against the floor. Joel collapsed face first on the ground and turned toward Calandra as he landed. His now lifeless eyes were frozen in painful shock.

Calandra pressed a hand to her mouth to suppress a scream and covered Alexa's eyes with the other hand. Kevin backpedaled and dropped down behind a bench forming one end of the barricade. He fired his eliminator. His first shot cut down the Stellar Guard officer who killed Joel.

Four more Stellar Guard officers burst through the main door. They ducked behind tall leafy plants flanking the entrance, using them as impromptu shields. Eliah turned and fired a melter at the nearest one, striking his upper leg with an acid pellet. The Stellar Guard officer screamed and sprawled across the floor. Eliah dashed toward the barricade. Multiple eliminator bolts ripped through his neck and back in mid-sprint.

He collapsed in a bloody heap.

Both army rangers took cover behind the barricade on the opposite end from Kevin. One Stellar Guard officer lobbed a wrist-length cylinder toward the barricade. It sprayed a liquid across the bench shielding Kevin from their eliminator bolts. Flames ignited at once as the liquid splashed along the bench.

A Cassian fire shell.

Kevin jumped backward to escape the flames. A second Stellar Guard officer raised an armored sleeve and fired a razor disc.

It found its target.

Kevin cried out and clutched his ribs. Blood seeped out from between his fingers. The eliminator spilled from his hand and landed at Calandra's feet. Her eyes darted from the weapon back to her friend. Her limbs became frozen as terror settled like a dense fog over her. Kevin crawled away from the flaming barricade as other colonists screamed and scrambled for cover.

Blood oozed between the fingers on his left hand and dribbled across the floor.

"Get out of here." He let out a ragged cough. "I'll hold them off."

Calandra snatched up the eliminator as a Stellar Guard officer started forward. She raised the weapon over her head and fired haphazardly in his direction. An eliminator bolt struck his left shoulder and knocked him backward. He staggered and fell, landing on his side.

Another Stellar Guard officer hurled a round object resembling a smooth stone over the burning barricade. A sudden bright flash followed. Calandra did not avert her gaze quickly enough. Their stun pebble stripped away her vision, leaving behind only blinding whiteness.

Unseen hands ripped Alexa from her grasp. She cried and inadvertently kicked Calandra's arm as they separated her from her mother. Calandra cried out and groped blindly for her little girl. Another pair of hands clamped down on her arms and slapped metallic restraints across her wrists. Her unseen captor yanked Calandra to her feet and gave her a hard shove forward.

She pinched her eyes shut and clenched her teeth because of pain produced by the stun pebble. Calandra's heart sank. She and Alexa were now prisoners of the Stellar Guard.

27

Tressek drummed his fingers on his chair's armrest and leaned forward. His brows knit together while studying the helm holoscreen. Waiting for a command from the chief sovereign to finally break orbit inflicted havoc on his already tense nerves.

Orbital surface scans revealed small pockets of humanoid life on the planet's three major continents. Survey data showed no evidence of anything beyond primitive civilizations on two continents. A different scenario unfolded on the third one. The fleet intercepted communication signals originating from its surface. Subsequent scans found evidence of advanced technology in two embryonic settlements. One occupied a broad plateau along an expansive ocean. The other lay on a flat plain bordering a dense forest. A considerable distance separated both settlements.

Beeps greeted his ears and the fleet commander's image materialized on Tressek's helm holoscreen. An exasperated frown graced her lips.

"Is this unwelcome news, Nikaia?"

He instinctively peered up at the bridge windshield expecting to spot something amiss. Nothing greeted his eyes except other ships belonging to the fleet positioned above the Land of the Three Suns.

"We made contact with a settlement on the planet's surface," Nikaia said. "It did not go well."

"What happened?"

"I told them to submit to our chief sovereign and assist us in obtaining the Staff of Onrai."

"How did they react to your order?"

"The one who spoke to me relayed a message from one of their leaders. They said we all could kiss their ass. I'm unfamiliar with that phrase, but I assume the intended meaning is a hostile one."

Tressek leaned back in his chair and rubbed the tuft of hair springing from his chin. He recalled hearing the same expression only one time before today. A humanoid alien whom Xttra and Bo'un brought back from Earth once uttered a similar phrase before a Stellar Guard tribunal. He objected to a pointed question during the tribunal's investigation into what went wrong with Xttra's first contact expedition.

Did aliens from Earth also dwell in the Land of the Three Suns? No. Not possible.

Tressek dismissed the thought as soon as it entered his head. Such a scenario made no sense. Tressek never heard of aliens from the Aramus system mastering faster-than-light travel. But the Earthian who joined his former crewmates was a known saboteur and dissident. If he were here, other rebels or dissidents must also be here.

They were right to be concerned about seeing the smuggler's ship in this system. How many of his ilk were stationed on the planet's surface working to undermine the chief sovereign?

"Nothing left for us to do except release thermal compasses," Tressek said.

"My thoughts mirror yours," Nikaia said. "I already reported to our sovereign. He ordered us to cease further communications and move forward with our plans."

"Should we break orbit and head to the surface?"

"Wait until I give the word. We'll send out thermal compasses first."

Her image vanished from the holoscreen. Tressek frowned. An endless wait grew longer. His eyes shifted over to the tracking sensors.

Seven vessels embarked into the upper atmosphere and released clusters of thermal compasses. Energy readings from these compasses would help the fleet pinpoint advanced technological devices in use on the planet's surface. Once they culled all necessary data, another wave of scout ships would swoop down and join the first wave to neutralize all advanced weaponry capable of preventing their landing. Ground transport troops would journey to the planet's surface once both earlier waves finished their assigned tasks and secure a safe landing spot for the chief sovereign's flagship.

A simple plan.

Until they met resistance.

Sudden bright flashes illuminated the atmosphere above the planet's northern hemisphere. Tressek's eyes slid down to a stationary screen on the helm. His sensors detected two unidentified vessels. Both ships blasted thermal compasses out of the sky before the compasses entered optimal scanning range.

"We must obliterate those ships at once." Dray's eyes darted to Tressek. "They'll destroy all our compasses!"

Tressek shook his head.

"Only when our fleet commander, or our sovereign, orders us to engage enemy vessels. Not a second sooner."

Dray said nothing. She simply nodded and refocused her eyes on a holoscreen before her, with fists clenched. Tressek urged patience with his words. But angst grew inside him as seconds and minutes ticked away. Each new explosion tightened his nerves into stiffer knots. Swarms of explosive projectiles rose from the surface. They joined the two enemy vessels in blasting one thermal compass after another into burning remnants.

Tressek's eyes slid over to a holoscreen map at the navigation station. Both enemy vessels and explosive projectiles originated from the plateau settlement. Other vessels were now climbing skyward to join the first ones. They began attacking the first wave of scout ships.

Nothing came from the forest settlement.

He scratched his head as he studied the map. Why did every attacking vessel launch from one specific region? Defending the plateau with force made sense if it housed the same relic which the chief sovereign sought. Unless their attacks were a clever diversionary tactic designed to draw the fleet's attention away from the relic's actual location. A deep intuition in his bones convinced Tressek the second scenario was the correct one.

"Open a channel with the fleet commander again." He glanced over at Dray. "I have an idea where we should start our relic hunt."

Dray did not hesitate and sent the signal. Nikaia reappeared on the helm holoscreen a few moments later.

"We just ordered the second wave to descend." An annoyed tone threaded through her voice. "Be patient, Tressek. Hold your position."

"We're playing right into their hands," he said. "All the attack vessels are launching from the plateau. None have launched from the settlement near the forest."

Nikaia's eyes blinked rapidly, and her mouth dropped open. She glanced down at a stationary screen on her console and met Tressek's gaze again.

"You're right. How did I miss this?"

"I barely noticed it myself. A thought struck me while studying the sensor data. If I wanted to divert unwanted attention from a specific place, staging attacks from another place would offer an effective distraction."

A knowing smile graced Nikaia's lips.

"You think the attack vessels want to draw us away from the forest settlement?"

Tressek nodded.

"Precisely. That's what I'd do in their position."

"You have new orders," Nikaia said. "Land on the plain outside the other settlement. My vessel and another will join you."

Her image vanished from the holoscreen. Tressek flashed a nervous smile and turned toward his navigator.

"Plot a course to the forest settlement. Let's try to avoid detection along the way."

Jo'ber gave him a slight nod and pressed multiple buttons on his console.

"We'll enter an atmospheric window on the planet's dark side." He gestured at a new route tracing across the navigational holoscreen. "Our sensors show no attack vessels there, so we'll improve our odds of reaching the settlement undetected."

"Let's hope that scenario unfolds," Tressek said.

Tressek pressed a white button on the helm console to activate his manual steering controls. Two cylindrical columns topped by spheres rose from the floor. He slid his hands into molded grooves embedded atop each sphere. Their vessel broke orbit and Tressek guided the scout ship to the planet's far side where moonlight and darkness swallowed sunlight.

Staring at shadowy land masses on this side produced a surreal feeling for Tressek. Strings of lights dotted Lathos anywhere day turned to night, marking countless cities and villages. The Land of the Three Suns offered a stark contrast. Aside from solitary lights flickering in random spots, the planet's dark side showed no discernible human activity. So foreign to his experiences on Lathos or Serbius. This quiet, peaceful darkness resembled how Tressek pictured nights on ancient Lathos in his mind. Tranquil and lonely in equal measure.

The scout ship plunged through the atmosphere and skirted along tops of rolling clouds. Light from a silvery moon orbiting the planet danced across shimmering lakes stretching across broad plains.

"I've never visited a planet with only one moon." Wonder tinged Dray's voice. "It's so strange not to see two moons sharing the same sky."

Moonlight quickly receded as their scout ship crossed over to the planet's sun-facing side. Tressek glanced at the holoscreen. Their sensors still detected no ships in their vicinity aside from the two Stellar Guard companion vessels on their flanks.

His plan was working flawlessly.

Tressek angled the spheres down and forward. Their scout ship gradually dropped in altitude, matching his gentle hand movements. It dipped below rolling white clouds and soared over a dense forest covering staggered mountain slopes. Their sensors detected a vast structure nestled near a waterfall deep within the forest. Tressek's crew searched for visual signs as their ship passed over scores of treetops while traveling southeast.

He caught a fleeting glimpse of a giant waterfall. The scout ship zipped over the area too fast for Tressek to study anything in greater detail. An unusual place to build a structure with so much water and a tangle of trees and brushes of varying red hues hemming it in on three sides. A greater purpose must exist for the structure. A purpose as shrouded in mystery as the planet itself.

Their ship passed over foothills filled with shrubs and wild grasses. The expansive village they sought covered half of a broad flat plain below the foothills. Mountain streams fed a small lake bordering the south end. Stone perimeter walls surrounded the village on the other three sides. Flocks of unidentified alien animals grazed in open fields outside the village walls.

No ships launched from the settlement to greet their arrival or resist their approach. The total lack of aerial activity struck Tressek as unusual.

"It's too quiet here." Dray confirmed similar thoughts ran through her mind. "Someone in that village had to notice three scout ships approaching."

"We should land and greet the village leaders," Tressek said. "Perhaps an alien race dwells here and will aid us in carrying out our mission."

Dray arched a brow and cast a sideways glance at him.

"Is that such a wise idea?" she asked. "Staying aboard the scout ship and communicating from a safe distance is standard Stellar Guard first contact protocol. We create needless risks otherwise."

"Time is not our ally," Tressek said. "Nikaia ordered us to go to this village. We must move quickly before attack vessels from the plateau discover what's happening and track us to this spot."

He tapped on the holstered eliminator hanging off his belt against his right hip.

"Besides, I have no intentions of entering an alien village unprepared and unarmed."

Dray brushed back a blonde braid from off her left shoulder and let out a worried sigh.

"I hope you know what you're doing."

Tressek frowned. He knew exactly what he was doing. Why did she insist on questioning his decisions so often? Dray acted and spoke as though she were the master pilot rather than his assistant pilot. Her inability to trust his judgement grew increasingly annoying. He never took reckless actions and always considered his crew's safety and welfare first.

Grazing animals scattered in multiple directions as the scout ship neared a field outside the walled village. A solitary herder watching over the herd glared up at the vessel and started forward. He froze in his tracks when the landing gear touched solid ground. The herder turned after some hesitation and raced toward the village wall.

"Stay alert," Tressek said. "I don't expect a warm welcome from these aliens."

He sprang from his chair. Dray followed on his heels.

"You need to stay here and watch the ship," he said without looking back. "Stellar Guard protocols."

"If we're not following one protocol, does it matter if we ignore a few others?" she scoffed. "Besides, I want to see what they're hiding in this village."

Tressek let out a resigned sigh. He should not let Dray's request stand. Giving in would only encourage her rebellious attitude. Still, Tressek wished to avoid an argument. He paused at the door leading to the cargo bay.

"Jo'ber, Tazlam, and Zarvash will stay here and guard the ship," Tressek said, turning to face his crew. "Kelum and Dray are heading to the village with me."

He lingered in the doorway until Dray powered down non-essential systems and caught up to him.

"Happy now?" Tressek asked.

She flashed a defiant grin.

"Perfectly."

Kelum opened the lower hatch and extended a ramp from the cargo bay. Tressek's eyes trailed across the field as he hurried down the ramp with Dray and Kelum and planted his feet on the soil of the Land of the Three Suns. Crimson grasses extended from the village wall into the foothills. The other scout ships found landing spots closer to the foothills. Eight Stellar Guard officers drawn from their crews approached the village.

Nikaia marched ahead of the others. She had drawn her black hair into distinctive Orontallan half-braids since their last communication. Single half-braids adorned each side of her head and two others extended over her neck. He never knew the fleet commander hailed from Orontalla. Tressek swelled with pride to know a fellow native of his home Ra'ahmian city occupied such a respected position in Delcor's chosen fleet.

"I tried to communicate before landing," Nikaia said as her group met up with Tressek, Dray, and Kelum. "No luck. No villagers responded to our transmissions."

"Then we'll knock on their door," Tressek replied.

She extended her hand toward the village wall.

"Lead the way, master pilot."

Tressek marched to the wall with the other Stellar Guard officers fanning out on both sides of him. A simple gate in the wall opened. Two villagers stepped through and stopped in front of the open gate. They crossed their hands, pressed them against their foreheads, and bowed their heads. An ancient Ra'ahmian expression of humility or submission. Their colorful headwraps, long shirts, and pants also incorporated simple Ra'ahmian designs.

These villagers were no aliens.

"You are not from this planet," Tressek said. "Who are you? How do you know Ra'ahmian customs?"

One villager, an older man, stepped forward. He raised his eyes briefly and cast them to the ground again with equal speed.

"We are a peaceful people." His voice trembled as he spoke. "We harbor no quarrels with Ra'ahm or Lathos."

"Why are you here?" Dray jumped in before Tressek had a chance to pose a follow-up question. "How did you find this planet? The Land of the Three Suns is hidden from almost everyone on Lathos."

Tressek flashed a half-frown at his assistant pilot. He did not appreciate her trying to commandeer questioning the villagers from him. Nikaia expressed her displeasure with a disapproving grunt.

The second villager, a teenaged boy, lifted his chin and opened his eyes.

"We are humble followers of Valadius." He squinted at Dray and Tressek. "We pattern our lives after the pure peaceful teachings of Ahm, the Divine Creator."

The first villager cast a worried glance back at the boy. Tressek instantly knew what stirred his fear. The boy volunteered secret information. One word stood out more than anything else.

Valadius.

They proclaimed themselves followers of a long-dead former prime oracle.

"Valadius is dead."

A biting sharpness permeated Nikaia's voice. The fleet commander walked past Tressek and stood toe-to-toe with the first villager. She raised his chin with her hand and forced him to meet her gaze.

"What are you hiding from us? What is your true purpose for being here?"

"Nothing…I…we…only…"

He struggled to form words, his eyes widening at the fleet commander emblem on her uniform.

"Where is the Staff of Onrai?" Nikaia pointed over his shoulder past the gate. "Is it inside your village?"

The old villager swallowed hard and pressed his lips together. He waved at the boy, warning him to stay back.

"Answer me. I command the chief sovereign's fleet. You will risk incurring his wrath unless you are honest with me."

Nikaia stared at the old villager with an intensity Tressek had not yet seen from her. She probed him with her eyes, daring him to flinch. When he did not answer, she pulled her hand back from under his chin and pivoted toward her subordinate officers.

"Search their village," Nikaia said. "Do not leave a stone unturned until we uncover what they've hidden."

She pushed the first villager to the ground and then shoved the boy aside with her forearm. Tressek and the other Stellar Guard officers followed her past the two frightened villagers and marched through the open gate down a narrow street.

Villagers inside the gate fled to dwellings surrounded by neck-high walls on both sides of the street. Nikaia drew her eliminator. Two officers flanking her activated mounted pulse cannons on their shoulders. The rest brought out eliminators.

Except for Tressek.

His hand lingered above his holster as fear washing over the faces of the villagers imprinted on him. They had no need to brandish weapons. No villager offered evidence of being armed or hostile. Dray shot him a puzzled look, visually coaxing Tressek to follow orders and not draw undue attention to himself. He finally complied and pulled out his primary weapon. But he let it hang loose in his hand, barrel aimed at the ground instead of pointing forward.

"We have taken possession of this village in the name of the chief sovereign." Nikaia cast her eyes from one side of the street to the other and spoke with a loud voice. "Bring your village leaders to us at once."

Sobs from children pierced the air. Tressek trailed the cries to their source. A few small children huddled with their mothers against a wall only a few steps ahead of him. Tears coursed down their cheeks as children clung to their equally frightened parents. Mothers glanced up at passing Stellar Guard officers with pleading faces and trembling lips.

What in Ahm's name are we doing here?

Uneasiness grew inside Tressek's mind. These people had done no harm. They were peaceful worshippers of Ahm. Nikaia's extreme reaction at learning of their connection to Valadius troubled him.

The Council of Oracles supported the chief sovereign as Ra'ahm's rightful ruler since the end of the Separatist War. Critical information had been withheld from him and his crew.

They marched for two and a half peds. Nikaia ordered villagers into the street and sent Stellar Guard officers to search their dwellings. Tressek and the others scoured homes on both sides of the street as they marched but turned up no weapons or clues to the staff's location.

"Spare us and leave this village."

A voice called out to the Stellar Guard officers from a wooden tower. It overlooked the perimeter wall bordering a dwelling ahead. Tressek cast his eyes up at the tower. An aged man with a thin white beard leaned against a wooden railing under a peaked roof atop the tower. A polished wooden staff rested by his side.

"It's not possible."

Disbelief permeated Dray's voice. The same sensation gripped Tressek. Valadius stood before them, wearing a purple cloak. He was supposed to be dead. Everyone on Lathos knew what happened. Radiation from a solar flare enveloped his ship and claimed his life while on a journey to Fengar. Tragic images and words from Tressek's childhood and intense mourning that followed lingered in his memory like menacing shadows.

This was no specter speaking from the dust. Valadius stood before them alive.

"Lead us to the Staff of Onrai," Nikaia said. "Your chief sovereign has journeyed here to claim what belongs to him."

Valadius folded his arms and shook his head.

"Delcor will never obtain the staff. Ahm decreed it shall not depart from the Land of the Three Suns."

If the prime oracle's return from the dead shocked Nikaia, she hid it well. Her eyes hardened like glass, and she clenched her jaw.

"That is not your decision to make."

Nikaia turned to the two Stellar Guard officers wielding shoulder-mounted pulse cannons. They seized two villagers from the street and shoved them to their knees. Each officer produced a remote that controlled targeting and firing. Both villagers bowed their heads and tearfully begged for them not to fire.

"Where is the staff?" Nikaia asked.

"I cannot tell you." Concern flooded his eyes as Valadius stared down at her from the tower. "The staff is not mine to give."

Nikaia glimpsed at both officers and nodded. They pressed buttons on their remotes. Electromagnetic bolts surged from both cannons and slammed into the villagers. Their faces and bodies contorted in agony, and they collapsed into the dirt.

"Where is the staff?" she repeated.

Valadius buried his face in his hands. Tressek's eyes shifted back to the sprawled-out villagers. Both were motionless.

Smoke rose from their chests.

An urge to vomit crept over him. Tressek fought back against his gag reflex. They bypassed the stun setting. Nikaia executed two unarmed villagers to prove a point.

Valadius got the message.

The prime oracle lifted his head and his tear-filled eyes fixed on the fleet commander again.

"I'll give you the answers you seek. First, promise me you will spare these people."

A crooked smile appeared on Nikaia's face.

"Surrender yourself into our custody, and we'll leave this village at once," she said, crossing her arms. "These are the chief sovereign's terms. Accept your fate or stand and watch your followers perish."

Valadius bowed his head.

"I will trust in Ahm and accept your terms."

He took up his staff and climbed down from the wooden tower. Tressek wanted to rush forward and end this madness before they incurred Ahm's wrath. They made an oracle their prisoner. The prime oracle himself. Nothing good came from this action.

Valadius exited through a door embedded in the wall surrounding his dwelling. He ambled forward, leaning on his staff to support his quivering frame. Tressek's eyes trailed from one side of the street to the other. Villagers dropped to their knees with bowed heads. Tears trickled down their cheeks. The former leader of the Order of Ahm would be dragged away like a criminal.

He sacrificed himself to save their lives.

Dray gnawed on her lower lip and stared wide-eyed at Valadius as he drew closer. Her silent terror perfectly matched horrified feelings spreading through Tressek. A quiet, somber realization washed over him.

Xttra and Calandra were right all along.

28

Xttra leaned against the terrace railing and stared at the rolling farmland. He scratched his head and shot Malar an irritated frown. Finding a suitable farm outside the Daraconian village was no simple task for a new refugee. Many local villagers in Rodadan viewed Ra'ahmian exiles with endless suspicion.

One couple accused Xttra of being an agent working for the chief sovereign. They were convinced Delcor sent him to their isolated community specifically to sow chaos and breed violence. Few listened to his story and most resisted his efforts to purchase a farm for his parents. Half a dozen villagers turned Xttra down before an impoverished aged farmer finally agreed to sell him a tract of land.

Enduring such an ordeal amounted to a useless effort after seeing his father's reaction to his new farm.

Malar strolled around animal pens and checked out a pair of tall grain storage towers. He listed off one problem after another as he walked with Xttra. Malar also detailed how much time and labor correcting these issues required. His knowledge of farming did not cover as much ground as his father's expertise, but Xttra remembered enough to understand when Malar exaggerated problems for dramatic effect.

He let out an exasperated sigh when they returned to the house.

"I spared no effort in finding a suitable farm for you and mother," Xttra said. "Why do you dismiss my gift as an insult?"

He turned and faced the doorway leading out to the terrace and stared at Malar. His father rested his back against a door post and scowled at him with folded arms.

"This is not my home. It will never replace what your mother and I built with our own hands. What you forced us to leave behind in Ra'ahm."

His blunt response stung Xttra. Malar's lack of gratitude and unchecked anger was appalling.

"I did my best given the circumstances," he said. "What more do you want from me?"

Malar approached the carved fraxa wood railing and rested a hand on the top rail. He pressed his lips together and released a weary sigh.

"We had a good life. A peaceful life. Why did you bring Delcor's wrath down on our clan again?"

"Someone needed to oppose him. He's a dangerous tyrant unfit to rule Ra'ahm."

Malar answered him with a cynical laugh and shook his head. His face wore the same jaded and irritated look he showed when Xttra accidentally wrecked their new harvester as a child.

Xttra hated that look.

"You're too idealistic for your own good, my son."

"Am I?"

"Listen to me: You cannot oppose him."

"Why not?"

Malar slapped the railing.

"He has countless allies and unmatched power! I tried to end his rule when he first became sovereign. I ended up being a mere ictus bug he easily flicked away."

Xttra turned away from Malar. He closed his eyes and pressed a closed fist to his lips. His father seemed content to hide from his failures. Too many years living on a farm outside a tiny village because of paralyzing fear.

It never needed to be this way. Xttra always silently resented living a simple farm life. Not because of a distaste for farming or a lack of exciting activities near his home. Now he understood why it gnawed at his soul.

Cowardice.

"You should have fought him harder," he finally said, facing his father again.

Frustration filled Malar's eyes as he stared at Xttra. He answered him with a dismissive hand wave.

"If I had done as you suggest, you would not exist." Malar turned away and faced the Aurora Mountains clustered along the distant horizon. "Opposing him destroyed my life. Your mother and I fled from Luma to guarantee our survival. You're alive because of the difficult choices we made. Now your recklessness returns danger to our door."

He wheeled around and scrunched up his face when he laid eyes on Xttra again. Xttra's hair grew increasingly damp. Water started trickling over his eyes and nose. He brushed it from his face with his fingertips.

Xttra gasped with sudden violence. His eyes snapped open. Images of Malar and the farm evaporated into the humid salty air. Water sloshed against his partially submerged dart's outer hull and seeped through a broad crack running from top to bottom on the windshield. A pool formed inside the vessel, grazing the top of his upside-down chair.

A safety harness held Xttra against the chair. His head throbbed worse now than when his dart first crashed into the tide. Blood rushed to his skull while pinned upside down for so long until his head felt ready to burst. Xttra braced one hand against the outside edge of his chair while he fumbled for the harness release button. The harness retracted with a sudden burst. He twisted in mid-air as he plummeted from his seat and splashed down into the shallow pool forming below.

Bubbles escaped through Xttra's lips, and he pushed off from the ceiling of the dart. He swam toward the rear exit door through the deepening pool. Xttra finally popped his head above gathering water near the door and inhaled sharply.

Water pooling inside the dart shorted out the electrical system controlling the motion sensors. The exit door would no longer open on its own. Xttra unhooked his cutter from his belt. He activated the blue laser and jabbed the blade into a narrow crack between the door and the wall. Steam billowed upward and sparks flew as the laser sliced through door locks. Xttra pressed down through each lock, withdrew the blade, and switched off the laser again.

He slid the cutter back into its sheath on his belt and wedged his fingers into the crack. Xttra let out a few loud grunts and clenched his teeth while prying the door open. He pushed it backward until he shoved the door most of the way into the slot designed to house it when motion sensors were online.

"Calandra will never let me hear the end of it if she finds out I crashed," Xttra mumbled, laughing to himself.

He wiped sweat from his brow with his armored sleeve. She feared for his safety many times over the last seven years. He hated to add crashing over an alien ocean to the growing list of concerns cluttering her mind.

Xttra hoisted himself through the open doorway and climbed past the sleep quarters and cargo bins. He braced himself against the side of the inner hull and carved out an escape hole in the rear hatch with his cutter. A jagged metal block popped loose and plummeted from his wrecked ship, landing with a huge splash, and sinking into the depths. He pulled himself through the hole and plunged into choppy water buffeting the dart.

Are any colonists aware my dart was shot down?

This question plagued Xttra as he worked to pull his arms and legs through chilly ocean water. He kicked off his boots to aid his swimming and rounded the side of his wrecked vessel toward the shore. The frothy surf soon grew shallow enough to plant his feet on solid ground again. Xttra tried to charge out of the water and staggered forward. Reaching the beach, he collapsed face first. Sand grains plastered his sopping wet clothing from his shoulders down to his ankles and coated exposed skin on his hands and face.

Xttra lay sprawled out on the sand, as motionless as a stranded piece of driftwood washed ashore. Water licked his upturned heels. His body ached from head to toe. He drew heavy breaths while his eyes remained half-closed. Both boots washed onto the sand only a few steps from his legs, deposited by a crashing wave.

Good. A small but useful blessing from Ahm. I won't need to climb over jagged rocks back to the plateau in my bare feet.

Scaling cliffs overlooking the ocean became a much simpler task with some sturdy footwear—even a pair of drenched boots. Xttra pushed off his arms and rose to his knees before collapsing backward into a sitting position. His face and chest left a deep impression in the wet sand. Xttra smiled. It reminded him of a mold cast in fresh clay.

He cast his blue eyes skyward, shielding them with his forearm. The main sun hung lower on the horizon with evening approaching. No visible sign of enemy ships flying overhead. If any scout ships tracked him, they must have turned back once his dart crashed. Xttra counted their absence as fortunate. He had no safe place to hide if a ship doubled back to finish him off.

Xttra scrambled to his feet and staggered over to his soggy boots. Water dripped from his clothing, forming a dotted trail behind him. He sank again to his knees and pressed his hands against his temples, pinching his eyelids shut.

If only he had medicine on hand to dull the stabbing pain. Xttra left medicine on board the partially sunken dart but did not think he could swim in and back out again. When his aches ebbed sufficiently, he opened his eyes again and slid the boots back over his toes and heels. The footwear squished from excess water when he stood and planted both feet on the sand.

Xttra plunged his hand inside his chest pouch and drew out his arca vox. Water also leaked out from the pouch. He silently prayed the circular communication pad still functioned within normal parameters. It was engineered to be waterproof, but Xttra questioned if that remained true after swimming in a salty ocean. He pressed the crystal activation button near the bottom. An empty holoscreen materialized with a violent flicker and vanished with equal speed. Xttra pressed the button two more times. Nothing happened.

"So much for being waterproof."

Diving into ocean water rendered his arca vox useless. Xttra hurled the device to the ground with a shout and trudged toward the cliffs. No time to linger and mope about bad luck.

Delcor's fleet outnumbered Cascadian ships three to one even after he and Bo'un destroyed multiple vessels. Reaching the Earthian colony took priority over everything else. What remained of the fleet had no doubt landed on the planet's surface. Concern for his wife and child pierced his heart. He hoped Calandra and Alexa remained safely concealed in their underground bunker, undiscovered by Stellar Guard patrols. If only he could speak with Calandra to assure her that he was alive.

A whoosh overhead greeted his ears.

Xttra stopped and squinted at the sky, again shielding his eyes with his left forearm. A lone vessel passed under a cluster of white clouds. Was it Earthian or Ra'ahmian? The sheer distance between ship and beach made answering his question impossible. Xttra squinted at it anyway. The vessel suddenly rolled to its side and plunged into a downward trajectory.

Toward the beach.

Xttra's heart started racing. His eyes trailed over the cliffs for a suitable spot to hide. No crevice or cave caught his eye. What could he do? He only had an eliminator, a cutter, and two armored sleeves—one holding razor discs and the other carrying an arm saber. Small weapons offered scant protection against a spaceship bearing plasma cannons. Outer hull features grew sharper as the ship morphed from a gray metallic dot to a giant vessel. Xttra recognized the sharp triangular nose blending into rounded sides.

A scout ship headed straight for him.

His limbs stiffened and he closed his eyes.

I will survive this ordeal, he vowed. *I will reunite with Calandra and Alexa.*

Running promised no better outcome than standing his ground and waiting for the inevitable. Their weapons would cut him down long before he reached the cliffs. If Xttra ran, he died. If he stayed, he became a prisoner of the Stellar Guard.

Facing the second scenario was not markedly better than the first. Still, he understood enough about the inner workings of scout ships from his past Stellar Guard training to feel optimistic about escaping from captivity. For Calandra's sake and Alexa's sake, he chose to survive and save other battles for a different day.

Plumes of sand exploded outward around the scout ship as it landed on the beach. He dropped his arm from his forehead and raised his armored sleeve. Four or five razor discs were in the chamber. That's all he needed. Xttra was ready for a scenario where a few Stellar Guard officers came out of the ship firing.

The lower hatch opened, and a ramp extended down to the sand. Xttra steadied his index finger near the button triggering the razor disc launch mechanism. His eyes hardened into a fierce stare.

"Whoa! Hold your fire."

Sam emerged from the open hatch with hands raised. Xttra scrunched up his eyes and nose as confusion permeated his mind. How did Sam gain possession of a scout ship? He lowered his armored sleeve and let his arm fall to his side.

"We weren't sure we'd find you alive out here," Sam said. "When we discovered your spaceship crashed near the shoreline, we feared the worst."

Xttra cracked a grin.

"What can I say? I'm resilient."

Three other Earthians carrying rifles trailed Sam down the ramp. They were clad in familiar military uniforms. Xttra battled soldiers dressed in similar attire when he made first contact with Earth, only these uniforms were red instead of green. Sunglasses concealed their eyes, but side-to-side head movements revealed they surveyed the beach in both directions for signs of hidden enemy troops.

"You can thank the rangers for this spaceship." Sam pointed to the soldiers. "I never thought they could storm a Lathoan vessel and seize control of the damn thing, but they proved me wrong."

"I deserve some credit," a voice behind him said.

Xttra glanced past Sam's shoulder. Bo'un stood at the top of the ramp. His smile melted into a frown when he met Xttra's gaze.

"I returned to the colony too late to do anything." A slight tremor gripped his voice. "By the time I arrived, they were already gone."

Xttra stiffened like a stone column. A chill raced down his spine.

"What do you mean?"

He knew exactly who Bo'un referenced. Xttra wished he misheard him or Bo'un misspoke. A nightmare was unfolding. He could not wake from this one and escape.

"Your wife and daughter were abducted by the Stellar Guard." Bo'un confirmed his fears. "We don't know where they were taken."

Xttra sank to his knees. His face contorted and he unleashed an anguished shout. He struck the bottom of the ramp with both fists. Tears trickled down his cheeks.

Calandra and Alexa were Delcor's prisoners.

29

Her eyes ached long after Calandra gradually regained her vision. She squinted and pressed her right hand against her forehead while resting her elbow on her knee. Both her mouth and throat had grown drier than desert sands. Calandra smacked her lips to stimulate new saliva production.

Magnetic restraints circled her wrists. Other restraints bound her legs around her ankles. Calandra's captors confiscated her gear and her chest pouch before tossing her inside this cell. They now had possession of Marteen's parchment. Reclaiming it offered one more challenge among an avalanche of crises.

Alexa.

Calandra's green eyes widened, and she straightened up on the hard molded wood bench. Where was her little girl? Her eyes darted from wall to wall searching for evidence of Alexa's presence.

Awful images and sounds clawed their way to the surface in Calandra's memory. A flash of blinding white light. Forceful sobs as Stellar Guard officers ripped Alexa from her arms. Being led away with an eliminator pressed to her spine, not knowing if Kevin or the colonists hiding with her were still alive.

She found Alexa huddled inside a back corner cage in their cramped cell. Those awful setaworms locked up her child like a dangerous wild animal. Tightly clustered metal bars fused to the floor formed two sides and the wall formed the other two sides. A flat metal slab enclosed the top of the cage and offered negligible room for movement.

Alexa could not stand inside the cage without hunching her back. She sat with her back pressed against the wall, hugging herself. Alexa dipped her chin to her chest and sobbed.

"I'm here," Calandra called out. "I'm still with you, sweetheart."

Alexa lifted her chin. Her watery eyes settled on her mother. Despair flickered to hope in an instant.

"Miama!"

She crawled forward and tugged at the bars.

"Help me! Let me out!"

Tears welled up in Calandra's eyes. She cursed the magnetic restraints binding her limbs and restricting her movement. Alexa needed her. Their sadistic captors purposely separated mother and child. Calandra refused to let these monsters prevent her from comforting her frightened little girl.

She lurched off the wooden bench and dragged herself across the cold hard metallic floor. Calandra winced and clenched her teeth while sliding on hip and shoulder closer to the cage. Fighting immobile limbs to aid her forward movement dug hard metal edges into the flesh around her wrists and ankles. It supplied a cruel burst of pain. She bit her lip to stifle her urge to cry out.

Calandra vowed to be strong for Alexa's sake.

She stretched her arms toward the cage and pressed her fingers against the bars. Alexa wrapped her tiny hand around the four metallic fingers of Calandra's artificial hand and grasped them tight.

"I love you, my little flower," Calandra said. "Through worlds without end."

A metallic whoosh greeted her ears and added light flooded the cell. Calandra cast her eyes at a freshly open door. Two heavily armed Stellar Guard officers stepped inside the cramped cell. Their eyes drifted to the floor and swam with disdain for her.

Calandra harbored similar hostile feelings for her captors. If her limbs were free, she would attack those monsters without a second thought. What they had done to her and Alexa redefined cruelty. Their actions were blatant torture.

One Stellar Guard officer approached her and kicked Calandra in her ribs. She winced, eliciting a satisfied smile from him.

"Your sovereign demands we bring you before him," he said. "You will soon taste the fruits of your treachery."

"My treachery?" Calandra fumed. "Delcor is a tyrant. A murderer not fit to rule Ra'ahm."

Her harsh words concerning the chief sovereign invited a second hard kick against her ribs. She let out an involuntary groan.

"Spare us your lies," the second officer said. "Your poisonous face and voice afflict Ra'ahm like a plague, but we're immune to your words."

The first officer seized her arm and forcefully pulled Calandra to her feet. When she reached eye level, she spit in his face. He wiped fresh saliva off his nose and stared at his open palm. His eyes met hers again and he unleashed a forceful slap across her left cheek. Only his other hand grasping her arm prevented Calandra from falling to the floor. Unable to rub away the sting where he struck her, Calandra contorted her jaw and greeted him with a defiant stare.

"You should praise Ahm I don't simply execute you now," the first Stellar Guard officer said. "The chief sovereign will supply a fitting punishment. He will award you the traitor's fate you deserve."

Both Stellar Guard officers marched her from the cell, leaving her restraints in place. Calandra peered back over her shoulder at Alexa and fought their efforts to push her forward, squirming like an orange spinefish to free her arms from their tightening grasp.

"Don't leave her there alone," she said. "She's a little child. She's scared."

"You should have thought about that before you brought her to this planet with you."

The second officer's callous tone suggested Calandra herself created the trauma they inflicted on Alexa. Calandra ached to cram these setaworms inside the same tiny cage they reserved for her little girl. How did Xttra ever take pride in serving with the Stellar Guard? Many cruel monsters populated their ranks. All blinded from recognizing truth by their unhealthy devotion to an evil ruler whose actions served only himself. He emboldened minions to commit unspeakable crimes in his name.

Her captors marched Calandra down a dim corridor. Twin rows of rectangular running lights lined each wall, one near her hips and the other above her head. Their reduced luminosity told Calandra they imprisoned her aboard a grounded scout ship running only essential systems to conserve energy. Were they still close to Cascadia? Did any colonists survive the invasion?

Xttra.

Calandra shuddered. She encouraged him to climb into a dart and directly attack the fleet. The Stellar Guard launched a successful ground invasion. Did they shoot him down? She could do nothing for Xttra if he needed help. She had no way of knowing if the man she loved body, mind, and soul was alive or dead.

Why did I tell him to go and fight?

Remorse seized Calandra and clutched at her chest with the strength of a mokai's talons. Xttra should never have left their side. Kevin stayed on the ground to protect her and Alexa. Then a razor disc cut him down before her eyes. Surely, her Earthian friend bled out from his wound—inflicting a loss that grieved and haunted her. Would things have turned out better if Xttra were present?

"How can you sleep at night?" Calandra turned and stared down the Stellar Guard officer on her right. "You attacked and murdered innocent people. All for the sake of helping Delcor tighten his grip on power."

"Ignore the rebel," the Stellar Guard officer on her left said. "She only seeks to tie your mind in knots and lead you astray with her lies."

"It is terrible to think for yourself." Calandra distorted her voice to exaggerate his authoritative tone. "You may learn the powerful man blinds your eyes for his own benefit."

Her mockery brought forth another hard slap across her left cheek, striking almost the same spot as before. This slap stung in equal measure. Still, Calandra pressed her lips tight and strained to conceal a visible reaction to their abuse. She would never give them the satisfaction of believing they were wearing her down.

Two doors slid open at the end of the corridor and revealed a scaled-down version of Delcor's throne room from his palace in Luma. An ornate table decorated with an engraved treema rested against a wall to her right. An equally lavish senosa wood chair stood atop a square granite platform. The back wall platform rose parallel to Calandra's ankles above the surrounding floor. Sapinoa hair cushions, dyed with a golden hue, covered the chair. Narrow granite pillars rose from the platform's rear corners. An intricate mokai statue with harsh stone eyes and spread wings topped each pillar.

Such a grandiose display impressed Calandra at one time. Those days had long since passed. Seeing this room's trappings only reinforced Delcor's vileness and his oppression of Ra'ahmians while enriching himself.

A door behind the platform opened. Delcor entered the room and stepped up to the platform. Two guards trailed him. His lips formed a pompous smile when he laid eyes on her.

"Ahm has smiled on me this day," he said. "The would-be rebel who sought my destruction is bound in restraints and delivered into my hands."

Calandra refused to avert her eyes. She stared, unblinking, at his devious and sanctimonious face. Delcor thrived on intimidation and fear. Those tactics would not work on her. She resolved to make herself into a stone before him.

Immovable.

Unbreakable.

"You found favor with Ahm?" she scoffed. "You invaded a peaceful planet. Murdered countless innocent people. You do not please Ahm. You have grieved him."

The Stellar Guard officer standing on her right struck her cheek a third time.

"Kneel before your sovereign."

Calandra cast a sideways glance at him and scowled.

"I would rather die."

Delcor answered her declaration with a brief chuckle. He settled into the cushioned chair and crossed his arms. His guards flanked each side of his chair. The Stellar Guard officer on her left kicked Calandra behind her left knee. It buckled and she dropped to her knees.

She winced.

"Your wish will be granted when the time is right." His eyes sparkled with amusement. "Other pressing matters require my attention first."

"Matters such as caging my daughter like she's a dangerous animal? She's a child. Far too young to understand what is happening to her and why."

Delcor leaned forward and clucked his tongue.

"She is in a cage? That is a terrible thing. I certainly authorized no such action in my name."

His eyes shifted over to the Stellar Guard officer who forced Calandra to her knees.

"Release the child at once and bring her before me. This is not the way of Ra'ahm."

Both officers quickly marched from the room, leaving Calandra involuntarily kneeling before him. Delcor's arrogant smile melted into a stoic frown when the door slid shut again.

"I never expected to find you on this planet," he said. "You are like a sliver trapped in my hand. A nuisance. An irritation. Like a sliver, I will remove you, cast you away, and you will be forgotten."

Calandra instinctively glanced down at her restraints before her eyes settled on him again.

"You will fail. I journeyed here to the Land of the Three Suns to guarantee your failure."

Delcor pushed off his chair's armrests, rising to his feet. He stepped off the platform and approached her before stopping an arm's length away.

"My failure? I am not bound in restraints, kneeling before my sovereign and silently praying he will show me mercy."

Calandra's scowl deepened.

"You are not my sovereign. You are not worthy of such an honor."

Delcor pinched his lips together and took another step forward, staring down his nose at her. He puffed out his chest, making every effort to tower over Calandra.

"I will always be your sovereign. In life and in death."

Beeps emanated from under the platform. Delcor snapped his head toward the sound's source and waved a personal guard forward. The guard pressed a button on a short horizontal column running parallel to the chair. A long slot opened on the platform and a holoscreen materialized before the chair. A young man with slight blond curls, shorn away on the sides and back of his head, appeared on screen. His uniform bore a master pilot's insignia. Delcor passed through the image and stepped back on the platform. It flickered briefly before returning to normal.

He turned and faced the holoscreen.

"Your troops captured another valuable prisoner, my sovereign." A celebratory smile crossed the master pilot's lips. "He is now boarding your flagship. Shall I send the prisoner back to you?"

Delcor rested his hands on his hips and flashed a quizzical frown. "Who is this prisoner, Nihu?"

"He claims to be Valadius, prime oracle of Ahm."

The chief sovereign gasped. His eyes widened and lips parted like one who witnessed a dead man crawl out from a tomb before his eyes.

"Valadius is here? On this planet?" His voice grew quieter. "How is that possible?"

Nihu glanced over his shoulder at a crew member standing offscreen. He shrugged when his gaze returned to Delcor.

"I thought he died from the solar flare accident—we all did. Perhaps he's an impostor? But he does resemble an older version of Valadius—judging by images I've seen of the former prime oracle."

Delcor stared at the holoscreen, saying nothing. His eyes drifted past Nihu, and past Calandra herself, to an unseen point beyond the room. She sensed true fear rising within the chief sovereign as silent seconds multiplied into minutes. One man in the galaxy with power to end his reign still drew breaths.

"Bring him before me," Delcor said, breaking his self-imposed silence. "I will deal with this so-called prime oracle myself."

Nihu's image vanished and the holoscreen receded. Delcor turned and retreated to his chair. A smile crept across Calandra's lips.

"Your lies are unraveling," she said. "When your troops see Valadius lives, they will know you deceived an entire planet. They will no longer surrender their eyes and ears to you."

He leaned back in his chair and cast an icy stare at her. Calandra had not seen the chief sovereign act so visibly scared and frustrated since her speech inside the assembly chamber after she fled from Ra'ahm.

His angst warmed her heart.

The door to Delcor's room slid open again. The cruel Stellar Guard officers who brought her here earlier reentered with Alexa. One tugged her by the arm. The other cradled their left hand.

"This rotten child bit me," he said, grimacing, as the door closed behind him.

Calandra glared at the injured Stellar Guard officer.

"Good. I wish she could inflict worse pain on you. You deserve worse than a child's bite."

Alexa squirmed out of the other officer's grasp and hurried to her mother. Her arms encircled Calandra. She yearned to shatter her restraints and embrace her daughter with equal enthusiasm. Fresh tears brimmed in her eyes.

"I love you, miama," Alexa whispered.

"I love you so much." Calandra lowered her head to meet Alexa's eyes. "You're forever my little flower."

Delcor rose abruptly from his chair again.

"You are all witnesses to my mercy." He stretched his hand out toward Calandra. "I reunited mother and child. And the little girl is unharmed."

Calandra snapped her head upward.

"This is not a righteous act on your part. We are both still your prisoners."

The door slid open again. Three more Stellar Guard officers marched inside, surrounding Valadius. They had confiscated the old oracle's staff. Magnetic restraints circled his arms, but not his legs. One officer held Valadius by the arm as he walked gingerly toward the platform. She instantly recognized him.

Tressek.

Calandra counted it fortunate Xttra was not here to reunite with his former crew member. It would pain him to see Tressek so blindly compliant in carrying out the chief sovereign's reprehensible plans.

Delcor cast his eyes at the ceiling. He licked his lips as his gaze trailed back to the prime oracle.

"You are an ancient shell of the man you once were," he said. "Life has not favored one who fled from his people rather than honor his holy station."

His taunt masked a tangible unease from being in the prime oracle's presence. Calandra stared, unblinking, at Valadius. His advanced age made it impossible for him to stand without a slight hunch in his back. But unlike many others, Valadius met Delcor's eyes and refused to cower in his presence.

"You should never have journeyed to the Land of the Three Suns," he said. "This is a sanctuary of peace. Your presence in this hallowed place disturbs Ahm."

Delcor's scowl deepened.

"I am his humble servant. You affirmed the right to rule Ra'ahm belongs to me and my clan alone."

Valadius' expression remained steady and unafraid.

"My blessing no longer rests upon you. You already know as much. No man who secretly murders his father and slaughters innocent people to secure his throne will retain the right to rule Ahm's people."

Delcor clenched his jaw and started pacing before Valadius. Fury snuffed out fear in his eyes.

"That is not your decision to make. One decision alone rests in your hands."

"What decision do you speak of, Delcor?"

"You will reveal where the Staff of Onrai is hidden so I may claim what is rightfully mine."

Valadius closed his eyes for a moment, as though carefully considering his words. Calandra's heart raced as she grasped the situation unfolding before her eyes. She had uncovered Delcor's nefarious scheme to murder the prime oracle early in his reign. Who would stop him from completing his plan now?

"I am forbidden to lead you to the staff or reveal its location." Valadius opened his eyes again. "Ahm decreed the staff will remain undisturbed and hidden while time stands."

"Fine. I will find it myself." Delcor stopped pacing and wheeled around. "You are a fallen oracle and a traitor to Ra'ahm."

He motioned to his personal guards. They marched past Delcor and stepped off the platform. The two guards raised armored sleeves.

Arm sabers sprang forth at the wrist.

"Execute him."

Both guards lunged forward. One plunged his blade through the belly of Valadius. The other pierced his heart. The prime oracle gasped and staggered forward. Blood gushed from both wounds. Valadius collapsed on the floor and his right arm struck the platform.

His eyes fell on Calandra as the final spark of life fled from him.

Her eyes grew wide as plates, and she cried out in horror. Alexa screamed. Delcor sank back into his chair. His hardened eyes and stoic frown settled on Calandra.

"You witnessed mercy and you witnessed justice, Calandra Menankar. The power to decide rests with me alone."

"You murdered him." Her voice trembled as those words left her mouth. "You slaughtered the leader of the Order of Ahm."

"I posed a test. He failed."

Delcor reached into his robes and produced a trique. He activated the holoscreen and turned his device so the screen faced Calandra. A thermal image materialized before her, showing an ancient building standing near a giant waterfall amid a dense forest.

"No matter. Our thermal compasses found the place where we believe the Staff of Onrai lies hidden."

His frown morphed into a satisfied smile.

"You and Valadius will share the same fate," Delcor said. "But I will delay your punishment so you may witness my ultimate triumph. You will mourn your foolishness and curse your failure with your final breath."

Calandra dropped her head and refused to meet his gaze. An awful stifling gloom settled on her soul. Everything she had done to fight against Delcor made no difference. All her sacrifices, along with sacrifices from her clan and her friends, were in vain.

He had beaten her.

30

A numbness enveloped Xttra's entire body. He stared, unblinking and silent, at the opposite wall inside the confiscated scout ship's cargo bay. Xttra slumped down against a water vapor tank and refused to budge from that spot during the journey back to Cascadia. His reality brought his worst nightmare to life. Calandra and Alexa languished as prisoners of a tyrant. They were at a despotic ruler's mercy—a man driven to exact revenge against anyone he perceived as his enemy.

Xttra failed them.

In an hour when they needed his protection, he was not at their side.

"She never gave up."

Xttra gave Bo'un a cursory glance as he crouched beside the tank. His eyes slid back to the opposite wall. Grief stifled every word resting on Xttra's tongue.

"Her relentless hope and determination were inspiring," Bo'un continued. "Calandra refused to believe you were dead. For an entire year after your abduction from Fengar, she searched for you, prayed for you, and fought to bring you home."

"What good came from it for her?" Xttra closed his eyes and lowered his head. "Her life would have turned out better if she had never known me."

"Don't ever say such an awful thing again." An unexpected sharpness threaded through Bo'un's voice. "You know that isn't true. You bring a deeper purpose to one another's lives. Your shared experiences molded you into the good people you are now."

The lower hatch opened. Xttra's eyes followed the ramp extending to the ground. Bo'un's words pierced through his whole soul with an arm saber's sharpness. Everything he said was true.

Calandra and Alexa molded him into the best possible version of himself. Now they counted on Xttra to save them from a perilous situation. Giving into despair would doom his little clan. Darkness inevitably yielded to light. With Ahm's help, he would find his wife and child and bring them home again.

His eyes slid back to Bo'un.

"Calandra and Alexa are alive. I know it in my heart. I won't rest until they are safe with me."

Bo'un smiled and rose to a standing position again.

"We'll save them." He extended a firm hand and helped Xttra to his feet. "Even if mounting a rescue requires cutting through every one of Delcor's minions."

A scene of pure devastation greeted Xttra's eyes outside the scout ship. Smoldering holes scarred three cylindrical towers at the heart of Cascadia. Piles of stone and glass surrounded standing remnants of blackened walls and floors. Plasma cannons and ion torpedoes reduced many smaller dwellings to burnt shells and rubble. Only a handful of buildings escaped destruction. Lifeless bodies were strewn through scattered rubble. Xttra recognized Stellar Guard uniforms on a few bodies. Earthian clothing adorned the rest.

"Delcor's fleet broke through our defenses," Sam said. He trailed Xttra and Bo'un down the ramp. "We did our best to push them back. His ships left most of our colony in ruins."

"How many reached the ground?" Xttra asked. "16 ships were still airborne when my dart was shot down."

"Eight landed in Cascadia," Sam said. "Unfortunately, three troop transports were among those ships. We fought dozens of enemy troops street to street."

Xttra's eyes trailed across decimated structures after stepping off the ramp. No scout ships or ground troop transports crossed his vision. Only remnants of vessels shot down earlier. No visible evidence showed Stellar Guard troops held ground in the Earthian colony. Their absence further frayed his nerves rather than soothe raw emotions still churning inside him.

Where were Delcor's minions lurking?

"Where did the Stellar Guard go?" Xttra's eyes drifted back to Sam. "I see no patrols in your colony."

"We forced them to retreat."

An Earthian soldier walked past, greeting him with a grim stare.

"Our ranger platoon suffered significant casualties," the Earthian soldier continued. "But we held our ground and inflicted heavy damage. Those alien bastards fled with their tails between their legs."

Sam loudly and deliberately cleared his throat.

"Watch what you say about aliens around here, Lt. Gates. We're not all from the same planet."

Lt. Gates grunted and flashed an exasperated frown but did not press the issue.

"Sorry, sir. I'll be more sensitive to their feelings."

His flat caustic tone told Xttra the Earthian soldier had zero concern for offending or angering non-Earthian species. Sam's worries were equally irrelevant to Xttra. He did not waste a second sweating over what Earthians thought of him. Only their actions truly mattered.

A sharp stabbing pain cut through his right ankle as Xttra walked with Sam and Bo'un toward a fourth tower. Their destination suffered only minor structural damage compared to other adjacent towers. He winced with each step forward. His gait betrayed a pronounced limp.

Bo'un stopped and pivoted around when he noticed Xttra had fallen behind. His efforts to mask his pained expression from Bo'un proved unsuccessful.

"Are you injured?"

"My ankle is a little sore. Nothing serious."

Sam also stopped and wheeled around.

"Let's get you to our medical clinic. Lily can examine your ankle and get it feeling better."

Xttra's mind instantly flashed to Calandra's artificial arm. Lily was likeable and friendly by Earthian standards. But he did not trust Earthian medicine for a second after what befell Calandra.

"I'll take my chances," he said. "My ankle will feel better with movement."

"Nonsense," Sam replied. "I'm willing to bet that's a sprained ankle. Lily can slap on a wrap or brace and give you some aspirin to dull the pain while it heals."

Xttra glared and stabbed his index finger at Sam.

"If I lose my leg, there won't be a planet distant enough where you can hide from me."

Sam closed his eyes and rubbed his forehead.

"Our understanding of differences between Lathoan and Earthian physiology has improved dramatically." He opened his eyes again. "You have no reason to worry."

He turned on his heel and marched away without giving Xttra a chance to respond. Bo'un shrugged. He wrapped Xttra's arm around his shoulder and helped him take weight off the injured ankle.

They followed Sam into the cylindrical tower. A half-dozen heavily armed army rangers patrolled the ground level. He led Xttra and Bo'un past the stone-faced rangers to the tower's second level.

They entered through glass doors and Sam led them past a long desk and down a corridor holding a series of small rooms.

Lily emerged from a room near the end of the corridor. She wore a white lab coat and held a cup filled with a steaming brown liquid in one hand. Her disheveled hair and heavy eyes betrayed her own nightmarish ordeal, treating scores of casualties following the attack on Cascadia. When Lily laid eyes on Sam, a worried frown deepened on her lips.

"Please don't tell me we have more casualties. I passed the limit of what I can handle a few hours ago."

Despair filled her voice. Lily sounded as beaten and exhausted as she appeared.

"How many died?"

Somberness gripped Xttra's voice. His former hatred of Earthians ebbed as he witnessed their willingness to stand against Delcor's fleet. These colonists put their lives on the line for a noble cause. It pained him to see them also suffer at the hands of a tyrant.

"33 confirmed dead. Seven others are in critical condition—including your friend."

Xttra froze and stared at her with wide eyes.

Lily did not need to identify his friend. Kevin had been conspicuously absent since Sam and Bo'un arrived to rescue Xttra from the crashed dart. Grief over the danger Calandra and Alexa faced consumed Xttra so deeply he gave no thought to anyone else until this moment.

"Kevin?" Xttra forced himself to ask the obvious painful question. "What happened to Kevin?"

"He's in rough shape." Her voice cracked. Tears brimmed in her eyes. "Kevin is fighting to stay alive, but I don't know if he can pull through. He's lost so much blood. I'm sorry."

Xttra clasped his hands behind his head. Treating a sore ankle turned into an unimportant concern on learning of Kevin's status.

His eyes darted over to Bo'un, then Sam. Somber frowns painted their faces.

"Where is he?" he asked.

"I'll take you to him." Lily beckoned at him to draw closer. "Follow me."

She led the others to a room near the middle of the corridor. Lily pushed the door open and revealed Kevin lying motionless in a bed. Tubes burrowed under the skin on his left arm and connected to hanging bags filled with blood and other vital fluids. A beeping machine standing behind his bed tracked heart and lung function. Closed eyelids concealed unmoving eyes. A breathing tube hung out of his mouth.

"An unidentified weapon tore through his ribs and multiple organs." Lily grimaced while she recounted his injuries. "His right lung collapsed, and he lost a ton of blood. It's a miracle he survived long enough to bring him here to the clinic."

"Is he stable?" Sam asked.

"I medicated him to induce a coma several hours ago. He was moving too much and pulled out his PICC line. We are doing all we can to save him."

A helpless anger consumed Xttra. He owed an eternal debt to Kevin. His Earthian friend saved Calandra's life on two separate occasions. He sacrificed everything to help them escape from Earth. These life-threatening injuries came from guarding Calandra and Alexa. Kevin did not deserve to suffer through this ordeal following his selfless bravery.

"Don't give up." Xttra approached the bed and grasped his friend's hand. "We need you. Our lives will be empty without you."

His anger over Kevin's sacrifice burned with great intensity, spreading the flames through Xttra's mind and heart. Words meant to encourage his friend to keep fighting for his life echoed powerfully in Xttra's own ears. His admonition applied to Xttra himself just as much.

He would not give up.

Not now.

Not ever.

Calandra and Alexa were still alive. His heart grasped this hopeful thought with an iron grip and did not let go. They needed him in this dark hour. Finding his wife and daughter and saving their lives mattered more than searching for an ancient relic.

"I'm bringing them home." His eyes locked on Kevin. "Your suffering for their sake will not be in vain."

Xttra released Kevin's unresponsive hand, letting it drop to his side again. He wheeled around and faced the others. Determined expressions rested on their faces.

"You're not in this alone," Bo'un said. "Whatever it takes, we'll find them."

31

alandra stared unblinking at the floor of her cell. She rested against the end of a molded bench and faced the sealed cell door. Her ankles and her natural wrist ached from being bound. The magnetic restraints placed tremendous stress on her brittle bones. She had gone longer than a day now without taking her regimen of bone strengtheners and tried to position herself to relieve pressure on her bones.

Stress fractures were a growing concern.

Alexa slipped between Calandra's restrained arms and crawled into her lap. She pressed her head against her mother's chest. Calandra gazed down upon her daughter. She longed to free her arms and hug her little girl. She did her best to soothe Alexa's troubled soul, but words which sounded reassuring in her head rang hollow passing between her lips.

Still, Calandra persisted in her efforts to comfort her daughter.

"Diada will find us soon," she said. "He'll charge through that door and lead us to safety. Trust in Ahm. He's watching over us."

Alexa lifted her chin. Her sad blue eyes settled on Calandra and her bottom lip jutted out.

"Will the mean men hurt Diada?"

The same question troubled Calandra. One among a countless swarm bombarding her mind and weighing down her soul. She had to assure Alexa that Ahm would keep Xttra safe. But Calandra struggled to believe such a thing herself.

Delcor's guards cut down Valadius before their eyes. If a man once chosen as prime oracle met such a fate, how would Xttra succeed in evading the chief sovereign's wrath? Had Ahm forsaken them all?

"He is safe," she finally said. "And when he rescues us, we'll all be safe together."

Calandra dipped her chin and kissed Alexa's forehead. She pinched her eyes shut and her shoulders drooped. Sleep eluded Calandra since the Stellar Guard officers thrust her into this cell. Exhaustion gripped her from head to toe, but she obtained no relief. Endless worried thoughts drove away slumber.

A whoosh signaled her cell door opening. Calandra cracked open her eyelids as the door sealed again. An unexpected visitor stood before her.

Tressek.

"What are you doing here?" She greeted him with an icy stare. "I suppose your turn to interrogate and torture me has arrived."

He frowned. His eyes darted wall to wall and trailed across the ceiling before settling on Calandra again.

"I see no active image sensors. I don't think they're watching us."

Calandra's eyes narrowed and her brows knit together. She instinctively shifted her arms, trying to cover Alexa like a mother dochu guarding a nest housing her hatchlings.

"What are you planning to do?"

Tressek drew a stout metallic tube from a pouch on his belt and pressed a button. A thick tine with intermittent grooves sprang out from one end. He crouched down and inserted the tine into a pinhole opening in her ankle restraints. A light above the opening shifted from blue to red. The magnetic locks disengaged, and her restraints clattered to the floor with a light thud.

Calandra stared at him wide-eyed.

"I came here to rescue you," he said. "We have a route off the chief sovereign's flagship, but little time remains before they grow aware of our plan."

"Your plan?"

"My crew is helping me. We're all traveling the same path together."

The door slid open with a whoosh again. Tressek straightened up and glanced over his shoulder. A blonde-haired woman wearing Abidosian braids peeked inside the doorway. An assistant pilot's insignia adorned her uniform. Calandra had seen her once before. She was one of three Stellar Guard officers who brought Valadius before the chief sovereign.

"Is our path clear?" he asked.

The assistant pilot cast a sideways glance down the corridor and nodded.

"I mapped out a path to reach the cargo bay unseen. I disengaged image sensors along our path and on the other side of the ship. Bringing those sensors back online will divert attention away from us."

"And the aerorover?"

"I had to get creative to make space for four people. But it's fully geared and ready to fly back to our ship."

"Excellent work, Dray." Tressek smiled and gave her an appreciative nod. "Grab those magnetic restraints on the floor. We may need them later."

Dray scooped up the empty ankle restraints. Calandra glanced down at the other restraints still circling her wrists and back up at Tressek.

"What about my wrists?"

Tressek shook his head.

"Not yet. This will only work if they believe you're our prisoner. Don't worry. You'll be free of those restraints soon enough."

Calandra's eyes drifted down to her wrist restraints again. She wanted to believe him, but he never shared his motivation for freeing her and Alexa. Why were he and his crew risking their Stellar Guard careers and their lives to defy Delcor? It aroused her suspicions that a different sinister plan lurked in the shadows.

"Why are you helping us escape?" she finally asked. "I'm grateful for what you're doing, but you're choosing to aid an enemy of the chief sovereign. You know what your actions entail for you if we're caught."

"He robbed a prime oracle of his life." Tressek's tone turned somber. "No true servant of Ahm would dare commit such an unspeakable crime. Delcor does not deserve our allegiance."

Dray cast her eyes at the floor and nodded.

"He must be stopped." Her voice descended to a near whisper. "We will do our part to end his rule."

Hope spread through Calandra anew upon learning what sparked their change of heart. Delcor had become his own worst enemy. Ruthlessly executing Valadius turned the hearts of an entire scout ship crew against him. If one crew opened their eyes, surely others would follow the same path?

She roused Alexa from a light slumber and encouraged the little girl to crawl off her lap. Tressek and Dray both extended a hand and helped Calandra to her feet. Then, Dray hoisted Alexa and planted her back in Calandra's arms.

"Let's hurry," Tressek said.

He and Dray flanked each side of Calandra. They attacked the corridor with a deliberate pace. She resisted the urge to let her eyes wander while navigating the corridor. Calandra forced herself to stare straight ahead and match their strides. Her nerves tightened as distance between the four and her cell increased.

"Where are you taking those prisoners?" a gruff voice called out behind her.

They stopped in their tracks. Tressek and Dray both wheeled around and faced a Stellar Guard officer. Calandra kept facing forward. She gnawed on her lower lip. Their plan was not working. One Stellar Guard officer had already become suspicious. How long before others joined him and tried to detain them on Delcor's flagship?

"The chief sovereign assigned my crew to prepare the adult prisoner for transport," Tressek said. "She will join the trek to the forest sanctuary."

Silence greeted his explanation. Calandra took deliberate calming breaths. Panicked thoughts pelted her like hard rain, soaking every inch of her mind.

He doesn't believe Tressek. What will he do to us?

She glanced down at Alexa. Her daughter partially hid against Calandra's shoulder, peeking one eye out at the Stellar Guard officer standing behind them.

"He wants her to join the trek?" the gruff voice asked.

"That's correct," Dray said. "We must hurry. The chief sovereign wants to boost our search efforts before the colonists regroup."

"I will delay you no further," he replied. "May Ahm smile upon you."

Calandra listened intently, tracing his footsteps until the corridor fell silent again. Tressek and Dray turned and signaled a restart in their march to the cargo bay.

"I'm surprised he believed you," Calandra said. "I was convinced he'd detain us to verify your story."

"I had the same worries," Dray said. "And I'm not certain we've successfully crossed that last bridge yet."

Every second they spent navigating Delcor's flagship only intensified the tenseness gripping Calandra's nerves. Her anxiety stopped her from speaking. Calandra fully expected a restored image sensor to capture their escape, leading Stellar Guard officers to flood the corridor to prevent them from reaching the aerorover.

To her relief, no one else impeded their entry into the cargo bay. A systems officer stood inside the bay, checking power conduits connecting to the bridge. She gave Calandra a cursory glance and quickly refocused her gaze on an exposed conduit.

The systems officer wheeled around again with equal speed and stared straight at Calandra. A suspicious frown washed over her lips.

Her eyes settled on Tressek.

"Where are you taking those prisoners?"

Dray stepped in and repeated Tressek's earlier explanation to the other Stellar Guard officer. The systems officer tilted her head at the assistant pilot and narrowed her eyes.

"I better verify this with Nihu. Don't go anywhere."

She turned on her heel and marched over to an audio terminal linked to the ship's internal communicator. Dray shot a worried frown at Tressek. He clenched his teeth and pulled out his cutter. Tressek tiptoed forward and turned the polished stone handle away from his body. He raised his arm to ear level and struck the back of the systems officer's head in one fluid stroke.

She collapsed in a heap on the cargo bay floor.

Calandra's eyes followed the woman's body as it struck the ground. She cast an alarmed look at Tressek.

"Is she dead?"

He shrugged and stuck the cutter back on his belt.

"I don't think I struck her that hard." Uncertainty threaded through his voice. "She'll probably wake up from this with only a bad headache."

Dray opened the aerorover's passenger door. She helped Calandra and Alexa crawl into the rear cargo space behind the bucket seats. Alexa fit fine. Calandra had to draw her knees toward her breasts and duck her head to fit into the cramped space.

Tressek's assistant pilot helped make such a tight squeeze less frustrating by finally removing the wrist restraints. Calandra turned her wrists and stretched out all her fingers, both natural and artificial, once free from the restraints.

Tressek dragged the unmoving systems officer back over to the power conduits and positioned her body to appear as though she accidentally struck her head while at her post. He dashed to the aerorover, climbed in the driver's seat, and pressed the engine start button.

"I wish we had enough time to search for a guide I obtained," Calandra said. "I tucked it in my chest pouch before Delcor's fleet invaded. It holds valuable knowledge regarding the sanctuary housing the Staff of Onrai."

Dray dug into her own chest pouch and extracted a reddish-brown parchment.

"Are you talking about this parchment?"

Calandra gasped.

"How did you find it?"

Tressek smiled and glanced over his shoulder.

"The chief sovereign ordered us to use the parchment to guide our aerial search for the sanctuary. We didn't have a chance to return it before we decided to follow Delcor no longer."

He turned and faced the open lower hatch again. Tressek threw a control knob forward on the main console between the bucket seats and extended both wings. He drew the knob backward. All four magnetic wheels retracted against the aerorover's belly, and the vehicle lifted off the cargo bay floor. Tressek pushed the knob forward a second time and the aerorover shot through the open hatch.

A genuine smile crossed Calandra's lips for the first time since her abduction from Cascadia. Tressek and Dray breathed renewed life into her fight against Delcor with their courageous actions.

32

An urge to repeatedly slam his fist against the wall simmered inside Xttra. He wanted to scream at Erica until his voice grew hoarse. The Cascadian governor exposed herself as a complete fool. Her reaction to his detailed search and rescue plan showed a callous disregard for the lives of his wife and daughter.

Lily did not hold back in expressing her outrage.

"You're condemning a mother and her child to an untimely death." Her voice increased in pitch while staring down her fellow Earthian. "How do you expect us to rescue them without providing any military support?"

Erica crossed her arms and pressed her lips into a weary frown.

"I'm considering a bigger picture here," she said. "Cascadia lies in ruins. We suffered a tremendous loss of life. The remnants of our ranger platoon must stay here and defend our colony in case fresh waves of spaceships arrive to attack us."

Xttra leaned over an orange hardback chair, gripping it forcefully until his knuckles turned white. Rescuing Calandra and Alexa by himself would be virtually impossible. His restraint burst like a dam after an earthquake. He straightened himself, raised the chair, and hurled it across the room. The chair crashed against the opposite wall, plastic cracking on impact.

Erica flinched.

"Are only Earthian lives valuable to you?" he shouted. "Delcor plans to execute my wife and daughter. You're wasting time and jeopardizing their lives with your stubbornness."

Shallow rapid breaths followed his outburst. Fire filled Xttra's eyes. Did this woman have a child? Would she embrace the same indifferent attitude if her own child faced this situation?

"We already tried to help you once." Erica's tone grew icy. "Look where it got us. Cascadia does not have enough resources left to stage a full-scale counterattack. There's nothing more I can do."

Sam pressed his palm to his forehead and stared at her in disbelief. "Nothing more you can do? There's so much more we can do."

"Look around us, Sam." She thrust her right hand at the nearest window. Destroyed buildings cluttered the landscape outside all the way to the colony's border. "An entire squad of rangers perished defending the colony. Only two squads are left from the platoon. They may not withstand another attack. Sending one with you will leave us hopelessly vulnerable if the hostile aliens return."

"If this alien dictator finds the weapon he's seeking, it won't matter if 24 soldiers or 24,000 are guarding Cascadia," he said. "He will gain an upper hand forever. Checkmate. Game. Set. Match."

Erica rolled her eyes.

"I'm in no mood to be spoon-fed extraterrestrial folklore. It's superstitious nonsense. You want to believe that shit? Be my guest. I refuse to stake the lives of our colonists on fairy tales any longer!"

"Do you think he'll stop with his home planet?" Lily asked. "If that tyrant can obtain a means of increasing his grip on power, what will stop him from conquering Colonia? Or Earth?"

Erica crossed her arms and shook her head.

"If he wants a fight, we'll give him a fight—when we're ready to fight."

Xttra marched to the door leading out into the Cascadian shipyard. He stopped and turned on his heel, facing Erica again.

"I don't care if the staff exists or not," he said. "I do care about protecting Calandra and Alexa. They will never truly be safe while Delcor lives and reigns. I'll find them again, and I'll destroy him. And I won't let you stand in my way."

Xttra wheeled around and marched off without waiting for a response. He did not want to hear another word from that fool's mouth. The control tower door slid open and sealed shut behind him again. His shoulders slumped. He needed a new search and rescue plan that did not rely on Earthian military aid.

One persistent thought lingered with Xttra for several hours while he formulated a new plan for rescuing his wife and daughter. Delcor redefined the meaning of vindictive. Calandra once shared with Xttra how she learned the chief sovereign planned to secretly murder everyone who returned from Earth in retaliation for Doni's death. His disregard for justice and thirst for vengeance, ironically, opened their eyes and inspired their opposition to his rule.

Xttra frowned at a few distant broken dwellings beyond the window and shifted in the cushioned bench seat he occupied. He counted on the same vindictive spirit driving Delcor now.

The chief sovereign would love nothing more than to humiliate him and Calandra with his ultimate victory. A sudden execution far from Lathos held no pleasure compared to the bliss of forcing the couple to witness him obtaining the Staff of Onrai. It amounted to a simple equation for Delcor, Xttra reasoned. They weakened his standing in Ra'ahm. He would be satisfied with nothing except making them suffer.

Delcor's arrogance would be his undoing. Xttra uncovered the final piece completing the puzzle. Only one place stood out as a focal point for his search.

"I know where they are."

He sprang to his feet from the bench inside Lily's dwelling, casting his eyes around to see who was listening. Xttra gathered in her home earlier with other trustworthy individuals willing to aid his search and rescue mission. Sam and Lily simultaneously lifted their heads from laptops on a nearby table.

Their eyes settled on him.

"Where?" Sam asked.

"Delcor wants me and Calandra to taste bitter defeat as much as he wants to obtain the staff," Xttra said. "Since she's his prisoner, he will force her to witness him acquire the relic."

Lily rose from her chair. Her eyes widened with excitement. A hopeful smile graced her lips.

"So, we'll find your family and find the staff in the same place," she said.

"Precisely," Xttra replied.

Bo'un rose from a couch nestled against a wall on the opposite side of the room.

"Do we know which ruins or ancient structures house the staff?" he asked.

Xttra approached Sam's laptop and turned the screen toward himself.

"My guess is the cliffside structure in the forest bordering Genahm," he said. "I never had a chance to study the guide Marteen gave us, but it makes sense Valadius settled near the staff given his insistence on dissuading anyone from searching for it."

"Where's that parchment?" Sam asked. "We should take a closer look at what it says."

Xttra frowned. He remembered where he last saw the parchment. Calandra rolled it up and stuck it inside her chest pouch before Delcor's fleet attacked Cascadia.

The guide would offer no help now.

"Calandra has the parchment." A newly deflated tone drained the energy from his voice. "I can't imagine it's in her possession any longer."

"We'll have to get along without it," Lily said.

Bo'un shook his head.

"Marteen said the guide shows how to navigate the sanctuary's internal defenses," he said. "If we go in there blind, we risk serious injuries...or worse."

"What do we do?" she asked.

"We'll find Calandra and Alexa first." Xttra clapped his hands together. "Everything else comes second."

Loud, panicked barks greeted his clap. Lily snapped her head toward a round pillow on the floor beside the couch. A calf-high animal with a short square muzzle, black nose, and tan floppy ears stood on the pillow and stared at Xttra. A distinct nervousness filled the animal's deep brown eyes.

"Calm down, Scout." Lily crossed the room and stooped down in front of the pillow. She scratched Scout on the head. "You're safe now, boy."

Xttra returned the animal's stare with a wary look. He ignored Scout while the animal slept. Now he wondered if Lily's pet intended to attack him.

"Don't worry about him." She glanced back at Xttra. "Scout is a sweet dog. He's gentle with people—like all beagles. The poor little guy is a little traumatized after suffering through loud bombs and persistent laser fire."

Xttra sympathized with her beagle's anxiety. Bella also appeared frightened when he checked on her earlier. Similar feelings bombarded him. Xttra waited for the other shoe to drop, as Kevin often said, expecting their situation to take an unexpected turn down a worse path.

"Beagles are scent hounds, right?" Sam asked. "We should bring Scout with us. He can help track Calandra and Alexa."

Lily straightened up again and pursed her lips.

"Scout gets distracted when he's out running around. Even if he picks up their scent, he'll ignore it once he discovers a more fascinating aroma."

"Let's take him along as a watchdog," Sam said. "He can alert us if Delcor's goons try to get the drop on us in the forest."

Xttra glanced at the dog again and smiled.

"We don't have this animal species on Lathos. This may work to our advantage. They wouldn't know what to make of him."

Lily knelt in front of Scout and rubbed his ears.

"You ready to go outside, boy? We're going for a walk in the forest."

He jumped off the pillow and started panting. Xttra welcomed any help in their search—even if that aid took the form of a beagle.

33

Xttra circled above the forest near Genahm in an aerorover. His cautious approach along the tree line turned out to be unnecessary. He found no sign of Stellar Guard aerial patrols. Xttra witnessed considerable activity on the flat plain Genahm occupied. Remnants of Delcor's fleet besieged the peaceful village. Troops ransacked homes inside the walls, forcing panicked villagers to assemble with hands behind their heads in narrow streets. A sick feeling gripped his belly as he surveyed the scene playing out below him. The chief sovereign never ignored an opportunity to impose his tyranny on peaceful, defenseless people.

"I count eight ships near Genahm." Xttra squinted at sensor tracking data on his console screen. "Five scout ships, two ground force carriers, and Delcor's flagship. They're using the plain as a staging area."

He took solace at seeing visual evidence of a reduced fleet. The Earthians did an admirable job of defending Cascadia. They destroyed or captured half of the remaining Stellar Guard vessels after his dart crashed. He would need to channel that fighting spirit on his own. Erica's refusal to send a full squad of rangers left his search party severely outnumbered compared to surviving Stellar Guard troops under Delcor's command.

"Do you see a path we can use to reach the sanctuary undetected?" Sam stared out a side window, eyes fixed on the ground. "I can't tell from this height which parts of the forest are occupied."

Xttra lacked a clear answer to his question. Tracking Stellar Guard troops from this altitude presented major obstacles. Dense clusters of crimson and scarlet treetops obscured natural trails and the aerorover's engine interfered with handheld thermal sensors. They would need to rely on thermal trackers on the ground—and Lily's dog—to illuminate a route through the alien forest.

Fortunately, Sam negotiated with Lt. Gates to permit their use of the captured scout ship. Gulah offered to fly the search party out in his star cruiser. Xttra struck down his well-meaning suggestion. A Confederation vessel would never blend in sufficiently among Ra'ahmian ships to land near the forest without raising alarm.

Flying in with the scout ship and its complement of aerorovers alleviated that problem.

"Our best strategy is to land in a meadow or clearing above the waterfall," Xttra said. "We'll climb down the cliff and enter the sanctuary from above."

"Won't they see us coming from a mile away?" Sam's eyes filled with concern as he refocused his gaze on Xttra. "We're making ourselves easy targets from that height."

Xttra shook his head.

"Delcor's troops are entering the forest from the foothills. We'll have the higher ground. They'll be easier targets for us if we hold our advantage. Bo'un and I can easily cut down attackers."

Sam licked his lips and gave him a wary nod.

"I'll take your word for it."

Xttra activated his replacement arca vox and instructed Sam on how to use the circular communication pad. Once the Earthian grasped how each crystal button functioned, he had him send messages to Bo'un and Gulah relaying the plan. They selected a rendezvous point four peds east from the waterfall. Xttra chose a pristine meadow he spotted on his first sweep over the alien forest. Scores of trees surrounded the meadow on three sides. A broad river feeding the waterfall formed the fourth border. It offered a perfect starting point for approaching the waterfall undetected.

Xttra flew his aerorover above the river, tracing the churning water winding around pockets of crimson trees and grass shrouded rocks. An unsettling feeling seized him. The whole forest exuded a peaceful and beautiful vibe from above. In some respects, this place mirrored the mountains where he landed during his first journey to Earth. Xttra prayed those eerie similarities were not an omen foretelling a similar nightmare awaiting him here.

Beeps from his arca vox grabbed Xttra's attention. He cast a quick glance over at Sam.

"Bring up the holoscreen."

Sam's hand hovered over the arca vox while he studied the buttons again. The Earthian struggled to retain Xttra's earlier instructions, glancing up at him in a silent request for help.

"The bottom button." An impatient tone threaded through Xttra's voice. "Press the bottom button."

Sam finally activated the arca vox. Bo'un's image materialized on the holoscreen. A concerned frown slipped through his steadfast gaze.

"Landing in this meadow may not be a wise idea," Bo'un said. "It's not as undisturbed as you thought."

Xttra's eyes shot from the holoscreen back to the forest. Another aerorover sat in the meadow, parked near a small brook flowing out from a pocket of trees toward the river. He glanced back and shot Bo'un a puzzled look.

"That isn't Gulah's aerorover," Bo'un said. "I don't know who's down in the meadow. I'm not certain I want to find out."

Xttra wanted to find out.

What was a lone aerorover doing in a secluded meadow so far removed from Delcor's fleet? Sending unprotected Stellar Guard officers out this way made no sense from a strategic perspective.

He circled the meadow a second time. Both doors opened and a pair of Stellar Guard officers exited from the parked vehicle. The two quickly faced the aerorover again and helped two others climb out from the rear cargo space. One was far too small to be an adult.

Alexa.

Xttra let out a gasp. He found them. His wife and child were in the meadow.

Fear quickly swallowed joy like a hungry animal devouring a fresh meal. Why were Calandra and Alexa brought out here? Did these Stellar Guard officers intend to carry out a quiet execution? If this was their intention, it only increased the urgency to mount a rescue.

"Are you seeing this?" Xttra blurted out his question. "Alexa and Calandra are outside that aerorover. We need to land now!"

Bo'un glanced away from his holoscreen. A similar desperate mixture of happiness and concern filled his eyes when he returned his gaze to Xttra.

"Lead the way," he said.

Xttra guided his aerorover down to the meadow. Everyone outside the parked aerorover ducked behind the vehicle as his magnetic wheels touched down amid spongy red grass. Xttra exited his aerorover with eliminator in hand. He gave the bolt chamber a cursory glance. It held a full charge of blue laser bolts.

A Stellar Guard officer with Abidosian braids peeked over the other aerorover's hood. Her intense blue eyes settled on Xttra. She crouched behind a front magnetic wheel, ready to spring out like a treema and attack.

The passenger side door on his aerorover opened. Xttra turned on his heel and waved at Sam, motioning for him to stay back.

"This doesn't need to turn violent." He faced the partially concealed Stellar Guard officer again. "Return my wife and child unharmed to me and I'll leave in peace. You have my word."

"Xttra?"

A hopeful lilt threaded through the voice speaking his name. His heart soared when Calandra rose to her feet from behind the parked aerorover.

"Calandra!" he shouted.

She raced around the end of the vehicle. Xttra jammed the eliminator back in its holster and sprinted forward. He swept his wife up in an embrace and spun her around. Xttra set her down again. His lips parted and pressed against hers in a warm passionate kiss. His hand trailed through Calandra's disheveled auburn locks.

Xttra pulled away from her lips a moment later and glanced over her shoulder.

"Where's Alexa?"

The little girl sprang out from behind the aerorover upon hearing her name. Xttra and Calandra invited her into their embrace. He planted a kiss on Alexa's cheek.

"I'm so happy you're both safe," Xttra said. "When I learned you were captured, I almost lost hope."

"I clung to the thought of you rescuing us to endure this ordeal," Calandra said. "It carried me and Alexa through dark moments."

Both Stellar Guard officers circled around the aerorover and cautiously approached the happy little clan. Xttra did a double take, instant recognition filling his eyes.

"Tressek?"

His old systems officer stood before him. Tressek's uniform now bore a master pilot's insignia. But he still owned the same cheerful expression and recognizable tuft of hair sprouting from his chin.

"How did you find us?" Tressek asked. "We came to meet up with my crew after Dray and I rescued your wife and child. We never expected to run across you in such a secluded place."

"You rescued Calandra and Alexa?"

Xttra walked forward and wrapped his former crew member in a hearty embrace.

"Thank you. I'll always be in your debt."

Plumes of grass and leaves rose from the ground in Xttra's peripheral vision. He turned as the captured scout ship's landing gear touched solid ground. Gulah had parked his aerorover within walking distance of Xttra's aerorover. The scout ship touched down further up along the same small brook where Tressek's aerorover landed.

Lily's dog Scout bounded down the ramp before it fully extended into the grass and jumped off the end. The beagle let out an enthusiastic bark, dropped his nose to the ground, and started investigating new scents. Lily followed on Scout's heels, clutching a long leather strap in her left hand. She caught up to the beagle and connected the strap to a collar circling the dog's neck.

Bo'un emerged from the cargo bay last. A broad smile washed over his lips when he spotted Calandra and Alexa. He sprinted across the meadow and embraced them both.

"It's a relief to see you safe again," he said. "We all worried so deeply about you and little Alexa."

Xttra's smile dropped off his face, yielding to a concerned frown. He turned and faced Tressek again.

"Did you say you're waiting for the rest of your crew to come to this meadow?"

"I sent word for them to bring my scout ship here."

"Is Delcor aware you betrayed him?"

His former systems officer flinched at Xttra's second question. Tressek averted his eyes from him, staring at rolling clouds.

"I took great care to conceal our plans from his loyalists. Only my crew knows."

Xttra exchanged worried glances with Calandra and Bo'un. They dealt with treacherous crew members before. Tressek's escape seemed too effortless.

"We better get this show on the road."

Sam's words cut through a growing tense silence. He finally joined the small grouping near Tressek's aerorover after taking a moment to gaze upon the meadow and capture images on his smartphone.

"Now that we've found Calandra and Alexa," Sam said. "Let's go back to Cascadia and plan our next step."

Xttra studied the scout ship as he mulled over Sam's suggestion. It made sense for him to infiltrate the sanctuary with Bo'un and Tressek. Gulah could fly the others back to the colony on the scout ship. He wanted to keep Calandra and Alexa safe.

"I think you're right, Sam," he said. "I will return to the forest with Bo'un and Tressek, and we'll infiltrate the sanctuary without putting anyone else at risk."

Dray marched up to him and crossed her arms. Her eyes hardened into a fierce stare directed at Xttra.

"I'm equally capable of finding this relic. You can't shut me out from the search. I won't let you shut me out."

He sighed.

"Look, I'm not trying to…"

Xttra trailed off and froze. His eyes shot over to a cluster of trees west of the meadow. A second scout ship flew over the treetops. It descended toward the meadow.

"Here's my crew now," Tressek said. "We'll figure out who goes where once they land."

The newly arriving ship landed facing the other scout ship. Tressek turned and started walking toward the vessel. Landing gear extended and the lower hatch door opened. Xttra's right hand instinctively dropped to his side and rested on his eliminator.

"We need to leave this meadow at once." Xttra snapped his head toward Bo'un. "Get everyone back on our scout ship."

Bo'un turned and sprinted in that direction. Calandra shot Xttra a concerned look.

"What are you doing?"

His eyes slid over to her, horror enveloping each one.

"This is a trap. I feel it in my bones."

"Nonsense." Tressek waved dismissively without looking back at Xttra. "I trust my crew completely. You should do the same."

The lower hatch door opened. A Stellar Guard officer marched down the ramp and stopped at the bottom before stepping off into the grass. Blonde curls adorned his head, but he had shaved his hair to the skin on both sides. Xttra's eyes fixed on his uniform insignia.

A master pilot's emblem.

"Nihu?" Surprise gripped Tressek's voice. "What are you doing on my scout ship?"

He halted a few steps short of the ramp. Nihu beckoned for him to draw closer. His frown deepened and disgust seeped into his eyes as they fixed on Tressek.

"You're a worthless traitor," Nihu said. "Did you believe the chief sovereign would not discover you liberated a prisoner who has spent four years trying to overthrow him?"

Tressek stiffened, legs rooted to the ground. Other Stellar Guard officers joined Nihu on the ramp, forming a column behind him. He raised his left armored sleeve.

"I will give you a traitor's fate."

A razor disc launched from the sleeve with a metallic hiss. Tressek let out a violent gasp and clutched his belly. He turned to run and staggered to his knees. Blood dribbled between his fingers and over his bottom lip. Nihu marched forward and plunged his arm saber deep into Tressek's back. Screams and cries from his friends reverberated in Xttra's ears as his former systems officer slumped face first into the spongy meadow grass.

Delcor set a trap and they walked right into it.

34

alandra shielded Alexa's eyes with her hand as Tressek turned to flee from Nihu. Those tender eyes already endured far too many awful sights. She did not want another haunting image added to her daughter's memories. A lump formed in her throat as Tressek's violent demise unfolded and she bit on her lower lip to suppress a quiet rage bubbling inside her. Nihu cut Tressek down for his sincere change of heart without an ounce of remorse.

A monster equal to the ruler he served.

Nihu refocused his hardened gaze on the others after withdrawing his bloodied blade from Tressek's back. His eyes instantly found Xttra.

"Xttra Oogan. This is perfect. Now I'll dispense the justice you've eluded since returning from Earth."

Xttra's eyes narrowed. His hand stayed flush over the eliminator handle, ready to draw at a moment's notice.

"Should I know you?"

Nihu retracted his arm saber and raised the other armored sleeve again.

"I'm Nihu Zell—remember my name as you meet your fate, you worthless setaworm."

His last name struck a familiar and frightening chord with Calandra. Doni Zell.

Her heart raced faster once she made the connection. Nihu sought revenge for Doni's death on Earth seven years earlier. His saber side hand retreated to a button above the left elbow.

"You should have never killed my father."

Xttra drew his eliminator and fired off a quick shot in one fluid motion. Nihu recoiled and staggered backward. He clutched at his throat where the eliminator bolt struck and stumbled to the ground in front of the ramp. His eyes glassed over as blood gushed out from the hole under his right hand.

"You should have stayed on your ship," Xttra said.

The other Stellar Guard officers standing on the ramp sprinted into more defensible positions and fired their weapons. Xttra and Dray dashed toward the nearest aerorover, matching their adversaries bolt for bolt as they ran. Calandra scooped up Alexa, keeping her body between her child and the Stellar Guard officers while sprinting in the same direction. Sam and Gulah took cover behind a second aerorover. Lily, Scout, and Bo'un reached the scout ship and sprinted up the ramp. Scout frantically barked and whined as they fled, tugging at the leash in Lily's hand.

Calandra ducked down behind the aerorover next to Xttra. He pulled out his arca vox and handed it off to her.

"Tell Bo'un to take off without us," he shouted over the unfolding chaos. "I'll fly you out in an aerorover."

Calandra stared wide-eyed at him. Bolts from eliminators and melter pellets peppered the vehicle serving as their impromptu shield.

"They're shooting the aerorover," she said.

Xttra clenched his teeth and raised his left armored sleeve. In a brief dance-like circular turn, he rose and fired a razor disc over the vehicle's hood, before completing the spin and dropping back down behind the vehicle. An advancing Stellar Guard officer groaned and slumped to the ground, clutching a fresh gaping hole in his belly.

"We'll take one not currently riddled with holes," Xttra said. His eyes remained frozen on Stellar Guard troops trying to swarm their position.

Sam and Gulah dashed up the scout ship ramp in Calandra's peripheral vision. She punched Bo'un's contact code into the arca vox. His image materialized on the holoscreen.

"Xttra says to take off." Shallow panicked breaths threaded between her words. "We're flying out in an aerorover."

Bo'un raised his brows. His mouth dropped open.

"What does he think he's doing? He can't evade a scout ship in an aerorover."

"I can if I fly between trees," Xttra said, ignoring Bo'un's image while seeking another opening to fire at the Stellar Guard officers. "They would be foolish to follow me into the forest in their scout ship."

"That's reckless!" Bo'un said. "You've lost your mind."

His words mirrored Calandra's thoughts. Weaving through dense clusters of trees inside an aerorover endangered their lives as much as staying and fighting Stellar Guard officers.

"This isn't the proper time to argue," Xttra said. "Return to Cascadia and bring back whatever help you can find. More scout ships will arrive any minute. I'll purchase us more time. Go!"

Bo'un's image vanished from the holoscreen. Calandra's lips deepened into an anxious frown. Trees could be as deadly as any pursuing vessel to a speeding aerorover.

"He's right." She clutched Alexa a little tighter. "You're being too reckless. Lance and I crashed an aerorover into a ravine filled with trees. We barely survived."

Xttra ducked down again after firing off two more eliminator bolts. He shot her an irritated scowl.

"Trust me. You know my piloting skills. I flew us through a giant planet's gravity well under pressure. We survived unharmed. Don't you believe I'll keep us safe flying through a forest?"

Calandra stared at him in disbelief. Of course, she trusted him. She did not trust the trees grew far enough apart for their aerorover to pass through the forest unscathed. Xttra tempted fate with his brash attitude. Surviving earlier brushes with death meant nothing when taking unnecessary risks.

"We run on my signal," Xttra said. "I'll slice off a door to use as temporary body armor while we sprint for the other aerorover."

Dray ducked down after firing her eliminator again. She flashed an exasperated scowl.

"Tressek was right about you."

Xttra narrowed his eyes.

"What did he say?"

"What do you think? And here I thought he exaggerated his stories from his time on your crew."

Bo'un's scout ship lifted off the ground and shot skyward a moment later. Anxiety squeezed Calandra like a giant hand crushing her inside its palm. They were the only ones left in the meadow to deal with what remained of Nihu's cohorts.

Xttra unlatched his cutter from his belt and activated the blue laser circling the volcanic glass blade. He jammed the blade against a hinge raising the aerorover door. Sparks flew as he sliced through the hinge. Dray lobbed a Cassian fire shell over the aerorover roof while Xttra cut. Her fire shell landed between the aerorover and the nearest Stellar Guard officer, sending up a wall of flame and billowing smoke in front of the vehicle.

"Nice work." Xttra shot Dray an approving smile. "That gives us an added layer of protection."

The aerorover door fell forward into the grass after Xttra sliced through the last hinge. He studied the fallen door for a moment before pressing the cutter blade against the window's upper edge. A straight-line incision formed behind the laser as Xttra trailed the cutter across the glass. He carved out a square section of glass and lifted it away from the door. Xttra tossed the cut glass aside and knocked out remnant pieces with his armored sleeve. He latched the cutter back on his belt and hoisted the door off the ground.

"Is everyone ready?" Xttra asked.

Calandra did not feel ready. Her nerves kept tightening into taut knots. Nihu brought more than a standard scout ship crew with him. More Stellar Guard officers marched out from the ship's cargo bay. Xttra and Dray had cut down five, including Nihu, with their weapons.

Calandra counted 12 outside the ship.

Freshly planted shield markers forming a half-circle around the vessel now protected the Stellar Guard officers. Each metallic marker consisted of a stake topped with a glass ball. The ball held an electromagnetic coil. Stellar Guard officers methodically planted new markers to expand the energy shell outward while drawing closer to the aerorover.

"Stay by my side as much as possible," Xttra said.

He positioned the aerorover door as a shield over his exposed side. Calandra held Alexa close inside her arms and flanked his other side. Dray slid behind Xttra and helped bear the weight of the metal door. They stumbled along at a brisk pace toward Tressek's aerorover parked near the small brook.

Thuds and hissing metal bore witness to eliminator bolts and melter pellets spraying the door. None cut through the metal far enough to strike vulnerable body parts. Xttra's plan was working. They had already covered two-thirds of the ground between their original position and the other aerorover without suffering a scratch.

A sudden overhead whoosh greeted Calandra's ears. She cursed herself for not keeping watch above and jerked her head skyward.

Her heart sank. A ground force carrier descended toward the brook. Aerorovers flanked both sides of the vessel.

Their only chance to escape had vanished.

***

Silence reigned inside the ground force carrier. Calandra stared at new restraints encircling her ankles. Her renewed hope for prevailing against Delcor fled, snuffed out like a weakened candle flame. She shared a tiny detention cell bench with Alexa and Dray. Xttra sat on the floor beside the bench. Calandra wrapped her arms around her little girl. No comforting words rested on her tongue or entered her mind. Only a natural inclination to encircle her daughter in a protective embrace.

"We'll find a way to prevail." Xttra finally pierced a stifling silence. "Delcor will not beat us."

Calandra lifted her chin and gazed at him. His lips formed a hopeful smile. His weary eyes betrayed a hidden wave of frustrated fear.

"Prevail?" she shot back. "Have we truly made a difference? The Staff of Onrai is within his grasp. Every measure we've taken to oppose Delcor has failed."

Xttra cast his eyes down at the magnetic restraints circling his wrists.

"The outcome hasn't been what we wanted," he said. "But my resolve has not faltered. I'll fight Delcor to my final breath. I know you will too. If we die, we'll die knowing we chose a better path."

An appreciative smile graced her lips. His bravery amid such dire circumstances was inspiring. A small part of her wished for a release from pain and heartache a final breath promised. But Xttra offered a flicker of hope their battle would turn in their favor and peace would return to their lives.

Their detention cell door slid open. A Stellar Guard officer entered the room. Holding Alexa close, Calandra rose to her feet. Xttra and Dray mirrored her action. Restraints bound their ankles and wrists. No restraints circled Calandra's wrists this time around. Xttra negotiated with a Stellar Guard commander to let her keep her wrists free to care for Alexa. She admired his ability to stay calm and negotiate without insulting Delcor or the Stellar Guard. The commander granted his request.

Three other Stellar Guard officers followed the first. They flanked the prisoners and led them from the cell down a dim corridor.

"Where are you taking us?" Dray asked.

"Our sovereign ordered you brought before him," the lead officer said. "Your fate is in his hands now."

Xttra rolled his eyes and sighed.

"Don't be so dramatic. Old Delcor is a desperate tyrant facing dwindling time. Our fate will be better than his...and yours."

Calandra pinched her lips together to prevent a surprised laugh from escaping her mouth. She loved Xttra's appropriation of Kevin's derisive nickname for the chief sovereign. His bravado lifted her gloomy spirits.

The lead officer turned and marched up to Xttra. He slapped him hard across the right cheek.

"I don't care who you once were in the Stellar Guard. You are nothing now, Xttra Oogan. Nothing."

The lead officer signaled to his fellow officers to move forward. They marched down the corridor, leading the prisoners into a docking bay holding a half-dozen small vessels. Calandra recognized the two aerorovers used to helped corner them in the meadow. Their captors brought them down a ramp leading out of the carrier.

Calandra squinted when she stepped off the ramp. She wished she had the sunglasses Lily gifted to her to block the mid-day glare from twin suns. Scarlet and crimson trees adorned foothills beyond the ship. A river meandered down from the foothills and looped around the far side of Genahm before emptying into a lake bordering the south end of the village.

"Bow before your sovereign," a voice called out.

Every Stellar Guard officer in the vicinity promptly obeyed the instructions. A few crossed their open palms and pressed them against their forehead as they bowed. Calandra, Xttra, and Dray refused to drop their heads.

A lectian rolled past the assembled troops. The vehicle resembled a vertical box with wheels. Tinted windows adorned the upper half on all four sides and a peaked roof topped the vehicle. A metallic emblem rose from a central spire on the lectian's roof. The emblem depicted Ra'ahm's national symbol—a golden sun with rays spreading in all directions hovering above a flying Mokai.

The lectian stopped on the bank of the mountain river. A door facing Calandra opened, revealing the chief sovereign. He sat on a single cushioned chair before a navigational console. A small set of steps descended and settled in the grass. Delcor had discarded his usual royal robes for a custom Stellar Guard uniform with the Ra'ahmian symbol as his emblem. His personal guards approached and flanked each side of the chief sovereign after he stepped out of the vehicle.

Delcor flashed a triumphant smile when he laid eyes on his new prisoners.

"Ahm delivered you into my hands. Now you will be blessed to witness me seal my right to rule his people forever. Lathos and the Land of the Three Suns will both know the love of Ahm."

"You never had a right to rule Ra'ahm," Calandra shot back. "You're a liar and a murderer."

His eyes hardened into a fierce stare for a moment. Delcor quickly shook his head and countered with a derisive laugh.

"First, I must reclaim stolen property."

Delcor snapped his fingers and jerked his head toward a personal guard on his left side.

"Search the prisoners. One is concealing a parchment that belongs to me."

The guard stepped forward and carried out Delcor's command. He searched Calandra, Xttra, and then Dray thoroughly—finally drawing out Marteen's parchment from Dray's chest pouch. A distressed frown crossed her lips as he handed the parchment to the chief sovereign.

"Excellent work." Delcor unrolled the parchment and briefly glanced at the text. "Now we will enter the forest to obtain the staff."

"Your will is forever our will, my sovereign," his guard said. "May Ahm lengthen your rule to match your days."

Calandra shuddered at those sycophantic words. How many times had she uttered similar phrases before she opened her eyes to the truth?

Delcor and his minions crossed a foot bridge connecting to a trail leading into the forest. Thick horizontal ropes formed handrails and stout vertical ropes linked the handrails to a series of connected wood planks. The primitive rope bridge only supported foot traffic. Delcor refused to leave his lectian behind and walk through the forest. He ordered his personal guards to carry the vehicle on their shoulders and wade through the river along the bridge to the other bank.

"I wish one of his guards had the spine to sink his lectian into the river," Xttra said. "Let Ahm prove his 'chosen' status by fishing him out of the water."

His dark humor masked an obvious discomfort woven through his face from walking in restraints. A persistent pain attacked Calandra's legs for the same reason. The Stellar Guard officers guarding them made no move to remove their restraints while forcing them to walk at a brisk pace. Her arms ached from carrying

Alexa to spare her the cruelty of a forced march. Calandra had no way to track how many peds the group walked while following a winding river deeper into the forest. One ped alone was torture under these conditions.

A cool breeze caressed her cheeks. Thunder from distant cascades of roaring water greeted Calandra's ears, mixed with a river churning and crashing over a smooth rock bed. Clusters of trees thinned as the group drew closer to the waterfall itself. The riverside trail soon led into a giant bowl-shaped depression.

Towering cliffs flanked a turbulent white curtain. Patches of red moss decorated the cliffs from crest to base on both sides of the giant waterfall. Foaming and churning water generated a near-deafening roar while cascading down into an expansive plunge pool. Mists arose from the pool itself, encircling the bottom of the falling curtain of water.

"I've never seen a greater waterfall," Xttra said. "This is magnificent."

The giant waterfall took Calandra's breath away. Her eyes climbed to the crest where the river plunged over colossal cliffs. This place evoked the grandeur present in ancient descriptions of the Land of the Three Suns more than anything else she had seen on this planet. Calandra's eyes drifted back down to Alexa. Her daughter stared wide-eyed at the cascading water, transfixed by its natural beauty.

The lectian opened again. Delcor disembarked from the vehicle with Marteen's parchment in hand. His guards alerted his other minions to his presence. They greeted the chief sovereign with a fresh wave of bows.

"We have reached our destination," he said. "Let those designated to enter the sanctuary accompany me."

Calandra turned her head as Delcor strode past with his guards still flanking him. Her eyes settled on the sanctuary.

A gray stone facade protruded from a cliff facing the sun-drenched side of the waterfall. The facade resembled the stone temple in Genahm but bore larger proportions than its village counterpart. Stone blocks formed a tower consisting of four equilateral triangles, each smaller than the preceding one. The largest triangle forming the base dwarfed Delcor's sprawling palace in Luma. Ahm's seven-point star crowned a spire rising from the uppermost triangle. Unlike Genahm's temple, the surrounding cliff swallowed this structure's backend like a giant mouth past the central spire.

The Staff of Onrai lay hidden inside that sanctuary.

Multiple jabs in her back compelled Calandra to trail Delcor. She cast her eyes toward her husband and saw Stellar Guard officers coercing Xttra and Dray into the same forced march. The chief sovereign fulfilled his promise. He truly intended to compel them to witness his ultimate triumph.

35

Lights sprang to life inside the sanctuary's main chamber. A single row circled the chamber at eye level. Calandra studied the partially embedded spherical lights adorning all four walls. Hidden motion sensors activated each luminous orb. What powered the lights? Solar energy or hydropower were the most realistic options for such an isolated structure. She noted no visible solar collectors or hydro converters outside the sanctuary. Of course, Calandra did not actively seek out those items before entering the ancient structure.

Her thoughts led her down a different path.

"Those Wekonn rebels spared no effort to conceal the staff from prying eyes."

Calandra snapped her head toward Xttra and frowned at his comment. Did he expect the Staff of Onrai to decorate the chamber like a painting or sculpture?

"It will be revealed," Delcor said. "Your failure will be complete soon enough."

He raised Marteen's parchment over his forehead and flashed a condescending smile at Xttra. Calandra silently fumed at his gloating demeanor. The chief sovereign intended to taunt them at every step until the staff came into his possession. Then they would be expendable.

Delcor brought the parchment down to eye level and unrolled it again. He squinted and mouthed words as his index finger trailed down the record.

The chief sovereign scowled.

"Riddles fill this parchment. If I wanted riddles, I would've brought my copy of the *Book of Ahm* with me."

"What is the riddle, my sovereign?" a female voice asked behind him.

She spoke with a humble tone, eager to offer help while seeking to avoid stirring up his anger with an implicit suggestion he needed her assistance. Calandra turned away from Delcor and laid eyes on a Stellar Guard officer wearing four Orontallan half-braids. Her uniform displayed a commander's insignia.

"Only eyes of faith will see what Ahm has hidden." Delcor recited words written on the parchment. "We all have faith. Even traitors claim to follow Ahm. Now tell me, Nikaia, what do you make of this passage?"

"I hesitate to guess, my sovereign."

Nikaia returned Calandra's stare with a stony glare. She averted her gaze and studied the chamber's layout. Her eyes trailed over a long stone back wall, interrupted by two evenly spaced doors. An altar shaped like a giant metal chalice capped a fixed platform before the doors. It towered like an inanimate guard, daring visitors to pass.

"Try the doors," Delcor said. "If they are locked, we will cut through them and carve our own path forward."

Nikaia and three other Stellar Guard officers approached the doors. Calandra and Xttra both shuffled forward as much as their ankle restraints allowed and gazed at the other side of the giant chalice. A spout protruded from the chalice's base and hung over a small metallic finger bowl. No dust, mineral deposits, or rust caked either spout or bowl. Both were in immaculate condition despite being many hundreds of years old. Xttra stared at both objects and a puzzled look crept over his face. Calandra shared his bewilderment.

What purpose did the spout and bowl serve?

A sudden painful shout grabbed her attention. Calandra snapped her head toward the now open doors. Flames sprang to life inside one doorway, veiling the path forward. The other showed a second inner chamber. A violent flicker rippled through the doorway as her eyes settled on it, revealing a holographic image.

Only three Stellar Guard officers now stood at the doors instead of four.

"What do we do?" Nikaia asked.

"Send the prisoners through," Delcor said.

Xttra raised his restrained arms in protest.

"If you want to kill me, remove my restraints first. Let's make it an even battle."

Calandra's eyes trailed back to the giant chalice. Clear water trickled from the spout into the bowl. Once the vessel filled to the brim, the water ceased flowing.

"What does the parchment say below the first passage you read?" she asked, glancing at Delcor.

"Why should I tell you?"

"This is an obvious riddle to be solved," she snapped. "You won't claim your prize until you solve it, will you?"

Delcor scowled and cast his eyes down on the parchment again.

"It has a drawing of the chalice and says below the drawing, 'Drink living water and quench the flames of your thirst.'"

Calandra gazed at the bowl and then at the flames obstructing the doorway to the right of the giant chalice. Her eyes brightened and a smile emerged.

"I have the answer."

Delcor lifted his chin and met her gaze.

"Tell me."

Calandra raised a finger and shook her head.

"Remove our restraints first."

"How dare you try to manipulate our sovereign?" Nikaia marched to within arm's reach and drew her hand back, striking Calandra across the cheek. "His will is your will. Obey him."

Calandra shrugged. Her movement stirred Alexa who rested her head against Calandra's shoulder.

"Figure the riddle out yourself," she said. "If I die, at least we'll die here together."

Delcor's scowl deepened. He motioned to his guards, and one drew out a restraint deactivator, the same device Tressek used to free her earlier.

Calandra's smile broadened as the restraints dropped off her ankles. She instantly stretched sore leg muscles. Wrist and ankle restraints on Xttra and Dray both fell to the floor soon after. Delcor had confiscated their arms and gear, leaving only the flex armor under their clothing untouched. She counted the number of armed servants of the chief sovereign.

Impossible to fight or flee.

"Weapons ready," Delcor said, instructing his minions. "They pose an insignificant risk outside their restraints but are still foolish enough to oppose our common purpose here."

Calandra handed a sleepy Alexa to Xttra and approached the giant chalice. She scooped up the bowl and pressed the rim to her lips.

"Shouldn't you cast that water into the fire?" Dray asked. "Makes more sense than drinking it."

Calandra paused and shook her head.

"That makes sense to me too, but it isn't what the guide wants us to do. And I know why."

She tipped the bowl forward as her lips parted. The water was strangely ice cold. It tasted refreshing crossing over her tongue and splashing down her throat. Calandra left a portion of the water inside the bowl and approached the flames.

"Wait!" Xttra shouted, preparing to run after her. "What are you doing?"

"Trust me," she said. "This isn't what it seems to be."

Calandra stepped up to the doorway and held out her arms until the fire licked the front of the bowl. A port opened above the flames and a blue light appeared. The light scanned both her and the bowl before disappearing with equal speed.

At once, the flames vanished. Calandra let out a relieved sigh. She was right.

And still alive.

A second inner chamber lay beyond the doorway.

"Faith requires trust in the absence of certain knowledge," Calandra said, smiling back at Xttra and Alexa.

She carried the bowl through the doorway. Xttra, Alexa, and Dray—prodded to go first—followed. Delcor and his people came through last. Calandra noted the rest of the group crossed through without trouble. The sensor must have automatically deactivated the flame trap after scanning her. She set the bowl aside on a protruding ledge. Another row of eye-level lights running along the chamber walls sprang to life.

This second chamber featured three corridors deep inside the room. Two broad corridors flanked a narrow central one. Thick columns divided the central corridor from its larger parallel siblings. Medium-sized circular white stones poked up from the square gray stone block floor at even stride length intervals. These stepstones created a path through each corridor. Each circular stone bore an ancient Aracian symbol, etched deep into its polished surface.

"Aracian script?" Xttra expelled an irritated sigh while staring at the stepstones. "I'm tired of seeing those symbols everywhere."

"What does your parchment say concerning this chamber, my sovereign?" Nikaia asked, facing Delcor.

Calandra noted Nikaia spoke with greater courage now. A threat of punishment for insubordination did not hang over her. Not while Xttra and Calandra herself—whom Delcor considered true rebels—were present.

Delcor gazed intently at the parchment. A smile crossed his lips as he read.

"Treasure the words of Ahm, for he illuminates the true path," he said, looking up at her.

Nikaia returned his gaze and promptly turned to Calandra. Many others in the chamber did the same. Calandra cast her eyes on the stepstones. The symbols served a purpose. What purpose? Xttra crouched down, with Alexa still in his arms, and tapped the nearest stone with his finger.

It started glowing.

"These are guide stones." He glanced over his shoulder up at Calandra. "I think we're supposed to touch the corresponding stones one at a time as we pass through the correct corridor."

"Sounds simple enough," Dray said.

She started toward the right-hand corridor. Dray planted a foot on one guide stone, then another. When she extended her left foot to step on a third stone inside the corridor, Xttra sprang to his feet.

"Stop!"

His loud voice bounced off the chamber walls. Dray pulled her foot back and froze on the second stone.

"Keep going," Delcor said. "We solved the riddle. No sense standing idle in this chamber."

"Ignore him," Xttra replied. "If you take another step into that corridor, you'll die."

Calandra's mouth fell open and her eyes widened.

"How can you be certain?"

Xttra beckoned to one of Delcor's personal guards.

"Toss a small object into either wide corridor. Doesn't matter which corridor. Take your pick."

A guard flanking Delcor's right side glanced over at the chief sovereign. He gave a reluctant nod. The guard dug into a pouch on his belt and tossed a little ball compass. It rolled over the guide stone ahead of Dray. The stone glowed and a whoosh followed.

A massive horizontal blade cut across the corridor from a slot in the left wall. It completed its deadly path and cut back to the point of emergence, vanishing once again. A trap door then opened under the stones and the compass plummeted into a darkened pit below. The door raised again after a few seconds and the path forward appeared as safe and clear as before.

Dray stared wide-eyed at Xttra, visibly shaking.

"The riddle said Ahm himself illuminates the path," Xttra said. "Not his words. We need to search for specific stones spelling out his name."

Xttra returned Alexa to Calandra and approached the narrow middle corridor. Calandra stared at Aracian symbols on each stone. The first three leading into the middle corridor spelled out Ahm in Aracian script. Xttra stepped from stone to stone, moving forward after each one lit up under his feet. Her breathing quickened. Calandra hoped his intuition proved correct.

He passed through the corridor unharmed.

Xttra turned and beckoned to her to follow. Calandra took a deep breath and dashed forward with Alexa, matching his stone touching sequence. Dray followed on her heels. Another relieved sigh escaped Calandra's lips when she joined Xttra on the other side.

"What kind of sanctuary is this?" she asked. "I've never encountered a temple or sanctuary of Ahm rigged with death traps."

Xttra cast a glance back at Delcor. His eyes trailed forward again to Calandra.

"Those other places were not designed to safeguard an ancient relic from being used as a world-conquering weapon," he said.

Lights illuminated the third chamber, revealing detailed murals covering the front facing wall and side walls. Calandra's eyes settled on the mural gracing the near wall and she studied the artwork. Mural images detailed the creation of Lathos and showed Ahm directing Onrai to construct the staff bearing his name. She could spend hours studying these murals and absorb only a small part of the mysteries they revealed.

"I don't believe it. The staff really exists."

Amazement threaded through Xttra's voice. Calandra glanced over at him. His mouth hung partially open. Her eyes trailed to where he stared.

A massive platform with long flat stone steps on all sides occupied the back end of the chamber. Giant circles formed a symmetrical pattern in four directions on the platform floor, originating from a central altar built with metallic components and cut stones. A long polished wooden staff stood atop the altar. Metallic fingers emerged from the staff and wrapped around a clear oval stone on the top end.

This staff perfectly matched descriptions of the Staff of Onrai in ancient records she studied.

"The time has come to claim what rightfully belongs to you, my sovereign," Nikaia said.

Delcor gave her an approving nod. Nikaia started forward and climbed the steps. A hopeless feeling welled up inside Calandra. The chief sovereign would soon claim his prize and lengthen his rule to match his days. Three rebels stood against him and his armed guards, unarmed and outnumbered. How could she or Xttra stop him from leaving this sanctuary with the relic?

"I think I activated another sensor," Nikaia said. "The platform is scanning me."

Calandra gazed at the Stellar Guard commander. She stood frozen inside a circle on the platform floor. Small ports had opened on each side. Blue lights zipped up and down her body.

"Back away from the platform," Xttra said.

He retreated from the stone steps, falling back to a position near the chamber's entrance. Calandra and Dray mirrored his actions. Delcor and his minions ignored the warning.

The ground trembled, and an artificial crack opened around the circle where she stood. A clear tube rose from the crack, trapping Nikaia inside. It continued to rise straight up, soon locking into a matching slot in the ceiling. Nikaia's eyes widened. She pounded her fists against the tube.

"Cut me out of here!"

Her shouted plea barely registered above a whisper through the tube's thick transparent material. Calandra's eyes drifted down to Nikaia's belt line. A sheathed cutter hung from her belt, but sheer panic had overtaken her common sense.

"Tear apart that tube," Delcor said. "Free her."

The circle beneath Nikaia's feet grew redder. She cast her eyes downward and screamed. Nikaia beat her fists against the tube again. Tears streamed down her face.

Flames ignited inside the tube.

Calandra and Xttra exchanged horrified glances. She quickly shielded Alexa's eyes with her hand. Nikaia's screams grew more intense. Blue-white flames climbed her legs and spread over her body. Flesh and bone melted like candle wax. When the blaze finally flickered out, charred weapons, bone remnants, and ashes formed a pile atop the circle. A dull roar sounded. The pile flew skyward and vanished through a slot in the ceiling.

"Maybe Valadius spoke the truth concerning Ahm's decree." A trembling lilt permeated Calandra's whispered voice. "The platform burned her to ashes."

Xttra shook his head.

"Ahm had nothing to do with this." His eyes trailed from ceiling to floor. "Wekonn rebels set these traps—presumably to prevent Wekonn soldiers from reclaiming the relic."

Delcor stared at the spot where Nikaia perished. A deep scowl crossed his lips. His eyes drifted to the altar holding the staff and back down to Calandra and Xttra.

"A prisoner will go next," he said.

"What?" Calandra's voice climbed several decibels. "We all witnessed what happened. You're not obtaining possession of the staff. It's over."

His scowl morphed into a crooked smile.

"Maybe Ahm will smile on you and choose to not strike you down."

Delcor motioned to his guards. Two marched over to her. One snatched Alexa from Calandra's arms. Alexa screamed and grabbed at her as they ripped the little girl away. Calandra and Xttra both cried out. The other guard drew his eliminator as they rushed forward, stopping them from taking her back.

"You volunteer, Calandra Menankar, to fetch the staff for your sovereign," Delcor said. "If you resist, I shall send the child in your place."

A lump formed in Calandra's throat. Tears brimmed in her eyes and Xttra's eyes. Alexa sobbed and cried out for her parents. The chief sovereign's brutality knew no limits. He was ready to condemn their child to death. Calandra despised him with all her heart. But she would do what she must do to save her little girl.

"If I go," Calandra said. "I want to know what else the parchment says. I won't step on that platform blind."

Her voice grew forceful yet threatened to break under her swelling emotions.

"Your request is reasonable," Delcor said.

He cast his eyes down at the parchment and mouthed a few words while trailing his finger across the document.

"Ahm will grant knowledge and wisdom to one who writes his name in their mind and their heart," Delcor said, reading the words aloud.

Calandra wiped away her tears and cast a fearful glance at Xttra. What did this latest riddle mean?

Her eyes darted from wall to wall. She spotted two freestanding pillars before a specific section of the colorful mural. It depicted a conduit of light descending from a seven-pointed star and piercing through ashen clouds. An open shelf embedded inside each towering pillar held sealed glass vessels half-filled with translucent purple paint.

His name written in their mind and their heart.

"I know what I need to do." Calandra turned back to Xttra. "Help me apply paint to my forehead and chest."

Xttra answered her with a puzzled stare.

"What is that supposed to do?"

"His name must be written in my mind and my heart," Calandra said. "This test requires me to place a visible symbol of Ahm on my head and on my chest to reach the staff."

They dashed over to the pillars together. Xttra unsealed a vessel and dipped his index finger in paint. He drew the seven-pointed star on the designated spots. She clasped his hand tight but dared not kiss or embrace him for fear of smudging the paint and ruining the symbol.

Calandra glanced at her frightened daughter and offered a reassuring smile.

"Don't be afraid." She caressed Alexa's cheek. "I will be safe."

She turned away and climbed the platform steps. Calandra paused on the same circle where Nikaia stood earlier. Blue lights emerged on both sides and scanned her from head to toe. They flickered after passing over the symbols and vanished. Smaller circles converging at the altar ahead of her illuminated in succession.

Calandra followed the lit path. When she paused on the final luminous circle, an energy shell surrounding the relic dissipated. She reached out and plucked the staff from atop the altar. Her heart raced as her hands clutched the relic.

Calandra drew the Staff of Onrai to her chest.

36

Calandra's eyes trailed over the Staff of Onrai. Aracian symbols adorned the shoulder-high staff, carved into the polished wooden surface with meticulous precision. These symbols detailed the relic's origin and purpose. No one outside of Genahm had laid eyes on the staff for hundreds of years. To both see and touch it now filled Calandra with a thrill of discovery that subdued her fear, anger, and sadness for a moment. She trailed her metal hand across the stone topping the staff, pondering what secrets it held. Her eyes settled on the stone itself.

It began to emit a white ethereal glow.

"The stone is glowing," she said.

"Your task is complete," Delcor replied. "Bring the staff down to me."

Calandra did not bother acknowledging the chief sovereign with so much as a cursory glance. His voice sounded distant, as though emanating from a far-off room. Her eyes remained transfixed upon the glowing oval stone. The stone's luminosity increased.

Light diffused from the stone, shrouding Calandra from head to toe. An indistinct bright whiteness enveloped her face.

Calandra found herself inside a conduit of pure light. Three screens materialized before her, forming a panoramic view. Random scenes played across each screen. Jumbled, out of focus images greeted her eyes. Calandra stared at the screens, trying to make sense of what she was seeing. Images gained clarity and color becoming vivid while unfolding in real time before her.

The assorted images intrigued Calandra. She recognized some. The relic sensed her thoughts and connected to her life. Did the images pertain to her past or were they drawn from her future? One screen started replaying forgotten childhood memories. Another screen displayed images from moments not yet experienced.

Some were joyful. Others were haunting.

The panoramic screens and surrounding conduit of light vanished in a violent flash. A harsh tug tore the staff from her grasp. Calandra let out a sudden gasp as her eyes readjusted to the light and color of the sanctuary chamber again. Delcor stood before her, wearing a brazen smile. Translucent purple paint forming the symbol of Ahm adorned his forehead and his chest.

His left hand grasped the Staff of Onrai.

"I claimed what rightfully belongs to me," Delcor said. "Now you have truly failed."

He gestured toward the steps. Delcor's guards had their weapons trained on Xttra, Alexa, and Dray. Calandra reluctantly climbed down from the platform. The chief sovereign followed on her heels. He raised the staff aloft when he touched the chamber floor again.

"I will be as Ahm himself." Delcor's voice echoed through the chamber. "Those who rebel against me are now dying embers amid cooled flames."

Stellar Guard officers surrounded Calandra and then forced every prisoner to retrace their path back through the sanctuary.

One of Delcor's personal guards continued holding Alexa, refusing to relinquish her to Calandra. Her eyes darted between Xttra and Alexa as she contemplated how to survive this situation. Stopping Delcor from staring into the stone became more important than anything else. Once he gained the knowledge he sought, nothing would end his rule.

Distracting him was the only weapon she had left.

"You will never conquer Lathos," Calandra said. "Ahm will not allow a liar and murderer to gain equal footing with him."

Delcor answered her with a derisive laugh.

"Ahm has smiled upon me from the beginning. I rule in his name. Now he will deliver Lathos to me and my clan forever."

"How will you rule an entire planet when you're never leaving this one alive?" Xttra replied.

Delcor signaled to his minions to halt inside the outermost chamber. He motioned to his personal guards, and they forced Calandra, Xttra, and Dray to their knees before him.

"We will carry out their execution now," Delcor said. "Capture their deaths on a holocaster so Ra'ahmians may bear witness to their deserved fate later."

The guard carrying Alexa set her next to her parents. Xttra wrapped his arms around the sweet little girl whispering his love for her in Alexa's ear. Calandra bit down on her trembling lower lip and swallowed hard. Delcor's personal guards lined up before the prisoners with eliminators drawn.

He elevated the Staff of Onrai a second time.

"I will relish uncovering every secret this relic holds," Delcor said. "And you will die knowing your treacherous efforts to dethrone your true sovereign failed to—"

Tremors shook the sanctuary walls, interrupting his gloating speech. A din of shouts and explosions followed from outside the sanctuary. The melee was faint against the waterfall at first but soon increased in volume as it drew nearer. Hope welled up inside Calandra. Bo'un and the others arrived with reinforcements from Cascadia.

And not a moment too soon.

The main entry door flew open. Three stun pebbles spiraled into the chamber.

Xttra snapped his head toward Calandra.

"Shield your eyes."

She pressed her forearm over her eyes ahead of a blinding flash of white light. Pained shouts erupted through the chamber and bodies dropped against the stone floor. Calandra's heart pounded when she uncovered her unaffected eyes. Half of Delcor's personal guards and many of his Stellar Guard officers lay sprawled on the floor, clutching their eyes. Xttra's arm shielded Alexa's face at the cost of protecting his own eyes. A painful grimace twisted his face and he let out a groan. Dray, Calandra, and Alexa all avoided making eye contact with the stun pebbles and were unaffected.

Several familiar faces entered the sanctuary. Bo'un, Gulah, Lily, and Sam all appeared—accompanied by a team of four Earthian soldiers.

"Delcor has the Staff of Onrai!" Calandra shouted. "Don't let him peer into the stone!"

Sam instantly raised an Earthian pistol and fired at the chief sovereign. Delcor screamed and dropped the staff. It bounced off the floor and rolled out of his grasp. He fell backward as a chunk of flesh and bone sprayed out from a fresh hole in his left hand.

"Free the prisoners." Sam glanced at Bo'un. "I'll grab the staff before—"

He let out a sudden gasp. Eliminator bolts fired by one of Delcor's personal guards with unhindered vision struck the Earthian in the neck and chest. Sam collapsed in a heap on the chamber floor. His shocked eyes fell on Calandra as he took his final breath.

"Destroy them!" Delcor shouted, panting hard.

Lily helped a still-blinded Xttra and Alexa retreat behind the giant chalice. Bo'un and Gulah confiscated weapons from Stellar Guard officers still blinded from stun pebbles and tossed them to Calandra and Dray. The Earthian soldiers engaged the Stellar Guard troops who escaped temporary blinding in a battle. Smoke and dust simultaneously billowed out of the walls and climbed up from the floor amid a steady stream of plasma bolts and Earthian bullets. Shouts, pained screams, and the deafening boom of Earthian guns reverberated off the walls, creating a frightening cacophony.

Calandra's eyes slid over to the chief sovereign. Delcor crawled toward the staff and snatched it off the floor. He scrambled to his feet, blood dripping from his wounded hand, and fled into the inner chambers. The personal guard who killed Sam followed him through the doorway.

A troubling image from the staff flashed through Calandra's mind. Legions of Lathoan ships, now under the chief sovereign's command, lay waste to the Land of the Three Suns and slaughtered all life on the planet.

"We can't let Delcor flee this sanctuary." She ducked behind the chalice. "If he survives, he will return and destroy this planet."

Xttra blinked repeatedly and shook his head as his vision gradually returned. He inhaled sharply. Lily held up three fingers.

"Can you see me?" she asked. "How many fingers am I holding up?"

"Yeah, I'm fine," he said, looking around. "Does someone have a weapon I can use?"

Lily tossed him an eliminator, showing mild surprise when he snagged it out of the air. His sight had fully returned. Calandra held a second eliminator in her hand. She turned and glanced at Lily.

"Please keep Alexa safe until we return."

Her Earthian friend nodded and huddled against the chalice with Alexa, clutching an Earthian pistol. Xttra charged through the doorway to the second chamber. Calandra followed on his heels.

A plasma bolt struck Xttra in the upper arm as he entered the chamber. He grunted and stumbled. Calandra fired a bolt over his shoulder as he fell, clipping Sam's killer in the chest. Xttra regained his footing and put a bolt through the personal guard's left eye right as he raised an armored sleeve. The guard stumbled forward and collapsed face first at Xttra's feet.

Delcor fired an eliminator at Calandra, striking her leg. She winced. Her flex armor absorbed the bolt, but it still left a coin sized hole in her pants. She and Xttra simultaneously struck him with eliminator bolts. The chief sovereign let out a brief shout and staggered over to a column separating the narrow middle corridor from a wider one. Delcor leaned against the column, trying to regain his balance. A pair of fresh holes in his uniform revealed his own flex armor protecting his ribs.

Xttra and Calandra circled Delcor from opposite sides and stopped in front of him. Both pointed their weapons squarely at his face.

The chief sovereign laughed amid heavy breaths.

"It has come down to this." Delcor's eyes trailed from his fallen weapon up to Calandra. "If you slay me, what becomes of you? Once my blood stains your hands, you will never find peace."

Calandra narrowed her eyes and tightened her grip on her eliminator handle. A scowl deepened on her lips. Delcor destroyed countless lives without remorse. He murdered tens of thousands over a lifetime. His hypocrisy had become unbearable.

"Peace will find us after you draw your final breath," Xttra said.

Delcor licked his lips. His eyes darted over to the Staff of Onrai leaning against the column next to him. Fresh blood streaked across the polished wood.

"Grant me mercy," he said. "I will show you the same. Ra'ahm needs a steady hand to guide her. You will chase peace from our people if you slaughter their ruler."

Calandra shook her head.

"Your will is not my will."

Delcor lunged forward to snatch up the eliminator. Xttra and Calandra fired one bolt after another into the chief sovereign, blasting holes through his forehead, throat, and uniform. Delcor fell forward, blood streaming down his face and chest, and sprawled across the floor.

Ra'ahm no longer shouldered the burden of his oppressive rule. They too were free.

A huge weight lifted from Calandra's shoulders as she dropped her eliminator and stared at his lifeless body. She and Xttra no longer had to live in fear or hide. They could regain their lives and raise Alexa in peace.

Xttra approached the Staff of Onrai and snatched it up from its resting place against the column. He turned the shoulder-high staff over in his hands, studying the symbols carved into the wood. Calandra peered at the stone atop the staff again. She perceived the direction his thoughts traveled concerning the fate of the staff.

The wrong direction.

"We can't destroy the staff," she said. "I hate to admit it, but Valadius was right. We need to preserve the Staff of Onrai and leave it hidden in a safe place."

Xttra cast a sideways glance at her and a disappointed frown washed over his lips.

"This relic is too dangerous in the wrong hands," he said. "Few places are more isolated than this sanctuary. We found it. Delcor found it. How much time will pass before a worse tyrant succeeds where he failed?"

"This isn't meant to be a weapon," Calandra replied. "The staff is a valuable tool in the right hands. What I learned by gazing into the stone convinced me we cannot destroy it out of fear."

She drew closer to Xttra and clasped his hand tight, offering a reassuring smile. He glanced away, his eyes settling on the stone again.

"What did you see?" Xttra glanced over at her, his brows knit together in consternation. "When you gazed into the stone, what did you see?"

Calandra had no simple answer. If she spent many hours recounting every image she saw inside the conduit of light, her tale would only scratch the surface of what she experienced. Her eyelids snapped shut as she contemplated what the Staff of Onrai revealed.

"Everything passed before my eyes."

"Everything?"

"My entire life. Past, present, and future—exactly as the ancient legends promised."

Xttra fell silent. Sounds of battle faded beyond the chamber. A call demanding surrender—uttered by Bo'un—greeted her ears. Calandra blocked out what lay beyond the chamber. She reopened her eyes and refocused her gaze on Xttra.

"What I learned gave me hope," she said. "Hope for a better world. One we can help build together."

"I want to see what you saw," he said.

His eyes settled on the staff again, this time focused on the clear stone atop the relic. A white glow returned to the stone. Calandra flashed a hopeful smile. Once Xttra witnessed the same things she had seen for himself, he would better understand the value of protecting and concealing the staff.

Building a better world required their unity.

alandra returned the Staff of Onrai to its home atop the altar. A calm assurance swept through her as she exited the innermost chamber with Xttra. They took the right step forward. Delcor was slain. The Cascadians decimated his fleet. Ra'ahm's next chief sovereign would not be foolish enough to try to complete Delcor's quest. The Staff of Onrai lay undisturbed for many centuries. Now the tool forged by Ahm could fade back into the realm of myth until the staff served its true purpose at a future time.

Delcor's death stamped out the will to fight among his surviving Stellar Guard troops. Calandra and Xttra dragged the chief sovereign's bloodied lifeless body out of the sanctuary. Faced with the sight of their fallen leader, and armed Earthians, the remnants of his fleet quickly surrendered.

Their surrender liberated Genahm. Villagers greeted Xttra, Calandra, and their allies as heroes and saviors when they passed beyond the walls surrounding the downtrodden colony.

A torrent of emotions unleashed inside Calandra after they disarmed every surviving Stellar Guard officer and made them prisoners. She embraced Xttra and shared a joyful kiss with him. They drew Alexa into their embrace and kissed their daughter. Emotional hugs with Lily, Bo'un, Dray, and Gulah followed.

"I prayed so long for this day," Bo'un said. "Now that it has arrived, it almost doesn't feel real to me."

"It is real," Calandra said. "This is no dream. It is a wonderful, real day."

Another hero's welcome awaited the group when they returned to Cascadia. Surviving colonists greeted them with smiles and cheers after their scout ship landed in the colony's shipyard.

Sorrow intertwined with joy in celebrations at both places. Genahm villagers mourned the death of Valadius, who sacrificed himself in a futile effort to turn away Delcor's troops. Survivors in Cascadia mourned fellow colonists who fell while defending the Earthian colony.

One specific death resonated hardest with Calandra. Sam stopped Delcor from using the Staff of Onrai at the cost of his own life. His heroism washed away whatever bitterness lingered in her heart against him. Sam redeemed himself. She sought out his heartbroken family to tell them the value of his sacrifice.

Calandra approached Sam's daughter and his grandson Jared following an Earthian rite honoring the dead. Surviving colonists gathered in a small field at twilight and lit a series of stout white candles. Each candle symbolized a colonist who perished at the hand of Delcor and his invading fleet.

"Sam Bono was a good man," she said, approaching his family. "I wish I recognized his true nature sooner. But now I will never forget."

She knelt before Jared and gazed into his teary eyes. The young boy clutched a candle symbolizing Sam. The tiny flame flickered as a gentle breeze brushed the wick.

"Your grandfather sacrificed himself to save us all," she said. "He's a true hero."

Sam's daughter swallowed hard and mouthed the words 'thank you' to Calandra. Jared cast his eyes at the grass surrounding his feet and nodded.

Colonists trickled away to dwellings or temporary shelters. Calandra, Xttra, and Alexa made their way to Kevin's hospital bed. She blinked back tears seeing her friend in his comatose state. Calandra pushed a chair over to the bed and sat beside him. The squeaking chair stirred no reaction from Kevin.

"We stopped Delcor." Calandra grasped his hand. "His rule is at an end. Everything you did mattered."

His eyes remained still beneath closed eyelids. Beeps from the machine monitoring Kevin's heart and lungs echoed in her ears. Calandra wondered if he heard her words. She wanted him to hear, to see, and to speak again. They fought for this day together.

"You can't leave us." Her voice grew choked with emotion. "Not now. We are alive because of you. Our lives will be empty without you."

Calandra raised Kevin's hand and pressed it to her brow. Tears trickled down his wrist.

"Why won't Uncle Kevin wake up?"

She cast her eyes down at Alexa. Her daughter stood next to her chair, her lower lip jutting out and tears glistening on her cheeks.

"He wants to be awake, sweetheart." Calandra wiped her eyes with her other hand. "But the bad people hurt him, so he needs to sleep."

She refocused her gaze on Kevin, studying his silent face. He made countless sacrifices for her, Xttra, and Alexa. Kevin abandoned his home planet and his people to bring them safely back to Lathos. He risked his own life and freedom a second time to stop a Stellar Guard assassin from executing Calandra. Watching him fight for his life ripped apart her soul.

Kevin earned a better fate. Ahm owed him a miracle.

"Please stay with us," Calandra said.

A somber silence settled in the room. She made no effort to turn away or stand. Calandra looked at leaving the room as abandoning him to his fate.

Kevin's eyelids fluttered.

Her heart raced faster as both eyes cracked open. A breathing tube rocked as Kevin tried to move his tongue and lips, preventing him from speaking. His eyes found hers and Kevin gave her hand a gentle squeeze.

A relieved, radiant smile washed over Calandra's lips. She glanced at Xttra. Joy also permeated his face. He raced from the room, calling for Lily, and reappeared with her a moment later.

Lily's eyes brightened when they settled on Kevin.

"You're one hell of a fighter," she said. "Look at you. Eyes finally open."

Describing him as a fighter did not go far enough.

Kevin was a hero.

***

Calandra gazed at Gulah's star cruiser through a control tower window in the Cascadian shipyard. Xttra and Bo'un spent a week helping Gulah repair damage the vessel suffered while fending off the invading Stellar Guard fleet. They impressed her with their speed and efficiency in preparing it to handle safely traversing through wide swaths of deep space again.

"The colonial council voted to not allow any prisoners to return to your home planet."

Calandra turned toward the door when she heard Lily's voice. A distinct nervousness filled her eyes as she entered the room. She licked her lips and her eyes drifted to the same expansive window overlooking the shipyard.

"Is keeping them here a wise idea?"

Letting hostile Stellar Guard troops return to Lathos was not an option. A few prisoners breathed out threats, vowing to avenge their fallen sovereign and return with a larger fleet to crush Cascadia. Holding them captive on the planet also posed a serious threat. Dray claimed Delcor restricted immediate knowledge of the space bridge to his fleet. If loyal prisoners escaped custody and fled back to Ra'ahm, they could use their knowledge to instigate a long and deadly interplanetary war.

"Erica wants to confer with Earth Defense Bureau leadership before making a final decision on their destination," Lily said. "She favors shipping the prisoners to Earth. I wouldn't sleep well at night sending a bunch of hostile Ra'ahmians there either."

"What do you think should be done with them?"

"Colonia has tons of uninhabited land. I suggested we confiscate any technology they could use to flee the planet and settle them on an isolated island with enough food and supplies to start their own colony."

Lily's suggestion seemed more humane than Erica's proposal. Calandra labored to convince the prisoners they were making a terrible mistake. They had the power to change their fate. One scout ship crew followed Dray's lead in renouncing their allegiance to Delcor and settled in Genahm. They surrendered their weapons, made an oath to stay on the planet, and embraced a peaceful life.

The remaining prisoners refused.

"Maybe it is for the best if we isolate them in a spot where they will pose no serious threat," Calandra said. "Perhaps when enough time passes, isolation will purge blind devotion to Delcor from their minds and hearts."

She turned away from the window and gazed at a small enclosure where Alexa played with Bella. Calandra smiled as her mind flashed back to the happy reunion between her daughter and the little cala. Alexa held out her arms and excitedly called out Bella's name. The diminutive animal trotted over when she heard her voice, greeting her with an enthusiastic coo and flicking her bushy tail as she ran. Excitement had not dimmed on either side as Calandra watched them play now.

"Gulah's cruiser is ready to fly us back to Daraconiah. I tried again to convince him to let me pilot the ship."

Calandra laughed as she glanced over at Xttra. He flashed a bemused smile at her as he entered the room with Bo'un.

"I failed," he said.

"You're all leaving?" A dejected tone overtook Lily's voice. "I don't think I'm ready for this."

"That was always our plan once we ended Delcor's rule," Xttra said, glancing at her. "Lathos is our home."

Lily ran her fingers through her wavy brown locks and frowned.

"Is it still your home?" she asked. "Will you be safer now than before? You created a power vacuum with Delcor's death. One an ally or heir will readily fill—a successor who may hunt you like Delcor himself did."

Calandra's smile faded from her lips. In her zeal to end Delcor's reign, she devoted minimal thought to a new chief sovereign. Delcor left behind a wife, children, and many powerful allies in Ra'ahm.

An expansive pool of potential successors.

If a successor loyal to Delcor later learned of his slaying, they would seek revenge for his death. Calandra quickly realized she, Xttra, and Alexa would not find a moment of peace back on their home planet if such a likely scenario materialized.

Her eyes slid over to Xttra. He rubbed his chin and stared skyward. Xttra soon met her gaze. She found the same recognition in his deep blue eyes. They could not return to Daraconiah and resume their lives on Lathos as though nothing happened. Their circumstances changed forever.

Life on their home planet had grown too dangerous.

"What will we do?" Bo'un asked. "Word of Delcor's death will reach Ra'ahm one day. When that word arrives, the collective wrath of his clan and their allies will be unrestrained."

Lily's eyes darted from Xttra to Calandra. She swept her arm toward the control tower window.

"Stay on Colonia with us. Help us rebuild Cascadia. It can become your home as it has become mine."

Live among Earthian and Confederation colonists? Calandra internally recoiled when Lily first suggested the idea. Many Ra'ahmians harbored a deep-rooted enmity toward the Confederation and grew to revile the northern tribes long before waging the Separatist War. Similarly, Earth held many horrors buried deep in her memory. But Lily and Kevin proved honorable Earthians existed. Sam showed how even adversarial Earthians could eventually become allies and friends.

Did her future entail a home in the Land of the Three Suns? Calandra closed her eyes. Images from the staff swarmed her mind. Her and Xttra. Alexa. Disjointed scenes from their future lives together. Some appeared connected to Lathos, others bore links to Cascadia.

Calandra struggled to place the deluge of images in a meaningful context. No obvious chronological order manifested itself and offered a helpful clue about their future occurrence. Perhaps if she returned to the sanctuary and gazed into the stone atop the staff again, she would gain clarity.

No.

Calandra's eyelids snapped open. She and Xttra promised one another they would never disturb the Staff of Onrai for selfish personal gain. It must stay hidden and protected.

"Is this what we're supposed to do?" Calandra mused, glancing at her husband. "Is our future here rather than on Lathos?"

Xttra averted his gaze. His eyes trailed along the ceiling. Did he also revisit visions the staff showed him? Calandra wondered how they influenced his thinking.

She got a faster-than-expected answer.

"The future is forever in motion." Xttra's eyes settled on her again. "We will make our own future. An ancient staff will not steal my ability to choose my own path."

Calandra inhaled sharply and sighed. She struggled with not knowing.

Faith requires trust in the absence of certain knowledge.

Her words to Xttra in the sanctuary permeated Calandra's mind again. Embracing an uncertain future stood out as the ultimate act of faith. Staying on Cascadia offered their most realistic hope for a peaceful life.

Xttra offered up an encouraging smile, showing Lily's offer resonated with him in the same manner it did with Calandra.

"Do you need an astronomer and a master pilot in your colony?" she asked.

Lily smiled.

"I think we can work something out."

Xttra turned and faced Bo'un. He clasped his wrist and placed the other hand on Bo'un's shoulder.

"What will you do once you return to Lathos?"

"I will discuss resettling in the Land of the Three Suns with Selia," Bo'un said. "It won't be the first sacrifice we made together, but I want to live in a place where peace is attainable."

Calandra embraced Bo'un one final time before he departed for Gulah's ship. After checking on Alexa, she returned to her spot at the control tower window. Xttra clasped her hand, and they watched the star cruiser climb skyward until it was no longer visible to the naked eye.

Their path led to a new home. One, Calandra hoped, where their little clan would find lasting peace.

THE END

ALIEN WORDS PRONUNCIATION GUIDE

Names:

Calandra (Kaw-lan-druh)

Xttra (Ex-tra)

Delcor (Dell-core)

Valadius (vah-lay-de-us)

Janthore (Jahn-thor)

Sarianna (Sar-e-ahn-na)

Giljax (Gill-jacks)

Oogan (Ooh-gun)

Menankar (Men-ann-kar)

Jemanoah (Gem-ah-noah)

Nihu (knee-who)

Bo'un (Bow-un)

Onrai (Ahn-rai)

Tressek (Tress-ek)

Gulah (Goo-law)

Aginon (Ag-e-non)

Kujoth (Coo-jaw-th)

Eliah (E-lie-aw)

Nikaia (Nick-aye-ah)

Galjokk (Gaul-jock)

Malar (Mah-lar)

Jo'ber (joe-bear)

Locations:

Lathos (Lay-thos)

Ra'ahm (Ray-ah-m)

Wekonn (We-con)

Rubrum (Rube-rum)

Aramus (Air-am-us)

Taircona (Tare-con-ah)

Aracian (ar-ay-she-un)
Abidosian (abi-doze-ian)
Fengar (Fenn-gar)
Sabadan (Sab-ad-ann)
Orontalla (Oar-on-tall-ah)
Daraconiah (dar-ah-co-ne-ah)

Luma (Lou-mah)
Animo (ann-e-moe)
Daracos (dar-ah-cos)
Khuara (Coo-are-ah)
Ashmuth (Ash-moo-th)

Plants, Animals, & Technology:

Ebutoka (E-boo-tow-kaw)
Cala (Kaw-lah)
Sapinoa (Sap-eh-noah)
Setaworm (see-tah-worm)
Senosa (See-nose-ah)
Fraxa (Frax-ah)
Arca vox (arc-ah-vox)
Syri'nai (sear-e-nye)
Treema (tree-maw)

Russakin (Roose-ah-kin)
Ictus (Ick-tuss)
Dochu (Doh-chew)
Kerval (Cur-vahl)
Odoco (Oh-doh-co)
Trique (Try-cue)
Mokai (Moe-kye)
Chitha (Chee-th-uh)
Arcodon (Arc-oh-don)

ABOUT THE AUTHOR

Being a storyteller is second nature to John Coon. Ever since John typed up his first stories on his parents' typewriter at age 12, he has had a thirst for creating stories and sharing them with others. John graduated from the University of Utah in 2004 and has carved out a successful career as an author and journalist since that time. His byline has appeared in dozens of major publications across the world.

John has published several popular novels. His debut novel, Pandora Reborn, became an international bestseller on Amazon and ranked as the no. 1 horror novel in Japan for a brief time. His novel Alien People earned distinction as a Top 100 new release and Top 100 bestseller in multiple science fiction categories on Amazon.

John lives in Sandy, Utah. Bookmark his official author page, johncoon.net, to receive news and updates on his fiction. Subscribe to his newsletter, Strange New Worlds, http://johncoon.net/subscribe, for original short fiction, poems, and articles. You can connect with John on Twitter (@johncoonsports), Instagram (@jcoon312), and Facebook (@jcoon).

Printed in Great Britain
by Amazon

41316583R00202